A Brand New Me

For much of Shari Low's working life she was a nightclub manager, standing on club doors arguing with crazy drunk people in Glasgow and Shanghai. She now lives in Scotland with her husband and two children and spends her days writing books, screenplays and two weekly columns for the *Daily Record* newspaper. It's great – but she does miss the crazy drunk people . . .

For further information on Shari Low, visit her website at www.sharilow.com and visit www.BookArmy.co.uk for exclusive updates.

Praise for Shari Low:

'Hilariously addictive.'   *Closer*

'Feisty fun.'   *The Mirror*

'A thrilling page turner that grabs your attention from the off. Highly recommended.'   *The Sun*

'Great fun from start to finish.'
                    Jenny Colgan, author of *Operation Sunshine*

'There are just two words for Shari Low: utterly hilarious. I laughed like a drain.'
                    Carmen Reid, author of *Late Night Shopping*

By the same author:

The Motherhood Walk of Fame
My Best Friend's Life

SHARI LOW

A Brand New Me

AVON

This novel is entirely a work of fiction.
The names, characters and incidents portrayed in it are
the work of the author's imagination. Any resemblance to
actual persons, living or dead, events or localities is
entirely coincidental.

AVON

A division of HarperCollins*Publishers*
77–85 Fulham Palace Road,
London W6 8JB

www.harpercollins.co.uk

A Paperback Original 2008

1

First published in Great Britain by
HarperCollins*Publishers* 2008

Copyright © Shari Low 2008

Shari Low asserts the moral right to
be identified as the author of this work

A catalogue record for this book is
available from the British Library

ISBN: 978-1-84756-017-9

Set in Minion by Palimpsest Book Production Limited,
Grangemouth, Stirlingshire

Printed and bound in Great Britain by
Clays Ltd, St Ives plc

Mixed Sources
Product group from well-managed
forests and other controlled sources
www.fsc.org Cert no. SW-COC-1806
© 1996 Forest Stewardship Council

FSC is a non-profit international organisation established
to promote the responsible management of the world's forests.
Products carrying the FSC label are independently certified
to assure consumers that they come from forests that are managed
to meet the social, economic and ecological needs
of present and future generations.

Find out more about HarperCollins and the environment at
www.harpercollins.co.uk/green

An enormous thank you to the brilliant Sheila Crowley for being the most encouraging, inspirational agent a writer could have. Thanks too to the Avon team: Maxine Hitchcock, Keshini Naidoo, Sammia Rafique and Sara Foster for their stellar support and help along every step of the way.

Huge hugs to Gemma Low, who still hasn't disowned me despite the fact that it's really embarrassing that your step-mother writes about sex stuff.

As always, Sadie Hill, Rosina Hill, Liz Murphy, Paul and Beccy Murphy and Anne Marie Low have been not only family, but great friends as well.

And finally, if it's true that the best mates are the ones who can make you laugh even when it's all going ceremoniously tits up (okay, I might have made that saying up), then mine are truly brilliant: Carmen Reid, Lennox Morrison, Janice McCallum, Linda Lowery, Wendy Morton, Pamela McBurnie, Sylvia Lavizani, Mitch Murphy, Gillian Armstrong, Frankie Plater and Jan Johnston.

To Danny Murphy, our incredibly handsome new nephew, who won't be allowed to read this until he's at least thirty!
To John, who knows he is everything, always . . .
And to my boys Callan & Brad, for being hilarious, outrageous and endlessly cuddly.
Now can one of you please learn to make tea.

Prologue

'Three . . . two . . . one . . . Happy New Year!'

The champagne corks popped, streamers fell, the music blared, lovers embraced, their hearts overflowing with joy as they welcomed in another year . . .

But unfortunately all that happened on the TV.

In my living room, three twenty-something friends sat shrouded in dejection, watching the celebrations on the box, each clutching a sparkler in one hand and a drink in the other.

'We are officially the saddest people on the planet,' I muttered.

'No, we are not!' argued Stuart.

Over on the other couch, Trish burst into a faux-tragic rendition of 'My Heart Must Go On'.

'Okay, now we are,' said Stu. 'Right, Trish, one verse and a chorus and that's it. My ears will start to bleed any minute.'

His voice got louder with every word as he endeavoured to be heard over the noise of poppers and whistles coming from next door. Even my neighbour Mrs Naismith was having a much wilder time than us, which, given that she was in her seventies, was taking the night to a whole new level of depression.

A wave of something suddenly consumed me. In hindsight it was probably several large glasses of Rosé Cava, but at that moment it absolutely felt like it was something real – something important. 'I'm making a resolution,' I announced.

'Here we go . . . ' grinned Stuart, consulting his watch. 'Two minutes, three seconds – that's a record.'

I ignored him and spoke up so that I could be heard over the noise of Trish going down with the *Titanic*.

'My dear saddo friends, this is it – this is the year I stop being unfulfilled, skint and single. I'm going to find the perfect job, the perfect man, the perfect life. Oh, and sex – I'm going to have bloody great sex!'

I stood up with a flourish and dramatically raised my glass to propose a toast . . .

'Wow!' spluttered Stu and Trish in perfect synchronisation.

I was gratified by the enthusiastic reactions from my audience.

'I know,' I continued, in the solemn, dignified manner of a politician announcing that he was running for prime minister, 'it's a huge challenge, but I'm determined.'

'Leni, get out of the way of the telly! We weren't wowing you, you daft cow – you've made that same speech every year since 1998. We were wowing at the poor bloke playing the bagpipes. A gust of wind just flicked up his kilt and he flashed the entire watching world.'

Trish had now ceased channelling Celine Dion and dissolved into a puddle of giggles. 'And I don't rate his chances of getting a date tonight.'

Stu automatically leapt to the defence of his fellow man. 'Look, it's cold out there – give the guy a break.'

I thumped back down on the couch just as Stu and Trish's laughter escalated due to the antics of the demented presenter, who was now making the whole situation even more hilarious by trying to hold down the front of the undeniably cute piper's kilt with a large microphone.

Fabulous – the announcement of my life-changing mission had been gazumped by an event that would feature on those *TV's Naughtiest Blunders* until the end of time. Although . . . I suppose they did have a point. Yes, I had made similar resolutions before, but this time I absolutely, definitely meant it. I did. This was going to be the year that I changed my destiny, and the only way to do that would be to take chances, be bold, be fearless, and relentlessly look for opportunities everywhere. Starting right now.

I wondered if there was any chance of getting that piper's number?

1

Wired to the Moon

Four weeks later...

'Leni, do you truly believe that the stars control your fate?' asked the woman in front of me. The same woman that had positioned her desk according to the laws of feng shui, studied my feet, cleansed my chakras, and taken a snapshot of my aura. And that was just at our first meeting.

This was the second and final interview and she'd upped the stakes by comparing our Chinese horoscopes, reading my retinas, analysing my star sign (Libra), and asking me to join in a meditation session to connect with our higher selves. To be honest, my higher self just wanted to know if I had the job and whether or not it came with private healthcare, because if I sat with my legs in the crossed position for much longer I'd have a groin strain that would require urgent medical attention.

In the meantime, I nodded in what I hoped was a Zen-like fashion at Zara Delta, spiritual guru, author, television celebrity and founder of the web's most popular astrology site: www.itsinthestars.net.

Other than the cosmos, Uranus, Neptune and whatever other paranormal forces that may or may not have been involved, I had Trish to thank for getting me in front of

4

Ms Delta. After four years in catering college, Trish had abandoned her idea of becoming a chef in her final year, when a particularly challenging work placement made her realise that putting her own rather volatile personality in close proximity to notoriously temperamental creatures in a confined space stacked with lethal weapons could one day lead to the need for a defence lawyer. Instead, she'd taken the admin route and worked her way up to Food & Beverage Manager of a very swanky London hotel, before buckling to her love of all things shallow and showbiz by accepting a job as Hospitality & Catering Manager at *Great Morning TV!*, a role that involved meeting, greeting and catering to every whim, request and rumbling stomach of the show's stars and guests. Want all the blue M&Ms out of the bowl? Trish would get it done (although she might offer several suggestions as to where the offending sweets could be stored, all of which would require surgery to remove). If a Hollywood A-lister required her macrobiotic bran to be served by Buddhist monks on skateboards, Trish was the one who nipped down to the temple to deliver a crash course in street sports. A soap star showed up drunk, in the night-before's party clothes, having somehow lost her knickers along the way? Trish's trusty supply of coffee, aspirins and granny pants came to the rescue. It was rumoured that she even supplied a notorious movie-star bad boy with the medication to cure his crabs after a traumatising incident involving a pre-show shower, suspect residue on a towel and several minutes of stomach-churning screams (all his). She had so far refused to confirm or deny, but since the day of the alleged incident there had been a pair of Marigolds in her desk drawer.

In short, there was nothing she couldn't arrange for the pampered prima donnas who beamed into the televisions of the British public every morning, the biggest prima donna of them all (according to Trish) being Zara Delta, the show's resident astrologer, who popped in at the end of every week to deliver her starry predictions.

Thankfully for me, though (depending on how you felt about working for a temperamental astrologer who believed her menstrual cycle was controlled by galactic forces), Trish had put her personal feelings to one side when, on the first Friday back at work after our New Year's knees-up, Zara had stormed into the green room late, screeching that her PA had 'buggered off to the Turks & Caicos' with a boy-band member over the New Year break and failed to return. Like a true friend, Trish had bolted right over to her, armed with a tray of Danish pastries, and told her she knew of the perfect replacement for her erstwhile assistant. That would, apparently, be me. Although, I'm not sure how my five years of experience in the marketing department of City Plumbing Supplies (although I solemnly swear I didn't come up with the slogan *Our Toilet Fittings Won't Drive U Round the Bend*') qualified me for a job as a celebrity PA.

True to form, when she'd called to give me the news, Trish's honesty had been about as subtle as a nuclear missile with PMT.

'Look, it's not like you've got any other options on the table. And she's desperate – she'll take anyone. She's really been left in the lurch.'

'Trish, I hate to point out the obvious – but if Zara was any good at her job, wouldn't she have seen it coming?'

'Leni, do you want the job or not?'

I'd hesitated. The truth was that I probably didn't. You see, much as my vino-fuelled rant at New Year had been made with wholehearted conviction, as Stu had sweetly pointed out, I did make that announcement on an annual basis. However, courtesy of a lifelong aversion to taking

6

risks of any kind, my resolution for change never lasted longer than the New Year hangover.

I'd love to be adventurous and relish the thrill of spontaneous acts, but I've enough self-awareness to realise that I'm, well, a bit of a plodder. I'm comfortable with familiarity. I'm consistent. Predictable. I even occasionally relish boredom. And on the rare occasions that I do make a concerted effort to be more daring and open to life's experiences, my 'New Challenges' gene gives up after five minutes and goes back to lying on a couch munching crisps and watching reality TV.

'Leni? LENI?!' Trish's voice had boomed from the handset.

As her agitation had emanated up the phone line, my eyes had flicked to the book sticking out of my handbag: *Ten Steps to a Whole New You*. Waste of a tree and £6.99, because I'd finished it on the tube that morning and had realised that the old me was still rooted to the spot. My anxiety levels had slid upwards as I mentally prepared myself to utter the 'thanks, but no thanks, you're a great pal, good of you to think of me' platitudes.

'Trish, thanks . . . '

I'd lost track of the conversation, because right at that moment the head of design, Archie Botham, arrived, beaming in such a proud manner you'd swear he'd either won the lottery or given birth to the second coming. As he'd slapped a mangle of plastic down on my desk, I'd realised it was neither.

'This ballcock will revolutionise toilets,' he'd declared, with all the excitement of someone who realised he was a shoo-in for a Nobel Prize for Sanitary Ware Design. 'Draw us up a provisional press release, Leni,' he'd demanded in his thick Lancastrian accent. 'Aye, girl, this is really going to put us on the map. I'm calling it The Botham Ballcock.'

They say that when your life is about to end you get

flashbacks of the highlights. I suddenly realised that if I, Eleanor Olive Lomond, aged 27, got killed by a dose of salmonella in my chicken mayo baguette one lunchtime in the foreseeable future, the last thing I'd see was my name at the bottom of a press release announcing superior flushing technology.

'I'll take it!' I'd blurted.

'The ballcock?' asked Archie, with more than a hint of puzzlement.

'What?' bellowed Trish.

I'd gesticulated to the phone sandwiched between my neck and shoulder and motioned to Archie to give me a minute. He'd backed off, clutching his revolutionary invention to his chest.

'I said I'll take it – the job,' I'd whispered, anxious not to burst Archie's euphoria by alerting him to my potential desertion.

'Wise decision. She'll have to interview you first, though.'

'Just tell me when and where.' I could do this. I could. I'd just taken one giant step (albeit with Trish pushing from behind), and all I needed to complete the rest of the ten steps to a brand new me were courage, determination . . .

'And you might have to tell her you're a firm believer in the paranormal – you've seen her on telly, she's on a one-way ticket to Loon Central.'

. . . and bold-faced lies.

Thus I came to be sitting in front of Zara Delta, nursing a debilitating groin strain while channelling Zen. I felt it wasn't an opportune time to tell her that the only Zen I knew owned our local kebab shop and was under investigation by Environmental Health.

In the manner befitting a wonderfully efficient PA (and to take my mind off the fact that this was only the second interview of my adult life), I'd meticulously researched the do's and don'ts of successful interviews. Embarrassing revelation, number one: *Ten Steps to a Whole New You* wasn't a one-off random purchase. In fact, there was a good chance that I was single-handedly responsible for keeping the entire self-help industry afloat. Other people read gossip mags. Some collect stamps. I've got a high-grade habit that involves lots of books with the words '*Steps*' and '*Dummies*' in the title. By rights, I *should* be able to manage any situation in one minute, unleash the giant within me, and be capable of doing a PowerPoint presentation while winning friends, influencing people, thinking positively and re-bonding with my granny.

The emphasis on that last bit being 'should'. Somehow those affirming bibles of improvement seemed to have an expiry date approximately eight hours after I'd turned the last page, when my inherent personality traits kicked back in and shifted my paradigms right back to the ones I was born with. Yet I couldn't stop reading them. I was like the shoe-holic who bought four-inch platforms in fourteen different colours even though she'd never wear them. To be honest, I thought I'd only be cured when I found a self-help guide to cure me of my dependence on self-help guides.

Unsurprisingly, none of the techniques or questions recommended in the self-help section came up during the first interview – well, I say interview, but the reality was that every time I spoke she shushed me and told me it was interfering with her attempts to connect our spiritual forces. That was a week ago, and now, to my frankly gobsmacked surprise, she'd called me back again. My spiritual forces must have been acting particularly slutty and welcoming all advances.

In the seven-day interval, my natural tendencies (the ones that were begging me to forget any crazy notions of new jobs and mad astrologers) were kicked to the kerb by intrigue, and the reminder that if I didn't make the change now I'd be contemplating Botham's Ballcocks right up to my pension years.

I'd read in *Prepare Yourself, the Job Is Yours* (£9.99 from all good bookshops) that employers form impressions within seconds of clapping eyes on you, so for our first meeting I'd gone a bit formal and pulled my eternally uncontrollable red, shoulder-blade-length hair back into a (only slightly messy) chignon, donned my one skirt suit (black, polyester, Primark, £19.99), a white top, and shoved my protesting feet into black court shoes with three-inch heels. Afterwards, I realised that the outfit probably gave the impression that I was about to serve her a chicken cacciatore at an Italian bistro. And since the heels made me about five foot eleven and a good nine inches taller than my potential employer, I decided to re-evaluate for our second meeting. This time I'd gone casual: black skinny jeans, ballet pumps, white T-shirt, soft grey merino wool wrap with my hair middle-parted, loose and wavy, completely undisciplined by straighteners. On Nicole Kidman, that hair is sexy, casual and straight out the pages of *Vogue*. On me it's a bird's nest straight out of *National Geographic*.

Suddenly Zara flicked her eyes open and inhaled dramatically. Was this it? Was this when she delivered her decision? Or decided that my higher self wasn't qualified for the post? Nope, eyes shut again, back in weird trance. Zara Delta: founder member of Wackos 'R' Us.

Or maybe that should be Hippy Throwbacks 'R' Us, given that Zara's wardrobe seemed to consist entirely of tie-dyed kaftans, straw flip-flops and headbands from which protruded a menagerie of flowers. Today there was a sunflower sticking out of one side, and three large daisies

10

had wilted on the other side, drooping towards her shoulder. Her thick mahogany hair flowed down to her waist and she wore enough blue eye-shadow to kit out an entire Abba tribute band. According to the press she was forty-five, but she looked younger – obviously all that serenity and inner peace was allowing her to circumvent frown lines and wrinkles.

While she carried on with strange humming thingies, I contemplated my surroundings and realised that, compared to my current place of employment on a dilapidated industrial estate on the outskirts of Slough, working here would be stellar. Literally. The office was in a grand Georgian townhouse in Notting Hill, the kind of building that looked like it housed a stockbroker, his interior-designer wife and three children called Palomina, Pheronoma and Calispera. But any preconceptions had to be dumped at the door, the one that was carved with ancient Mongolian warrior symbols in a bid to ward off evil spirits, negative forces and any local yobs armed with cans of spray paint.

The huge oblong entranceway looked like a mini planetarium. The carpet was black, the walls and ceiling were the colour of the night sky, and fluorescent stars covered every surface. It wasn't so much a professional office, more the view from the flight deck of the Starship *Enterprise*. In the corner, a receptionist sat behind a futuristic silver desk, illuminated only by one desk lamp and the flashing red squares on the switchboard. The first thing that had struck me was how miserable she looked – not surprising given that the lack of sunlight probably made her a shoo-in for rickets.

Zara's office took up the entire first floor and suitably reflected a zany TV New Age guru who looked like a cross between a Woodstock refugee and Cher in her 'Turn Back Time' years. The walls and ceiling were draped with rich red

11

silks, giving the whole space the vibe of an elaborate Bedouin tent. Huge plants sat in every crevice and corner, while ornate Persian rugs covered almost every inch of the ebony wood floor. Two trees had given their lives to make her inordinately wide desk, both of them cut vertically in half and then laid side by side – a concept that might have worked a little better if the branches had been removed. Instead, about fifteen feet of shrubbery filled a whole corner of the room. The rest of the floor was covered with the same oversized cushions that Zara sat on now; massive squares of intricately embroidered, rich damask in shades of deep ochre interspersed with small tree stubs that doubled as tables.

Still, at least (unlike the poor, pale, vitamin-deprived receptionist) she had three huge sash windows that filled the room with natural daylight. Or they would have if it wasn't six o'clock on a January night and pitch dark outside.

Suddenly, Zara jumped up, grabbed a large, gilt-engraved chalice from her desk and headed towards the window I'd been staring at just seconds before. Spooky. Was that a coincidence? Or a bit of psychic prompting? Oh my God – could she read my thoughts? Think nice things, think nice things . . .

She wrenched up the window and held the chalice outside.

Okaaaaay . . . So was she:

a)   dealing with a cup of tea that was too hot in a sound ecological fashion by using rainwater to cool it down;

b)   contravening Health & Safety legislation by passing out a liquid refreshment to a window cleaner who bucked the industry norm by working nights;

c)   actually, there wasn't a c) because I couldn't think of another logical (or otherwise) reason that she had her arm thrust out of a first-floor window on a cold, dark January night.

'Father Moon,' she wailed, 'send me a sign that I am walking the correct path, the one that leads to the destiny that your wondrous powers will deliver.'

My chin incurred skid marks as it ricocheted off the floor. She was, quite literally, howling at the moon. I didn't need Father Moon's divine powers to tell me that this woman was about as stable as a vibrator on a hammock. In a hurricane.

Suddenly, she slammed one hand over the top of the cup, brought it back inside and turned to me, her victorious grin clearly conveying that whatever the bloke in the sky had done, she was chuffed about it.

Gliding across the floor (she appeared to move in a Dalek fashion, due to the barefoot/ long kaftan combination), she brought the chalice to me and gingerly lifted her palm to show me what was inside. 'He sent one to us,' she announced, her voice all breathy with joy.

'Don't be ridiculous, there's nothing in there, you mad, mixed-up loon!' I retorted. But only in my head. In real life I was too stunned to speak and instead just sat with a facial pose that gave her full view of my fillings.

I stared at the inside of the chalice. Nothing. Empty. Void of all contents.

'He sent us a moonbeam,' she gushed.

Of course. A moonbeam. I should have noticed.

'Leni, that's a sign.'

I waited for her to add, ' . . . that it's time for me to have a long lie down in a dark room until the magic mushrooms wear off.'

'It's a sign that we are on the right path,' she continued.

I was beginning to understand why her previous assistant had decided that the right path for her was the one that led to Heathrow Airport.

I attempted an encouraging, receptive expression, one

you might give to a four-year-old who'd just confided that her imaginary friend was having a quick shower before dinnertime.

'So, Leni, are you absolutely sure that you want to work here?'

Noooooooooo!

So of course I said, 'Definitely.'

Look, it didn't involve flushing, I'd broken the habits of a lifetime by actually getting this far, and it paid fifteen grand a year more than my current job. I'd already decided that as long as it didn't involve sacrificing my firstborn child then I was taking the position.

She sank back down onto her cushion and resumed the meditative position: her legs crossed, eyes closed and her fingers upturned on her knees, thumb and middle finger pressed together.

'And you're open to the new challenges and experiences that destiny will bring?'

I nodded again, resisting the urge to make the atmosphere a little more dramatic by adding a 'hmmm'.

'Then welcome to our team. I'm delighted to have you here and I think we'll work together in perfect harmony.'

My higher self gave a silent cheer and embarked on a Mexican wave. I'd done it! Sure, it was bizarre and it was just a little bit terrifying, but the most important thing was that I was no longer facing a heady future in ballcocks. I was PA to Zara Delta. And so what if I didn't know her rising moon from Saturn's ring – I'd wing it somehow. After all, how tough could it be? I zipped all my doubts in a mental file, labelled it 'This Job Makes No Bloody Sense Whatsoever', filed it away and allowed myself a brief moment of self-congratulation – a month into the New Year and already I was on my way to fulfilling my resolution to change everything about my life. And, let's face it, this was about as different as it could get.

Zara opened her eyes and gave me a benevolent smile. Maybe working for her would be fine after all. Perhaps I was just a little overwhelmed by her eccentricities and idiosyncrasies and in a few weeks she'd seem perfectly normal.

'Be here next Monday, six a.m., for Tai Chi, affirmations and a full briefing on your first assignment.'

'Er . . . *assignment*?'

'Yes. You will of course fulfil the normal role of a PA, and I expect you to be by my side on a daily basis. You'll only be asked to work in the evenings if your presence is essential. But you do realise that your role also involves an element of practical research?'

I didn't. So, naturally, I nodded.

'Can I ask, Zara, exactly what the research will involve?'

'It's quite simple, dear. My project for this year is to write a new, pioneering book on the relationships between men and women. There are so many lost little stars out there and it's my calling to set them on the celestial journey that will lead them directly to their soul mate.'

Aaaaw, she was like Cilla Black with mystic powers.

'I believe that I've developed a new way of interpreting the signs using a combination of ancient Chinese philosophy, psychology, rune stones, mathematics, planetary alignment and the instinct and intuition that I was gifted at birth. And I'm going to use my methods to redefine and reinvent current dating techniques. Forget speed dating, forget all those matchmaking websites – I'm going to write a defining, ground-breaking, revolutionary guide to wooing a partner depending on his star sign.'

I thought it probably wasn't the time to enlighten her that Mills & Boon were on the phone asking if they could have the word 'wooing' back.

A book on landing men depending on the date they were born? It was ridiculous. Trite. Insulting. Wasn't the modern woman far more evolved than that? Didn't we have principles, emotional intelligence and the savvy to find a partner based on like-mindedness, inherent compatibility and how great his abs were?

I had a sudden insight as to why I was still single.

'So what exactly will I need to do?' I had a flashing premonition of endless, mind-numbing hours spent in libraries collating information on all the astrological traits and characteristics. I'd then deliver expansive reports to the divine Miss Delta so that she could harness the mighty investigative powers of solid research, an enquiring mind and moonbeams.

'It's simple, Leni. I need to hone and test my theories and include references to practical examples and real-life cases in my book. So, over the next few months, I need you to date twelve men, one from each of the signs of the conventional zodiac.'

'Whaaaat?'

My peachy-clean aura threw a major strop. No way! Forget it. I was not pimping myself out for some ludicrous, half-boiled book by a TV celebrity with a head like a neglected flower basket.

'You will of course be paid extra for all evening work, and there will be a bonus on completion of each of the twelve studies. So – can I assume you accept the challenge?'

I was outraged. I was insulted. But I was also skint, desperate to get out of plumbing and losing the feeling in my legs. So . . .

'Hmmmm,' I replied.

2

Aligning the Planets

'So?????'

Their little faces were the epitome of expectation.

'I got the job!' I replied gleefully, joining in an exaggerated group hug thing that almost toppled them off their bar stools. They'd been waiting in the pretentious, overpriced wine bar around the corner from Zara's office for the last two hours, so they were already struggling slightly with minor issues like balance and staying upright.

'Told you she was desperate!' Trish exclaimed helpfully.

That's the thing about Trish – I love and adore her but she went to the Joseph Stalin School of Friendship. She's brutal, thoughtless, self-obsessed, and prone to dictatorial behaviour. However, unlike Mr Stalin she's also funny, kind and, underneath the complete lack of compassionate social skills, she has her friends' best interests at heart. We've known each other since our first day at college in London, when I bumped into her as she wandered along the corridor outside the catering department clutching a toffee pavlova (yes, the stains came out eventually). Surprisingly, given her truculent disposition, we've never fallen out, although that's probably because I'm subconsciously aware that if I crossed her there's every chance she would dismember me while I slept.

17

The first thing that struck me (after the pavlova) about her was that she was so different from my group of friends back in the sleepy suburb of Norfolk where I grew up. In my little gang of middle-of-the-road, normal, everyday pals, not one of them had a navy-blue Mohican and wore Doc Marten boots with long flowery dresses. She looked like the love child of Sid Vicious and Laura Ashley. In fact, that had been a major puzzlement when her husband Grey first met her. Let's just get this out of the way – he's a fireman. No jokes about large hoses, sliding down his pole or relighting his fire, please – that kind of shallow innuendo does nothing but demean the role those courageous men play in today's society. But he is a big hunka hunka burnin' love who could set any female's knickers alight.

Anyway, they got together after he was called to her apartment by a neighbour who spotted thick smoke coming out of Trish's window. A few bee-baws later he was carrying a semi-conscious Trish out of her front door while the plug-in, hot-wax kit that she'd inadvertently left on after trimming her bikini line burnt down her kitchen. Electrical fault, apparently. Thankfully, she was fine, but when she regained consciousness while waiting for an ambulance, Grey asked her why she was wearing boots with a nightdress. They've been together ever since that moment and she vowed right there and then that she'd never again wear floral prints, men's boots or well-trimmed nethers.

Now her wardrobe is more Kate Moss on a slightly lower budget – a hip, eclectic and edgy combination of vintage and high-street jeans, T-shirts, waistcoats and various other chic pieces that definitely shouldn't work together but somehow on Trish they just do. Meeting Grey also brought about the last of the Mohican. Her hair is now a screaming shade of scarlet and shaped into a razor-sharp asymmetric chin-length bob, a style that's maintained in pristine fashion by our mutual best chum Stuart. Another college relationship that's lasted the distance, we met Stu when he advertised for hair models in the first month of his hairdressing course. Trish and I, fuelled by the combination of permanent bed hair, cheap cider and empty bank accounts, went along, and despite the fact that he bestowed upon us crew cuts that made everyone around us view us in a whole new light (if you're reading this, Julie McGuiness, thank you for the k.d. lang poster), we've been friends ever since.

Oh, and just in case you were doing that whole stereotype thing, Stu is as straight as Russell Brand with the horn. However, he is . . .

'That's great news, Leni! I'm so proud of you! But stop the hugging, honey, because this virus I've got might be an airborne one so best to keep your distance.'

. . . a hypochondriac. Or should I say, the post-millennium version, a cyberchondriac. First sign of a sneeze and he's on the computer inputing his symptoms into medical websites, and the next thing you know he's claiming bubonic plague and ringing a bell before he enters the room. Still, much as the web does invariably throw up the most dramatic diagnosis, we're glad he's finally binned the old-fashioned medical dictionary. When he was addicted to that he'd get stuck on the same letter for days and go into psychosomatic meltdown. That terrifying week back in 2002 when he contracted piles, pleurisy and pregnancy will be etched on my memory forever.

We keep hoping that he'll meet his perfect woman and the security will rid him of his morbid obsession, but so far all attempts to set him up with a member of the nursing profession have met with a premature end. He once got as far as a third date with a geriatric nurse but she dumped him in the middle of an episode of *ER* when he asked her to talk him through a prostate examination. And not in a good way. It's a shame really because, neurosis aside, he's a grounded, cool, entirely macho six-foot-tall specimen of gorgeousness with close-cropped black hair, piercing green eyes and an abdominal rack so tight you could play bongo drums on it. Of course, he'd never let you for fear of cracked ribs, punctured lungs and internal bruising.

Oh, and he's successful. Courtesy of his achingly hip salon, he's a rising star (vertigo, altitude sickness, anxiety) in the hairdressing world (nits, life-threatening finger cuts, inhalation of toxic perm lotions). He styles Chelsea mothers, precocious teenagers, a few daytime-telly celebs and does the weekly makeovers for *What?!!* magazine. Trish has vowed that she'll get him the *Great Morning TV!* slot one day, but that often involves whisking viewers off to sunny climates so he'll have to overcome his fear of flying first. Not only is he terrified of the actual big steel tube/plummet to death scenario, but he's phobic about germs since he heard that aircraft ventilation systems simply recycle the air, spreading everyone else's bacteria. On the plus side, his in-flight panics often have a silver lining – if first class is quiet, he regularly gets upgraded because the stewardesses are worried that the sight of a terrified grown man sweating in a medical facemask might upset the other passengers.

I hopped onto a bar stool next to them – but not close enough that Stu's highly virulent Ebola virus could kill me before I'd had a large glass of wine and a packet of Nobby's Nuts.

I gave them a full debrief and they were, by turn, astonished, enthralled, proud and . . . horrified.

'You have to *what*?' Trish almost spat her vino across the table.

'You're not doing it,' Stu commanded, like a stern parent forbidding underage drinking, discos and any contact involving the pelvic region.

'Right then, Dad, I won't – but only if you increase my pocket money this week.'

'I mean it, Leni, it could be dangerous. Twelve men? Do you know that statistically at least two of them will be carrying a sexually transmitted disease? Not to mention that there's a high chance that at least one will have a criminal record.'

For a macho guy he really did get hysterical sometimes (anxiety disorder, raised blood pressure, wrinkles).

Now that he was looking at me with an expression that sat somewhere between horror and disbelief, with a helping of concern thrown in just to make me feel even worse, my teeth started to grind. Of course he was right. And deep down I knew it. Taking this job would be utterly insane. Dates? I couldn't go on twelve dates. I'm the woman who takes weeks to decide to try a new washing powder – and even then I feel bad for the old one. But then . . . My mind flicked to the pile of books at the side of my bed. Shouldn't I feel the fear and do it anyway? Shouldn't I fake it until I make it? Shouldn't I take those ten steps to a new me? Aaaaaargh! Shouldn't I stop reading bloody self-help guides and actually put some of their theories into action instead?

It was time for me to get a life – one that I actually bloody liked. I could do this. I could. I was feeling the fear so it was time to get on with it.

I decided to bluff bravado.

'Stu, I'm not going to sleep with them, I just have to date them. You know – dinner, bowling, art galleries and stuff like that. And how bad can it be? Look at my track record in picking men. Ben? Married. Donny? The Olympic World Champion in the field of Unmitigated Boredom. Gary? Ran off with my chiropodist. Goliath? Tried to snog Trish at last year's birthday barbecue.'

21

'I warned you not to go out with someone called Goliath – bound to have inferiority issues,' she piped up.

'Thank you, Dr Jong,' I replied curtly.

'You're still not doing it. It's way too dangerous, and besides, you'll hate every minute of it. This just isn't you, Len,' Stu demanded, thumping his bottle of Bud on the square pod we were gathered around.

He was so, so right – so irritatingly, bloody annoyingly right. My emotional pendulum swung back from 'fearless' to 'realistic' – there was no denying that when God doled out adventure and ambition, I had refused with a, 'No thanks, I'll stick with consistency and predictability.'

I threw back a few of Nobby's finest to break the emotional tension of it all. Take the job. Don't take it. Take the job. Don't take it. I used to be indecisive but now I wasn't so sure. Once again, aaaaaaargh!

'Oh, for fuck's sake stop being so dramatic,' Trish argued. 'She'll be fine. She might even meet someone who's slightly elevated above her usual selection of losers and reprobates.'

Shucks. I didn't know whether to be grateful to Trish for the encouragement, offended by the observation, or horrified that she didn't seem at all perturbed that I might meet an axe-wielding maniac.

But her observation had already crossed my mind.

I was twenty-seven years old and I'd never had a serious/ humming-the-wedding-march/ flicking-through-bridal-magazines type of relationship. The longest one had been the two years I'd spent with the (as yet) only man I'd ever been in love with: Ben (sob – sorry, still can't think about him without involuntary gulp and flaring of nostrils), the gorgeous stranger I'd met on a train a couple of years after I'd finished college. We were definitely world leaders in the 'unlikeliest couple of the year' award. Me: reserved, prone to wimpish behaviour with an adventure rating that never went any higher than trying a new muffin in Starbucks. Him: a serving marine, six foot four inches of testosterone-oozing manliness who – bearing in mind that he was a trained killing machine – had the sweetest, most caring nature. Unfortunately, at the end of two years I discovered that he also had a wife and child in army barracks in Felixstowe. Turned out that the majority of his 'covert manoeuvres' took place well away from the front line. Handling the Taliban must have been light relief after the stress of juggling a wife and a girlfriend, neither of whom had an inkling about the other until . . . nope, I didn't even want to think about it. I threw back some more nuts and mentally fast-forwarded to the brutal aftermath that mostly consisted of me lying on the bathroom floor sobbing into the shower curtain, wishing hell and damnation of the entire male species. Since then, I'd just drifted along, embarking on a few flings with obviously incompatible blokes just to give myself a break from serial singledom.

In hindsight, what I should have done was loaded up a backpack and taken my mind off the heartbreak by trekking across Nepal seeking religious enlightenment. Or headed to the Great Barrier Reef to discover the wonders of nature and shallow sexual couplings with long-haired Australian surf dudes. Instead? Same job for years, unexciting love life, and I still lived in the same Slough/Windsor border, one-bedroom flat that I'd been renting since I first moved there. Actually, it was more Slough, but if I hung out of my bedroom window at a forty-five-degree angle clutching a set of binoculars, I could just about make out the castle. Not that I had. Well, only that once, and Mrs Naismith from next door had been holding my ankles to prevent me from plummeting to my death.

I took a long, deep breath, and in the manner of a fearless superhero (aka Nobbygirl), adjusted my jaw to a position of strength and determination. There was no way I wanted to look back on this moment and regret that I hadn't grabbed the new opportunity with both hands (or at least the one hand that wasn't busy chucking salted protein nibbles down my throat).

What had I vowed to do at New Year? Carve out a brand new me. And given the reminders of my mundane, deathly boring life and my deeply unsatisfactory romantic history, I was surer than ever that a little bit of crazy unpredictability was exactly what I needed to change my life.

And Zara Delta was definitely a little bit of crazy unpredictability.

Great Morning TV!

'Now, Zara, I believe you've got an exciting new project that you're working on this year and you need our help,' said Goldie Gilmartin, the nation's favourite sofa queen. In her mid-forties with a stunning auburn pixie cut and a body that was no stranger to the gym, Goldie bore more than a passing resemblance to a young Liza Minnelli. The British viewing public loved her, and with her sassy style, forthright manner and compassion-where-it-mattered, she was close to being declared a national treasure.

'I have, Goldie, and it might just be the most important thing I've ever tackled. I don't want to give too much away, but let's just say I think I may have the answers for all you single girls out there looking for Mr Right.'

Goldie grinned as she turned to camera. 'Maybe there's hope for me yet.'

Goldie's single status had long been a source of interest to the gossip mags. What they didn't realise (and we did – courtesy of Trish's insider information) was that for years she'd been happily having an unorthodox and wildly adventurous relationship with a six-foot-two stripper with the body of an Adonis who was almost twenty years younger than her.

'Goldie, first book off the press is all yours, darling!' Zara promised, before turning to the camera. 'What I need from our viewers are single men. Ladies, is your brother, son or even dad living on microwave dinners for one? Or are you a single guy who is fed up with the dating game? Come on all you loveless gents out there, drop me a line, tell me a bit about yourself, enclose a photo and you could be lucky enough to get chosen to participate in a fabulous new challenge where we'll set you up on the all-expenses-paid night of your dreams. Dating agencies charge thousands of pounds – we might just be able to find your perfect partner and we'll do it for free. Intrigued? Well, all will be revealed when my new book is released at the end of the year, but in the meantime I can promise you this – if selected you'll be in for an adventure that might just lead you to your soul mate.'

'Great, Zara, thank you for that,' interjected Goldie as she wound up the segment. 'Now come on, guys, write in – and if there's anyone that catches my eye I might just be calling you myself!'

3

Star Gazing

'Morning, Leni. Zara needs her schedule for today, her new crystals collected from Swarovski on Bond Street, and can you arrange for a cleaning team to blitz the house – she had a few people over last night and it got a bit crazy. Oh, and we've come up with a match on the manhunt thing – I've left the details on your desk.'

'Sure, Conn, no problem.'

He grinned as he squeezed past me on the stairs. I waited until he was out of sight.

'Chicken tikka baguette,' I shouted to Millie, the pale-faced receptionist who, underneath the anaemic complexion, coal-coloured hair and dour exterior, was actually very sweet and funny – although I did worry that if she didn't see daylight soon she was facing a future blighted by osteoporosis.

'Nope – cheese salad on brown, no mayo,' she countered in a thick Glasgow burr.

Conn's head suddenly reappeared at the top of the stairs.

'Sorry, Millie, forgot to say . . . could you order lunch for me? Cheese salad sandwich will do.'

Millie did a triumphant double wobble of her eyebrows in my direction.

'Sure, white or brown?'

'Brown,' he replied. 'And no mayo.'

'Cream buns are on me at lunchtime then,' I replied ruefully. How did Millie do that? I'd been working for Delta Inc. for a fortnight and so far Millie had whipped me every day in the sandwich challenge. I wasn't taking it lightly. Maybe I should start taking notes and work out if everyone had a regular favourite depending on the day, week and position of the moon. And I wasn't being facetious with that last one, because in this office that was probably the most likely scenario.

Our admittedly immature game had started on my first day, when I was introduced to Zara's son and manager Conn in the reception area. There are only two highly descriptive, all-encompassing, suitably formal adjectives to use when attempting to sum him up: hubba hubba.

I'm five foot eight, and even in my highest ankle-straining heels (eBay, ridiculously impractical panic buy for city plumbing Christmas party, can only be worn in presence of crash mat and paramedics) he towers above me. His shoulders are the approximate width of the average pavement, he has sallow young Marlon Brando-type features and his topaz eyes glint brighter than those horrible bloody stars in reception. But the most remarkable thing about him is his hair – dark, long and windswept, it's not so much Led Zeppelin, more the shoulder-length cut adopted by Jon Bon Jovi after he got a bit older and decided that heavy-metal hair was costing a fortune in conditioner.

According to Zara, Conn was born when she was sixteen, so he's twenty-nine now – yet, despite being only a little older than me he has a composed confidence that makes him seem much more mature than his years – a disposition that renders him perfect for his role as Zara's manager. And yes, I could tell all that from the five conversations we've had since I started here two weeks ago. Oh, okay, I

28

confess – a couple of times I accidentally listened in when he was chatting to people on the phone, courtesy of the hopelessly inefficient phone system that allows you to cut in on anyone's call. I'd complain it was intrusive and invasive to privacy, but then, if Zara is as good as she claims, doesn't she always know what everyone is thinking anyway?

A shiver ran up my spine to accompany that now-familiar mental mantra – think nice things, think nice things . . . Most employees give an occasional thought as to whether or not their boss will check their desk drawers. Some people even worry about management installing spyware on their computer to check their emails. Me? I'm too busy fretting that Zara can see right into my mind and that I'll get fired because some irrepressible brain cells will blurt out, 'Hey, you in the dodgy kaftan, you're a few decades too late for Woodstock.'

I made my way up to Zara's office and opened the door with not a little trepidation. The thing is, you just never knew what you would find. One day last week she had been dangling a large kite out of the window, convinced that the patterns it made in the air would tell her whether or not she should book a spiritual retreat to Mongolia next Christmas. Yesterday I'd walked in on her in deep conversation with a goat. Yep, a goat. I'm still contemplating whether the NSPCA would find anything untoward about a grown woman demanding to meet and vet (no pun intended) the animal that will be supplying her morning beverage. Archie Botham and his ballcocks seem positively mainstream compared to this.

Thankfully, this morning there was no livestock in sight – just Zara, in a fluorescent pink boob tube that flared at the waist into a full-length gown, complete with matching headband. As always, she came to greet me, placed her palms against mine and closed her eyes tightly.

'Let the cosmos deliver a fruitful day of peace, progress and harmony.'

I said it with her, trying my best not to feel like a twat and just to be grateful that the day had started well. I'd already come to realise that she'd ignore me when she was upset or furious about some cosmic problem, but when she was on the sunny side of the street she liked to perform our little morning affirmation. It was just one of the quirky little rituals I'd come to consider run of the mill. There'd be hell to pay if she realised that I hadn't checked my aura for celestial darkness since a week last Tuesday. And I didn't suppose she'd appreciate the book that was tucked safely out of sight in my rucksack: *Surviving a Crazy Boss – a Guide to Creating a Positive Working Environment.* It was doing the trick. I was more positive than ever that Zara was bonkers. Sudden scary thought: would she sense the book was there? Did she know I was thinking about it?

I switched to efficient PA mode, while thinking nice things. Nice things. Nice thing number one: I actually enjoyed working there. The hours were fine, the job was interesting, and despite the fact that Zara could switch from the epitome of serenity to ranting egomaniac in less time than it took me to read my horoscope, I'd so far managed to avoid her wrath. Nice thing number two: the salary was great and lots of interesting things happened every day. Nice thing number three: the ... Conn. Whoa, that just slipped out there. But okay, I will admit that working in close proximity to *GQ* man did occasionally stir the ...

Alarm bells shrieked inside my head and the voice of doom yelled, 'DO NOT THINK SEXUAL THOUGHTS ABOUT A MAN WHEN HIS PSYCHIC MOTHER IS STANDING IN FRONT OF YOU!' Beads of sweat formed on my upper lip as I rapidly shut down the mental porn channel and reverted to capable secretary mode.

'Your schedule for today is already on both your computer and your BlackBerry and I updated it last night before I left. You're in the office all day today and you have three private readings – one is with a Mrs Callow from Bridgend, standard six hundred-pound fee for the hour. The second is with the competition winner from last week's *Great Morning TV!* competition – it's a freebie so I told them you'd only see them for half an hour, as you said. And the third is with Sher DeMilo – she's just been dropped from *EastEnders* and she was hysterical when she called. What should I charge her?'

Zara closed her eyes and was silent for a moment, then 'A thousand pounds – she'll make more than that opening a new supermarket.'

Did I mention that I'd discovered yet another surprising and fairly scary truth about Zara? Her image might be one of superior spirituality, she might be an earth goddess, she might even live within the principles of karmic equality, but when it came to her bank balance she was as astute as a supremely gifted accountant.

'Conn asked me to pick up your crystals and organise the house cleaning, so I'll do that while you're with your first client. Is there anything else you need me to do?'

'Yes, could you find out the dress code for the *TV Times* awards and ask Mrs Chopra to come in to discuss my outfit please.'

I made a note on my pad. Far from sourcing all her clothes in vintage markets and on her Third World travels (as many of her press articles claimed), Zara actually had most of them made by Mrs Chopra, a lovely little Indian lady who ran a sewing business from her two-bedroom terraced house in Hounslow.

I made my way over to my desk and chair – sorry, my *cushion and tree stump* – in the corner. As my coccyx thumped onto the floor, I reminded myself for the tenth time to pick up a pair of those cycle pants with the padded buttocks. Not a wardrobe item that I'd ever considered I'd need in my professional career.

My eyes immediately went to the red file in the middle of my desk. Or should I say bark? Anyway, no time for semantics because my brain was suddenly beating to the sound of da dum. Da dum. Da dum. Da dum. Then the hand tremors started and a solid mass formed in my throat making swallowing impossible. The da dums were speeding up now. I decided to add a defibrillator to the next office supplies order.

Da dum. Da dum. For two weeks I'd forced myself into denial, hoping that Zara would change her mind, think of a new plan, or get run over by a bus before I had to go through with this ludicrous project, but now the reality was in front of me in black and white – the first of the candidates selected from the bag of replies Zara had received after she'd announced to Goldie that she was looking for blokes who wanted to find their Miss Right.

At the moment I was definitely channelling Miss Absolutely Bloody Wrong.

A new wave of panic began to rise from my toes and stopped somewhere around my aching posterior. Why had I ever thought I could do this? Why? This wasn't my role in the universe. In our daily existence, Trish took care of 'fearless, outrageous and blunt to the point of abuse', Stu took care of 'gorgeous, thoughtful, funny and hip', and I took care of 'safe, dependable and predisposed towards the uneventful'.

I pulled out an A4 sheet of paper with a photograph attached to the top. 'Harry Henshall', the title announced. My stomach gave a lurch as I looked at the photograph and realised immediately that he was not exactly my type. Not that I had a 'type', as such (other than unreliable and prone to compulsive lying), but Harry looked like a boy-band member . . . ten years after they'd had a number thirty-two in the charts and split up to pursue solo careers.

I scanned the biography as quickly as possible, panic now at waist height. Harry, it transpired, was twenty-eight and worked in manufacturing for a fabricated panels company, and enjoyed reading, sport and socialising in his spare time. Panic was now competing with thudding heart. It was one thing mortally dreading this whole project, but I was even higher on the terror scale now that it was a reality.

Harry. Leni and Harry. Harry and Leni. Nope, wasn't feeling it. I couldn't do this. I couldn't. Very attractive sweat bubbles popped up on the palms of my hands to keep the nausea in my gut company. I wondered if I could get my old job back?

'Ah, you found it then,' Zara observed as she hovered over me. 'We thought he looked like a nice chap. He's a Leo.'

I wanted to add, 'Who could also be running late for a meeting with his probation officer.' I kept it to myself.

'Now, as I've explained before, I've devised a new way of reading the stars that will revolutionise the current stereotypes that modern astrology holds for each sign – so I'm not going to give you any advice or background on his astrological character traits before the date. I want you to go in there with no expectations or knowledge whatsoever.'

I presumed that she meant no expectations other than the two I already had. Number one: if Harry had time to send his dating profile in to a telly show then he probably wasn't beating potential girlfriends off with his love-stick; and number two: fear would kill me before I got there anyway.

'Now, you have to leave absolutely everything on the date up to him – where you meet, where you go, what you do.'

There went my plan to have a quick drink and then leave – out of the pub's bathroom window.

She thrust a sheet of A4 paper in front of me.

'And we do have a few guidelines we'd like you to follow. Obviously you are representing the Delta brand, so we expect you to behave in a manner that won't reflect badly on us.'

I had to really focus to stop my eyes rolling. This was the woman who had decided to illustrate her femininity by painting the huge canvas that hung in the hallway with her nipples. She had made a client cry last week when she'd told her that her missing Chihuahua had gone to the big kennel in the sky. And she charged celebrities up to three times the going rate. Yet she was concerned that *my* behaviour would reflect badly on *her*? Shit, she was looking at me with a really weird expression. Quick, nice things! Think nice things. Bloody, bloody bugger! It was bad enough having to go through with this mad, crazy notion without the constant bloody worry that Zara was reading my mind!

I couldn't do this. Right now, I just wanted to put my head between my legs and wait for the terror to subside. I had a sudden urge to pen my own autobiographical, inspirational guide that others could learn from: *Feel the Fear . . . then Shake Until Your Nose Bleeds*.

'Now, are you sure that you're up to the challenge, Leni? Conn and I had a chat and we absolutely realise that this is a rather unusual requirement, so we thought that a bonus of two hundred pounds per night was appropriate, plus of course we'll pay for all your expenses including transport there and back.'

Urgh, it really annoyed me that she thought I could be bought. I had morals! I had values! And I had a student loan/overdraft combo that was currently sitting at a couple of thousand pounds and could be wiped out by these lovely two-hundred-pound bonuses.

It was decision time. Two choices. Quit or go through with it. Quit. Go through with it. Quit. Quit. My opinions and concerns rose to a crescendo, and were then silenced by a thundering mental roar of Trish's voice demanding that I pull myself together. I had to do this. I couldn't quit after just a few weeks – where would that leave me? In the dole queue, skint, and thoroughly depressed that I'd let the prospect of twelve perfectly harmless evenings (with potentially axe-wielding maniacs) deprive me of the most interesting and lucrative job I'd ever had. Deep breath. Deep breath. And for the 243rd time in recent weeks, a silent vow of, 'I can do this.'

'Nope, it's fine – I'm definitely up for the challenge,' I assured her with an accompanying rallying sweep of my arm for added effect. I could do this (number 244).

'We'll also be providing the gent with a hundred pounds to spend – although he can of course exceed this amount at his own expense. You can withdraw the money from our petty cash account and courier it over to him on the afternoon of the date, together with a confidentiality agreement similar to the one you signed when you started here – saves dealing with the admin side of things when you're out together.'

Great – now they were actually paying blokes to go out with me and then making him promise to keep it a secret. As if I wasn't already at an all-time low, a thousand pounds of Semtex just attached itself to my ego and self-detonated.

Zara swept off to her first appointment and I slumped at my tree stump, the list sitting there like a death warrant waiting to be executed.

There were ten points on it, in bold, cold black and white:

1. *A comprehensive report must be written after each meeting (template to follow).*
2. *To ensure that the session is as spontaneous as possible, the candidate is not to be prompted, prepared or manipulated in any way.*
3. *Each meeting must last several hours, the content of which to be decided entirely by the candidate.*

4. *Details of this project and of candidates must not be discussed with anyone outside Delta Inc.*
5. *Physical contact with candidates should not be initiated.*
6. *Any physical contact initiated by candidate should be rejected but noted to be used in analysis.*
7. *To preserve the integrity and atmosphere of each date, direct questioning should be avoided. However, during the course of the evening, as much information as possible on previous dating history should be attained. Family and work history should also be attained.*
8. *No personal information, contact details, company material or discussions should be shared with the candidate.*
9. *Post-date contact with any candidate is strictly forbidden.*
10. *Project deadline: 31 May.*

I reached for the phone and punched in Trish's number. She answered on the first ring.

'I officially want to kill myself,' I blurted, before she could pipe in with anything as mundane as 'Hello'.

'Dollface, I love you madly but I've got twenty minutes to rustle up a butterscotch and raspberry cheesecake out of no-fucking-where because that demented twat chef on the cookery slot came in pissed again and dropped the fucking dessert. Thank fuck it's pre-recorded. So, what's up?'

Did I mention that Trish is in training for the next Olympics? She's competing in the highly demanding category known as 'repetitions of the word "fuck"'. So far only Gordon Ramsay, Billy Connolly and a few successful porn stars are her major threats.

'It's this whole dating thing, it's totally freaking me out.'

There was a sigh at the other end of the phone. 'Oh, for bollocks' sake, Leni – you've got a great new job, you're single, you're hopeless at picking men, and this might just turn out to be a great way to meet a guy.'

In other words: Pull. Yourself. Together.

'Am I just being a pathetic coward?' I asked, hoping for some soothing words and a gentle massage of my self-esteem. I realised too late that I'd phoned the wrong friend. Ego-boosting and feel-good encouragement were Stu's department.

'Absolutely! Now get a grip and just get on with it. Got to go – I've got some real problems to deal with here. Kiss kiss.'

You can't beat a comforting word from a friend in a time of need.

I took another look at Harry's photo and then picked up the phone. Somehow, my shaking digits wouldn't quite press the buttons. Should I do it? Or not? Not. Definitely not. But what were the options? Back on the nerve-racking interview market, more upheaval, more change and no guarantees that I'd get a position that I actually liked at the end of it? Or unemployment, rent arrears, and not even the money to buy an inspirational tome called something like *101 Careers That Will Make You a Millionaire.*

I did the deep-breathing exercises that Stu had insisted on teaching us in case we ever found ourselves in a position where cardiac arrest was imminent.

Zero . . . One . . . My shaking fingers slammed the phone buttons as I punched out the numbers on the sheet in front of me.

Okay, Harry Henshall, panel salesman from Milton Keynes, let's see if you're just about to meet your soul mate.

4

The Leo Date

'Hey, love – give you fifteen quid for a quickie!' The offer, generous but unprompted, came from a crowd of blokes in a minibus that stopped at traffic lights next to where I stood, freezing my extremities off on the corner of Piccadilly Circus.

I was so glad I'd taken the advice of Millie on reception and pitched my dress code at 'cold weather casual': dark boot-cut jeans, high black leather boots and a black polo-neck jumper, with a knee-length thick wool coat. Although the cold coming through the soles of my boots was making me shiver, it was still a much wiser choice than the jeans, strappy sandals and glittery top I'd been planning on wearing. But then, what did I know about dating clothes? I hadn't been on a blind date since, well, ever, and I couldn't remember the last time I'd been out on the town in London.

I'd always hated coming into town at night (too crowded, too impersonal and far too expensive for a late-night taxi back to Slough), but since Harry was travelling from Milton Keynes, I thought I should meet him somewhere convenient and this was the first place he'd suggested. I hobbled from foot to foot, trying to get some heat into my veins, my mind distracted from my imminent pneumonia by the familiar trains of panicked thought that were flashing through it: what was I doing here; I didn't do things like this; I didn't thrive on excitement; I didn't get fired up on adrenalin; I definitely didn't take unexpected events in my stride; I was a creature of habit that hated surprises and would rather undergo organ removal without anaesthetic than put myself in a potentially embarrassing situation.

This angst ran in conjunction with an in-depth, highly convoluted, complex internal dialogue that went along the lines of, 'Stay. Go. Stay. Go. Stay. Go. Stay.' To make the voices stop, I'd just conjured up a mental image of Archie Botham beaming with pride over his new invention when my mobile phone rang.

'Tell me you're not going through with it!' Stu begged.

'Stu, I have to,' I answered patiently, giving no clue as to my inner turmoil. 'It's my job.'

'It's borderline prostitution! Where are you now?'

'Standing in Piccadilly Circus waiting for him.'

'Leni, it's far too bloody cold for that. You could come down with hypothermia. Or you could get frostbite in your digits. That happened to Ralph Fiennes on his expedition to the North Pole. He ended up amputating his fingertips with an electric saw in his garden shed.'

That was the thing about Stu – he was generous with his hypochondria and liked to share it around.

'Stu, first of all, Ralph Fiennes is the bloke from the Harry Potter movies and he's never, as far as I know, attempted a one-man expedition across a polar icecap. Ranulph Fiennes, the explorer, may have done that. But I'm sure he'd be the first to acknowledge that my fingers are highly unlikely to meet the same fate as his while tucked into screaming-pink fake-fur mitts in the middle of Piccadilly Circus.'

'Excuse me, are you Leni?'

I lifted the phone away from my ear and turned to the new arrival. My first reaction was that he looked just like the guy in the photo . . . about, oh, fifty pounds ago.

He gave me a big smile and stuck out his hand. 'I'm Harry, pleased to meet you.'

With my non-telephone hand I reciprocated, taking in his eager smile and seemingly happy demeanour.

Okay, so he wasn't Orlando Bloom. He wasn't even *Hollyoaks*. But he *was* wearing clean jeans, brown Timberland boots and a black felt jacket, a stripy scarf, and despite the lack of resemblance to his photograph, my initial gut instinct was that he was fairly inoffensive. Plus, he was so overweight that if I had to flee for my life he'd never catch me. 'Leni! LENI! *LENI!!!!*' came an increasingly agitated voice from the phone.

I quickly put it to my ear. 'Look, Stu, Harry's arrived so I have to go.'

'Have you got the pepper spray I bought you? And keep your mobile on. And remember to say what I told you right at the start. And remember, if you're in a pub, don't eat the peanuts – the bacteria will kill you. And . . . '

'Have to go now, Stu. Bye-ee.'

'Leni, LENI, *LENI!!!!*'

I pressed the 'end' button on the phone and took a deep breath as I remembered my promise to Stu, extricated after he'd spent three hours lecturing me in person the night before.

'Sorry, that was my big brother on the phone, he's very protective. To be honest he's been a bit unstable since they stripped him of his world kickboxing title after they discovered he was wanted for arms possession.'

I couldn't believe the words were coming out of my mouth. My face was beaming and my left eye was doing the twitch thing that it always did when I was lying. I so, *so* wasn't cut out for this.

I half-expected Harry to turn pale, hail a taxi and run while he still had his kneecaps. To his credit he didn't seem too perturbed and breezed right over it.

'Sorry I'm late,' he apologised, 'I had to wait in for the courier to bring the money and some forms to sign before I met you tonight, and he didn't show up till after five. So . . . you said that I had to decide what we'd do?'

'That's right,' I agreed. Okay, in that last sentence he'd apologised for something that wasn't his fault and sought reassurance on the night ahead – didn't that demonstrate a little insecurity? Perhaps I could tick serial killer off the list.

'And it should be something that I'd normally do when I take a bird out?'

I nodded again. 'Absolutely. Just be yourself.' Tweet.

'Are there, like, secret cameras following us or anything?' he asked, looking around nervously.

'No,' I reassured him, 'it's just me. But I can't be sure my brother isn't hiding behind a lamppost.'

His eyebrows shot up and he scoured the street to the left and right.

'Kidding!' Awareness alert – save terrifying jokes until you have a better understanding of his personality.

Right, it was time to get this going – I'd stood on a pavement corner for long enough. I was cold, I was hungry, and although meeting Harry face-to-face had taken my anxiety levels down from 'potentially fatal' to a manageable 'hating every minute of this', I was still desperately in need of some Châteauneuf du Dutch Courage.

'So, Harry, what's the plan? Where are we going?' Assertiveness, showing interest, encouraging personal expression: thanks to a stressful afternoon swotting over *A*

41

One Way Ticket to Successful Dating, I knew I was displaying three of the ten essential skills for a successful night.

'Well, if it's honestly all down to me . . . '

'It is,' I reassured him (number four – reassurance).

'Then I'm taking you somewhere that you'll have an absolute blast!'

A blast.

At least he got that bit right.

5

Shooting Stars

Bang!

Everyone in the room cowered in mortal fear as the killer paused on his lethal mission. We'd already watched him shoot three unarmed men, and countless others lay dead as a result of the grenade that he'd used to announce his arrival. Now he'd run out of bullets and had stopped to reload. One desperate man tried to take the opportunity to escape, but he was too slow. The maniac took aim and fired, sending another victim to the morgue. Silence again while he watched. Waited. Poised and ready to continue his manic spree.

'Can you pass me my Diet Coke, Leni – can't take my eyes off this cos the SAS will storm in any minute now.'

I reached over for his can, sitting on a nearby ledge next to mine. There was a sudden thunderous noise – nope, not a crack team of special forces making their entrance, just my stomach rumbling, reminding me that it was 11 p.m. and I still hadn't eaten. The Twix from the vending machine hadn't quite filled the meal-sized hole.

Three hours after I'd met Harry and what had I learned? I now knew that there was a giant amusement arcade in London's West End. I realised that standing for long periods of time in high-heeled boots led to the kind of discomfort that required painkillers and a foot spa. I had been educated in the fields of mass murder, unarmed combat, battle strategies and simulated cage fighting. And I had a sneaking suspicion that there was a very good reason as to why Harry was still single.

Still, at least I wasn't alone. I was sharing this special night with around one hundred teenage boys, several security guards and a large party of Japanese tourists.

I vaguely remembered a similar night somewhere in my dating past – but then I had been fourteen and had to be home before my ten o'clock curfew or my dad would confiscate my Boyzone DVDs.

Apparently, Harry's post-pubescent self was still alive and well and intent on rivalling the death toll of a Third World despot before the night was out.

I blamed myself for not objecting to Harry's plans.

Actually, I didn't – I blamed Zara bloody Delta for landing me in this in the first place.

On the plus side: all feelings of anxiety had now been squashed by the realisation that Harry wasn't going to judge me, scare me or drag me into a candle-lit basement and mutilate me in some kind of Satanic ritual. On the downside: I'd just wasted a whole night of my life that I could have spent engaged in educational, humanitarian pursuits – like watching Horatio in *CSI Miami* catch bad guys by putting his sunglasses on and taking them off in a brooding manner.

I hadn't sat down, I hadn't eaten, I hadn't laughed, I hadn't flirted and I hadn't had a single conversation of note with my prospective suitor. Instead, I'd stood beside him and watched as he played arcade games for approximately – I checked my watch – 195 minutes. Harry, on the other hand, had run the full gamut of emotions – he'd been joyful, sad, ecstatic, furious, determined, triumphant and homicidal.

44

'Shit!' he exclaimed, throwing down the life-size AK-47 and taking the cola from my hand, 'outnumbered – sixteen SAS – didn't stand a chance.'

Oh, I hate it when that happens.

'Want to go for a burger? I've still got twenty quid left.'

What does it say about my life that right there, right then, that felt like the best offer I'd had in weeks?

We went off to the nearest junk-food emporium and he treated me to a double bacon cheeseburger.

Harry dumped the tray on the table. 'You know, I've had a really good time tonight – you're really easy to talk to,' said the man who had been responsible for eradicating several thousand people from the face of the earth while barely saying two words to me.

'Er, thanks.'

'And it's great the way that you got into the whole arcade thing. Most chicks don't even give it a chance. They don't know what they're missing.'

Torture. Death. Blood. Gore. Guts. Armageddon.

'So what's all this about, then, this dating experiment?'

I shrugged my shoulders. 'Not sure. I just work for Zara, and all I know is that she's writing some kind of relationship book and I'm helping out with research.'

'So you're not actually single and looking for someone then?'

'I am. I mean, I'm single . . . ' The senses that hadn't been numbed forever by three hours of death and destruction were warning me that an awkward moment was imminent. I decided to round up a posse of excuses and head it off at the pass.

' . . . but I'm not really dating. Just focusing on my career right now. I'm only doing this so that I can add a research element to my CV.'

Harry had the decency to look sad. For a gun-wielding

maniac he was obviously well in touch with his sensitive side.

'So, if you don't mind me asking, what made you apply for this?'

'Blokes at work. Last month I dared my mates Jammy and Kegsy to flash their tackle at the CCTV cameras in the High Street. The month before, Dudsy had to buy ten boxes of Tampax in Boots the chemist. Daft tossers thought they were stitching me right up making me do this. Wait till I tell them I had a bloody brilliant time. Ha!'

I felt utterly blessed and flattered that I appeared to be rating above indecent exposure and the bulk buying of feminine hygiene products.

'So do you need more photographs of me or anything like that?'

I shook my head. 'Nope, I don't think so – apparently all the case studies in the book will be anonymous.'

His face fell.

'Something wrong?' I asked.

He shrugged his shoulders. 'Nope, it's just that I was kind of hoping that this would be an ongoing thing. A hundred pounds, a night on the town, a hot bird – I could get used to this.'

Sadly for Harry and the balance sheet of the Coin Slot Amusement Centre, I knew that I couldn't.

'So, anything else about you that I should know?' I prompted, mindful that I was under orders to get as much background info as possible. 'You said on your application that you were into sports?'

He put down his large double whopper and fries, took a slug of his full-fat coke and then burped.

'Darts. I play for the pub darts team.'

And there was me thinking that he'd done a quick four-hundred-metre hurdles before he came to collect me.

46

'And I'm a total god on the PlayStation – nobody, and I mean nobody, can touch me on Grand Theft Auto IV. My firepower is awesome.'

I realised that somewhere out there was the perfect woman for this man . . . I just hoped that she got parole soon so they could get together.

'And reading?'

'The usual stuff . . . ' he chomped, giving me a full view of the mastication process.

The usual stuff? Thrillers? The odd John Grisham? The occasional Harlan Coben?

' . . . you know, *Nuts*, *Zoo*, stuff like that. Do you want an ice-cream? I've still got a fiver left.'

'Go on, spoil me!' I replied with a smile. Romance might be out of the question, love and lust were a definite non-starter, but after hours of hunger, if I could at least get my blood-sugar back up to a level that ruled out the possibility of fainting, I figured that would be a bonus.

He sauntered off to the counter, checking his cash the whole way. When he returned, he threw down a little surprise. 'Had enough left for a donut as well.'

I was getting luckier by the minute. 'Do you mind if we go outside now – my lift will be here in a minute.'

'One of your mates?' I asked.

'Nah, my mum. She didn't want me travelling on the tube at night – said she'd drive down after her line-dancing. She gets jittery if I'm out late at night. Called the police once, but I'd just had a few too many and my mates had left me in a wheelie bin outside the front door.'

Outside, I shook his hand as a taxi pulled up.

'Thanks, Harry, I had a really, er, interesting time.'

Well, there was no point in being rude. Besides, my mortal fear of confrontation was up there with the tendency to plod on my prevalent characteristics scale.

47

'So I can't get your telephone number or anything then?'

Aw, bless, he was swinging from foot to foot in some kind of nervous shuffle – I knew that feeling all too well.

'It's just that there's this really cool arcade in Milton Ke—'

I shook my head. 'I'm sorry, Harry, it's more than my job's worth. But thanks.' I jumped into the taxi, but before it drove off he stuck his head in the window.

'Okay, but if your brother ever fancies a pint, get him to call me. Wouldn't mind picking his brain . . . you know, about the whole arms possession thing.'

I leaned towards the driver. 'There's a twenty-quid tip if you get me out of here before I start to hyperventilate.'

My head thudded back onto the upholstery as the car screeched off.

I took a deep breath. Okay, let's not overreact – morbid fascination with violence aside, he was fairly polite. And I hadn't needed to use my pepper spray once.

However – cue depressing music and feeling of doom – he was only number one, so I still had eleven more dates to go.

Little did I know that I'd one day look back on Harry as being one of the more normal ones.

PROGRESS SUMMARY: *IT'S IN THE STARS* DATING PROJECT

CONCLUDED		
LEO	Harry Henshall	Morbid fascination for simulated violence

EMAIL

To: Trisha; Stu

From: Leni Lomond

Re: If last night's date had a personal ad, it would read like . . .

Male, 28 (maturity age 13–16), Leo, cuddly, seeks like-minded female with endless supply of pound coins for fun-filled nights wiping out entire civilisations with big plastic fake guns. Must be technologically skilled: proficient on PSP, Xbox, PlayStation, Wii and Nintendo DS (please note that I am the 'God of Milton Keynes' on all of these systems), and have interest in weapons of mass destruction. GSOH, likes fun dares and practical jokes – can supply own wheelie bin. Very sociable, has many friends with adolescent nicknames and can't wait to add girlfriend called 'Knockers' to the list. Ideal partner will therefore have knockers of substantial size. Must be good cook with wide range of specialities: burgers, chilli, fish and chips, donuts, pizza, and should be able to drink until they fall down or vomit, both of which will be captured on mobile phone and posted on YouTube. Family values important – expect to live with parents until middle age.

Most romantic gesture: sharing bargain bucket of KFC while playing two-player game of Ninja Warriors 3.

Ideal holiday: Blackpool, Las Vegas, terrorist training camp.

6

Earth Calling Zara

'I don't know what you're complaining about, at least he bought you a donut,' Millie spluttered through tears of laughter. 'I mean, that's true devotion for you.'

'Listen, don't mock,' I replied with faux seriousness. 'At least now if I ever want to annihilate a small country I know the very person to call.'

We were off again, giggling away under the starry evening sky – at nine o'clock on a February morning.

My nose began to twitch and I suddenly realised that we weren't alone. Conn. Or, rather, Conn's gorgeous, sexy scent – I believe it's called Hubba Hubba for Men.

'So, how'd it go last night, Leni – did you have a good time?' With those deep, undulating tones he could get a job in TV doing the announcements between *Coronation Street* and *The Bill*.

'Lasagne, baked potato,' Millie hissed, out of earshot of the new arrival.

I spun around just as Conn started walking up the stairs, his athletic gait effortlessly straddling two steps at a time. I automatically flushed as in my mind's eye his clothes fell like a stripper's to the floor, and his beautifully toned, naked arse continued to climb the stairs. If he turned around there was every chance my cervix would explode.

Why did he have that effect on me? I mean, it wasn't as if I'd never seen a good-looking man before. Ben, my beautiful, perfectly formed cheating-bastard marine, had been the type of guy who made every female in the room stop and stare. Stu was handsome in an almost Californian/*OC* kind of way. Although, naturally he'd never live there because the sun could cause skin cancer and he'd once read that the whole cast of *Baywatch* came down with a horrible bug after swimming in the sea off the coast of Malibu.

Anyway, Conn . . . nope, no idea why he made my heart beat faster and my sweat pores open.

'Erm, no, it was . . . ' I started to reply, but I was too late – he'd already disappeared out of sight. Memo to self: try to take less than a week to answer Conn's questions.

I pondered for a moment. It was Wednesday. Last Wednesday I specifically remembered him requesting pitta bread, chicken legs and hummus. I laid out my prediction with a smug grin and was just congratulating myself on my astute observation when the phone rang.

'Yes Conn? Sure. Okay, one lasagne, one baked potato. No problem.' Millie replaced the phone with a giggle. 'Millie – one, Harry's girlfriend – zero.'

Aaaaargh! How did she do that?

I swatted her across the head with the morning mail and headed off up to the office, took the customary deep breath before opening the door, and . . . I swear you couldn't make it up. The music hit me first: a wild, chaotic cacophony of drums. In the middle of the floor was Zara, topless except for a huge, chunky wood necklace, wearing a flowing terracotta-coloured skirt adorned with what looked like African symbols. Next to her was a huge, beautiful black man, dressed similarly to Zara, every muscle perfectly

52

defined and his skin glistening with moisture. Providing the musical contribution were two blokes in the corner, battering away on huge steel drums. My eyes darted back to the stage show – Zara and the bloke were gyrating in some kind of hypnotic tribal dance, both of them in perfect sync, making it obvious that this was a well-practised routine. Some warning would have been nice. Most PAs run a danger of catching their boss sneaking an illicit bacon butty in the morning. Or perhaps calling their secret date from the night before. As far as I could remember I had never heard anyone comment that they'd walked into the office in the morning and come face to face with their boss swinging her hooters to the accompaniment of two steel drums.

Her gaze suddenly swung to me, her expression irritated. Fuck! She definitely could read my mind. Think nice things. Think nice things. Exit. Exit. Exit.

I motioned that I'd be next door in one of the consulting rooms and made a quick departure. Once there, I picked up my phone to dial into the voicemail, only to hear Conn's voice.

'No, that's not a problem – she'll deliver the full manuscript early June and a quick turnaround suits us perfectly. No, no, I understand – we don't want to miss the Christmas market either so we're happy to commit whatever time is needed.'

Zara's book. I got a little rush of excitement. Despite the sheer craziness of it all, I had to admit there was something quite thrilling about being involved in this world of celebrity and media. For years I'd promised myself that one day I'd take the day off work and persuade Trish to let me visit the *Great Morning TV!* studios, but now it was part of the job to go there every Friday with Zara. On the first occasion, Trish had had to steer me to a dark corner so that I wouldn't risk the embarrassment of being struck dumb when the bloke who used to be in *Where the Heart Is* spoke to me. On the second visit, I was so busy gaping at Tom Hanks plugging his new movie that I thudded into the catering table, causing a whole avalanche of food to go sliding to the floor in front of a room full of people. Bad point: there were many people to see my mortification. Good point: if Trish had followed through on her promise to kill me there'd be plenty of witnesses for the prosecution.

I listened to Conn for a few seconds before gently replacing the receiver, trying to ignore the fact that the hairs on the back of my neck were standing on end and there were the definite beginnings of a very strange sensation in the pit of my stomach. I barely had time to gasp when . . . suddenly he was there, sitting on the edge of the desk in front of me and, oops, he'd forgotten to put his clothes on again. 'Leni . . . ' he whispered, before leaning over, slipping his hand around the back of my neck and pulling me towards him. He kissed me, his tongue slowly, sensually finding mine, his teeth nibbling gently on my bottom lip, his body ready and waiting to . . .

Stop! In the name of office pervs, what was going on with me? It wasn't even 10 a.m. and already I'd had two daydreams involving a very naked man. I definitely had to have sex soon, as neglected libido is now causing disturbing hallucinations of a genital nature.

Distraction. Needed a distraction. I pressed a button on the phone to get a different line, entered a code to switch my calls to this extension, then dialled into my mailbox.

'You have seven new messages.' Seven? I never got more than two and one was usually my mother phoning for a chat.

I pressed '#'.

'Leni, can you call me back – I'm a bit worried because I haven't heard from you since last night.'

Aaaw, it was so sweet that Stu was worried. I'd meant to call him but when I got home the night before my mobile was out of charge and I'd fallen asleep before I'd given it enough juice to make a call. I'd thought about getting a landline installed but there was a £145 connection fee and it always seemed unnecessary when I could talk all evening for free on my mobile. Talking of which . . . I felt around in my bag for my phone. Damn. Must have left it on the charger at home.

I pressed delete, then # again.

'Leni, me again – call me back.'

He sounded a little more urgent this time.

Delete. #.

'Leni, okay, I'm getting seriously freaked out. Call me.'

Delete. #.

'Leni, if I don't hear from you in the next fifteen minutes, I'm calling the police.'

Delete. #.

'No, I'm not, I'm going round to your flat. If you're lying behind the door it should be someone who loves you that discovers you.'

I rolled my eyes. *And the Oscar for 'Most Dramatic Friend in a Crisis' goes to . . .*

Delete. #.

'Okay, I'm going to leave in ten minutes. Just as soon as I get these roots done.'

Delete. #.

'Leni, I . . . '

I didn't get to hear the rest of my message because the phone burst into life with the ring of an incoming call. I pressed 'receive'.

'Hello, Leni speaki—'

'OH, THANK GOD! THANK GOD!!!!'

The words came tumbling out, the voice raspy, the breathing out of control.

'Stu, calm down, I'm fine. I just got into work and was about to call you back.'

'CALL ME BACK?!!!'

It wasn't an exclamation or a question – more an outraged outburst.

'I'VE BEEN CALLING YOU SINCE EIGHT O'CLOCK THIS MORNING!!!'

I checked my watch – 10.30 a.m.

'Stu, I just got in. They let me start a bit later this morning because of the date last night. Anyway, thanks for being concerned, but there's no need, honestly, I'm absolutely fine. Didn't you get my email?'

'EMAIL!!!! I've been too bloody busy preparing myself to identify your body to check my bloody emails!'

Silence. I had no idea what to say to him other than, 'Well, happy days, I'm not on a slab in a fridge.' How could I have been so thoughtless? I knew how he worried yet I'd sent him into a full-scale panic. Cue familiar large cloud of guilt.

'Look, why don't I come over to the salon at lunchtime and I'll bring your favourite paninis and those Belgian chocolates you love from the deli. My treat.'

I'd already had my first salary cheque so I was feeling flush.

There was a long pause, then . . . 'I, er, won't be there.'

'Why, where are you?'

I was baffled. I was sure he'd said he was at the salon in one of his calls – the one before he said . . . Oh no.

'I'm at your flat . . . ' he answered awkwardly. One of my heartstrings pinged. How sweet was he? I was so lucky to have such a caring, sweet friend – even if he did veer towards the hysterical in times of stress. But my flat was only fifteen minutes from the salon, so surely he'd make it back in plenty of time for lunch? Unless . . .

'. . . and I'll need to wait here for the joiner. You never liked that front door anyway, did you?'

Once again, my mind drifted back to New Year's Eve when I had bemoaned the lack of excitement and adventure in my life. A few weeks later? My boss flashing her baps at me first thing in the morning wasn't the craziest thing to happen in my day. I was beginning to think excitement and adventure were overrated.

A strangled yelp came from the other end of the phone, followed by a clearly discernible, 'What is going on here, young man?'

It was the unmistakable sound of Mrs Naismith on the warpath. The mental image of five foot two inches of septuagenarian, topped with hair the same colour as her varicose veins, giving Stu a stern dressing down, almost made the destruction of the door worthwhile. I could hear him blustering out excuses but she was having none of it. Since the day I had arrived from Norfolk she'd appointed herself as a cross between my guardian and a neighbourhood watch service. She kept an eye on my flat (most of the time!), stopped in for regular chats and frequently cooked for two, leaving half outside my door for when I came home. She was an absolute gem – one that was about to serve time for threatening behaviour, going by the bollocking she was giving Stu.

I hung up, leaving Stu to face the wrath, just as Conn came in clutching a large sheaf of papers packed into a clear file. I tried unsuccessfully not to blush.

'There you are!'

'Yes, Zara is, er, busy next door, so I thought I'd work in here for a while.'

At least I think that's what I said. It was difficult to hear over the noise of the butterflies in my stomach and the whooshing in my head.

He put the file in front of me.

'This is the debriefing document for the date last night. I'm sure you'll appreciate that we need to know every detail so that we can do effective analysis and comparisons.'

How about comparing my . . .

'Are you okay, Leni? You seem a bit . . . pale.'

Right on cue, my face flushed bright red. 'No, I'm, er . . . er . . . '

Inarticulate?

It was difficult to tell who was the most uncomfortable, but I was putting my money on me.

'Right then,' he answered with an understanding nod, although I've absolutely no idea what he understood – other than the apparent fact that his mother had hired the most moronic PA since time began. He came around to my side of the desk and half-sat, half-leaned, in exactly the same position as I'd imagined him before. If my body was a thermometer, the mercury would have shot out of the top like a burst pipe.

'Can you do something for me?' he asked.

Note to tongue: please re-enter gob.

'Can you send flowers, mmm, I think orchids would be best, to Annabella Churchill, with a note saying, "Thank you for a wonderful time last night. Eternally yours, Conn."'

My pencil scribbled away on my pad, the shaking making it look like it was written by me in my geriatric years.

'And can you also arrange some for Courtney Caven and Penelope Smith; here are their address details.'

His Eau de Hubba Hubba had now permeated my entire space and was making me giddy.

'Of course. What note would you like with those ones?'
He was such a gentleman – so sweet, so chivalrous.

'The same.'

Such a player.

So while I was putting myself in potentially life-threatening peril (it was the hormones, they were making me a bit hysterical), he was having it off with three – count them – *three* other women.

Focus, Leni, focus. This was work, not the problem page of *Cosmo*, and the last ten minutes had thrown up tasks that needed to be addressed. I called the florist, organised the blooms, then clicked on to amazon.co.uk and ordered *How to Make Him Notice You – a single girl's guide to standing out from the crowd*.

The file Conn had left on my desk was next. After three hours, six coffees and the loss of my will to live, I finally completed twenty-two A4 pages recounting practically every minute and detail of my night with Harry. I would have gone home for a lie down, only I didn't want to get in the way of the joiner.

Instead I called Trish.

'Fancy lunch today?'

'Can't – I'm working an extra shift covering *Wacky Women*.'

It was one of my favourite shows – a panel format of five celebrity females discussing the day's top stories and celebrity gossip, headed by Kim Black, a fifty-something actress/comedian who got more outspoken and outrageous with every passing year.

'And besides, I wouldn't miss this, even for you – Kim has had a boob job and the producer is going mental because she needs a whole new wardrobe. They've come to blows once already, and now she's screaming in her dressing room that if her lawyer isn't here within the next thirty minutes she's not going on. Oh, and she's asked me to get her a cattle prod from the props room, so I'm thinking this isn't going to end well. God, I love TV. Phone Stu, I'm sure he'll be hard up for someone to have lunch with too.'

Trish was like a scud missile to the ego every time. The door opened behind me so I hung up quickly.

'Finished?' Conn asked with a smile. Thud. Thud. Thud. Sorry, heart overruling head and all significant motor skills.

'Uhuhhh.' Including vocal cords.

'Great – I'll just take the file away then.'

'Uhuhhh.'

'Thanks, Leni. We'll start looking for number two.'

I was going to repeat my reply, but I'm guessing that it was fairly predictable.

'And Leni, you do remember that this is all strictly confidential and that you signed an agreement that it cannot be discussed outside the organisation?'

I did. And I'd never, ever, breach company security by divulging classified information to unauthorised sources.

Never.

Ever.

At least, not during working hours.

Great Morning TV!

Goldie Gilmartin closed off the interview with Jeremy Sinclair, the MP for Cornwall and Devon, a rather rotund, flush-faced human personification of a walrus who was making a public apology to his wife after being caught by a Sunday tabloid snorting cocaine from an intimate part of his twenty-one-year-old girlfriend's anatomy.

'So, just to re-emphasise one point, Goldie,' said the walrus, in a weary yet pompous monotone. 'I sincerely apologise to my party, my constituents, my mother, and all those who have placed their confidence in me over the years. But, most of all, I'd like to apologise to my wife, whom I love very much and who has pledged to stand by me for better or worse.'

Goldie reached over and shook his hand.

'I wish you well, Jeremy,' she said sincerely, 'and good luck to your lovely wife Leticia.'

Jeremy nodded gravely. The shot closed in on Goldie as she spoke directly to camera, an undeniably cheeky twinkle in her eye. 'And don't forget, the other party in this affair, Araminta Delouche, will be with us tomorrow morning to give her version of events. But first . . . '

The camera panned out again, this time a little too quickly, and the audience got a full view of Zara, standing to the side of the set, waiting to take Jeremy's chair, but not succeeding because he was frozen to the spot with a horrified expression on his face, astounded that his young bit of fluff had secured airspace on the country's primetime morning show.

The unmistakable image of a researcher dragging him from the set would have the nation talking for the rest of the day.

As always, Zara ran through her weekly predictions, forecasting love, joy, excitement, doom, gloom and disaster for the various signs.

'Thank you, Zara. And thanks too for that accident warning for all us Taureans – I think I'll make sure I stay at home this weekend,' she said with her trademark grin. 'Now, you wanted to make another announcement about your forthcoming book.'

'That's right, Goldie. As I've mentioned before, all you single girls out there have something to look forward to at the end of the year, because I'm working on a top-secret book that will revolutionise relationships forever. Brace yourselves, girls!' she added, giggling conspiratorially.

'But in the meantime, I need some men . . . '

'Don't we all, Zara, don't we all,' Goldie joked.

'I need you single men to write in, tell me all about yourselves and take part in this revolutionary research. Or of course you can log on to my website at www.itsinthestars.net, Britain's most popular website featuring a full range of Zara Delta merchandise.

'Now, we're especially looking for Scorpios this week, and as I've said before, all expenses will be paid and you just might have the best night of your life. So, mums, sisters, aunties, grannies and all you bachelors out there, get writing . . . and don't forget to enclose your birth date and a photograph.'

While Zara paused for breath, Goldie swept in to wrap the slot up.

'And that's all we have time for. Stay tuned for Wacky

Women, *who'll be discussing the male contraceptive pill in a show entitled, "Would You Really Trust Your Reproductive Health to a Species Who Can't Remember What Day the Bins Go Out?"'*

7

The Scorpio Date

'Who wants to hear the best gossip since I revealed that two current affairs reporters had been caught in an Edgware crack den with three Thai lady-boys, doing unmentionable things with boom microphones?' Trish twiddled her cocktail stick between her fingers, her eyebrows in the 'you'll never believe it' position.

'We're all ears,' said Stu, grinning.

'I know, but surgery could correct that.' She ducked to avoid the beer mat that was propelled in her direction. 'Guess which clean-living sports icon I heard indulging in a little powder-snorting in the gents toilets at the studio this morning? I'll give you a clue – if his missus finds out there'll be a fair amount of police brutality involved.'

'Noooooooooooo,' we both blurted. It could only be Dirk Bentley, legendary heptathlete, now married to Karen Cutler, publicity-loving Chief Commissioner of the Metropolitan Police.

It took a few minutes for the news to digest before the obvious question surfaced.

'Trish, why were you in the gents toilets?'

'Grey stopped by after work. Honest to God, his shift

pattern is a nightmare – have you ever tried having a healthy sex life when you have opposing work schedules?'

Stu and I spontaneously joined in a collective, 'Eeeeeeeeeew!'

'You had sex with your husband in the toilets at work?' Stu groaned.

'My office has a large window – I'd have shocked the staff,' she deadpanned, then turned to me. 'So anyway, what time are you meeting the next victim?' she asked, while sucking a cherry off a cocktail stick.

'STOP!' Stu interrupted. 'Trish, look at that manky bloke behind the bar.' He pointed in the direction of the greasy-haired grunge fan who had served us.

'Yeah, so?' asked Trish, unimpressed.

'He was the one who put the fruit on that cocktail stick, the one you're sucking up like a Dyson. You might have survived doing naked things in a toilet this morning – and incidentally, that mental image will probably scar me for life – but if you swallow that germ-oozing cherry you'll be down with a bacterial stomach bug before the night's out.'

Trish rolled her eyes. 'Stu, you're a male hairdresser – aren't you supposed to be frivolous, glib and full of scandalous gossip?'

'You're female – aren't you supposed to be caring, emotional and compassionate?'

'Good point, well made,' Trish laughed, as she threw the rest of the cocktail garnish in the ashtray.

'Right, children, that's enough,' I interjected, my anxiety and apprehension manifesting itself as sharp irritability. 'I'm meeting him at eight o'clock. I told him to come in here, so keep your eyes on the door for a Matt Warden, five foot nine, age thirty, tall, brown shaggy hair and brown eyes. Looked a bit like Paolo Nutini in his photo. His hobbies are going to gigs, listening to music and playing in a band,

and he has the unequivocal honour of being my Mr Scorpio.' With that, I picked up my glass of white wine and downed it in one. My nerves and self-esteem might one day recover from this, but I wasn't so sure about my liver. I thumped the glass back on the table then slipped my hands under my thighs so no one would notice them shaking. I couldn't stand another lecture from Trish, and I didn't want to freak Stu out any more than he already was.

Right on cue, Stu subconsciously started to massage the left-hand side of his beautifully rounded pectoral muscle. One of the up sides of being obsessed by your health is that you tended to surpass the government guidelines on nutrition and exercise.

'I still can't believe you're doing this. I swear my stress-induced heart attack will be on your conscience.'

'Can I have your record collection and your Prada Messenger bag when you pop your clogs then?' Trish asked.

He ignored her. 'Man alert, man alert – potential date entering building.'

I spun around to see the bloke whose photo I'd studied that afternoon making his way towards me. I was glad that once again I'd taken Millie's advice and gone for slouchy jeans and trainers, because Matt was dressed in the same ultra-casual style.

I'd given him a description of myself on the phone, and since I was the only fairly tall redhead with a Rolling Stones T-shirt in the immediate vicinity, he spotted me right away. I hopped off my stool and smiled as he approached me (which sounds very casual and relaxed . . . if it weren't for the fact that my legs buckled at the knees and only a swift grab by Stu saved me from rank indignity).

'Leni? Thought so – I'm Matt.' He smiled to reveal a perfect row of glistening teeth.

Stu coughed behind me, so I made quick introductions,

then got Matt out of there before I could change my mind or Stu could do anything to jeopardise the date. He'd been threatening all night to slip Mr Scorpio a telephone number, say it was the National Leprosy Helpline and advise him to give the number a call if he developed any suspicious rashes within five to seven days of meeting me.

Outside, the wind took my breath away – a natty distraction from the now-familiar shaking hands, dry mouth and sick feeling in my stomach. I could do this. I could. How bad could it be? At least Matt was easy on the eyes and had so far shown no unnatural interest in computer-simulated weaponry.

I decided to plunge right in before my nerves took hold and I either froze up or started to babble.

'So what would you like to do?'

'Well, if it's okay with you . . . ' Caring. Considerate. Consultative.

' . . . my band got a last-minute gig and . . . ' Cancelled.

'Sure, it's no problem, we can meet another night, it's fine, really, no problem, fine,' I babbled.

He laughed and spontaneously leaned over and put a finger to my lips: presumptuous, but strangely I felt absolutely no compulsion to complain.

'I thought – again, if it's okay with you – that maybe you'd want to come along. It's only an hour-long set, and then maybe we can go and grab something to eat later. I know a great little Italian place near the club we're playing in – nothing fancy but it does a great lasagne.'

Okay, so now I'd been further demoted from 'date for hire' to 'groupie'.

Fabulous!

I'd been waiting for this moment since 1995, when I'd discovered a teen mag feature entitled: 101 Ways to Meet Your Favourite Band. I'd tried all 101 of them and never got any further than a signed photo of the drummer from Blur and the threat of a restraining order from a band who had a number 16 hit and then split due to 'creative differences'. Deep down I always wanted to be one of those cool girls who hung out with musicians. You know, standing at the side of the stage basking in their spotlight, the thrill of the live gig, going from town to town on the tour bus, in a hedonistic world of indulgence and decadence. So my inner rock chick was head-banging in joy at the prospect of being with the band, and it didn't matter in the least that I'd never heard of them or that when we got to the tiny club there were only about fifty people in the audience. When we walked in and everyone turned to stare, a thrilling shot of adrenalin turned my cheeks purple (a look that was, thankfully, camouflaged by the dim lighting).

Nirvana blasted from the music system as Matt grabbed a couple of beers from the bar and then took me over and introduced me to the rest of the band, all crowded around a huge amp at one side of the stage and sporting the same image: funky T-shirts, slouchy jeans and bed-hair. The reason that there was a disproportionate number of females in the audience was blindingly clear.

Oh, the thrill of it. Miss Anxious Plodder, 2009, was now a hip, trendy groupie who was getting on down with a happening band. Groovy.

Yes, I realised that my internal dialogue had tripped back to the Sixties, but I didn't care – I had a feeling that tonight was going to be unforgettable.

How right I was . . .

8

Stars in Their Eyes

'I'd like to dedicate this last song to someone special. This is for Leni . . . '

The crowd went wild, although it might have had more to do with Matt peeling off his T-shirt than dedicating a tune to some female they'd never met.

Taking a purely objective viewpoint, I could categorically confirm that The Black Spikes were absolutely brilliant. Turns out I hadn't been far off when I'd said Matt resembled Paolo Nutini. They had the same hypnotic, gravelly vocals, although Matt's music was more in the vein of the Red Hot Chili Peppers. As he flipped between rock numbers and a few soulful, heart-melting ballads, I wondered if it was still etiquette in situations such as these to throw one's knickers at the stage (I suspected that wanton act was the reason that, despite having lust-worthy looks and a great voice, Stu had never pursued a music career – he'd be up there in a surgical facemask hosing down the stage with disinfectant).

To thunderous applause, Matt gave a final wave and jumped off the stage, clearly buzzed up and looking more alive than anyone I'd ever seen. I suddenly realised that this was why I had embarked on this whole life-change plan.

Worry and hesitation be damned! This was what I'd been talking about when I had made that New Year's resolution to change my life. Right here, right now, this was what I'd been missing for so long – the excitement, the high, the grinning until my jaw hurt. I'd done it!

'What did you think?'

I decided to play it cool. 'OH MY GOD YOU WERE AMAZING AND I'VE NEVER SEEN ANYTHING LIKE THAT AND YOU SHOULD HAVE A RECORDING CONTRACT AND YOU JUST WERE SO SO SO BLOODY BRILLIANT.'

I was playing it cool in a hysterical, babbling sort of fashion.

He grabbed my hand. 'C'mon, let's get out of here. Let me just get a quick shower in the staff room and I'll be right with you.'

He tugged my arm and steered me in the direction of the side of the stage, then through a black door that led out of the madness.

'Grab a seat, I'll be two minutes.'

Now, that statement might sound utterly innocuous, but – I realised as he flipped open the top button on his jeans and then started on the zip – it depended on what he was planning to do for those 120 seconds and whether or not I'd be forced to witness it or participate. The euphoria was now punctured by just a few shards of apprehension and doubt. Do not panic. Do not panic. Was there a fire-alarm glass I could smash while my inner groupie came to terms with the fact that she was all talk and no action?

We were in a square room, about ten foot by ten foot with coat pegs lined along every wall and a menagerie of hold-alls and backpacks on the floor. In the corner there was a shower, with only a tattered pink curtain protecting the modesty of the user. The flush of mortification started at my toes and worked its way up until puffs of steam were being ejected from the neck of my T-shirt.

And still he was unzipping, unzipping . . . Where the bloody hell was the fire alarm?

Suddenly he stopped, laughing as his glance went downwards and he realised he'd almost flashed me. 'Oh shit, sorry! I just . . . I mean . . . shit, you must think I'm a complete maniac.'

A firmly toned, unbelievably cute maniac with the voice of an angel who'd just scared the crap out of me.

I shrugged, hoping I came across as blasé, cool and collected. Granted, the steam framing my purple face may have given the opposite impression.

'Okay, close your eyes and I'll tell you when to open them again. Unless you want to wait outside, but the pub's mobbed and there are no seats in the corridor out there.'

'No, no, it's . . . erm, fine. I'm cool.'

Uurgh – did I really just say 'I'm cool'? Who did I think I was – Shaft?

I closed my eyes and listened to the unmistakable sounds of clothes coming off and a shower going on. All the while he was chatting away, giving me the history of the band, how they were hoping that they'd get spotted by some A&R people this year, how they wrote their own music and . . .

I tuned him out. Differences between males and females, number 2,343: he's in the shower, thinking of nothing deeper than whether to use coconut shampoo or just give his hair a quick going-over with the shower gel, meanwhile I'm sitting five yards away thinking that this is the loveliest guy I've met in a while and yes, I definitely fancy him and would he ask me out again and what would I say and then what would I do about the other ten dates because surely he wouldn't want me to go on them and maybe I could broach it with Zara because surely she'd understand. Of course, I'd repay her with free tickets to his gigs when the band had made it big and I'd become a bona fide rock chick with a lifestyle to match. There'd be the customary large mansion in Sussex that was forever getting picketed by adoring fans, while a team of people organised us and arranged the annual summer move to the beach chateau in St Tropez. I'd get to wear leather trousers, even when they were out of fashion. I'd never worry about what people thought of me, because rockers just don't care. Money would roll in and life would never, ever be dull, because there would always be other rockers hanging around doing wild things like having orgies on revolving beds and vomiting in the swimming pool. We'd give interviews to *OK!* magazine where he'd say that he knew our relationship was real because we'd met when he had nothing, and I'd be able to let go of all the hesitation and shyness because I'd be cocooned in a comfort blanket of love, devotion and excitement. And we'd always be with friends because I'd employ Stu as our medical advisor and stylist and Trish as our cook. Although I would have to check the food for arsenic as I reckon she'd be so bitter about my money, fame and private jet that she might be unable to resist the urge to poison my curly fries.

'Okay, you can open your eyes now.'

I hesitated, suddenly fearful that this was going to be one of those horrific moments caused by a cataclysmic difference in expectations. Was I going to flip up my lids and be confronted with him standing bollock-naked, muscles flexed, with his microphone in a state of expectant erection?

'Leni, really, it's fine to open your eyes.'

I took a deep breath and sneaked one eye open just a millimetre. Phew. Fully clothed.

'So let's go. Hungry?'

Strangely, my appetite seemed to have vanished.

'Starving!' I'd read somewhere that men enjoy the company of women with an enthusiastic attitude to food.

My hunger – previously suffocated by excitement and physical attraction – was resuscitated by the lasagne, which was, as promised, magnificent. We shared a huge bowl of tiramisu and were on to our fourth or fifth glass of wine when I realised something: this was the best night I'd had in years. Forget that I was doing this as part of my job, forget that I'd only met him four hours before; I now understood what people meant when they claimed to have an 'instant connection' with someone. Matt and I just clicked, and every well-worn cliché seemed to apply – I felt like I'd known him for years, we were two peas in a pod, we were on the same wavelength, I was flying without wings . . .

Oh God, I was starting to think in Westlife lyrics – time to stop drinking.

'I just have to nip to the loo.'

It was only when I got up that I realised we were holding hands. When had that happened?

Water. Cold. On face. Now.

I stared in the bathroom mirror for a few moments. Calm down, Leni, calm down. He's gorgeous, he's cute, he's the most amazing guy you've met in years . . . what was I missing out? Oh, yes, *he's in a band!!!!!* My experience and judgement when it came to members of the opposite sex had been fairly inaccurate in the past, but this was different. Forget the *OK!* magazine deal and the vomit-filled pool in Surrey – even if he never made it bigger than dingy clubs in Camden, I really, really wanted to see him again, and I absolutely, definitely, positively knew that he felt the same.

I brushed my hair, dabbed on a quick coat of Juicy Tubes pink shimmer, grinned inanely at my reflection for a few seconds and then left the loos. To think I'd been so nervous about tonight, and just look how brilliantly it had turned out.

As I pushed through the door to the now almost deserted restaurant, he had his back to me so I didn't feel too self-conscious about the running commentary in my head: . . . *look at the way the light catches his hair . . . that colour of blue looks great on him . . . he's ordered another bottle of wine so he must be having a good time too.*

I was almost right behind him when I realised three things:

a) He was on the phone.

b) He hadn't heard me approaching.

c) He wasn't speaking to the features team at *OK!*.

Even from a couple of feet behind him, I could clearly hear every word.

'Baby, I'm sorry and I won't be much longer, I promise. No, she's not totally stunning, she's just normal-looking. Ordinary. Nothing like you, babe. Look, I told you, this is for the band. It's all about contacts, baby, and this one could get us a gig on that morning telly show. Exposure, that's what we need, then the record companies will be lining up. Honey, you know I wouldn't, I promise. Why would I want to shag anyone but you, huh? This is just networking, babe, taking advantage of the opportunities.'

I was glad I already had my bag over my shoulder because a whole 'fumbling for my belongings' episode would have completely spoiled the effect. Plus, then he might just have seen how upset I was, and that would have been the biggest tragedy of all.

Instead, I just kept on walking in the direction of the door, and I promise it was just an inexplicable reflex action that caused my left arm to flick out and knock a whole bottle of Shiraz into his lap.

He sprang up, dropped the phone and yelped out a high-pitched 'What the fuck!!!?'

I automatically did what I always did in situations that called for a cunning reply with an acerbic tongue. A mantra of '*What would Trish say, what would Trish say?*' tore through my mind all the way to the door. As a blast of freezing cold air hit my face, I suddenly knew.

I turned to face him, his chiselled features now contorted with blind fury.

'You know, Matt, your band was okay . . . but to be honest, it was really nothing that special.'

And then I cried all the way home, totally irritated that I'd been such a twat. If this was change, adventure and excitement, I'd happily go back to my rut.

PROGRESS SUMMARY: *IT'S IN THE STARS* DATING PROJECT

CONCLUDED		
LEO	Harry Henshall	Morbid fascination for simulated violence
SCORPIO	Matt Warden	Lead singer, lying arse

EMAIL
To: Trisha; Stu
From: Leni Lomond
Re: If last night's date had a personal ad, it would read like . . .

Male, 30, Scorpio, wannabe rock star with all the pelvic thrusting moves, could charm the knickers off a nun, talented, good looking, ambitious, and will stop at nothing to get what he wants. Has own leather trousers. Prepared to sacrifice dignity, morals and sperm in the name of success. Very sociable, with large network of friends, and happy to screw them over or sell them out to get to the top. Would like to meet powerful, well-connected, open-minded female with job in A&R department of a successful record company, who wouldn't mind sharing him with existing girlfriend. Or Simon Cowell. Revolving bed and Surrey mansion a bonus.

Applicants to apply in person at local shit-hole pub, Saturday night, 8 p.m. – tickets £5.

The Daily Globe, Female Section, 20 February

Interview with Zara Delta, Sage to the Stars,
by Camilla Beaufort-Dodds

The first thing that strikes me about Zara Delta is her inner glow – but not quite in the way you might imagine. I soon discover that the inner glow is caused by two small battery-operated green light-bulbs that she has placed within her cheeks, in order, she informs us, to harness the powers of 'light energy' – a practice she claims calms her mind and rejuvenates her inner life-force. She made no comment as to whether or not she was concerned about the potential health hazards that could be caused by holding two live batteries in her gums.

Ever the professional, however, I see that she has had the foresight to colour-coordinate her flashing cheeks with her dress of choice today – an elaborate green kaftan adorned with what she informs me are ancient Masai symbols, a garment that was gifted to her by the tribal head of a small village during a recent private trip to Africa.

Thankfully, Zara removes the light-bulbs before our conversation begins; however, I do confess to being slightly alarmed when she suddenly clenches her eyes shut and the tone of her voice plunges dramatically.

'You've had a recent loss,' she informs me in hushed tones. 'And it involves ... it involves an animal ... a very dear, beloved animal.'

It seems prudent to confirm that yes, only a few weeks before, we had indeed lost Crackers, the horse on which I'd cantered since childhood. I was deeply comforted when Ms Delta assured me that he was in a better place where he could gallop freely, unburdened by the pains of old age.

Surely such perception and insight into the lives of others must be a devastatingly emotional burden to bear?

Zara nods wearily, her frame slumped in exhaustion after our opening exchange.

'Sometimes it is difficult,' she agrees, 'but it's also a very special gift that I feel so privileged to have been given. And I feel it is my duty to use that gift to improve the lives of others.'

She pauses to take a sip from a wooden clay pot on her desk, containing a mix of herbs and cleansing roots – a recipe, she tells me, that she discovered many years ago while living among the people of the Andes.

'That's why I've decided to write my latest book – a relationship guide that will revolutionise the modern woman's approach to searching for their perfect partner. Today's women have lives that are busier than ever – they're juggling careers, hectic social lives, personal fitness and family obligations, leaving them little time to focus on what really matters: finding love. This is where I will help. I will give them a foolproof plan that will identify their needs, and then show them how to fulfil their dreams. This book will, quite literally, change lives.'

Sadly, our conversation is brought to a premature end by an assistant who interrupts to inform Zara that a certain A-list household name needs her urgent advice. As she rises, she re-inserts her inner glow and hugs me tightly.

'I'm so sorry to cut this short, but that's another conse-quence of this gift – I have to go to those who need me.'

And if you are one of the thousands of women who need Zara Delta, her book will be available in all good bookstores in December.

9

The Aries Date

'Maybe this one will be better,' Millie said, as I filled her in on the details of my next trip to Dating Hell Central.

'Are you saying that because you really mean it, or are you just trying to keep my spirits up with moral support and false hope?'

'Definitely moral support and false hope,' she replied with a giggle. 'Is it working?'

'No,' I said bluntly.

The fortnight since my Scorpion disaster had been a roller-coaster of emotions that had finally derailed a couple of days before, when Trish had sat me down, swept aside the first ten drafts of my resignation letter, tossed away my new copy of *How to Spot a Tosser with Your Eyes Shut*, and given me a stern talking-to.

'Look, you can't bail out on this now. Yes, you met a nasty little shit, but so what? At least you got paid for meeting him. In the past you regularly met nasty little shits on your own time. If it wasn't for these dates, would you or would you not want to keep working for Zara?'

I'd nodded reluctantly. Okay, so it was like entering a parallel universe on Planet Space Cadet every day, but at least it didn't focus on the stark, banal reality of toilet fittings. And the alternatives still didn't bear thinking about – more interviews, more new environments, more upheaval, and no more pornographic fantasies involving boss's hot offspring.

'Okay, your personal life now – do you or do you not want to go out on dates, meet new guys, and, in the words of the late, great Freddie Mercury, find somebody to love?'

I'd nodded again.

'And did you solemnly swear in this very room on New Year's Eve that this was going to be the year that you broke out of your comfort zone and achieved your goals?'

I blew my hair out of my eyes and briefly wondered if other people had a best friend so fierce that they regularly made them sweat under pressure. Trish had so blatantly missed her calling in life. She should have a job that would allow her to use her skills at the highest levels – for example, as a military interrogator. Or a high-class dominatrix.

'Then get over yourself. So one was a dickhead – do you know how many dickheads I went out with before I met Grey? Loads.'

I knew she was trying to make me feel better – using methods taken straight from the *Sado-Masochistic Guide to Friendship* – but I wasn't convinced. Yes, her Grey was a lovely guy, kind, sweet and funny (I was choosing to momentarily overlook the penchant for sex in public places), and I'd love to meet someone like him, but let's face it, what were the chances of a Grey-esque sweetheart writing in to *Great Morning TV!* and landing at my feet? Slim. I'd only ever met one man that I'd loved the way she loved Grey, and . . . well . . .

'I still miss him, Trish. And when crap stuff like this happens I miss him even more.'

She'd softened for a moment. More than anyone, Trish knew how devastated I'd been when I'd discovered that

Ben was married. She'd spent weeks pushing the hair off my face while I exhausted the global stock of man-size Kleenex.

'Look, that's done. It's gone. So pick yourself up and just bloody get on with it. And I say that from a place of love.'

I'd mulled over her gentle advice. She was right. Broken heart aside, I'd had two bad experiences on the dating front, but I'd been paid for them and they had both taught me valuable lessons (stay away from blokes with arrested development and a penchant for computer-generated warfare; and lead singers are all devious, egotistical knobs).

Millie's voice brought me back to the present as it sing-songed with a, 'Good morning, Conn. Zara is upstairs and she asked if you could pop in and see her as soon as you arrive.'

'Thanks, Millie. Morning, Leni – ready for another big night tonight?'

'Absolutely,' I replied. 'Can't wait.'

'Great. I read your report on the last one – sounds like you had a rough time. Sorry about that.'

'Oh, it was nothing – nothing that I couldn't handle,' I assured him, with an accompanying swatting gesture. Millie folded her arms under her bosom and fixed me with an amused, incredulous stare that lasted until Conn licked my face, thrust me against the wall, devoured me with wild abandon (twice), made my earth move (just once), then climbed the stairs, his beautifully carved, naked buttocks clenching with every step.

Okay, so maybe he just gave me a distracted, encouraging smile and went to his office.

'Nothing? It was "nothing" then?' she probed, hardly able to contain her enjoyment as I squirmed.

'Oh, don't you start – I've already got one ruthless, mocking pal, thank you.'

'I think Leni is trying to impress a certain tall, dark, handsome gentleman.'

'I am not!' I replied indignantly. 'It's purely professional. I just want him to think I'm really good at my job, that's all.'

I gathered up the morning mail and took a few steps towards the stairs, when I realised . . .

'Conn didn't say what he wanted for lunch today.'

'Oh, I think he'll be going out.'

Ah, I had her! I already knew that Zara had taken temporary residence in an upmarket day spa, and that Conn was planning to work in the office all day before meeting Zara at 7 p.m. and going off to a fundraising ball they were attending that evening. Zara had donated a raffle prize of an hour's free consultation, and in return they'd been invited to the star-studded meal prepared by Jamie Oliver and a team of dinner ladies from Southend.

'Nope, sorry but you're wrong,' I argued, thrilled to bits that for the first time I had the upper hand, 'and I do believe that you'll receive a call any minute requesting . . . '

Right, it was Thursday. What did he have last Thursday? Think. Think. Think.

'Vegetable soup with a crusty wholemeal baguette,' I announced with a flourish and just a smidgen of smugness. Cue one departing smidgen as I got halfway up the stairs and met Conn coming back down them.

'Change of plan, Leni, I've got to meet with the event managers for tonight because they want Zara to do a live reading and I need to organise the set. I'll be out for the rest of the day, but you can get me on my mobile.'

It was official: what I knew about men could be written in capitals on a Post-it note. N.O.T.H.I.N.G.

'Oh, and can you send champagne to these four ladies,' he thrust a sheet of notepaper with contact details scribbled in red pen towards me, 'and organise for the house, pool and gazebo to be cleaned today. Thanks, Leni.'

Off he went, all suave and official, while giving me backwards glances that oozed wanton lust. Okay, so I was imagining that too.

I trudged up the rest of the stairs in the manner of a death-row inmate en route to the chair with the big plug. And ten hours later, as I waited for Daniel Jones, 25, an accountant from Teddington, I was wishing someone would flick the switch.

If this was such a 'nothing', as I'd blurted to Conn, then why was my heart thumping like a boy racer's Corsa? And the less said about the sweat patches I suspected were forming around my hotspots, the better. This was hell. Hell. I didn't want to be here. I wanted to be at home, lying on the couch, munching HobNobs and watching old episodes of *Sex and the City* with the volume up really loud, so it drowned out the Barry Manilow DVD that Mrs Naismith next door played on a nightly basis.

Still, at least tonight's rendezvous was local, so that would make it easier for the murder squad to track down my address book to obtain details of my next of kin. When I'd called Daniel to make arrangements and reaffirm that the content of the date was entirely up to him, I'd mentioned that I lived on the Slough/Windsor border, and straight away he'd suggested we meet at the bus station in Slough. My first reaction was that it was sweet that he didn't want to make me travel; my second was that I was fairly certain that I wasn't heading for an evening of five-star luxury and opulence.

'Leni?'

The voice sounded warm (somewhere between your favourite male friend and a *Blue Peter* presenter) with definite overtones of apprehension. At least we already had something in common.

'So, er, what would you like to do then?' he stuttered anxiously after we'd done the awkward introductions.

That threw me. 'It's, er, up to you,' I reminded him, trying desperately to suppress my tendency towards nervous irritation. I had enough to worry about, what with making conversation, keeping mental notes and trying not to crumble into a full-scale panic attack, without making decisions about the logistics of the night.

After a tortured gap of hesitation, he took the hint. 'Well, er, let's go for a drink first then.'

Oooh, what did he mean by 'first'? Maybe I had made a rash and incorrect assumption. Had he made reservations at a nice restaurant? Did he have plans for a swanky night of gastronomic indulgence?

'And then you can decide what kind of food you feel like: Indian, Chinese, pizza . . . '

Cancel all thoughts of swanky plans.

After a few on-the-spot shuffles we set off, strolling through the windswept metropolis that was the Slough pedestrian precinct. In the manner of an undercover operative (Mission Un-bloody-believable), I flicked some covert glances in his direction and committed the details to memory: auburn spiky hair (Jake Gyllenhaal meets hair gel), khaki combat trousers (well pressed, new) and pale brown cashmere v-neck jumper – fairly attractive, in an understated kind of way. And you could tell he'd made an effort. It was an image that said 'thought has gone into this', as opposed to 'dragged out from under a pile of pizza boxes and a week's worth of washing'.

'This is, er, a bit weird,' he'd perceptively observed, acknowledging that neither of us was entirely sure how to start a conversation based on a blind date set up by a mad woman on the telly.

I nodded, hoping that he'd point us in the direction of

a suitable destination before my feet began to ache. Damn those heels. I'd ignored Millie's advice (comfortable boots, skinny jeans) and gone for smart black trousers and my favourite vertigo-inducing eBay specials. Big mistake.

But back to the jolly, comforting tones of our strained silence.

'Are you cold?'

'No, I'm fine, thanks.'

More silence.

'What about there?' he blurted, pointing to an outwardly respectable-looking wine bar with several loved-up couples in plain view behind the shop-style window.

I shook my head. It might look okay, but thanks to a tip-off from Trish (obtained via a temp-agency waiter who supplemented his student grant by working in the TV studio canteen and acting as a naked butler for wife-swapping parties in the suburbs) I knew it was a major pick-up joint for swingers, doggers and deviants. Call me old-fashioned, but I felt that the prospect of being propositioned for a foursome by an ageing history teacher and his middle-aged nymphomaniac wife didn't seem like it would be the best way to spend the next few hours.

I shook my head. 'What about in there?' I pointed to a quiet little pub on the other side of the road. 'I've been there a few times and it's okay, I suppose.' It was either that or bunions that may well have crippled me for life.

We were barely in the door when he started ranting effusively. 'Great choice, it's lovely, brilliant, top option.'

It was a tiny pub with beer coasters on the tables and a telly showing the snooker in the corner – I doubted it had ever been anyone's 'top option'. Nevertheless, I appreciated his encouragement and enthusiasm and it took the prospect of the rest of the evening down from 'crippling dread' to 'might be just about bearable'.

'I hope you don't mind that I didn't plan anything – I wanted to wait and see what you liked first.' Sweet. Accommodating. A faint whiff of a cop-out.

'What can I get you to drink?' he continued.

'A white wine, please – dry if they have it.'

'Wow, that's what I drink. How bizarre.'

Indeed.

'And I hope you don't mind me asking, but do you think I could have a packet of peanuts – I haven't had time to grab anything since lunch.'

'Not at all – I fancy some myself.'

Once again, I give you Mr Sweet and Accommodating.

I watched him as he curved his way round a table of sixty-something bingo players and three old men poring over the horse-racing page in a newspaper, and I couldn't help wondering why he was here. He seemed fairly hygienic, he was personable and acted friendly enough, albeit in a shy, self-conscious kind of way. Did a guy like him really struggle to meet someone in the real world? Or did he have some deep-rooted personality flaw that I'd yet to discover? Dear God, please don't let it involve body parts stored in his deep freeze.

He returned with the drinks and we settled into the now-familiar small talk about Zara's book, the dating project and *Great Morning TV!*, before he swayed the conversation into more personal stuff with a, 'So, Leni, tell me more about you.'

Ten points deducted off the dating scale for clichéd questioning.

'What would you like to know?' I asked breezily, while mentally preparing a completely fictitious profile just in case he was contemplating stealing my identity and selling it to Eastern European gang lords so they could obtain false passports for use in sex-trade trafficking. Note to self: must get irrational thoughts under control.

'What kind of music do you like?'

I made the snap decision that this would be of no relevance whatsoever to Customs and Immigration or whoever dealt with passport applications.

'I think Amy Winehouse is great.'

'Me too! *Back to Black* was a classic.'

More things in common!

'And I like loads of bands: Nickelback, the Killers, Razorlight, Snow Patrol . . . '

I started to worry that his constant nodding would result in a severe case of whiplash. Call me psychic, but I was beginning to spot a pattern here.

We were both drinking white wine, both eating Nobby's finest, our body language identical, and he'd agreed with every single thing that I'd said.

I decided to test my rapidly forming theory.

'I think Pete Doherty's a bit of a tit though.'

'Completely! Totally agree.'

'And I love listening to classical stuff in the bath.'

'So relaxing, isn't it,' he nodded.

I had to stop myself from throwing in that I fancied Howard from Take That!, just in case he agreed and was forced to re-evaluate aspects of his core personality.

He went on to concur with my favourite colour (blue), my favourite car (Ferrari) and my dream holiday (a week on Richard Branson's Necker with the entire cast of *Grey's Anatomy*, U2, P. Diddy and Mary J. Blige).

I was starting to feel just a little uneasy. This was either the non-identical twin from whom I'd been separated at birth, or the most intense, creepy sycophant I'd ever encountered. At the moment I was veering towards the latter. I had a feeling that if I said that my favourite hobby was collecting skin cells from polar bears' scrotums, he'd have the swabs and test tubes ready by the end of the night.

I spotted that his glass was empty and made a desperate attempt to break the cycle of question, answer, agreement.

'Let me get you a drink – another white wine?' I asked.

He shot out of his chair like his buttocks were on fire, and spat out a panicked 'SIT WHERE YOU ARE!'

The three old men in the corner lifted their heads from their papers.

'I'll get it!' he blurted, before bustling off to the bar and returning with fresh supplies.

I was starting to feel seriously freaked out now – I think it was the fact that the force of his outburst had rattled my fillings. I'd read about guys like this before – usually in the court reports of stalking trials where some woman had flicked open her curtains to find the face of a bloke she'd bumped into at Tesco's fish counter pressed up against her window.

'Daniel, you, er . . . ' Careful, Leni – think of a nice way to say this. 'You seem like a lovely guy, so can I ask you why you would want to apply for a date?'

Mad or sad? My heart was racing again. Which was he: mad or sad?

He didn't say anything for a few long, *long* minutes.

Eventually, he shrugged.

'Zara Delta said she could find me the perfect soul mate and I've just got to the stage where I think that would be nice. But somehow . . . well, somehow it doesn't seem to be happening.'

I surreptitiously clutched on to my handbag and slipped off the skyscraper heels in case I had to make a run for it.

'To be honest, I don't really understand where I go wrong.'

'No idea at all?' I ventured, with the hesitation of someone who is desperately trying to avoid a deep and meaningful conversation.

He shrugged again. 'None. Every woman I've ever been out with always says the same thing – I'm too nice. And that's a bad thing, apparently.'

Ah, the mist was beginning to clear now. He wasn't mad, he wasn't particularly sad (okay, maybe just a little) – he was just a bit insecure and eager to please.

On some level I could relate to that. I was about to tell him so, but I'd opened some kind of emotional dam and now the floodwaters were gushing through.

'It's difficult, you know? I always find new situations really uncomfortable, so I get a bit over-anxious.'

You don't say . . .

He took a large swig of his wine before continuing. 'Don't laugh, but I even bought a book to see if that would help. One of those advice ones.'

Holy shit, I was right. I wanted to call my mother and ask her why she'd given away my twin brother. Oh. My. God. How had I not seen it? The questioning, the body language, the agreement technique to establish compatibility and commonality – this was Textbook Dating (the exaggerated version that tipped over into 'borderline scary').

Crap. Was this . . . *Was this what a night with me was like?*

'Daniel, can I be honest with you?' I interjected. 'You're trying too hard.'

Attention all dictionaries, we have a new definition of irony: Leni Lomond giving advice on the route to successful relationships.

'Forget the textbooks and just be yourself. Oh, and stop agreeing with everything everyone says – girls love a bloke who has an opinion of his own.'

'But I hate disagreements.'

Fuck, it was like looking in a mirror.

'But, you know, sometimes that makes you more interesting.'

I decided not to reveal that this confrontation was making my toes curl and my teeth clench, but to get it back to a level that was suitably superficial before I filled up and felt the urge to swap stories of decimated romances.

I thumped the table, making the three old guys eye us with undisguised irritation for the second time.

'Okay, Daniel, for the rest of the night I want you to do and say whatever you like. Assert yourself and don't be afraid to be honest, okay?'

He nodded warily.

'Right, I'm starving – let's go and grab something to eat.'

'What do you fancy?' he asked.

A longing for a chicken korma overtook me.

'Indian?' I replied hopefully.

'Perfect! Just what I was thinking.'

'Great! Let's . . . '

I was halfway out of my seat before reality dawned.

'Daniel, are you saying that because you really mean it or because you don't want to object?'

Rabbit. Headlights.

'I do mean it! Absolutely! I love an Ind—' Suddenly, his enthusiasm deserted him. 'You're right, I'm lying – the saffron in the curries makes me break out in a twenty-four-hour rash. Would a pizza be okay with you?'

Even our gormless giggles matched.

With a departing wave to the locals, we strutted out of the door in search of the heady delights of a stuffed crust.

The tension broken, barriers down, it was time to meet the real Daniel.

How could I have known that I was about to fall for him in a big, big way?

10

A Cold Moon Rising

'Excuse me, can you tell me where to find Leni Lomond?' The enquirer sounded anxious and agitated.

'Second cubicle on the left,' a male voice replied.

Suddenly, the curtain burst open and in tumbled Stu and Trish. They took one look at me and their faces fell. I must have looked like quite a sight. Thankfully, the X-rays had revealed that my nose wasn't broken, but it had received a mighty bang, and already the black circles were beginning to appear under my eyes. By tomorrow I'd look like my hot date had consisted of ten rounds with Ricky Hatton.

My right arm was already in plaster, encasing the wrist that had snapped like a twig when my weight, together with the collective might of three members of the Slough bingo squad, had landed on it.

Those bloody heels. Daniel and I had been leaving the pub when he'd made a gallant, chivalrous semi-lunge to open the door for me, a sudden act that – given the vertiginous heels – had forced me to hit the deck like I'd been shot by a sniper. Unfortunately, three large ladies had chosen that moment to leave, rushing to catch the 8 p.m. sitting at the Gala bingo, and it had deteriorated into a pile-up situation.

Trish was the first to recover her composure.

'I have to say, I've seen you looking better.'

I rolled my eyes and instantly winced with the pain.

Stu thumped a large hold-all on the bed next to me, causing me to wince again. He was avoiding eye contact, but I could tell it was because he was deeply uncomfortable – not least because he had a scarf tied around his face. I wasn't sure if he was here to collect me or to commit an armed robbery.

'Don't worry, honey, I've got everything here you need,' he promised, a statement that came out as dddddddodoooooogggggggennnnneeeeee due to the constricting nature of his facial accessory.

Great! I was dying to get out of these torn, filthy clothes and pull on something clean and comfy. Or rather, enlist the help of someone with the use of both their upper limbs to pull on something clean and comfy. But sadly, I soon discovered that 'everything I needed' didn't consist of jeans and a warm, snugly jumper.

Stu opened the zip on the bag and pulled out two Marigolds, which he quickly slipped on, followed by a large-sized bottle of antibacterial Flash, a medium-size sponge and a carton of disinfectant wipes. He immediately started washing down the bed, and then moved on to the nearby table.

Trish ignored him. 'So where's Date Number Three then? Away searching for a lawyer to defend the lawsuit?'

I couldn't help laughing, despite . . . ouch!

'Stop being so nasty, it wasn't his fault. He's actually really nice and he feels terrible. He's gone to the hospital canteen to see if he can find me anything to eat.'

'You are not eating anything from a hospital canteen! Here!' Stu reached into the bag again and pulled out two bananas, a wholemeal roll and a bottle of strawberry smoothie. 'Whole grains, potassium, vitamins – never too early to start the healing process.'

Just at that moment the curtain opened again, and a tentative Daniel entered, clutching a can of Coke, a cling-filmed roll and a Scotch pie.

'You know she'll be suing for assault,' said Trish, who for all Daniel knew could have rushed here directly from the offices of Scotland Yard.

His eyes widened and he was just about to stutter out a profession of innocence when I intervened.

'Don't listen to her, she's evil. And kidding. Daniel, these are my friends, Trish and Stu.'

Trish grinned and shook his hand, Stu just waved his squeezy bottle of Flash around in some kind of obsessive-compulsive greeting. It was a credit to Daniel's diplomacy that he didn't ask why Stu was dressed like a domesticated Dick Turpin.

I smiled at Daniel as I gestured to the clock. 'Daniel, it's one a.m. – I really don't mind if you go home now. I'm just waiting for the doctor to discharge me and then Trish and Stu will take me home.'

'Are you sure?'

'Positive.'

He held out his hand and then realised that my reciprocal limb was strapped to my shoulder. He shrugged helplessly instead.

'Okay, well, sorry. Again. I really am. And thanks for the advice you gave me before the . . . er . . . stunt work.'

Flashes of spontaneous humour – maybe there'd been some progress there after all.

'Don't worry, it was entirely my fault, not yours. And thanks – visit to Accident and Emergency aside, I had a really nice time.'

'Me too! And I'm not just saying that to agree with you,' he grinned.

Yep, definite progress.

He grabbed his jacket off a chair and waited patiently as Stu gave it a quick once-over with a disinfectant wipe.

'Leni, since we both had, er, a good time, would it be, er, okay if I called you, and maybe we could go out again?'

Time to practise what I preached. Daniel was lovely, but – Zara's rules forbidding post-date contact aside – I had to accept the truth: there was only room for one of me in any relationship. With double the deficiencies in assertiveness and drive, we'd never get anything done.

'Thanks, Daniel, that's really sweet of you . . . But, er, no.'

PROGRESS SUMMARY: *IT'S IN THE STARS* DATING PROJECT

CONCLUDED		
LEO	Harry Henshall	Morbid fascination for simulated violence
SCORPIO	Matt Warden	Lead singer, lying arse
ARIES	Daniel Jones	Unlikely to forge career as an assertiveness coach

EMAIL
To: Trisha; Stu
From: Leni Lomond
Re: If last night's date had a personal ad, it would read like . . .

BROKEN ARM.
BLOODY SORE WHEN TYPING.
PERSONAL ADS SUSPENDED.

11

Star-Crossed

Of all the places it could finally have happened, I'd never, ever have guessed it would be the cleaning supplies cupboard. It must have been something about the fumes from the floor polish.

I suppose I had Daniel to thank – if he hadn't tried to be so chivalrous, I wouldn't have fallen and so I wouldn't have broken my arm; therefore I wouldn't be wearing a hugely cumbersome plaster cast and I wouldn't keep knocking things over.

It was only 10 a.m., and already I'd inadvertently swept aside a large pile of mail, a goldfish bowl containing Zara's ancient Mayan meditation marbles (99p each on eBay – made in Taiwan), and a large cup of steaming cappuccino from the Coffee Bean down the road. Thankfully, I'd managed to jump out of the way before I got scalded, but the large puddle of brown goo that was spreading across my tree trunk needed urgent attention, thus a frantic search for paper towels in the cleaning cupboard had ensued.

'Come on, come on, where are you, come on, bloody hell, who's in charge of keeping this place organised?' It was a rhetorical question, given that I was the only person in the room.

'Leni, are you okay?'

Only person no longer. Maybe it was the effects of the painkillers, maybe it was the stress of the dates; it might even have been that I'd just wasted £2.75 on a cup of spilt coffee, but a huge, mortifying, dolloping tear splodged down and landed in the mop bucket below.

'Hey, hey, don't cry. What's going on?'

His voice was so sweet and full of concern that several dozen other big fat tears felt compelled to join the first one.

I didn't even register the first touch, and it wasn't until I was wrapped in his arms that I realised what was happening: Conn Delta, he of the hubba hubba, was comforting me in the salubrious surroundings of the cleaning cupboard – probably a fortuitous location, as he'd need some kind of stain remover to get rid of the trail of snot I was leaving on his Armani jacket.

We stood like that until the racking sobs finally subsided, and then for a few seconds more as I wondered how I could get out of this without fainting from mortification.

Dum dum. Dum dum. My ear was pressed against his chest and I could hear the steady rhythm of his heart. Maybe I'd just stay like this for a few moments longer.

I mean, what was the rush?

He murmured something into the top of my head. I had a sinking feeling it might be something to do with finding another job.

'What?' I whispered.

'You smell nice.'

Oh.

I dragged my face out of his pecs and looked up at him.

'Actually, I think that's the loo blocks for the toilets. Summer Breeze.'

His face crinkled into a huge grin, a grin that was coming

closer, and closer, and oh fuck really close, until . . . he snogged me. Yep, a full-on, hard, passionate, mouth-to-mouth tonsil tickle, and it came with accompanying sound effects of heavy breathing and astonished gasps (those were mine).

Eeeek! What was going on? I hadn't had a spontaneous snog in a cupboard since, well, *ever*. I was the woman who took twenty minutes to decide whether to have a HobNob or a Kit Kat with my tea.

'Oh, Leni . . . ' The murmured, sexy groan was emitted without loss of lip suction. And his hands had moved from my back and were now on either side of my head, his fingers deep in my hair, holding me to him.

This was nuts! It had to stop and I knew I had to be the one to stop it! I had to get a grip of this and restore some kind of sanity. And I would! Right after I'd whipped off his tie, wrenched open his shirt (one flying button almost taking out an eye), and given his chest a good wash with my tongue.

'Leni. Oh God, Leni . . . I want you so much.'

The fumbling sensation as I slipped my hand (the one at the end of the unbroken arm) inside his trousers probably informed him that the feeling was mutual. It all went a bit frantic after that. His hands pulled free from my hair and slipped up inside my black jumper, pushing up my sheer black bra and releasing my boobs. He ducked down, latching on to my right nipple, his tongue flicking the end of it while he hurriedly pulled my skirt up so that it . . .

'Aaaaaaaaaaaaoooooooooow!'

Shit! In the midst of the adrenalin and lust-fuelled animalistic passion, I'd attempted to grab his hair and instead had somehow missed and thumped him across the back of the head with my plaster cast.

How cruel, oh so cruel would it be if this was to be the

first time in my life that I was responsible for another human being's concussion?

A finger tracing its way along my inner thigh reassured me that he might be down (there), but he wasn't out.

The finger rose higher, higher, trying to find its path, forced to move right up to waist level by the ultimate barrier to desirability and passion that is fifty-denier tights. Tights! Bloody, bloody bugger! Why couldn't today have been the day I'd worn sexy hold-ups to work? Or seamed stockings? Or even jeans with a sexy little pair of silk tangas underneath. Nope – ugly, opaque tights with a gusset so thick it could protect my nethers from an invading army.

Riiiiiiiiip!

Make that past tense. Tights in tatters on the floor, the knickers soon followed (mercifully black, sheer, not resembling granny pants in any way). Using a combination of wriggling, pulling and pushing with feet, I'd managed to get his trousers down to his ankles, his – hang on until I get a good grip – oh dear Lord, his *almighty* cock springing free in the process.

'Turn around,' he gasped.

'What?'

'Turn around!' He did a push/pull thing, and in a split second I was facing the other way, his body pressed against my back, both arms curved around to the front of my torso, one hand cupped around my right breast, the other pushing its way inside me.

'You. Are. Fucking. Gorgeous. Leni, bend over, baby. Grab on.'

Er, to what? As I bent at the waist my hands frantically reached out for something to balance against. The first thing they met was a huge roll on the bottom shelf. Great – so *now* I find the paper towels.

The roll toppled over so my left hand clutched on to the shelf instead, my right hand still flailing until – clunk – it met something solid, at the very same time as I felt that almighty cock push inside me.

In. And out. In. Out. Oh, the sheer orgasmic bloody bliss of getting shagged in a cupboard while clutching on to a shelf and a Dyson. I would never again manage to do housework without a happy grin.

In. Out. In.

'Oh, Leni . . . '

'Conn.'

'Leni.'

'Conn.'

'Leni.'

'Conn.'

'Leni? *Leni, are you okay?*'

Hang on, that sounded . . .

'Leni! You're a million miles away. Are you okay?'

Noooooooooooooooo.

I could feel my pupils snap open as they adjusted to the daylight, and then refocused on the man who definitely wasn't behind me in a store cupboard.

Noooooooooooooo! I was sitting at my desk, and, standing in front of me, looking deeply puzzled, was Conn.

'Were you sleeping?' he asked, his tone somewhere between confused and amused.

'No! I was just . . . er . . . just . . . daydreaming. I think. Or maybe sleeping. Sorry, Conn, really, I've no idea. I'm just a bit drowsy. I think it's the drugs they gave me at the hospital, you know, for the pain.'

I threw up exhibit one for the defence, an arm encased in plaster. Unfortunately, in doing so I sent my nearby cup of cappuccino flying across the room.

'Shit! Oh, shit! Sorry! I'm really . . . ' I was up on my feet

103

now and halfway across the room. 'A towel! I'll just get some paper towels from the cleaning cupboard.'

'Do you know where they are or do you need me to come and show you?' he asked, his voice warm and friendly.

'No, no, it's fine!' I blurted, aware that I could send global warming to critical levels just from the heat emanating from my face. 'I've, er . . . been in the cleaning cupboard before.'

12

The Capricorn Date

I figured that by the laws of probability I was due to chalk up a successful date anytime soon – preferably within this millennium. I had a good feeling about Mr Capricorn, especially since Zara had allowed me to go through the pile of candidates and pick him myself – a decision that I had a hunch was the result of the combination of Conn's absence (he had three days of back-to-back meetings in the city centre), her inherent disinterest in anything that didn't directly affect her, and a modicum of employer/Health & Safety/broken-arm guilt. Actually, it was probably just the first two.

'So what am I looking for?' I'd asked her, as she'd pointed me in the direction of the large, bulging black plastic bag that Millie had just dragged into our office. The A4 sheet of paper taped to the front with the word 'CAPRICORN' in black marker-pen gave me a clue that this was our celestial, incoming-mail filing system.

'What's the criteria for selection of the candidates?' I'd continued, acutely aware that since this was a highly specialised investigative study, there were probably stringent requirements for each successful candidate.

'Oh, just whatever you think,' she'd replied with a

nonchalant shrug. 'As long as they fall within the star sign and the age range, that's all that matters. You might want to weed out the publicity-seekers, though – at least half of the guys who've written in are just doing it because they think it'll make them celebrities. I don't know where they got that idea.'

I chose not to point out that the applicants' hope of a new celebrity status might have sprouted from the fact that this was a TV-driven project with the promise that it would 'change lives', 'feature in a best-selling book' and deliver a 'new destiny'. The three candidates I'd already been out with were probably on the phone right now to Trading Standards.

Zara put down the large Spanish-style fan she was holding, took the wind chimes off her head (don't even ask) and stared at me with a dark, suspicious glint in her eye.

'Leni, is everything okay with you? Is there anything you'd like to discuss or share?'

Fuuuuuuuck! She did know what I was thinking! I was throwing out cynical aspersions and she was catching every bloody one of them. And if she knew that I was mentally mocking her, then chances were she also knew . . . My stomach began to churn with fear and dread. Yep, she knew that I'd fantasised about doing it doggie-style with the fruit of her loins.

'N-n-n-n-o, noth-ing,' I stuttered, face flushing. Earlier that morning I'd witnessed her threatening to strangle her Master of Tibetan Serenity because she discovered he was charging her double the going rate, so I didn't even want to think about what she'd do to me if she knew I was having fantasy sex with her son during working hours.

I returned to my familiar mantra. Think nice things. Think nice things. Zara is kind, Zara is wise, Zara definitely doesn't look like a pepperoni stick in that brown kaftan . . .

'Fine,' she suddenly announced, her demeanour switching immediately to sunny and bright. 'Well, get on with it then.' She gestured to the bin bag.

For the next three hours I read and sifted, while attempting to reassure myself that there was no way she was reading my mind and therefore no possibility that she'd sneak up behind me armed with a noose. But I made sure I was facing her at all times, just in case.

In the end it came down to an excruciatingly difficult decision between Chad, 28, a male model who included a topless photo showing a stomach so defined it could be used as a toast rack, and Craig, 31, a relationship therapist whose photo was an out-of-focus headshot.

I won't deny that my first instinct was to go with Chad – after all, how often would I get an all-expenses-paid night out with a bloke who modelled Lycra pants in the *World of Sport* catalogue? But in the end I decided against it on the grounds that my self-esteem had been given a big enough kick in the bollocks lately without spending a whole night face-to-face with someone who was far prettier than me, had a flatter stomach, and who had every girl in the room imagining him half-naked.

It did raise the question, though: if these guys both had the same star signs, then surely they had the same fortunes in store, and thus, taking that theory to a logical level, wouldn't the outcome of both dates be similar?

I tried to broach the same star sign/different fates question with Zara, but she brushed me off with a two-minute spiel on how conventional astrology is far too general and that was why her methods were far more successful. Then she crossed her legs, closed her eyes and launched into a Hindu chant, before falling into a deep meditation while she regressed herself back to one of her former lives – the one in which she was a fierce Viking warrior who was a great leader of men and conqueror of the seas. Ironic, since I'd once asked her if she wanted to take the ferry to a business meeting in Ireland and she balked at the idea, citing chronic seasickness.

Anyway, Craig won the toss, and I figured that even if we didn't hit it off, at least I might be able to tap into his professional knowledge and pick up tips on successful relations with the opposite sex. Or lack thereof.

We'd arranged to meet straight after work in a wine bar/gastro-pub in Notting Hill, and I followed Millie's advice and went for an 'office to night-time' look, despite the fact that I had absolutely no idea what that was. Apparently, it involved tarting up your office clothes (in my case a pair of black crepe trousers and a grey polo-neck jumper) by sweeping your hair up and adding glam, droopy earrings and kitten heels. And, of course, in my case, slipping a slinky black leg-warmer over the plaster cast that was still on my arm – an essential component when meeting someone new, as I didn't want them to make any assumptions based on the message Trish had written in marker pen on the plaster claiming that 'feminism means sitting on top'.

I arrived first, handy for picking the right spot, as far away from bright light as possible. The two black eyes had finally disappeared, but I still needed to pile on the slap to cover the dull yellow bruising that remained. By 6.30 p.m. the familiar nerves had started to kick in and I was already decidedly flushed. I said a prayer to the Gods of Blind Dating not to make this one awkward or uncomfortable, on the grounds that I deserved a break: I'd been a participant in this madness for almost two months, this was date number four, and I was only marginally less shaky now than I had been on date number one. If I got stressed and sweaty, there would be a foundation avalanche and my yellow complexion might give the impression that I had cirrhosis of the liver. Next date? The local branch of AA.

By 7 p.m., half an hour after our agreed meeting time, I was surrounded with groups of strangers, an eclectic mix of city suits and bohemian shabby-chics, all chatting and laughing and pretending not to notice the female with the plaster cast in the corner who had very obviously been stood up.

Oh, the humiliation. Capricorn Craig had only had a ten-minute phone call with me and already he'd decided not to go through with it. Well, I'd be bloody writing to him to demand the return of the hundred pounds that had been couriered to him that afternoon. Who'd have thought a relationship counsellor would have a side-line in extortion?

I decided to leave before I succumbed to the temptation to devour the little silver bowl of cashew nuts on the table in front of me – a rash act that would make Stu quarantine me for six weeks and demand that I take a course of high-dose antibiotics.

Suddenly, the bowl went flying, replaced by a bulging, weathered leather briefcase.

'Hello, are you Leni? You are, aren't you? You're Leni? You look exactly as I imagined.'

'I am.'

'Excellent. I'm usually right about these things. Apologies for my tardiness – my last consultation ran over, and it does of course take priority.'

I considered standing up, adopting an aloof expression, hissing, 'Too late, I wait for no man!' and flouncing out. Or perhaps I should just purse my lips and harrumph my bosom in an indignant manner then proceed to sulk for the rest of the night.

But of course, because (like Daniel, my long-lost twin brother) I suffer from a non-confrontational personality with a desire to please, I shrugged my shoulders, smiled, and lied that, 'It's no problem, honestly. I hardly even noticed you were late.'

He inadvertently nudged a couple of stockbroker types out of the way as he pulled out the chair next to me and thumped himself down. I was glad I hadn't dressed up too much as my non-flashy outfit perfectly matched his chocolate cord trousers and matching jacket with – oh good grief, I thought they were an urban legend – tan leather patches on the arms.

On the plus side: a clean white shirt, nice hands with trim nails, no obvious tattoos, and his slightly long black hair was attractive in a greying, unkempt kind of way.

On the down side (and yes, my ovaries were recoiling at the very sight of it): facial hair.

Facial hair. In the words of the modern-day philosopher and woman of words, Paris Hilton: 'Eeeeeeeew.'

And it wasn't the George Michael stubble, the Colin Farrell/*Miami Vice* moustache or the Musketeer goatee, it was the full 'pass my slippers, where's my pipe' beard.

I felt the hairs on the back of my neck crawl up in some kind of bizarre hirsute protest against the fuzz on his face. And forgive me for getting ahead of myself, but all I could think was, 'I'd rather eat contaminated cashews for a month than snog that.'

I know it's not rational and there are some perfectly nice men with beards – Noel Edmonds, Captain Birdseye and all the blokes in ZZ Top – but like gents with halitosis, body odour or any fetish involving pain or theft of undergarments, they're not for me. It was probably the consequence of a decadent night in my early teenage years when one of the boys in our gang smuggled an old Seventies porn movie into my house when my parents were out and the twelve teenagers packed into my lounge were given an introduction to the vagaries of oral sex when a bloke with a huge beard visited the parts of a buxom-blonde house-wife that non-bearded gentlemen couldn't reach. In fact, maybe it was just the dim lighting, but Craig the Therapist bore a highly disturbing resemblance to that porn plumber with the incredibly energetic wrench. I shuddered.

'Can I get you a drink?'

I snapped out of the memory of my teenage antics (that had cost me two months of pocket money and my tickets for a Blur concert when my parents had returned home unexpectedly early). 'Er, sure, I'll have a glass of white wine please – house wine's fine.'

He smiled, then headed off to the bar. Right, time to re-evaluate the situation. Lack of punctuality aside, he seemed genuine enough, and as a relationship counsellor he was bound to be interesting. And by focusing on something as superfluous as facial hair I was being downright shallow and superficial.

As I watched him weave through the masses en route to the bar, I chided myself for such immature thoughts and did some serious soul-searching.

Wasn't I a better person than this?

Wasn't I capable of looking past the superficial and appreciating a person's mind and soul?

Wasn't it time I grew up and stopped making petty judgements?

And if I commando-crawled towards the door, would I make it to freedom before he got back?

13

The Outer Cosmos

Sadly not.

Three hours later, the city/bohemian crowd had been replaced by groups of women on post-aerobic-class treats and groups of blokes on the pull. We'd moved through to the restaurant side of the establishment and I was happily tucking into my retro prawn cocktail while Craig filled me in on yet another one of his cases. Apparently, as long as no names were mentioned, he was free to discuss his clients at length and in detail. Infinite detail. Minute. It occurred to me that he was being overbearing, indiscreet and self-absorbed, but frankly I didn't mind, figuring that at least it avoided the risk of those first-date awkward pauses. And besides, in an hour or so I could leave, fill in my report, claim my bonus, tick another sign on my zodiac milestone and all would be well . . . just as long as in the meantime my bosoms didn't actually drop off with boredom and land in my retro fish dish.

I was debating whether or not to tell him he had oatcake crumbs in his undergrowth, when he suddenly changed tack.

' . . . And so that's why I decided to apply when I saw Zara spouting that ridiculous nonsense on the morning show.'

What? What had he just said? Focusing on the crumbs had made me completely tune out.

'So what I'd like to know is, what are these ridiculous techniques that she has allegedly discovered, and is there any logical merit to them whatsoever?'

'Pardon?'

There was a change in his body language and his demeanour appeared to shift slightly from 'pompous' to 'testy'. Or maybe it was the other way around. I'd given up halfway through *Body Language for Beginners* after realising somewhere around page seventy-five that the fact my body was horizontal and falling asleep meant I was bored rigid.

'I want some insight into exactly what ludicrous nonsense she is planning to write about. You have to understand, Leni, that it's the professionals in this field, my colleagues and me, who have to pick up the pieces of the failed relationships.'

'So let me get this straight. You applied for this because you thought you'd get insider information on Zara's book?'

'Yes.'

'But I don't know anything about it.'

He did a whole scoffing laugh thing that dislodged several small organisms from his beard. 'Of course you do.'

'I don't.'

'Are you seriously trying to tell me that you just go along on these meetings knowing nothing about them or the project they're linked to?'

'Er . . . yep.'

He looked at me with the kind of sad, disappointed expression you might give a puppy that had peed on the floor. I had a sneaking suspicion that if we hadn't already ordered dinner he'd be out of his chair and heading for the door.

'That's very trusting of you, Leni. Are you always so accommodating? I've been rambling on all night, so let's talk about you for a moment.'

'No, no, really, that's fine,' I reassured him. 'To be honest, I'm not that interesting,' I joked, then speared another prawn and switched back to 'good listener' mode.

He was silent for a moment, one long, glorious moment, before the bombshell hit.

'Have you always covered up your insecurities and self-esteem issues with self-deprecation?'

Pardon? He'd known me for three hours, I'd barely said a word, and yet now he was suddenly Dr Phil?

'Er, no,' I blustered jokingly. 'I really am this thick-skinned and difficult to offend.'

He sat back, oatcakes still dangling from each corner of his mouth, and regarded me with an intense stare.

'Now we both know that isn't true, is it? Tell me, what kind of relationship do you have with your father?'

God help us. All I wanted to do was get past my coq au vin and my arctic roll, then get home in time for *Friday Night with Jonathan Ross*, and instead I suddenly felt like the number-one suspect in *Taggart*.

I shrugged off the question with the briefest answer I could come up with, other than, 'bugger off, you're a twat.'

'It was and still is fine. He's a nice man.'

'Mmmmmm,' said Dr Freud. 'And since then? Married? Long-term relationships?'

Okay, now he was getting really annoying. I could almost bear it before when I could just listen while focusing on the distraction of delicious food, but now I was being robbed of that by his demands that I actually participate in the evening. Well, if I was going to have to share then I might as well get the benefit of some free professional opinions.

'One serious relationship, two years, his name was Ben,'

I said, incredulous that even after all this time the very thought of Ben caused an almost physical pain in the pit of my stomach. 'But he was married.'

'Ah, the attraction to the unobtainable, often another sign of low self-esteem,' interjected Freud just a little too smugly.

'No, I didn't know he was married,' I objected.

'Come on, of course you did – there's always awareness on some level. You didn't think to question the absences and the refusal to commit?'

Urgh. He thought he had all the answers, and I was beginning to lose the longing for the coq au vin.

'He was in the army. The marines, actually. I thought I was being loyal and devoted by waiting for him and tolerating the lack of time together. Turns out I was just being a sap.'

Appetite officially gone. And to my utter horror and eternal mortification, I realised that I was welling up.

'Tell me about your time together.'

That's it! How dare he pry into my life? I stood up, threw my napkin on the table and stormed out.

Or at least, that's what I planned to do. But somehow it came out as . . .

'Well, we met on a train, actually. I was going to Portsmouth for a plumbing conference, and he was on his way back to barracks after an R&R. I never normally speak to anyone on public transport – you know, too many weirdos, nutters, and that's just my pals . . . '

My attempt to use an immature joke to lighten the mood and divert attention from the one episode in my life that had left permanent scar tissue on my heart went completely ignored, so I succumbed to Dr Freud and gave him chapter and heart-bloody-breaking verse.

I'd almost become a *Daily Mail* statistic that day. I'd been sitting in a sparsely occupied carriage, brooding over the injustice that all the management team had been booked into first class, when in walked the ultimate cliché: baseball cap, zipped sweatshirt with the hood pulled up over the cap, and trousers that belonged on a sporting competitor as opposed to a teenage misfit with a glue-sniffing ring around his mouth.

He'd been walking past my seat when I'd suddenly felt something sharp pressed against my side, swiftly followed by his stinking breath on my face as he'd bent down to whisper in my ear.

'Give me your bag before I slice you.'

I froze. Had he really said . . . ?

'Give me your fucking bag now!' he'd hissed.

My eyes darted frantically around the carriage, but everyone was doing that British thing where they avoided eye contact at all costs, so no one had registered my situation. And besides, I hardly thought that two old ladies who'd been discussing their arthritis for the last forty-five miles would be proficient in disarming ASBO Andy.

The pressure on my side increased and catapulted me into action. I'd groped around with my free hand for my bag, when all of a sudden my attacker had moved slightly to the left and began to repeatedly bang his head off the table separating me from the empty seats opposite. It had taken me a few moments to realise that this action was being helped along by the huge hand that was grasping the back of El Thuggo's neck. The ensuing action was so dramatic that even the old ladies ceased ruminating over their ailments. One reached into her bag, and the next thing we knew, the kind of sound you would expect to hear signalling an incoming nuclear missile ripped through the cabin.

Seconds later, we'd pulled in at a station and the train

had been held up for one hour while the station police apprehended the youth, searched the carriage and took statements from all involved. Although all of this *Crimewatch*-type behaviour had only taken place after the long arm of the law had spent twenty minutes trying to switch off Ethelia Pancridge's personal panic alarm. In the end, they'd gone for the technical approach and thrown it out of the window, allowing it to be crushed by the 5.45 p.m. to King's Cross coming the other way.

It was only when the commotion had died down that I'd realised the intervening hand and forearm belonged to Captain Benjamin Mathers, Second Corps, Royal Marines. Ben was the kind of cartoon soldier that kids draw in battle scenes: six foot two inches tall, almost as wide across the shoulders, angling down past the visibly taught stomach to narrow hips. His light brown hair was shorn into a crew-cut, his skin was weathered to a deep shade of oak, and a flat row of white teeth sat above a sharp, square jaw-line. If I had to choose a physical specimen to protect our nation against hostile armies, terrorists and scumbag teenagers looking for glue money, it would be him. If I had to choose a perfect physical specimen with whom to engage in activities pertaining to the stimulation of the reproductive system, well, that would be him too. He was stunning. Beautiful. And much as love at first sight is an over-used cliché that is generally a gross exaggeration of reality, I have to say that my experience with Ben was the exception.

'Actually, I think it's more likely that a combination of the trauma of the incident and gratitude at being helped, manifested itself in powerful feelings of attraction,' interjected my date, now renamed *'Craig, the really annoying therapist'*.

It suddenly crossed my mind to wonder whether I'd get

117

a custodial sentence if I overcame my aversion to confrontation and forced the pepper shaker to make swift and repeated contact with the back of Craig's head.

I took a deep breath and carried on with the next instalment. I told him how we'd swapped contact details and addresses as we'd left the train, starting a correspondence that would become closer and more intimate as the months went on. Occasionally, he'd even managed to call from his posting in Afghanistan, and it was during one of those calls, late on a Thursday night, that the doorbell had rung. Large and potentially dangerous kitchen implement in hand, I'd tentatively opened the door, only to see him standing there clutching his mobile phone to his ear. He was everything I wasn't: strong, brave, spontaneous and adventurous. Oh, and married.

'I say again, don't you think that on some level you knew all along that he was married?' piped up my newly recruited relationship guru – the one I still wanted to batter to death with the pepper shaker.

I mean, give me strength! Of course I didn't know he was bloody married. I'd found that out two years later, when I'd decided to surprise him by showing up outside his barracks on the day he returned from the Middle East, just in time to see him exiting the compound with a little girl who looked around five years old holding one hand, and a tall blonde with a pneumatic chest holding the other. And the worst part was that he'd seen me. He'd noticed me standing there, and there was a brief, momentary flicker of shock before his eyes went dead. He'd looked right through me as they all headed towards the car park, jumped into a Jeep and drove off, leaving me standing there like the pathetic, sad imbecile that I was.

I paused, realising that there was a crushing pain in my chest, tears coursing down my cheeks and snot dripping into the remnants of the prawn cocktail. The waiter was also hovering nearby, clutching two main meals but obviously terrified to approach the table while I was in such obvious meltdown.

And Craig? His pretentious, professional demeanour was now slightly clouded by that look of blind panic that most men are genetically predisposed to when faced with an emotional woman in a public place.

But, like Daniel's cathartic experience on the previous date, the dams had been opened and now Niagara was pouring through. Or at least dripping into my dinner.

I carried on with the saga (yes, it was a tad self-indulgent, but then he'd rambled pretty much solo for the first half of the evening), telling Craig how there had been one phone call after that. Just one. When the phone had started to ring just after midnight a couple of nights later, I had known it was him. Stu had been staying over with me, and we'd just finished an epic run of *Pretty Woman*, *Top Gun* and *My Best Friend's Wedding*, while working our way through a Mexican village of Doritos and a valley of French plonk.

'Answer it,' he'd prompted.

'I can't,' I'd whispered, Dorito in mouth, paralysed with fear.

'You have to, Leni – you need closure.'

Aaaaaargh! Shaking, I picked up the phone and whispered, 'Hello?'

'Leni, I'm sorry.'

'Are. You. Married?' My voice was a low, tight staccato, caused by my windpipe constricting to the approximate diameter of a pencil lead.

'Leni, I . . . '

'Are. You. Married?' I'd repeated.

There was a silence, followed by a long sigh and finally a choked 'Yes'.

I'd hung up and Stu had held me tight for hours then put me to bed – but only, of course, after he'd removed all potentially dangerous objects from my room, then checked all my vital signs to reassure himself that I wasn't going to suffer a stress-induced stroke in the night.

The waiter got fed up of hovering and deftly removed our starter plates, replacing them with the main courses. My dried-up coq au vin looked as sad as I felt.

'And since then?' Craig asked, obviously a glutton for punishment.

'Nothing. Just flings.' I took a large slug of my wine as I realised that this had been the first time I'd told the 'Ben' story to anyone other than Trish or Stu. 'Short-term relationships with nice men who were never going to break my heart. And before you say it, yes, I realise that I choose to do that for a reason.'

Deciding that I sounded batty enough, I decided to omit that this was when the self-help obsession had started. *Moving On – Overcoming Heartbreak and Repairing Your Soul* had been the guide that went on to spawn a four-shelf collection on my bookcase.

Craig silently chewed on his undoubtedly rubberised chicken and mushroom pie for a couple of awkward minutes, before saying, 'Have you ever considered that perhaps it wasn't you who chose to have short-term, meaningless flings? Perhaps it was the men you were seeing who chose to keep it on that level?'

Okay, stop talking. Let's move on. I'd had a fifteen-minute, uncharacteristic revelatory outburst accompanied by deeply embarrassing tears and snot, but he was a relationship counsellor, so surely if anyone was going to be sympathetic and understanding it was him. And besides, he had asked me to tell him about it; it wasn't like I'd just volunteered the information on a whim.

However, I was ready to stop now. To move on to sunnier themes and superficial small talk. But . . . but I had to know what he was on about . . .

'I'm sorry; I don't understand what you're saying.'

He took a deep breath. 'Leni, I think you need to accept some truths.'

I nodded, figuring that after using his napkin to blow my nose after my meltdown, the least I could do was indulge him.

'In my opinion, the "short-term flings" that you refer to were probably kept within those boundaries not by you but by the men you were seeing. You see, that's often the consequence of dating someone who is, in essence, a habitual co-dependent with an inclination towards self-absorption and over-emotional reactions. In my professional opinion, I'd say that, despite your protests, you were attracted to Ben because on some level you knew that he was, if I may make an assumption and use colloquial terminology, *out of your league . . .* '

What??????????? Was he kidding me? Yes, okay, I might have got a tad overwrought. And yes, Ben was probably higher up the 'wow' scale than me, but I'd like to think that he loved me for who I was and could overlook the fact that it would have to be a dark, foggy night before I could claim to have more than a very glimmer of a resemblance to Cameron Diaz.

But self-absorbed? He'd *asked* me to tell him about Ben! And that was only after three and a half hours of listening to him while he talked about nothing but his inner bloody brilliance. If Trish were sitting in my seat right now she'd deck him. Obviously I was too busy being self-obsessed and co-dependent.

He reached out and took my hand in a nauseatingly patronising manner, and then started to speak in an even more nauseatingly patronising voice.

'So, Leni, what I'm about to say, I'm saying because I care, and I need you to understand that. Do you understand, Leni?'

No, no, NOOOOO, you obnoxious, ignorant, big hairy bastard.

But to avoid the risk of offence, I nodded in what I'm sure, again, was a self-obsessed and co-dependent manner.

'I think you need to work on yourself. I think you need to take time out, identify where your weaknesses lie, and fix them before you enter another relationship.'

Or I could just revert to plan A and kill you with the pepper shaker.

'And that's why I can't see you again, Leni. I can feel that already you're getting attached to me, even in the short space of time that we've been together tonight. And I know that you want more. I know that you see in me the same kind of protective instincts that you saw in Ben.'

I'm sure my chin was in my coq au vin at that point, given that all I actually saw was a fairly unattractive, pompous prick who was wearing half his dinner in his facial hair and leather elbow patches.

He kissed my hand with a dramatic flourish. 'And that's why I'm going to go now, Leni, because I don't want to compound the pain by letting you get even more attached. Because, you see, I don't have enough to give right now. I'm dedicated to my clients and to my growth as a human being, and I just don't have the emotional space to help someone else work through their issues and problems.'

Then (and how I wished I had a suitable receptacle for the contents of my stomach) he tried to soften the blow with a nauseating, 'But if I did have that energy to give, Leni, I'd give it to you. I'm sorry.'

He released my hand, stood up, retrieved his tatty briefcase, and said, 'Goodbye, Leni – and good luck.'

Exit Craig the therapist, leaving half a chicken and mushroom pie, a quarter of a bottle of wine and the most gobsmacked date in the free world.

After a few minutes of shocked stillness, I pushed my plate away and drained the wine bottle.

The waiter took the hint and cleared away the plates.

'Can I get you anything else, madam?'

'No thank you,' I replied. The restaurant was still fairly busy and I didn't want to take up his time by asking him to call me a cab. I'd just do what I always did and hail one when I got outside. Hardly the actions of a self-indulgent and co-dependent bloody woman!

A few minutes later the nice waiter returned with my coat and . . .

'Here's the bill, madam.'

'Didn't . . . didn't the gentleman I was dining with pay it on his way out?' I spluttered.

'Erm, no, I'm afraid not. Actually, he did refer to it.'

'What did he say?'

The poor, mortified waiter had the decency to flush bright red and stare at his shoes.

'He said you were to consider it his fee.'

PROGRESS SUMMARY: *IT'S IN THE STARS* DATING PROJECT

CONCLUDED		
LEO	Harry Henshall	Morbid fascination for simulated violence
SCORPIO	Matt Warden	Lead singer, lying arse
ARIES	Daniel Jones	Unlikely to forge career as an assertiveness coach
CAPRICORN	Craig Cunningham	Relationship therapist, incites violent urges

Have you spent your whole life waiting for that exciting, crazy guy who will sweep you off your feet and make you feel like the most special thing on earth? In that case you should know that you are deluded and should seek therapy. If, however, you are looking for a smug, patronising, irritating big bastard with a penchant for psycho babble, then this male Capricorn, chronological age 31, wardrobe age 61, would like to hear from you. I am highly articulate with extreme talents in the area of conversation: i.e. I have a masters degree in talking shite and I have been known to spout such intense drivel that my dates decide that jumping from tall cliffs would be a preferable activity to a night out with me. WLTM a woman who is turned on by the sight of crumb-encrusted facial hair and is driven wild by the sight of ancient academic-style clothing. Yes, come and slide down my elbow patches. Education, intelligence and the power of speech unnecessary, because quite frankly I don't give a toss what you think about anything anyway.

Please note that despite uncanny physical similarities, at no time did I participate in the filming of Seventies porn.

14

Sunburn

'Look, if it's any consolation, he'll probably die young as a result of a fur ball of beard hair accumulating in his oesophagus. Happens all the time.'

'Ah, honey, you really know how to cheer a girl up.'

I watched in the mirror as Stu took a deep, exaggerated bow. 'All part of our comprehensive and unique range of services. We can also test you for diabetes, pregnancy or ovulation while you're getting your blow-dry,' he added with a grin.

I'd like to hope he was kidding, but given that he was in personal possession of more medical supplies than the NHS, I decided not to probe any further. He went back to snipping away at my hair instead.

That was the great thing about having a best friend who was a hairdresser – free highlights, the latest cuts and a bit of pampering whenever you needed it. And in return, you just had to be outrageously . . .

'So you didn't shag him then?'

. . . indiscreet.

'No!' I yelped. 'Not that I would have anyway, but he ran out of the place like his arse was on fire the minute I started wiping snot on my sleeve. Honestly, some guys are just so difficult to please.'

After my ritual humiliation with Craig the hairy therapist, I might have been £54 lighter (every penny of which
I intended to claim back on expenses), but at least my sense
of humour had limped back, battered but not yet trampled to death, to rescue me.

Now, two weeks later, I'd popped in to see Stu for a cut,
blow-dry and catch-up. I loved Stu's salon. He'd spent ages
deliberating over names for it, ran a zillion suggestions past
focus groups, friends and family, researched competitors'
brands and contemporary themes . . . and then called it
Stuart Degas Hair. Yep, for a bloke called Stuart Degas, that
one came right out of left field.

No pun intended, but it was cutting-edge enough to appeal
to minor celebs, yummy mummies and a whole catwalk of
fashion types, but unpretentious and friendly enough to
appeal to students and staff from nearby offices. And me.

The salon had two storeys, both with distinct themes,
although three things remained constant in both: the shiny
silver floor that glistened like cut glass, the huge ornate
mirrors surrounded by battered steel frames that punctuated the walls, and the massive black leather chairs complete
with reclining action and a vibrating option. Stu maintained they were great for the lymphatic system.

Upstairs was a monochrome hi-tech emporium – or, as
Trish preferred to call it, Testosterone Central: huge plasma
screens showing sporting events, with blaring rock music
and staff in white T-shirts, scuffed-up biker boots and well-
worn jeans.

Downstairs was a gentler experience, with subtle background music, huge overstuffed zebra-print sofas and a lovely
team of achingly hip twenty-somethings who dressed all in
black and brought you tea and coffee at regular intervals.

I still found it difficult to believe that Stu had achieved
all this, although strictly speaking he'd had some help from

a windfall that had come his way just as we had got to know him at college. He'd never volunteered information about it and we were too early in our friendship to probe. Trish had, of course, demanded full disclosure several times since then, but Stu remained elusive. It was a bit of a co-incidence, though, that an unclaimed lottery ticket that was bought in his home town hit the headlines the weekend before he went home poor and came back rich.

But the money was only part of his success: his charm and talent brought the rest. And, of course, his unrelenting drive – fuelled, no doubt, by the harsh reality that he was single-handedly responsible for the turn-over and share prices of the world's top pharmaceutical companies.

My phone burst into life, and I hit the receive button.

'MC Madge, world-famous rap star/pain in the anus wants her dressing room painted violet; Goldie has somehow managed to burn off her fringe – I'm thinking it was something to do with a mid-life crisis and a pot pipe – and Grey's threatening to pick up a hooker if I don't get home by eight. Who the fuck would have my life????'

'Hang on, Trish, I'm just taking you off loudspeaker.'

Stu was practically on the floor laughing, and every other eye in the place was pointed in the direction of my beaming face.

'Loudspeaker? Are you kidding me?'

'Of course I'm kidding,' I lied, sending Stu off again.

'Thank fuck. Right, are you still with Stu?'

'Yes.'

'Can you ask him if he can come tomorrow morning at six a.m. to fix pot-girl's fringe?'

'Can you go tomorrow morning to fix po— Goldie's fringe?'

He leaned into the phone. 'For you, anything!'

'Then throw in some violet fucking paint and a hooker as well. Ciao.'

The line went dead and we took a few moments to recover before normal conversation resumed.

'So how was the holiday, and how's the gorgeous Sascha?' I asked between indulgent gulps of frothy cappuccino.

Stu had just returned from a fortnight in Marbella with a model-turned-make-up-artist he'd been seeing for the last two months. Even from another woman's point of view, and factoring in taste and extreme thin-thigh jealousy, there was no denying that Sascha was a goddess. She almost hit the six-foot mark in heels, and combined that boho-chic Sienna Miller vibe with Giselle-esque proportions. They'd got together at a photo shoot just after New Year, when Stu was styling hair and she was styling faces, and by combining their God-given good looks with their respective artistic talents they were permanently gorgeous and groomed to perfection. And it's not easy to admit that when you're sitting with no make-up on, scruffy jeans and an old sweatshirt, a cappuccino moustache, and hair that – until half an hour ago – looked like it had been baked in a microwave then styled with pruning shears.

Anyway, I had a great feeling about them, and if I were a betting woman I'd probably put money on this one going the distance.

'She dumped me.'

I now understood why God had been merciful and omitted to give me a gambling gene.

'No! What happened?'

He shrugged. 'On holiday, nothing in common.'

'You went into hypochondria overdrive, didn't you?'

You see, that was the thing about Stu: he managed to pretty much mask his little personality quirk to the outside world, creating this façade of being the hip, cool hairdresser guy who was too busy being Brad Pitt's younger, better-looking brother to worry about anything so trivial as a minor ailment. It was only in the company of his closest friends, an honour that fell to Trish and me, that he felt free to be a fully fledged, germ-obsessed, Dettol-carrying hunk of neurosis.

He shrugged again, this time with an extra edge of sheepishness, as he gave a half-hearted, obviously untrue, 'No.'

'Ah, that's why I love you – I sleep easy at night knowing that in our little trio of friendship I don't have the monopoly on neurosis. So what did you do?' I asked him, eyebrows raised.

'Nothing,' he replied nonchalantly.

'What did you do, Stu?' I repeated.

He stopped cutting, picked up the hairdryer, and started on the blow-dry, leaving me to lip-read his response. I reached over and flicked the dryer off at the plug.

'Pardon?' I replied archly.

He sighed indignantly. 'Okay, okay – I replaced all the cream in her factor two with factor fifty. She spent the whole bloody holiday fretting and obsessing over why she wasn't getting a tan despite lying in the sun for eight bloody hours a day. I mean, she was a malignant melanoma waiting to happen.'

I was laughing so hard that the other clients in the salon were turning to stare.

'Noooooooo! So how did she find out?'

'She caught me on the second-last day. Found me in the bathroom with the two bottles, a funnel and a pair of Marigolds. I think she thought I was trying to smuggle drugs in her suntan lotion. Or engaging in some kind of deviant sexual practice. I had to confess all.'

'All?'.

He nodded. 'The daily disinfection of the bathroom; the

insistence that all our food was overcooked; the secret tests on the swimming-pool water; the outright refusal to join the bacteria in the hot-tubs, the avoidance of aeroplane grub, the books on rare indigenous species of potentially dangerous insects, the telephone numbers of the nearest labs carrying antidotes . . . You know, all the usual holiday stuff.'

'Honey, the "usual holiday stuff" is an iPod, a passport and enough knickers for a fortnight.'

'Yeah, well, we can't all be as carefree as you, Miss Sob-in-Yer-Prawns,' he countered, grinning, as he fired up the hairdryer again. Ten minutes later, my mane was thick, shiny, and falling halfway between my chin and my shoulders in a style that was a slightly longer version of Trish's bob. Even my perpetual knee-trembles in the face of change had been steadied by the glossy, glorious image in front of me. He'd put it into a side parting and was now taking small sections at a time and sliding a set of bright pink GHDs down them.

Meanwhile I was musing out loud.

'You know, it's a shame we're not attracted to each other, Stu. That would just be too easy, wouldn't it?'

It was an incomprehensible twist of nature that we'd pondered many times. Stu was everything I could ever want in a guy: funny, kind, caring, house-trained and in possession of the kind of toned physique that I could happily stare at all day. We loved spending time together and I couldn't think of anyone I laughed with more. But sexual attraction? None. Void. Barren. On either side. If I was being really honest, I think that my subconscious realised that – strange idiosyncrasies aside – he belonged with some willowy model-type, and maybe on his side, his subconscious knew it too. But he'd never, ever say that out loud, and we both just put it down to a clash of opposing pheromones.

He flashed his row of perfect white pearlies. 'I know. It's a sad state of affairs, really. Not to mention totally inconvenient, because I wouldn't even have to spend a fortune trying to impress you,' he teased.

I swatted him with a brush. 'Yes you would! I'm not just a cheap, easy pick-up, you know!'

He stopped and stared at me with mock puzzlement. 'Really? Amazing! All these years we've been mates and the whole time I totally misjudged you.'

With that, he pulled my head back, kissed me on the lips and then thrust me forward, shaking my hair out with his hands as he did it.

The result was a perfect, casual long bob that I knew I'd never be able to re-create so beautifully.

I pouted in the mirror. 'You know I'm only your friend because you're a blessed genius with hair, don't you?'

He nodded solemnly. 'Yep, that and you like ogling my great arse.'

I bluffed outrage as my gaze moved down to inspect the merchandise.

'Actually,' I conceded with a grin, 'you could be right.'

I had a sudden thought. 'Oh, and Stu . . . '

'Yes?'

'Well done, I'm very proud of you – we smooched at least thirty seconds ago and you haven't run off in search of the antibacterial lip balm yet.'

He laughed as he delved into his pocket and pulled out a little tube, squeezed a little dollop of goo on his index finger and ran it around his lips.

I adopted my very best crushed expression.

'Sorry, honey, but you know what they say . . . '

'What do they say?' I replied petulantly.

'Pride comes before a cold sore.'

Great Morning TV!

Zara rounded off her weekly predictions by advising all Taureans to avoid over-spending that weekend as it could have long-lasting consequences – although she did add a caveat that David Beckham (2 May), Cher (20 May) and Barbra Streisand (24 April) probably didn't have to worry.

Goldie was just about to bring the show to a close when Zara smoothly interrupted her, forcing the producer to quickly switch back to Zara's camera.

'And Goldie, I forgot to mention this morning that we're still looking for volunteers for our pioneering celestial relationship guide that will be on the bookshelves later this year.' She smoothly turned to face her camera. 'We're on the hunt for young single men between twenty and thirty-five, and all you have to do, gents, is send in some information about yourself and a photograph. I'll study your profile, apply my pioneering new compatibility techniques, and this will allow me to hand-pick the girl of your dreams and send you off on the perfect date. You never know, gents, we might just change your destiny. Are you a Gemini? Or a Pisces? If so, we especially want to hear from you this week. So what are you waiting for? Full details are on the Great Morning TV! *website, or you can also get the information you'll need by calling my personal horoscope line on 0879 555 555. Calls cost one pound per minute from all landlines, mobile-phone surcharges may apply.'*

The focus switched back to the ever-smiling Goldie, who now had only a few seconds to wind up the show. And only the very perceptive would notice that she said goodbye and wished everyone a great weekend through very gritted teeth.

15

The Gemini Date

'Little black dress . . . '

'Which one?'

'The one I bought for my Uncle Dan's funeral. Actually, it's not so little because my mum would have killed me. Anyway, that, or . . . ' I threw open my wardrobe and pulled out my one other item of formalwear. 'Classic black trouser suit. Smart one. It's from Next, but as long as you don't get too close it looks like Prada. Have I told you how much I hate getting ready for these dates?'

'Only fifty-two times. Where are you going?'

'Nobu.'

'Oooooooooh, very in with the in-crowd,' Trish jeered, with more than a hint of sarcastic amusement. 'I'd go with the trouser suit. It says "aloof and in control . . . "'

'Which I'm definitely not.'

'Exactly! That's why you should wear it, you big wuss. And as an added bonus you don't have to shave your legs. Unless, of course, you plan on doing a Becker in the broom cupboard.'

'No, that's too obvious,' I replied tartly. 'Apparently blow jobs under the table are the in thing just now.'

'In that case, definitely the trouser suit – easier to bend.'

'Don't talk to me about bending – I've now progressed from daydreams to full-on nightmares and I had a particularly bendy one last night that I'm pretty sure has left me with a lifelong aversion to male organs and hairy faces.'

'Not a sentence I ever thought I'd hear,' she chuckled. 'So what happened?'

'Pamphlet edition or *War and Peace*?'

'Pamphlet – too much information might force me to freak out and stop taking your calls.'

'Okay, threesome situation – me, Conn and Craig the therapist.'

'Fuck, I can feel the bile rising.'

'Had the same effect on me.' Which was the truth. 'Anyway, got to go and meet my doom.'

I hung up and, despite strong and determined counter arguments from my self-preservation gene, couldn't help but relive the trauma of the mental movie that had premiered the previous night. I'd left work much later than usual because I had to wait until Zara had finished sweeping the office for bugs (and while this might sound like a procedure requiring high-tech equipment, Zara had actually convinced herself that she could do it just by tuning in to their frequency and sniffing them out. Needless to say, she'd yet to find any, but she had come across two mobile phones, a portable alarm and a kettle that were camouflaged by various cushions and shrubbery, so she was claiming a minor victory). When I finally got home, I treated myself to a gourmet dinner of a cheesy baked potato and schlepped off to bed with two weeks' worth of highbrow, intellectual celebrity magazines when . . .

Bang. Bang. Bang.

I leapt up, not even stopping to grab a robe, and ran

towards my door, yanking it open just six inches in a dual mission to a) find out who was there while b) concealing the fact that I was absolutely scud naked.

'Leni, I'm sorry – I was an idiot and I had to let you know how sorry I am.'

It was Capricorn Craig, his elbow patches completely in a twist, his expression aghast.

'How did you know where I lived?'

'Does it matter? What matters is that I'm here and I'm so, so sorry.' He was leaning against the doorframe now, utterly deflated. And, much as I wanted to rant about his arrogance and smugness, I realised that I had no right. Hadn't I been the one who'd unleashed a torrent of emotion on him? Hadn't I used him as a tweed-clad shoulder to cry on? I had no one to blame but myself.

'Goodnight, Leni . . . and I'm really sorry, and I just wanted you to know.'

'Stay.' The whisper was out of my mouth before I realised what I was saying. 'You can stay.' I pushed the door back and stood there, completely naked, utterly vulnerable.

He walked towards me and his lips fastened hard on to mine, pushing me back against the door, his breathing heavy, hot, passionate, his whiskers giving my lower jaw a free dermabrasion.

'Not here,' I murmured, bravery overtaking me as I took his hand, pushed the door closed and guided him towards the bedroom. We were almost there when he pulled me to him again, lifting me up so that I wrapped my legs around him, my heart thumping against his chest. One hand was behind my neck, the other under my buttocks supporting my weight as he reversed into the bedroom. There, he swung me round and . . .

'What the fu—'

He was staring now at the unexpected – the space in the

bed that he had anticipated occupying. The one that was, it seemed, already taken.

His arms dropped to his sides, sending me crashing downwards.

'So this is a bit weird,' I admitted sheepishly. 'But you know, Craig, you did say that I had to move on and take control.'

'What? Are you kidding? Is this some kind of joke? I'm out of . . .'

'Stay.' Good grief, where was this coming from? I didn't do deviant sex games. I was strictly a no pain, no kinky stuff kind of girl, yet now I was . . .

'What?'

I glanced over at the gorgeous, long-haired man who was lying in bed, obviously amused by this turn of events. Would he mind? Of course not. He was always up for new experiences in the field of hedonistic pursuits.

'It's fine with me,' Conn murmured nonchalantly, as if this happened every day of the week. Actually, that could be close to the truth.

I could see that Craig was fighting an inner turmoil, a conflicting dialogue raging between his brain and his libido, so I decided to help him along. As he stood there, stunned, frozen, I unzipped his trousers and let his anatomy speak for itself. I licked my finger, then slowly, teasingly, ran it along his solid shaft. He groaned with pleasure, his eyes closed, his head thrown back as the sheer bliss assaulted him.

After a few minutes of massaging his cock, I pulled it towards me, turned around, and used it in a gear-stick manner to guide him to the bed.

I climbed on top of the duvet, Conn immediately kneeling up behind me, massaging my breasts as Craig pulled off his jacket and his brown cord chinos, his eyes never leaving the scene in front of him, his cock never flagging. Gently, he pulled me towards him, kneeling down on the floor as he positioned himself in between my legs and lowered his head.

It was that Seventies porn movie all over again.

I gasped as his tongue flicked inside me, hitting my clitoris with relentless repetition. Meanwhile, Conn had bent down and taken one of my nipples between his teeth, biting hard, the pressure matching the intensity of the three bodies that were now moaning with pleasure. It was the most, the most . . .

Aaaaaaaargh!

I woke up with *OK!* magazine stuck to my face and had to spend several minutes scrubbing off the imprint of Paris Hilton's arse from my left cheek. The horror and revulsion were harder to shift.

※

Even now, just reliving the memory was making me physically shiver.

What was wrong with me? I'd always been a bit of a dreamer, but never on an X-rated scale. And not even my trusty *The Stories of the Soul – dreams & daydreams and how to analyse them* had a chapter on threesomes with your boss and a weird academic.

It had to be all the recent changes in my life – I was sure they were catapulting me into a subconscious turmoil that was manifesting itself in imaginary exploits.

What I really *wanted* to do now was to go to bed, sleep, and wake up calm and revitalised. What I really *had* to do now was to decide what to wear for another night of psychological trauma.

I went back to my deliberations. Millie had reckoned the

dress would be the best bet, and now Trish had said the opposite.

A little flutter of nervous tension ripped through my belly, although there was a definite mathematical shift now that I was meeting Jon, a stockbroker I'd chosen from the big bag of Gemini applicants. Actually, I hadn't so much chosen him as given in to the pressure of the relentless number of applications – eleven separate letters, all declaring his fervent hope that he got picked. The guy was either desperate or determined, but either way the postage outlay deserved a reward.

The emotional shift had come about when I'd called him and he'd suggested we have dinner at Nobu. Before each of the previous dates I'd been one hundred per cent in the 'dread and fear' bracket, but now there was a ten per cent portion of excited anticipation, which I suspected was down to my shallow gene doing the conga at the prospect of dinner in a swanky restaurant.

Perhaps it had been worth going through the pain barrier of the Rambo wannabe from Milton Keynes, the twat from the band, my non-assertive twin and Dr Phil to get to this point: a fabulous dinner in a famous restaurant with a guy who sounded like he wanted to treat me in style.

I pulled on the trousers, going for Trish's suggestion because – well, because she was always right, and if she ever discovered that I hadn't taken her advice I'd still be hearing about it when they were wheeling us to the lounge for bingo and custard at the old folks' home. I added a little black skinny-rib polo-neck (Top Shop, January sale, a tenner) and slipped on the jacket, covering up the elastic bandage that the hospital had advised me to wear for a month after they'd removed the cast.

I checked my reflection in the mirror: hair down and as close to Stu's original creation as I could manage with a quick shower and a going-over with my cheapo straight-eners. Make-up passable – carefully blended foundation, smoky eyes, pale, glossy lips, and I'd even had a go with a set of false eyelashes that had been on special offer at Boots. Feet: Trish's Gina peep-toes with the five-inch heels that she'd left the last time she'd had a few drinks too many and found herself in no fit state to walk in anything more perilous than my joke slippers (the ones with a large fake-fur hamburger on the front of each foot). Finishing touches: a quick squirt of Chanel No. 5 and the small diamond studs my parents had bought me on my twenty-first.

I ran my hands over each lapel, brushing away any dust or sprinkles of make-up. Yep, I thought, checking out my reflection from the left, then swinging around to get the back view. I actually scrubbed up pretty good. And Trish was right, I decided, as I grabbed my square black leather handbag (bought for impressing at interviews when I'd first left college) – the suit was definitely, definitely the best choice. This time, I absolutely had it right.

※

I wished I'd worn the dress.

My compulsive fear of causing offence had compelled me to arrive early, and as I sat in the bar I realised that the in-crowd were an eclectic bunch: there were stunning young females in designer boot-cuts and slinky tops, there were some very glamorous women in ultra-chic dresses and sky-high heels, there were some bohemian, casual outfits, all skinny denim and gypsy tops, but absolutely nowhere was there another person who looked like they'd just finished a day shift at the local undertaker's.

Except me.

Urgh, why did I always get it wrong? The very next day

Mr Ahmed at the local newsagent's was going to experience a profit spike, because I resolved to do a long-overdue trolley dash in the fashion mag section.

At least if I'd worn the dress I could have made a stab at the whole Audrey Hepburn look that was being carried off beautifully by a nearby twenty-something brunette, who was currently licking the palm of a calorifically-challenged and vertically-challenged bloke wearing more thick gold jewellery than a serial criminal could shoplift during breakfast, lunch or dinner-time at Tiffany's.

Thankfully, Gemini Jon arrived before I could take self-doubt to a whole new level. Or perhaps not. The first thing I noticed was his smile as he approached me: warm and open. The second thing I noticed was that with his blond ruffled hair and lean frame he wasn't a million miles away from a younger Kiefer Sutherland. And the third? Damn! What was he wearing? A black suit with a black T-shirt underneath.

One person all in black says bereavement; two says bank job.

'Hey, we match!' he exclaimed. Observant. 'Is that a good thing or a bad thing?'

'Depends whether anyone phones the police to report us. We do look uncannily like a criminal team that featured on *Crime Stoppers* last night.'

He laughed easily and without a trace of inhibition or self-consciousness. I liked that. It calmed my emotional overload of dread and fear and replaced it with the beginnings of a resolve to enjoy myself. It was only a few hours of my life (how bad could it be?), we were in a public place (what harm could I come to?), I'd spent two hours on Google researching the role of a stockbroker (to be used in case of awkward silences), and I'd already somehow managed to come out with one witty retort (didn't look like a complete cabbage). And as we were shown to our table, he stopped to let me go first (good manners), then reached around and pulled my chair out for me (very polite) and asked if he could get me another drink (caring, hospitable). After the blokes I'd been subjected to recently, my romance gene was putting out the bunting.

As always, the whole background to our meeting was the icebreaker, and I assured him that the salt cellar wasn't bugged, there were no cameras in the pot plants, and Zara wasn't about to suddenly burst in clutching a crystal ball.

Okay, deep breath, and time for the initiation of Zara's project rule number seven: . . . *during the course of the evening, as much information as possible on previous dating history should be attained. Family and work history should also be attained.*

'I hope you don't mind me asking,' said I, in a hesitant manner that probably made it clear that *I* minded asking, 'but what made you apply to take part in this?'

'Actually, I didn't.'

'You did.'

He was grinning now. 'I promise I didn't. However, my sixteen-year-old sister, who spends her life in pursuit of great new ways to humiliate and upset her brother, did. I think maybe I should call and tell her that it backfired big-time.'

Mmm, sweet and complimentary at the same time. My romance gene's street party was really kicking off now that I could strike 'publicity seeking' and 'desperate' off his list of potential characteristics and replace them with 'friendly' and 'flattering'.

'So how did you end up doing this, then?' he asked.

I shrugged my shoulders. 'I'm Zara's PA and it's part of the job – twelve dates, all with different signs of the zodiac.'

'How many have you had so far?'

'You're number five. I've already met Scorpio, Leo, Capricorn and Aries.'

He was genuinely intrigued. 'Are you enjoying it?'

I weighed up my options. Revealing any further information would be in direct contradiction of Zara's project rule number four: *Details of this project and of candidates must not be discussed with anyone outside Delta Inc.* And even if I was to be a rebel and disobey she who sees all, the polite and discreet thing to say was that it was all going swimmingly and I was learning valuable lessons that had deep anthropological significance.

This was a time for intelligent, rational thinking and making smart choices.

But somehow a fit of the giggles burst out, along with a whispered, 'No, I bloody hate it.'

For some reason he found this funny, setting us both off on such a snort of completely irrational hilarity that the diners at nearby tables couldn't resist a curious glance at Bonnie and Clyde.

An hour of easy conversation later, I'd discovered something utterly astonishing: he was . . . *normal.* Completely run-of-the-mill. No apparent hang-ups, craziness or tendencies towards deviance. Just wonderfully, spectacularly, reassuringly normal. He had one sister, originated from Devon, and had moved to London when he'd landed a job with a brokerage firm. He loved his mum and dad, lived in Islington, played squash, ran three miles every second day, liked to travel, drove a Mini and loved going to comedy clubs. And he had a quick, self-deprecating humour that somehow made being with him absolutely comfortable. Oh, happy days. The apprehension and the desperation to get the night over with joined my pre-date nerves at the wayside.

I excused myself and nipped to the loo. As soon as I was in the cubicle, I pulled out my phone and dialled Trish.

She answered after the first ring. 'Fucking shoot me – The Damnation Fires are playing on the show on Monday and they've just requested a Satanic priest and three live chickens. Why did I take this job?'

'No idea. Anyway, guess what?' I whispered, momentarily forgetting that she hated both whispering and trite questions.

'You've decided to become a lez and you're going down on Angelina's jolie as we speak?'

'I am. But other than that, this one's nice, Trish.'

'You said that about the singer.'

'I know, but this one's funny. And it's weird, but there's a . . . a kind of . . . connection.'

'Well, you've got a lot in common – you're both incapable of finding a partner using traditional methods.'

'Will you shut up? Anyway, phone Stu and tell him that I'm okay – he gets pissed off if I don't check in every three minutes when I'm on a date.'

'I will indeed, your ladyship. Now get back to Mr Wonderful – and remember what I told you . . . if you run out of things to say . . . '

'Yes?' I replied, racking my brain to remember what worthy advice she'd actually given me.

'Just slip under the table and unzip.'

I didn't bother informing her that this would be in direct contravention of Zara's project rule number five: *Physical contact with candidates should not be initiated*. Instead, I snapped the phone shut and left the cubicle, then made for the main washroom door.

'Excuse me . . . '

I turned to see Audrey Hepburn standing in the corner, looking mildly uncomfortable. She walked towards me and handed me a leaflet.

'Look,' she blurted out. 'Take this. I just want you to

know that I've been where you are – the whispering, the giggling, the sneaking around. Maybe this will help.'

And with that she turned and disappeared back into the dining area.

My gaze went to the leaflet and the headline at the top of the front page.

ARE YOU TRAPPED IN A CYCLE OF COCAINE ABUSE?
WE CAN HELP!

Why? Why would anyone think that? I skulked back out to Gemini Jon and placed it in front of him, whispering, 'Someone just slipped me this in the toilets. Apparently, I'm behaving suspiciously.'

We processed the development in a cool and objective manner – by bursting into another irrepressible fit of giggles.

I wiped away the tears of laughter and picked up my spoon. Right, time to calm down. Obviously the stress and pressure of this whole dating thing was tipping me over into an abyss of hysteria.

'Do things like that happen to you a lot – you know, bizarre stuff?' Jon asked, feigning wariness. At least I hoped he was feigning it.

'A few months ago the answer to that question would have been a definite *absolutely not*.'

'But now?'

'All the time. Honestly, it would take me all night to tell you . . .'

'Great!' he prompted with a smile.

Yes, a crack legal team could argue that some of the stuff I let slip in the following conversation was in contravention of Zara's code of omerta, but he was so interested, and not in an 'I'm pretending to be fascinated because I want to shag you at the end of the night' kind of way, or an 'I'm

146

really only feigning interest until I make an excuse about a sick budgie and get out of here' way. He was just, well, *lovely*.

And at least it kept the conversation flowing easily, avoiding the need to resort to Trish's methods of first-date relationship building.

'Do you believe in all the astrology stuff?' he asked as the waiter brought our desserts – pausing only to allow Audrey Hepburn and her sugar daddy to pass. She gave me a pointed, sympathetic glance, causing us to crease into giggles again the minute she was out of earshot.

I took a deep breath, blew the hair out of my eyes (Stu's haircut might look great but I was fairly certain I'd have conjunctivitis by the end of the week), regained my composure and answered his question with a shrug.

'I'm not sure, to be honest. I mean, I always check my horoscope when I read the paper, but I only choose to believe it if it's good. It's just not something that has ever been of major interest to me. Although it is now,' I added, almost as an after-thought.

'Why's that then?' he quizzed me.

'Well, because it is kind of fascinating. And Zara may be a little, erm, *eccentric*, but she's rated as one of the best astrologers in the country. People come from everywhere to get readings by her. There's no way that would happen if there wasn't some truth in what she predicts. Anyway, what about you – do you refuse to get out of bed before you know what the stars have in store for you?'

'Mmm, I'm not sure,' he said with a grin. 'I'm one of those people who trust facts and things that I can see or prove. Unless, of course, my sister is involved, in which case anything can happen.'

With that he grabbed both my hands and looked heavenwards, amusement in his voice as he whispered, 'Right then, powers of the cosmos, send us a sign, any sign, that we're just pawns in your great big game of celestial Twister.'

I leaned closer. 'Jon, what kind of sign are you looking for?' I asked quietly, going along with the game.

'Anything at all. Come on, cosmos, give us your best shot. Make something happen.'

Nothing. Nada. He shrugged. 'Guess I'll just have to go back to relying on charm and luck,' he said with a self-effacing grin.

That's when I suddenly saw the sign.

And at 8 p.m. on a Friday evening, the crowd of diners in one of London's swankiest restaurants had the ambience spoiled by a shrill, deafening screech.

16

Starry Starry Night . . .

'I'm so sorry, again, about the whole . . . thing. Well, you know . . . sorry.'

'Don't worry about it. I told you – it made the night extra-unforgettable. Although we might not want to go back there for a while. "A while" being the generic term for "ever".'

I couldn't believe it. He was alluding to us meeting again despite the fact that I'd thoroughly mortified him, caused a huge scene, ruined several dinners, attracted the attention of everyone in the restaurant and inadvertently slighted the reputation of a reputable establishment.

And why?

False bloody eyelashes.

Or, rather, the one small clump of my trendy new individual fake eyelashes that had somehow dislodged itself from my eye and fallen onto my dessert, leaving what looked like half of a tarantula sticking out of my sticky toffee pudding. All I had seen were four little legs wiggling away, and my morbid fear of anything with eight limbs took control of my reflexes. My shriek brought restaurant staff running, and first on the scene was a waiter who was of a similarly nervous disposition. He would forever rue the night that he had encountered a fake spider while carrying

149

a tray containing six meals intended for a nearby table of Parisian fashion-types.

We'd paid up and left shortly afterwards, embarrassed and increasingly worried that a very ostentatious, loud Frenchwoman would attempt to sue for the damage that a large portion of prawn tempura had done to her Bottega Veneta handbag.

When we'd got outside I was sure Jon would do that 'it's been great, nice to meet you, thanks for a lovely night and bye' thing, but, surprisingly, he suggested we head for the bar in the nearby Metropolitan Hotel.

'I'm supposed to find out all about your previous relationships, but in a subtle and devious way so that it doesn't seem like I'm interrogating you – so could you just do me a favour and confess all, because I'm rubbish at subtle and devious.'

He hesitated. 'You're not going to like this.'

'I'm not?' Crap! I knew he was too good to be true.

'Three marriages, seven kids.'

'You're joking!' I gasped.

'I am. But it's much more interesting than the truth.'

'Truth is good – let's stick with that.' Phew.

'Okay, let's go for bullet points:

- Never married.
- Four-year relationship when I was at university, but it ended when we realised that we wanted different things.
- Two-year relationship that ended when she was transferred to the New York office of her bank.
- Single now for three months.'

I mentally added 'consistent and trustworthy' to 'engaging, interesting and a great listener'. But then, I

150

suppose Trish did have a point: hadn't I thought all those things about Matt the singer?

However – and don't ask me how, given that we've already ascertained that my judgement skills are up there with my ability to, say, Morris dance while speaking in the national tongue of Kurdistan – Jon seemed different. More comfortable. Nicer.

'Miss, your taxi is ready,' the concierge informed me. Despite it being almost 2 a.m. he was still enviably perky.

Suddenly, Jon took one of my hands, and my thumping heart joined with my shaking knees in informing me that there was a definite possibility we were about to do that uncomfortable 'do we kiss/don't we kiss, and if we do, where shall we kiss: mouth or cheek?'

My internal voice (the one that had an honours degree in avoiding toe-curling situations) kicked in, and invoked Zara's project rule number six: *Any physical contact initiated by candidate should be rejected but noted to be used in analysis.*

'I have to go,' I said, with just a hint of sadness. I'd had a really nice night with a guy who hadn't brandished a weapon, insulted me, analysed me or caused any physical damage to my being – these were all major plus points.

'Leni, I had a really good time – you've no idea how nice I'm going to be to my sister for setting this up.'

Our gormless grins were in perfect sync.

'But I have to say the whole "dating the zodiac" thing bothers me a bit. I'm pretty open-minded, but I think my girlfriend going out with other guys might just cause me sleepless nights.'

Girlfriend? Had he said girlfriend? How bloody presumptuous! How borderline cocky! How, er, yep, once again I give you '*lovely*'!

'So, I wondered if we could see each other again when

151

this is all over. If you're still single, that is.' Aw, so sweet. He paused a little nervously, obviously working out what to say next. 'But in the meantime, maybe we could email and call and get to know each other better. Would that be okay?'

Sadly, I knew it wasn't. Zara's project rules, numbers eight and nine: *No personal information, contact details, company material or discussions should be shared with the candidate* and *Post-date contact with any candidate is strictly forbidden.*

It was impossible. It just wasn't meant to be. Wrong place, wrong time. Que sera sera. Then I ran out of clichés.

'I'd like that,' I blurted.

PROGRESS SUMMARY: *IT'S IN THE STARS* DATING PROJECT

CONCLUDED		
LEO	Harry Henshall	Morbid fascination for simulated violence
SCORPIO	Matt Warden	Lead singer, lying arse
ARIES	Daniel Jones	Unlikely to forge career as an assertiveness coach
CAPRICORN	Craig Cunningham	Relationship therapist, incites violent urges
GEMINI	Jon Belmont	Definite potential – secret plans to see again

DUE TO SHEER GORGEOUSNESS AND PLANS TO MEET AGAIN, LAST NIGHT'S SPECIMEN OF LOVELINESS IS HEREBY BANNED FROM HAVING A PERSONAL AD. IN THE MANNER OF A DEMENTED, SCARY CRONE, 'HE'S MINE, ALL MINE!!'

PS: Please understand that any bursts of irrationality have been caused by the trauma of recent dates. However, now that I've finally found the one decent, lovely, single man left in London, it's possible that this behaviour may escalate to stalking or a kidnap/hostage situation. In this event, please have me incarcerated before I can harm myself or others. Thank you.

17

Space Oddity

Millie stood, arms crossed, sceptical expression on her deathly pale face. Even from my perspective on the clueless bench in beauty-product world, I recognised that a wee dab of fake tan might be in order.

Her unique style always sat somewhere between Dita Von Teese and Morticia Addams. Today she was in Camp Dita, her hair in a side-parted glamorous quiff that curled on her shoulders, her lips scarlet, her bosoms high, above an eight-inch-wide belt that gave her a waist the size of one of my thighs.

'What?' I asked innocently.

'So what's wrong with him?' Cynicism was radiating from every luminous pore.

'Apart from the hump and the three legs, nothing,' I shot back breezily. 'He was nice. I liked him. And we're going to keep in touch, but don't tell Zara because she'll have her Spiritual Advisor for Forgiveness and Acceptance kick my head in.'

She mulled this over for a few moments. 'Just be careful, Leni – you have to be suspicious of the kind of guys who write in to TV shows.'

'He didn't write in, it was his sister.'

Her eyebrows shot up and dinged the bell at the top of the cynical scale. I distracted her from her negative vibes by plumping a white box in front of her. 'This week's lunchtime donuts. I've given up trying to out-guess the master and I can't take the daily humiliation any more.'

She smiled and raised her hands heavenward. 'And another victory is mine!' she rejoiced to the skies. Or, actually, to the fake, spray-on luminous stars on the deep navy ceiling.

I whacked her with a long cardboard tube that had come with the mail. 'Don't get too cocky there, stripper girl, because I'll work out your system one day.'

I trudged up the stairs. Monday morning. I could be faced with any one of a dozen scenarios. Zara might have had a restful, fulfilling weekend, in which case she'd ooze serenity and the day would pass in a tranquil haze. On the other hand, she could have had a frustrating, exhausting couple of days, and we'd spend the next eight hours walking the fine line between explosive and manic, with a pinch of un-bloody-reasonable thrown in just to keep things as volatile as possible.

She could have read about a new fitness breakthrough and might right now be suspended from the ceiling in a contraption that's probably illegal in several countries. Or she could have decided that she had an urgent spiritual message to give to a household name, and I'd have to hit the phones and endeavour to set up a face-to-face meeting. That was probably my least favourite option, as I was convinced that it had already earned me a place on the 'Nutjob' database of several celebrity security agencies.

Deep breath, deep breath. I turned the knob and swung the door open, smile fixed in place and a sunny 'Good morning, Zara' on the tip on my tongue, ready to face . . .

Nope, I definitely wasn't ready to face what I saw.

156

Zara's face. Just her face. It was the only part of her anatomy that was sticking out of a giant, six-foot-wide inflated ball. She looked like a prototype for a man-size space-hopper. Or a Zeppelin. That must have been it – she had obviously gone to sleep last night completely normal and woken up transformed into a gas-propelled balloon used in the early days of aviation.

'Morning Leni,' she bellowed, seemingly unaware that she could travel from London to France in two hours given a favourable headwind.

'Morning Zara,' I replied breezily, as if this was exactly the kind of thing that was happening in offices all over London this very minute.

'Juan is helping me balance my internal energies,' she explained. I think she might have been gesticulating to a small, dark chap sitting in the corner clutching a foot pump, but since I couldn't see her arms I couldn't be sure.

'How did the date go last night? Gemini, wasn't it?'

I nodded. 'Great. He was nice. I'll just take my laptop and go write up the report next door.' I figured it was the sensible thing to do. After all, I didn't want to intrude on her energy-balancing time. I wanted to give her space to focus on herself. And I was absolutely terrified that she'd accidentally burst, and then shoot around the room like an out-of-control torpedo, with potentially fatal consequences for both of us.

In the boardroom, I decided the report could wait a few minutes and called Trish, who answered with her customary, 'Make it snappy, I'm busy, busy, busy.'

'I love that my best friend always has time for me.'

She detected the wry sarcasm in my tone . . . and it had absolutely no effect on her whatsoever. 'I've told you before, between six a.m. and four p.m., Stu's your best friend. I only kick in when I finish work. And I can't deal with any drama today – Grey is on day shift and he kept me up half the night last night. I'm knackered. I swear to God he must be taking those blue pills. So anyway, last night's stooge didn't murder you and leave you in a bin-bag for rats to feed on? That's always a plus.'

'I thought so too. I told you, he was nice.'

'Nice? *Nice?* There's an adjective that'll whisk your knickers off every time.'

'I'd like to remind you that during this whole project my pants are un-whiskable.'

'Aw fuck, someone's just put a tray of bacon sandwiches in the green room!'

'What's the problem with that?'

'Today's guest is Fenella Smith McTartney. She's a militant veggie. Her people will go into orbit.'

'They might meet Zara there – she's dressed as an airborne bubble today.'

'That woman is fucking nuts. Oh, and listen, between us, after the show the other day there were some unhappy rumblings about Zara plugging the book and her phone lines. You might want to suggest she calms down on the self-publicity. Anyway, back to the important stuff, Miss Asbestos Pants. How long is it since you had a naked duvet wrestle?'

I wailed with outrage. 'What? I'm not answering that. Anyway, you already know the answer.'

'Yes, but by vocalising it, you might accept the tragic truth. Go on, round it up to the nearest year.'

'I. Refuse. To. Answer. I'm not discussing my sex life with you at nine o'clock in the morning.'

'Shit, you're uptight. Okay, but I'm just saying . . . If you get a hot one, there's nothing wrong with the occasional one-night stand for purely therapeutic reasons. Don't think of it as sex, think of it as an enjoyable way to exercise the pelvic-floor muscles.'

'You're depraved. And more than a little scary.'

'Fuck! Fenella has bitten into the bacon – she must have thought it was that vegetarian stuff. Have to go, doll, lawsuit pending . . . ' Click.

I replaced the phone, hoping that no one else in the building had fallen foul of our hopelessly rubbish phone system and inadvertently cut in and overheard any of that conversation.

How long had Trish known me? And had I ever had a one-night stand? Actually, there had been one, but I'd spoken to him in Starbucks every morning for six months so I preferred to view that as a long-term courtship . . . even though prior to meeting him one night in the pub and ending up in his double bed, the extent of our conversations had been, 'Good morning, what can I get you?' and 'I'll have a grande latte and a blueberry muffin.'

Nope, I think it was safe to say that my current investigation of the male species on behalf of the inflatable astrologer wouldn't extend to activities in the anatomical department.

Absolutely not.

Definitely no way.

I was sure of it.

Positive.

So it was only a matter of time before that theory went completely balls up.

Literally.

18

The Milky Way

'Leni Lomond? Hello again, good to see you. Come on through.'

In ten years' time I will remember breaking my arm; I will remember the hospital that I was treated in; and I will remember the grin of the male nurse who was my first point of contact on each visit.

According to his badge his name was David, but his colleagues called him Dave. Which, of course, I wasn't, so I just called him 'Nurse'.

He ushered me into his tiny room, furnished sparsely with a chipped teak-coloured desk, two orange plastic chairs, and a menagerie of medical gizmos. Over in the corner, stretching from one nicotine-coloured wall to another, was a half-drawn pale blue curtain with a brown leather trolley-bed behind it. Even the glare from the overhead strip-lights couldn't conceal that the room was dull, dull, dull.

And then there was Nurse David Canning, dressed in ultra-flattering designer blue overalls, with not a tuft of hair sticking out of the v-neck at the top. As far as I was concerned that was a good sign. There had been a male nurse back in the ER on my first visit who had looked like he was concealing Diana Ross under his top.

'It's just me that you'll be seeing today,' he informed me with a smile. 'This is the final visit, and we just want to check the mobility and swelling before we give you the okay to remove the bandage permanently.'

His eyes creased up when he spoke, immediately transforming him from 'average looking' to 'decidedly cute'. They were a deep blue and framed by long black eyelashes and . . . What was I doing? I couldn't believe I was actually checking out a male nurse in a *potential date*-like manner. This bloody experiment was taking over my life. Men had gone from the status of 'occasional distraction' to 'sole reason for being'. It was ridiculous. Yes, a partner would be nice. And yes, it would be lovely to have someone other than Trish and Stu to share weekends with. And yes, I suppose the odd multiple orgasm would be an acceptable way to spend twenty minutes or so, but I was getting sucked into a strange vortex of male appraisal that was far removed from my normal personality.

He did have nice eyes though.

Aaaaaaaaargh!

He gently peeled off my elastic bandage and placed it to one side. Then, cradling my forearm gently, he asked me to rotate my wrist clockwise, then anticlockwise. Next, he gently released his hold and we graduated on to fist clenching and finger flexing, then finished with gentle stretching and light lifting. My wrist was a perfect patient and completed all the tasks with ease.

Throughout the whole exercise, I was smiling inanely and surreptitiously watching his face as he concentrated on my hand action, his focus punctuated only by his subconscious habit of running his fingers through his thick, wavy black hair. That's who he looked like! I suddenly realised that he was the more normal, average-looking brother of that bloke Adam Grenier from *Entourage* – although obviously Nurse

Dave Canning was the sibling who made his parents proud by eschewing fame, fortune and Hollywood debauchery and dedicating his life to helping others.

'Full rotation, normal reflexes, minimal swelling – I think you're just about healed there, Leni.'

'Thank you.'

I had no idea why I was thanking him. Or why I'd somehow rested my arm on top of his.

'Sorry!' I snatched back my errant limb and – too fast – it caught the top of a mug that was sitting on the desk, sending torrents of coffee across a wooden surface. Unbelievable! Shouldn't I have left clumsiness back at puberty?

'Shit, shit, shit . . . sorry!' I exclaimed, this time wondering why I was apologising when the coffee had run in the direction of my lap and was now forming an unfortunate stain on the front of my light denim skirt. What was it with me and bloody coffee cups?

He grabbed a long stretch of blue paper towel from a dispenser behind him and bunched it up before thrusting it towards me. 'Here, you take care of your skirt and I'll get everything else. My fault, shouldn't have left that there in the first place.'

'No, no, it was mine . . . ' I countered, frantically dabbing and realising that all I was achieving was decorating the stain with loads of little blue fragments that were crumbling off the paper. Why did this always happen to me? Broken arms, panic-inducing eyelashes, spilt coffee . . . I wanted to glide through life on a wave of chic, effortless serenity, and instead I'd careered into yet another mortifying situation that had resulted in me appearing to have incontinence issues. Hadn't I studied *Decorum for Dummies* and *The Fine Arts of Composure and Confidence*? I could now confidently and without any bloody composure confirm that they didn't work.

Nurse Dave finished drying the desk and then lifted my sodden file and hung it on a bulldog clip suspended from the corkboard in front of him.

'I think I'll just leave that there to dry, and mark it up later,' he said, and, all credit to him, there was a hint of a smile where I'd expected an exasperated grimace to be. 'But in the meantime, you're free to go, and I don't think we need to see you back again, unless of course you have any prevailing pain or swelling, in which case just give us a call.'

'Thanks,' I blustered, my face still the colour of a raspberry ripple, 'and, erm, sorry. Again.'

'Don't worry about it. You take care.'

'I will,' I reassured him, apologetic smile still in place while I backed towards the door – in hindsight not my smartest move as it gave him a long, lingering look at the large brown stain that was still slowly spreading across my groin area.

I felt behind me for the door handle, pulled it open and quickly stepped outside, then pivoted 180 degrees and pulled the door shut behind me. Out in the corridor, I leaned back against the closed door, eyes shut, breathing deeply. How totally embarrassing. How completely mortifying.

Still, I thought, as I took a deep breath and attempted to calm my face back from a fierce impersonation of Revlon Red, my arm had been given the all-clear, so at least I'd never have to see him again.

Two seconds later, my buttocks hit the floor and I was staring up at the twinkly blue eyes of Nurse Dave. Lesson in exiting embarrassing situations, number 456: *Always flee the scene immediately – stopping to take stock, especially when resting against a door, may result in extension of deep discomfort.*

Utterly nonplussed, Dave bent down to pick me up with one hand, while he consulted the clipboard in his other hand.

'Sally Jane Stott?' he announced, in the general direction of the astonished people in the row of seats in front of us.

A gum-chewing girl of about nine, dressed like a Bratz doll except for the pink plaster casts on both arms, got up onto her sparkly pink platforms. By the time she reached us I'd managed to scramble back to an upright position and I moved to the left to let her past.

'Nurse Dave,' she whispered as she reached us.

'Yes, Sally Jane?'

Sally Jane gestured to me with a slight inflection of the head.

'Please don't give me whatever you gave her.'

I bolted out of there – at a speed that was probably prohibited within the hospital grounds – and made an executive decision. It was three o'clock, and I'd promised Zara I'd come back into the office to book her reflexologist, her osteopath, her African dance tribe and her body brusher (don't ask) for the following week. I'd need to drive to the train station and depending on the train times, it would take me at least an hour to get back to the office, so I wouldn't get there until four o'clock, and then, if I finished on time, that meant I was facing yet another commute – all for the sake of an hour's desk time. And it was all Zara's bloody fault I was at the hospital in the first place. Well, sod it. I'd had enough. I was tired, I was embarrassed, and my buttocks were killing me. I was fed up with putting life, limb and dignity at risk to please everyone else. Obedient, conformist Leni Lomond was bloody sick of being... obedient, conformist Leni Lomond. For once in my life I wasn't going to give a damn about doing the right thing.

Instead, I was going to do exactly as I pleased, and at that moment I wanted to take the necessary steps to remedy my general wellbeing.

Where was the nearest pub?

The Red Lion sounded like a darts-playing, beer-swilling emporium, but actually that couldn't have been further from reality. It was an ancient coach-house pub with stone floors along with thick, elaborate chintz curtains and battered oak furniture, where the mahogany-framed pictures on the wall were gently illuminated by the roaring fires in both the bar and the dining area. I'd left the hospital grounds (after stopping at the shop for a comfort-reading package consisting of *Take a Break*, *Cosmopolitan*, *Grazia* and *Heat*), pointed my yellow Nissan Micra in the general direction of home, and then stopped at the first pub I'd come to. Drinks in the afternoon at the Red Lion were probably the first step on the road to alcoholism, liver disease and an enforced stay in a rehab centre, but right then, right there, I really didn't care. Okay, there was a small part of me that was already feeling guilty, but I was trying to ignore it.

I ordered a glass of red wine (large), a packet of steak-flavoured McCoy crisps (larger) and found a huge, padded armchair in a corner, far away enough from the fire so that I couldn't continue on my general daily path of self-inflicted disaster by inadvertently setting myself aflame.

I snuggled into the copper-coloured chenille chair, plumped my chestnut Uggs on the matching footstool, switched off my mobile phone, took a huge gulp of the wine and opened a mag.

This was more like it. I know my New Year's resolution had been to inject some excitement into my life, but I had to face it, this wasn't the kind of excitement I'd envisaged. I closed my eyes for a second, conjured up a mental image of my office at City Plumbing, had an imaginary conversation with Archie Botham about his ballcocks and then involuntarily shuddered, my mood automatically lifting a few levels. There was a lot to be said for aversion therapy.

I took another large gulp of the Shiraz and turned my attention back to the magazine, ready to absorb myself in the story of Janette from Barnstable, who'd come back from Weight Watchers early one night to catch her husband having sex with her twin sister and her best pal at the same time. The poor thing had lost everyone she cared about in that very moment – but at least the trauma had also caused her to lose seven stone and win Slimmer of the Year. The moral of the story? Always enlist the help of your friends and family when you embark on a weight-loss programme.

This was working. An hour ago I'd been in the depths of despair, and now I was starting to feel like one of the privileged, chosen few. Who needed therapists when there were ballcocks, large bottles of red wine and magazines full of stories so awful they made your spirits soar by default?

'Be careful with that arm, I don't want you straining it with repetitive lifting.'

Nurse Dave. Standing behind my right shoulder. I started to turn around when . . .

'Stop! Don't move – I'll come to you,' he exclaimed, with a definite amused lilt in his voice. 'We don't want a repeat of what happened earlier.'

He stepped round so that he was standing directly in front of me. I was relieved to see that the blue overalls and the white shoes were gone, replaced with a pair of indigo jeans (clean and non-wrinkled), a loose black T-shirt (ironed and bearing a small Ted Baker logo) and what looked like suspiciously trendy trainers.

'At least the stain came out okay,' he observed, gesturing to the front of my skirt. I stood up, turned around and gave him full view of the large stain that, courtesy of a quick waistband shuffle, was now giving the impression that my incontinence was worse than first thought.

Two old ladies at a nearby table gasped and then continued to stare. I gave a small bow in Nurse Dave's direction. 'My aim is to entertain the masses with my episodes of serial humiliation.'

'You're very good at it,' he said, his voice oozing mock seriousness.

'It's a talent I've been cultivating for many years,' I told him solemnly, noting that a) the red wine had already kicked in and was delivering a healthy dose of irreverent boldness, and b) the two old ladies were still staring.

Irreverent boldness collapsed, exhausted after one witty comeback, and left an awkward, apprehensive silence for about five seconds. He was the first to cave. 'Can I buy you a drink?'

I motioned to the one already on the table. 'I've got one, thanks. If I get another one it just doubles the chances of an incident involving a red face and a mop.'

Wow, another sharp retort – normally in uncomfortable situations it took me ten minutes to think of a witty reply, and by that time the moment was long gone. Note to self – must drink more.

'Okay, I'll just get one for myself then.' Aw, he sounded almost shy there. Kind of bashful. I immediately regretted my refusal, positive that he was now going to head to the furthest corner of the bar and spend the rest of the afternoon avoiding me. Urgh, was I ever going to get it right? I went along with things I didn't want to, and then on the one occasion that I should have kept schtum, smiled and gone with the flow, I'd somehow taken the opportunity to come out with my first ever smart-ass comment. I was just one big social bloody dysfunction.

I exhaled deeply and stared at Aggie and Ethel, forcing them to finally turn away, then went back to my solitary mag-fest. What did it matter if I'd dropped Nurse Dave like a white-hot chip pan; I wanted to be alone anyway. I wanted to revel in the solitude, drink in the peaceful surroundings, let the overstuffed arms of the slightly smelly armchair carry away my cares . . .

'So can I join you then?'

'Sure, pull up a chair.'

'Are you sure you don't mind?' He checked his watch with the hand that wasn't clutching a newly purchased bottle of Budweiser. 'I'm supposed to be meeting my brother here in twenty minutes and I'd rather not sit on my own like a saddo.'

One. Two. Three . . . Cue furious back-pedal. 'Not that you're a saddo because you were here on your own. I mean, you're not. It's fine to drink here. On your own. Well, not every day, obviously, but sometimes it's fine, and especially today, because of, you know, the whole falling thing, and . . . '

I had to put him out of his misery. It was like we were caught up in some weird cycle of excruciation by osmosis.

'Please stop. It's like you've caught the crazy babbling bug from me and now you're in full flow,' I said, smiling.

He pulled over an identical chair to mine and sat down, leading straight into another one of those pregnant pauses.

'So, not working today?'

'So, finished work for the day?'

We both blurted at the same time, the equivalent of breaking the ice with a jackhammer.

'I'm playing hookie,' I told him. 'My boss is driving me

crazy so I'm seeking solace in magazines and wine. Like a saddo, obviously.'

He had the grace to match my teasing expression with a sheepish one.

'What about you, on a break?'

'Nope, finished for the day.' He held up his beer to emphasise his point. 'I'm on early shift this week, which I love, because it keeps me out of A&E and in with the nice, sober, regular people. Present company excluded, of course.'

'Hey! This is my first glass of wine. Although I do intend for there to be many more. But before you write out my admission slip to the detox ward, I promise you I don't do this very often. Never, actually, but I promise there are extenuating circumstances.'

He clinked his beer bottle against my glass. 'Well, I'm glad you decided to do it today. I'm Dave, by the way.'

'I know. It was on your badge.'

'Are you always that observant?'

'Only when it doesn't involve things that I can drop, squash or trip over.'

He smiled and checked his watch again. 'I've got fifteen minutes left before my brother gets here. Is that long enough to hear about those extenuating circumstances?'

'Sorry, no – it's a long, long list that can't be demeaned by rushing through it.'

Bzzzzzzzz. Bzzzzzzzz. Bzzzzzzzz. The mobile phone that he'd placed on the table burst into vibrate mode, sending it careering across the knotted oak surface. Just in time, he snatched it up and checked the screen.

'It's a message from my brother – he isn't going to make it,' he sighed. 'That's the third time this week. He's in the CID, so if a big case comes in they often have to work overtime.'

There was another five-second silence as I waited for him

169

to announce that he'd be going then. He drained his beer and then placed the bottle down next to his phone. 'I should really just get off home then,' he said.

No problem! I was looking forward to getting back to my magazines anyway. And I'd hardly touched my wine since he'd joined me. It would be nice just to sink into blissful oblivion again and resume repair work on my tortured soul. Or maybe I'd just have another packet of crisps and perhaps a Bacardi Breezer.

'Unless . . . ' he started.

'Yes?'

'Unless I got us both another drink and you filled me in on those circumstances you were talking about. Without rushing through them, of course.'

Before I realised what I was doing, my mouth smiled, my head went into a repetitive nod and 'Okay then, it's a deal' spouted forth.

As he wandered off to the bar, the irony of the situation didn't escape me. Last year I'd had a dating drought so severe it should have been given a government health warning. This year I was chalking them up even when I didn't want them.

Although this wasn't exactly a date, I corrected myself; this was more of a happy coincidence. Two vague acquaintances bumping into each other in a pub – that hardly made this an official date.

But, er, the bumping of intimate organs just a few hours later probably did.

19

Total Eclipse of the Heart

'Someone's changed the locks!' I wailed, as I slumped against the doorframe, defeated. Had I not paid my rent in time? Had I been invaded? Was there, right this minute, a gang of drug-addled teenagers sitting on the other side of my door, eating the contents of my fridge and raking through my knicker drawer while talking to their civil-liberties lawyer about their latest claim for squatters' rights?

Just as I was contemplating calling the Citizen's Advice Bureau, the door swung open and an amused face peeked through.

'You're at the wrong door, Leni, love. Had one or two sweet sherries, have we?'

'Sorry, Mrs Naismith.' Every sinew of my body cringed in embarrassment yet again. 'I'll bring you in a packet of Garibaldis tomorrow to make up for disturbing you.' At least, I'd like to think that's what I said, however, I was over a bottle of wine down and my cognitive powers were somewhat diminished.

'Och, no need love, you're fine. It's good to see you enjoying yourself. Am I not always saying you're only young and it's time you got a life?'

Indignity complete. I was receiving yet another life

lecture, and indeed a public one this time, from the well-meaning but brutally honest septuagenarian who lived next door.

I turned ninety degrees, hiccuped, pushed my key into the correct door and staggered inside. Then I realised that I'd left Nurse Dave standing next to Mrs Naismith, so I reopened the door and stood to one side to give him room to enter. Mrs Naismith watched him until he'd disappeared out of sight. Even in my confused state, I knew what she was doing: she'd once confessed it was her lifetime ambition to appear in a *Crimewatch* reconstruction, so she was just making sure she'd got every detail of the scene stored correctly in her mind.

'Straight ahead,' I directed (slurred to) Dave, then walked (staggered) behind him as he made his way through to my lounge. I had a sudden (delayed) realisation that I'd left my pyjamas from that morning lying on the couch. Great. He was about to be confronted with my Christmas present from Trish, flaming-red nightwear that announced I was 'Barry Manilow's Number One Fan' on the front. I made a mental note to show Dave that it then said 'So please give me drugs' on the back. Actually, maybe not – he might think he'd been coerced here so that I could blackmail him into giving me the keys to the A&E pill cupboard.

Even I could see that the room hadn't been diligently prepared for the arrival of guests. This morning's half-finished bowl of Frosties was still on the IKEA walnut coffee table. Purple IKEA cushions were scattered all over the cream IKEA sofa. The dust was thick on the IKEA walnut TV unit. My Billy bookcase groaned under the weight of my book collection. And the small balls of cotton wool I'd used to separate my toes when I'd given myself a pedicure the night before were now scattered all over the side table. The one I'd got in IKEA. All I needed was Ulrika Jonsson and Sven-Göran Eriksson and I could claim to be an official Swedish colony.

Other than being the place where flat-pack furniture came to die, my lounge, like the rest of the flat, was simply decorated with a goldish-coloured cord carpet and white walls. And a bit of green was added by those twisty plants that were called 'lucky bamboos'. I ignored the fact that since I'd got the bloody things I'd had nothing but strife and disaster. I should really return them to where I'd bought them: IKEA.

'I thought you said you had a view of the castle?' Dave asked.

Uh-huh. That's how I'd done it. I'd tempted him back with the immortal line, 'Want to come see the view from my bedroom?'

Kidding! However, the thought did make me dissolve into uncontrollable fits of hilarity, causing Dave, not exactly stone-cold sober himself, to stand in the middle of the room looking completely bewildered. That made the giggles even worse.

'It does,' I spluttered. 'If you're seven foot four and in possession of the Bubble telescope.'

Oh – shame, shame, shame – I swear I knew it was Hubble but it somehow came out wrong. That pretty much sums up why I never, ever drink without Trish or Stu.

'I'll get the coffee then,' I volunteered, following up on the real reason I'd given for luring him to my lair. Actually, it had seemed like a good idea at the time – the pub was closing, we were still in the midst of a great chat that had flowed seamlessly since his brother had informed him that he was standing him up, and in my wine-soaked mind it made perfect sense to carry on the conversation at home. Dave had already told me he lived with two doctors in the hospital's staff accommodation, so logic and a bucketful of Shiraz had dictated that we retire to Little Sweden.

I left him in the lounge and went into the kitchen to do the essentials: flick on the kettle and rest my forehead against the cool, soothing surface of the fridge door.

'Is it okay if I put a CD on?' he shouted.

'Of course,' I replied, emitting an internal scream that probably terrified the life out of every dog within a two-mile radius. Now he was going to open my CD player. Now he was taking out the disc that was already in there and staring at the wording on the front. And *now* he was racking his brain for excuses as to how he could make a swift escape from the woman whose choice of easy listening extended to Cliff Richard's Greatest Hits.

I wasn't even going to try to explain that it had been a Christmas pressie from Mrs Naismith – no stranger to the bargain bin at Woolies – and I put it on every now and then while I was in the bath (with the door firmly shut) just so she could hear it through the wall and take pleasure in the belief that she'd brought a new disciple to the Cult of Cliff.

It was amazing how the thought of three verses and a chorus of 'Bachelor Boy' could sober a girl right up. I didn't even get a head spin when I reached up into the cupboard for the coffee and the sugar, and I didn't spill a single drop as I carried the brimming mugs back through to the lounge.

'Two sugars and milk, wasn't it?'

His last drink at the pub had been a coffee and I'd obviously paid attention.

'Thanks. Sorry, I couldn't find any Barry Manilow,' he said with a straight face. Then burst out laughing.

'No, I keep Barry's stuff in the vault so it doesn't get damaged.'

I grabbed my pyjamas, tossed them over the back of the couch and then sat down.

'It was nice of you to bring me home. Thanks.'

He took a sip of his coffee, then pressed a button on the CD player.

'No problem. It's all part of the NHS service. Accident prevention – saves the paramedics coming out when you walk into a lamppost. But don't forget to go back for your car in the morning.'

Shit, my car! I'd forgotten all about it. I'd have to collect it on the way home from work tomorrow night.

He'd obviously had the good sense to change the CD because the opening bars of Dolly Parton's '9 to 5' filled the room. Have I mentioned before that I love country and western music? I just get cooler and more hip by the minute.

'First thing I came across,' Dave explained. Phew – I must have removed the Cliff CD last night. 'Except for Cliff Richard's Greatest Hits,' he added.

I flushed to a bright puce. 'Mrs Naismith next door – he's her favourite,' I stammered by way of explanation. 'She's trying to convert me.'

We sat in a comfortable silence for a few moments, before I opened with an ill-thought-out, 'My best friend Stu would love you.'

His instant reaction was to stop just short of splurting his coffee across the room and settle for tortured choking instead.

Not for the first time in the last hour, I was utterly confused, until he regained a limited power of speech and gasped out, 'But . . . but . . . I'm not gay.'

'NO! No, I didn't think you were! Sorry, you misunderstood me. My friend Stu would love you because he's a hypochondriac. He loves talking to people in the medical profession because it saves him from looking up his latest symptoms on the Internet. He's always convinced that all the typing will give him a repetitive strain injury.'

Nurse Dave was now staring at me with an expression that conveyed his deep conviction that I was certifiable. And so, obviously, were my friends.

Another silence.

'But my friend Trish wouldn't like you . . . '

Cue another horrified reaction.

' . . . but only because she doesn't like anyone.'

Stop talking. Stop talking right now. Why did I always have to translate nervousness into the rambling of incoherent nonsense? Thank God I wasn't a world leader or I'd end up wittering on about the latest bargains in Superdrug in the middle of crisis talks at the United Nations.

Thankfully, he interrupted me before I could spout another round of inane drivel.

'Can I kiss you?' he asked softly.

My mouth took that opportunity to clam up completely. Speak! Say yes! Now! Vocal cords, stand to attention! But hang on, what the hell was I doing here? I didn't do one-night stands. I didn't do random meetings. Were my experiences of the last few months finally chipping away at years of hesitation and fear of change? Was this project somehow changing the very fabric of my being, making me stronger and more resilient? Was Zara's barking-esque behaviour bringing me out of my shell?

Or was I just wellied and horny?

I knew I should say no. That I should definitely speak up with my objections.

So I nodded instead.

He leaned over, and to the soft, gentle, romantic sounds of 'I Never Promised You a Rose Garden', Nurse Dave puckered up and snogged me.

An hour later our fingers were still intertwined, my head had cleared, Dolly had been replaced by Snow Patrol and we were having a lovely time, alternating between kissing and talking. Although I had a sneaking suspicion that Mrs Naismith was standing against her wall with a glass to her ear.

'I should go,' Dave said softly, 'I have to be up early in the morning.'

'Okay,' I agreed, before boldly leaning over to kiss him again. 'You definitely should.' Another kiss. 'I'll see you out.' Another kiss.

Now his hand was touching my face while our lips were still locked, and then it slipped down and cupped my neck, unwittingly mimicking that bit in *Pretty Woman* where Richard Gere kisses Julia Roberts in the posh frock. Mmmm, I loved that bit. And I loved . . . this. This was good. Actually, it was better than good. If this was what you got on the NHS then I was never going private.

Okay, his hand was moving again, down the front of my neck, onto my breastbone, and there it stayed for ages. I wasn't sure if he was attempting to grope my boobs or give me CPR.

He pulled back. 'I really need to go, because if I stay here I'll want to do things to you that involve naked stuff,' he confessed with a shy smile.

'Okay then.'

He gave me one sweet final kiss, then pulled back and stood up.

'What are you doing?'

His brow furrowed in the middle, giving him cute little vertical wrinkles of perplexity.

'I'm . . . erm . . . going.'

And then, and I swear this has never happened before in all of my twenty-seven years, my whole being was possessed by the spirit of a Fifties sex siren, forcing me to glance down demurely, then look at him through hooded eyelids, while saying in a voice that I'd obviously borrowed from Mae West for the night, 'I meant "okay then" to the naked stuff.'

The unmistakable sound of smashing glass permeated through the wall from Mrs Naismith's flat.

He eyed me quizzically – not the reaction I'd expected when I'd just offered a red-blooded male a guided tour of my reproductive system.

'Are you sure? I mean, you had a lot to drink tonight, and we can see each other again and . . . '

I momentarily tuned out at that point to consider his argument. Yes, I'd had a lot to drink, but I'd pretty much sobered up now and was definitely thinking relatively clearly. Yes, we could see each other again, but then there was the slight obstacle of seven dates with other men that I'd yet to go on – how was I going to explain that to him? How long would the rest of Project Bloody Zara take? It could be months. In the end I considered the potential deed from all angles, and finally invoked an ancient law of physics to make the decision: when you can't remember what year it was when you last had sex, it's time to get your kit off and go for it.

I realised that he was still staring at me, waiting for a response to his objections – objections that I realised were an admirable attempt to be chivalrous and gentlemanly as opposed to being a heartless attempt to batter my ego to death.

I stood up and kissed him again. 'I'm sure.'

His tongue did a celebratory dance around my tonsil area. Time to turn on the really romantic, sexy stuff. 'Er, Dave?'

'Mmmm.'

'There's just one condition.'

'Mmmmm.'

'We have to turn the lights out because my bra and knickers don't match and I haven't shaved my legs for a fortnight.'

I never knew a bloke could laugh and kiss at the same time, and that it could be so damn sexy. Still joined at the lips, with me walking backwards, I guided him through to my bedroom, which, personal detritus aside, bore a striking resemblance to page 89 of the IKEA catalogue.

There was a rustling sound underfoot (that would be the magazine pile that never quite made it to the recycling bin), then a squirty sound (the contents of one bottle of baby lotion now sprayed across the wall), and finally a squashy sound as we fell, with all the grace and synergy of an Olympic synchronised-swimming team on banned substances, onto my white cotton waffle-effect duvet.

'Aaaaaaaaargh,' he yelled, frantically pulling something out from underneath him and holding it up. Even in the dark I could see the faint outline of *Office Fantasies: what they mean and how to make them come true.*

Do not let him read that. Do not let him read that. Nope, he was kissing me again, so I assumed he'd missed it.

The sensation of his hand creeping under my sweatshirt was very faint at first, and then, as he gained confidence, I felt the fabric being pushed firmly up.

'Zip! It has a zip,' I whispered urgently, followed by a fumble, fumble, fumble then a resounding howl as the zip caught a tiny fold of skin on my boob on the way down.

'Sorry, shit, sorry!'

'S'okay, don't worry.'

The sweatshirt was finally pushed off, leaving his hand to explore my bra. Inside my head there was a definite groan as I remembered that this was the first bra that had come to hand that morning. Even in the semi-darkness it was clear that it was orange (courtesy of a boil wash with my tangerine towels), and the under-wire on one side was missing. It had popped right through my jumper the last time I'd worn it and I'd just whipped the damn thing right out. I'd meant to bin it, but then this morning I had been in a rush and it was the first one I'd found and . . . aw, sod it, I'd just have to distract him and hope he didn't notice.

In a moment of (fictional cleaning-cupboard antics aside) uncharacteristic boldness, I reached for the front of his jeans and lightly traced my finger from button to groin, eliciting a deep moan of approval. I backtracked to the top again and somehow managed to flick open the button.

He was up on one elbow now, gently pulling down the cup of one side of my bra, his mouth then following his fingers and seeking out my right nipple. Time for a quick involuntary gasp of sheer wonderment, before I took my hand from his jeans, quickly slid it under my back, released the bra clasp and ping!

'Aaaaaw!'

Bugger, I should have waited until his face was removed from the general bra area before doing that.

'Have you still got both your eyes?' I whispered urgently.

'Leni, have you ever thought of having a paramedic on permanent standby?' he groaned.

I giggled. 'I think I'm taking advantage of our national healthcare employees quite enough for the moment.'

I managed to shrug off his T-shirt without strangling him, and then groped around, searching for the top of his zip. I grasped it, gently tugged it down and felt the definite emergence of his cock, constrained only by the fabric of what felt like cotton boxers.

My stomach was fluttering as much with ovarian excitement as it was with nervous disbelief that I was both doing this and enjoying it, while my hand felt its way back up to his waistband, ready to push his jeans off. This was it! I was about to be in bed with a naked man. While naked myself. I really should have been freaking out and horrified by this extraordinary activity, but I was far too busy with the serious contemplation of how fabulous it felt to have my nipples sucked in a Hoover-type fashion.

Noooooooo, don't stop. But he had. Still balancing on one arm, his body twisted and his kisses slowly worked their way down, down, further . . .

Panic stations! Panic stations! My brain emitted a noise that I imagined sounded exactly like an alarm that would go off when a nuclear missile was thirty seconds from impact. He was going down, doing that thing guys do because they think we'll be grateful and . . . stop! My toes were literally curling. I know it's not fashionable, I know we're all meant to be striking a blow for female equality, I know I was supposed to just open wide, lie back and enjoy the ride, but it just wasn't going to happen. He might be in my bedroom, we might be naked, he might have had a general chew around the breast area, but a mighty delve into the mighty bush was just a dropped inhibition too far.

But before I could gently steer or manoeuvre out of the path of imminent danger, my reflexes took over – namely the one connected to my knee joints, which flew up, making swift and sharp contact with his chin.

I was supposed to be making love to this guy, and instead he had a good case for charging me with breach of the peace, assault and grievous bodily harm.

'Sorry, sorry,' I whispered, as he froze in midair.

I knew I had to do something and fast or his mood would be irrevocably shattered. Losing several of your teeth from a whack in the face could do that to a guy.

I reached down. 'Come here and let me kiss that better.'

It was only when our faces were once again barely inches apart that I realised that I'd pulled him up by the ears – not a technique that I'd ever come across in the *Kama Sutra*.

But of course, since we were lips to lips, chest to chest, hips to hips, that meant *panic stations, panic stations . . .*

Thankfully, he reacted first this time.

'Leni, do you have a condom?'

'Right beside you, top drawer, bedside table,' I whispered.

More fumble fumble. My fantasy sex was definitely much slicker than the real thing.

'Hang on, I'll put the light on, but only on the condition that you don't look in this direction.'

His laughter was contagious. 'You are the craziest, funniest woman I've ever met.'

'I was going for gorgeous and irresistible,' I giggled.

'Yeah, you're that too.'

Our pupils just about had a seizure when the light flashed on, and my hand automatically flew to my eyes to protect them. I heard him pull the drawer open, rummage around, and then there was the unmistakable sound of rustling foil.

'Check the use-by date – those could have fossilised by now,' I warned him, palm still clasped firmly over eyes.

'It's 2011 – we're fine,' he reassured me, still laughing.

My eyes clenched even tighter when I heard the foil rip open. Watching a man I barely knew putting on a condom was almost as mortifying to me as the prospect of him having face-to-bush contact.

He was obviously still finding this whole thing highly amusing. 'Are you going to keep your eyes shut?'

'Absolutely.'

'Okay, it's done.'

I reached up to the switch above the headboard and flicked the light off. His mouth found mine again, his left hand gently massaged my right boob, my hands burrowed deep into his hair, and we sank into a blissful, ecstatic oblivion.

Slowly, gently, he moved on top of me, his leg gently pushing mine apart, allowing him to climb in between them.

Then tenderly, his lips never leaving mine, he rose up, higher, higher, until he gently, delectably slid inside.

And as my hands slid down and clutched on to his back, our two bodies locked together and perfectly, perfectly matched, I had a burning, irrepressible urge to ask him the most important question of all.

'Dave . . . ' I whispered, my breaths coming in short, ecstatic bursts. 'What's your star sign?'

Kiss FM Commercial Break. 6.45 a.m.

Backing track: the unmistakable sound of wind chimes, played over a slow, smooth instrumental piece by piano and strings.

Vocal: the raspy, sexy tones of a twenty/thirty-ish female with seductive tones.

So just how do you find a real man these days? Zara Delta, the country's most popular astrologer, knows exactly what to do, but she's not quite ready to reveal her secrets just yet. Instead, she's conducting the country's most comprehensive research on dating and relationships, and all you single men out there, she needs your help. What's in it for you? An all-expenses-paid night on the town with one of our gorgeous researchers, and you never know, guys, you might just find that love is where you least expect it.

So if you're between twenty and thirty-five, single and prepared to live it up for just one night, then call Zara on 0879 555 555.

Oh, and ladies, don't feel too left out – after all, Zara's research is on your behalf. In December she'll publish the ultimate definitive guide to finding the man you've always known that you deserve. He might not be Mr Perfect, but he'll be your Mr Right. *It's in the Stars* is set to be THE most sought-after book of the year, so don't wait and risk missing out – order your copy now by logging on to www.itsinthestars.net, and make this the first day on your journey to the man of your dreams.

20

Lunar Landing

'What. A. Crock. Of. Shit.' The disgust in Trish's tone was almost venomous as she flicked off the radio in her little office and slurped her Skinny Mocha Chocca from its Starbucks tin mug. 'I mean, what is this, the fucking 1800s?'

She leaned towards the radio, apparently so overcome with rage that she was under the misapprehension that dialogue directed at the silver boom box would, by some powers of reverse physics, be transmitted straight back to Zara.

'Haven't you ever heard of the suffragettes, you daft, insidious cow!'

Over in the corner, sitting on a bright purple beanbag chair, carefully trying to drink my latte without spilling any on the stuffed folder and pile of loose papers on my knees, I gingerly shrugged my shoulders. Bad move. And one that immediately diverted her wrath in my direction . . .

'Look, Leni, I know it was me who got you into this whole thing, and I thought it would be a bit of a laugh, and let's face it, you need all the help you can get when it comes to landing someone . . . '

'Cheers,' I nodded, my voice deadpan.

' . . . but this whole thing has turned into an exercise in

fucking degradation of the female species. I mean, what woman actually lives her life with the sole purpose of finding a man? Do they think we all wander around, tits out, preening ourselves like brainless fucking twats so that Mr Fucking Wonderful will whiz down and rescue us? Haven't we come further than this? I mean, really, haven't we fucking moved on from the time when a woman's sole mission in life was to land the right bloke? It's pathetic. And I can't believe that you're involved in this.'

'I refer you back to your original point – it's your fault I'm doing this in the first place,' I argued, in a low, mono-tone voice, desperate to adjust the volume level of the conversation as I was cognisant of the fact that if the shouting continued then it was a fair certainty that my eyeballs would crack, my brain would explode and my teeth would shatter and fall out.

'I know, and to be honest I didn't find it in any way offensive to start with. I thought it was just another daft idea Zara had dreamed up and one that might kill two birds with one stone for you . . . '

'The two birds being?'

'New job and the chance to meet new blokes. I didn't realise that she'd turn it into a full-scale propaganda campaign that sets the feminist movement back fucking centuries. And the irony is that it's such an obvious waste of time. What bloody woman of the new millennium would even by interested in this shit?'

I had two choices: keep quiet and concentrate on my internal monologue of 'Sweet Lord, make this stop', or light the blue touch paper that would probably result in my inevitable death.

'The book's only been available to pre-order for the last month . . . ' Sweet Lord, make me stop speaking now. 'And we've already had four and a half thousand orders.'

'YOU. ARE. PULLING. MY. PLONKER!!!!'

I wondered how observant she would have to be to realise that I was in absolutely no state to pull anyone's plonker.

'I GIVE UP. I FUCKING GIVE UP.'

'Look, Trish, not everyone has someone like Grey. You were really lucky when you met him.'

'I wasn't lucky; I set my fucking kitchen on fire.'

I decided to go along the flattery and mollification line. Much as I loved her, one of Trish's ultimate weak points (other than the Tourette's, the aggression and the homicidal tendencies) was her feeling of mild smugness that she'd met an amazing guy and had an equally amazing marriage.

'You know what I mean. A lot of women would kill for the kind of relationship you've got, but they're hard to find. Maybe women can have it all, but some just want to know the best place to find it, and Zara has tapped into that. Don't look at this as being a lot of desperate women who will try anything to find a bloke, look on it as appealing to efficient women who are prepared to entertain the notion that Zara might have found a way to cut out all the crap and go straight to the prize.'

I don't know who was more surprised – me or Trish. Where had all that come from? Since when had I added reasonable debate and informed argumentative skills to my CV? And since when had I defended the insanity that was Zara? Obviously getting wellied and shagged had addled my brain.

Trish's eyes narrowed, her nostrils flared, and she stared at me with a new intensity.

'What's happened to you?'

Rabbit. Headlights.

'What have you done? Something's changed. You're different this morning... You're...' Her eyebrows changed position and the evil grin of a Bond baddie crossed her face. 'You've had sex!'

'Haven't.'

'You have! Shit, no, don't tell me it was with one of Zara's stud squad.'

I resolved to remain silent and divulge nothing. That lasted for about ten seconds before I caved. I would have been rubbish in the war.

'A nurse from the hospital yesterday.'

'You're kidding! You're playing for the chicks' team? Christ, the world's gone mad. Only last week I found a twelve-inch strap-on in MC Madge's lilac dressing room, and now you've gone over to playing for Vulva United too? Fantastic! I always knew you'd get interesting eventually,' she gasped, loving every excruciating second of this.

I ignored the slur – my head hurt too much to argue. 'Such sexist stereotypes are beneath you, my friend. It's a *male* nurse, his name's Dave, and yes, we were engaged in biblical activities until . . . ' I checked my watch ' . . . about an hour and a half ago.'

'Eeeeew, mental picture I could have lived without there. Still, it could have been worse – you could have been getting rogered by MC Madge and the incredible foot-long dildo'. I loved how my friends made me feel warm and bubbly. 'Just tell me the non-genital stuff.'

I gave her the shortened version, given that the rest of her staff would be here in ten minutes and I wanted to get some work done before Zara rushed in for her slot with Goldie. We'd developed a routine on a Friday morning whereby we'd just meet at the television studios. Surprisingly, it had been Zara's idea, and she reasoned that instead of me travelling into the office and then leaving again an hour later to make my way to the studios, it made more sense for me to come directly here and work while I waited for her to get here from her early-morning hair-dressing, make-up and meditation session.

Somehow, however, I don't think that her definition of 'work while I wait' extended to imparting chapter and verse about my duvet antics from the night before to the demonic *Great Morning TV!* catering chief.

Trish listened, enthralled by the whole story, right up until the point where I'd woken up next to Dave that morning.

My cheeks were infused with a disturbingly unattractive shade of puce as I recounted what happened next.

When the alarm went off we had spun round to face each other. I won't go into details about what we'd been doing immediately before that point, but it involved extreme bendiness and the ability to hold one's breath for long periods of time.

'Wakey wakey,' I'd said lamely, flipping my body round so that all of me was pointing in the same direction.

He'd snuggled his face into the middle of my bosoms, with an accompanying laugh and a muffled, 'I don't know if you noticed, Miss Lomond, but we haven't been to sleep yet. At least I haven't. Did you nod off there during that last bit?'

I'd nodded and he'd tweaked my right nipple in revenge, before reaching over and kissing me.

'So now that I've given you a thorough examination I can assure you that you're in perfect health,' he'd joked. 'And what exactly do you think of our new healthcare services?'

'I think they should be available to everyone.'

He'd groaned and flopped back on the pillow. 'Better get working on my stamina then.'

He'd reached over and played with a lock of my hair, the one that was pointing straight at him. The rest of my crowning glory, courtesy of our indoor gymnastics, was doing a great impersonation of a burst sofa.

'I have to go,' he'd murmured, and I had been gratified to detect a definite tone of reluctance.

'I remember you saying that a few hours ago.'

'But this time I really have to – I start work in an hour.'

The bed had rocked as he'd kissed me then jumped up. I'd squeezed my eyes shut again. Yes, I know – it was fine for me to spend several hours doing pornographic things with a virtual stranger, but I'd flinched at seeing his willy in daylight. I had definitely been first in the queue when God gave out weird inhibitions and repressed behaviour.

As soon as I'd heard the unmistakable sound of a zip being pulled up, I'd opened my eyes and for the first time got a full, daylight view of a half-naked Nurse Dave. His pale skin was a striking contrast to his black hair, his abs and biceps were tight and defined, and as he'd twisted round and down to pull on his socks, I'd realised that he had a melon-sized tattoo in the centre of his back.

'It's a Maori warrior symbol,' he'd revealed sheepishly. 'I was eighteen and I'd never been out of London, but hey, it made sense at the time.'

I liked the tattoo, I liked that he'd been reckless, and I liked that he was open to admitting that he'd been a bit of a twat.

The inevitable awkward moment came when he'd pulled on his boots and stood up, ready to leave. 'Sorry for bolting, Leni, but I have to get home and shower before my shift starts.'

'It's fine, it's fine, don't worry. I'll . . . ' I'd blustered, and then realised that I had no idea how to finish the sentence.

'Can we do this again? I mean, not just the sex bit, although that would be great and I'd like to and . . . I mean, see each other, again, like, another night.'

And I also liked that sometimes he got just as tongue-twisted and incoherent as me.

'That would be good.'

Then the realisation had dawned. I still had seven more dates to go. I had no idea why I hadn't told him about it, but somehow, during the previous sixteen hours we'd spent together, there just hadn't been the right moment. Or maybe it was just that I still hadn't found a way to describe the scenario that didn't make me sound like a slapper. Or perhaps I just didn't want to say anything that would make him think less of me. Or judge me. Whatever the reason, right there in that moment I had a flash of déjà vu, the final conversation with Jon came into my head, and it made sense to me to postpone starting whatever we were starting until the dates were over with.

'But, look, Dave, I've got a thing going on with work just now – a project that's really intense and involves loads of working at night and it's a bit demanding. It's kind of why I had a bit of a revolt yesterday and went to the pub. Anyway, would it be okay to wait a few weeks until that's out of the way?'

His hesitation was clear. 'Leni, are you giving me the brush-off?' he'd asked gently.

'No, no, I promise! Trust me, I'm not a brush-off kind of girl. It's just difficult right now. But I'd like to see you again. Honest!'

He'd thought about it for a moment. *Don't say no. Please don't say no.* Then he'd grabbed a pen from my bedside table and scribbled a number on the front of this month's copy of *Glamour*.

'Call me when you can.'

I'd pulled the duvet up in a feeble attempt to mask the grin that was already making my jaws ache. He'd reached over, ruffled my hair, and then he was gone.

Body MOT: legs aching, stomach muscles tender, boobs happy, libido satisfied, brain ecstatic. Talk about famine and feast. I hadn't met anyone I liked in years and now I'd met two guys in two weeks.

Bzzzzzzz. Bzzzzzzz. Bzzzzzzz. Ring. Ring.

It had taken me a while to realise that the sound was coming from inside my flat, and another few moments to suss out that it was originating from under my bed. I'd scrambled over and thrust my hand down, fishing under the IKEA oak bedstead until I'd located the object that was spoiling my supreme moment of self-indulgent glory-basking.

The name flashing on the screen was CHARLIE. His brother? His best mate?

'Hello?'

Pause.

'Sorry, I must have dialled the wrong number.' Female voice. His sister? His aunt?

'Is it Dave that you're looking for?'

'Yes, is he there?' The voice was sounding more than a little perturbed now, and my spider senses of doom were starting to tingle.

'No, he's not. Er, sorry to be blunt, but who is this?'

'This is Charlie.'

'Charlie?'

'Yes, Charlie. I'm Dave's girlfriend.'

※

Trish's eyes literally popped out like those of the Amazonian frogs in that David Attenborough programme. 'You are kidding me!'

'If only.'

'What a shit!'

193

Thankfully, her rant was cut short by the arrival of Jessica, her second in command.

'Trish, the bakery has messed up again – they've delivered four hundred *pain au chocolat* instead of forty.'

'Which tosser signed for that?' Trish screeched.

'Me. Sorry. I wasn't paying attention.'

And that's when Trish did that astonishingly out-of-character thing that she pulled out when you least expected it. 'How's the baby doing?'

'Still the same. The doctors say it's croup and it'll pass, but he was up all night again.'

'Honey, you're exhausted, on you go home and get some sleep. I'll sort out the cake-fest. The homeless shelter up the road is in for a treat.'

There was the dichotomy that was Trish. Militant, fierce and high-grade combustible, but she did actually possess the compassionate gene. Jessica welled up with gratitude. 'Thanks, Trish, you're a star. I really appreciate it.'

Trish leaned over and hugged me. 'Gotta go, hon. But I'll be back later and we can work out an assassination plan for Dave the Dick.'

With Trish out of the way, I commandeered her immaculately tidy desk, thumped my folder in the middle then plugged in my laptop. As soon as it booted up, I opened up the Word function, step one to committing minor fraud. As I'd made my way to the studios that morning under a little cloud of Shiraz fumes and regret, I'd decided that I'd find one way to salvage a shred of usefulness from my night with Nurse Dave.

Now that I was entrusted with actually selecting the candidates, I could just tell Zara that in a fit of efficiency (and because I didn't want to bother her or take up her time, etc. etc.) I'd gone ahead and organised another date. It had become pretty clear that as long as another sign had been crossed off the list and there was a twenty-two-page report to show for it, neither Zara nor Conn would interfere in the process.

Zara wasn't due in for another hour, which gave me plenty of time to mock up an application letter from Dave and then write a comprehensive dating report, obviously omitting any reference to naked parts or orgasmic situations. If Zara or Conn did question it, I'd just say that he was one that I'd picked from the pile and that I'd misplaced the photograph.

Set to the melodic backing track of my grinding teeth, I got to work.

Dear Zara . . . blah, blah, blah, please pick me. Signed, David Canning.

I resisted the urge to write 'Devious Twat' underneath, and instead just printed the one piece of vital information that I'd so far omitted.

PISCES.

To: Leni Lomond
From: Jon Belmont
Subject: How's it going, Star Lady?

Good morning, Star Lady!

Just thought I'd drop you a line to see how you got on at the hospital yesterday. Are you now bandage-free? Strange, but I kept thinking about you last night. I know I've said it a few times already, but at the risk of sounding repetitive, I just wanted to say again how much I enjoyed our night together and that I'm lookin' forward to doing it again . . . just as soon as you reject all those other blokes!!!!

So how's the survey going? You said that you'd already crossed Capricorn, Scorpio and a couple of others off the list (sorry, can't remember − not that I wasn't listening to you but just get easily confused with all that zodiac stuff), so where are you up to now? I hope you've not found anyone who's made you forget the Gemini!

Sorry, just realised that sounded totally naff, but you know what I mean.

Is Zara still driving you nuts? Seems that she's everywhere just now talking about this book − you must feel good being a part of that. Your stories about her wacky ways were hilarious. Go on, I'm having an exceedingly boring day at work, so cheer me up with some more mad tales from the planetarium.

Better go . . . New York opens in ten minutes so gotta get my eye on the ball.

Write back soon! Today! Now!

Jon. Xx

PS: My sister says hi!

To: Jon Belmont
From: Leni Lomond
Subject: Re: How's it going, Star Lady?

Hi Jon,

Good to hear from you again, and yes, you're getting repetitive, but you're saying nice things so you're forgiven. Please say more ☺!

The bandage is finally off and I'm now free of the pressure of trying to coordinate my clothes with a white elasticated tube.

I continue to blaze a trail through the cosmos and have now scored Pisces off the list. It was a fascinating, unexpected kind of date with − believe it or not − a male nurse, but ultimately it was a bit of a disappointment. Not that I was in any way saddened by that because, as I mentioned before, this is an entirely professional project and not something that I'm doing for fun. Although, obviously, our date was fun. It was. Yes, I have the ability to say the wrong thing, cause offence and blurt out inanities even when using email. I really must make more use of the delete button.

It's a quiet day here today and I mean that quite literally. Zara has eleven Buddhist monks in her office, they are performing some kind of silent Tibetan ritual and no one else in the building has been allowed to speak since ten o'clock in case it somehow reaches Zara's ears and breaks her vibe. I'm tempted to burst into a rousing chorus of 'The Hills Are Alive with the Sound of Music' just to witness her reaction. However, I've got rent to pay at the end of the month so perhaps I'll give that idea a miss for now.

And, double strange, you popped into my head last

night too. I'm looking forward to seeing you when this craziness is over, although I might be all dated out so it would be nice to do something simple like go for a walk or chill out with a takeaway. Do stockbrokers do things like that? I have an image in my head that you're all adrenalin-fuelled and rush about all day shouting 'buy, buy, buy' and 'sell, sell, sell' into a mobile phone. If you could add 'two chicken fried rice and a packet of prawn crackers' to your repertoire that would be great.

Right, I'm going to go now because I'm rambling. Sorry about that. It's just a bit boring here today now that we've been robbed of the power of speech. I've finished all my filing, scored everything non-verbal off my To Do list, burnt off 300 calories by running up and down the stairs for twenty minutes, trawled eBay, and now I'm talking to you. Not that you're a last resort, because you're not.

Okay, going before I dig another hole . . .

Have a great day, Leni x

21

Jupiter's Moons

'Now, are you absolutely positive that it's okay, because there could still be a silent fracture in there. And did they do a scan? Because while the cast was on, a blood clot could have formed that could potentially grow, then dislodge, travel to your heart and kill you.'

Thankfully a racking cough cut Stu off in full flow before he could move right along to picking out hymns for my memorial service.

'What is it this week?' I asked, fully aware that 'oh, just a bit of a chest infection' wasn't going to be the answer.

'Don't know yet. Could be TB, could be pleurisy. But it could also be SARS or bird flu, in which case we're all fucked.'

Trish raised an eyebrow. 'Bird flu?'

'Look, it's only a matter of time. As soon as it mutates to a virus that can be easily transferred from person to person, we're going to see a return of the mass chaos that occurred during the 1918 outbreak. Scientists are predicting that fifty-five million people worldwide will die. It's got to start somewhere.'

'And you think it's going to start in the Third World environment of a shampoo section in a posh hairdressing salon in Notting Hill.'

'It could happen,' retorted Stu indignantly.

'Babe, I think you've been sniffing the perm lotion again. And Leni, stop spinning round, you're making me nauseous.'

I put my feet down immediately. I hadn't actually realised that I'd been spinning round aimlessly in one of the flash leather chairs while Stu was touching up Trish's roots.

'Right, wait until you hear this,' she blurted, dying to share her latest revelation. 'Malky Menzies, our celebrity chef? Tanked two bottles of red wine before breakfast this morning, vomited into his pre-prepared boeuf bourguignon and we had to phone The Priory to come and collect him. Thank fuck it was all off camera or school kids would have been eating their Coco Pops to the sound of "Yer fookin wankers! WANKERS! Where the fook's mah ladle?"'

I managed a (admittedly probably fairly pathetic) smile as I leaned back, flicked up the retractable headrest, pressed the button that made a foot-rest shoot out from underneath and then slouched down into a more comfortable position.

'Spit it out,' Trish demanded impatiently.

'What?'

'What's wrong with you? Other than the Grim Reaper here,' she gestured to Stu behind her, 'you're the most depressing person in here.'

I cast a glance around the deserted salon, all the staff long gone to their trendy wine bars, their Tae Bo classes and their part-time cage-dancing jobs. Stu attracted the kind of free spirits who like a bit of raunch.

'Trish, I'm the only *other* person in here.'

'No you're not – Grey's lying on the couch upstairs.'

Poor Grey. He'd worked a twelve-hour shift, during which he'd put out two house fires, a burning skip, assisted at a road traffic accident and used cutting tools to remove a road cone that was stuck on an eight-year-old's head. Trish had then dragged him, exhausted and mentally drained, along here on the premise of 'spending quality time together' and 'jungle sex later'. Five minutes after he'd arrived, he'd decided to spend quality time on the sofa upstairs while Trish got her hair done and insulted her friends. After spending all those long hours in the butch, life-or-death surroundings of an emergency service, I had the definite feeling that Grey found our rapid-fire gossip sessions too trivial for words. Trish usually only used the times when Grey was working nights and weekends to socialise with Stu and me, so these little snippets of his presence reassured us that he was a real-life person and not an inflatable imaginary husband that she kept in a cupboard.

'Come on, Leni – be sparkling! Be witty! Or at least tell us why you've got a face like a constipated camel.'

'Constipation is no laughing matter,' Stu interjected. 'It can be a sign of . . . '

' . . . me sticking that hairdryer where you'll need surgery to remove it. Shut up, Doctor Death, and let Leni tell us all about it.' She flashed her wrath in my direction. 'And it had better not be about that git from the hospital. I told you to chalk that one up to experience and forget about it. You just got unlucky,' she concluded, her tone softening at the end.

My heart plummeted – you knew you were in trouble when Trish was being very obviously sweet to you.

'I'm thinking about quitting my job.'

There. I'd said it.

Trish swiftly abandoned 'sweet'. 'Why? Why would you do that? The pay's great, it's a bit glam, it's never dull . . . '

'I know, I know, but I just think it's not me. Maybe I like things a bit dull.'

'Ballcocks,' Stu coughed.

'I don't have to go back to that. I could just get a job in

201

a normal company, one where I do normal things and have a normal job description.'

'Leni, where's the fun in being normal?' Trish sneered. 'Look, hon, this bloody ridiculous dating thing aside, working with Zara is a top job, not to mention a brilliant gig to have on your CV – but not if you chuck it in after you've been there for a whole ten minutes.'

She was right and I knew that, but she was overlooking the crux of the problem.

'So is it just the dating thing – is that what's making you want to leave?'

She was no longer overlooking the crux of the problem.

I pulled the sleeves down on my oversized navy jumper, and folded my arms as I shrugged. A body-language expert would be calling for Prozac by now.

'Oh for God's sake, Leni, why are you getting so uptight about this? It's just a few nights, and then it'll be done and you can get on with your life. You've got, what, five of them out of the way already?'

'Six. I lied and included Dave in the report.'

'So you're halfway there. Six more nights out, that's all, then you're done.'

'Why are you being so bloody positive about it – it's not long since you were claiming that this job was the biggest single affrontation to womanhood.'

'Did I really say that?'

'Yes!'

'Ah, don't listen to me! You know I talk crap when I'm having a bad day. Look, Leni – you're nearly there, just stick at it and then you can have a long and happy career as the craziest woman on the planet's PA – that's a dream job!'

It sounded so easy and simple, so how come it didn't feel like that? My pre-date anxiety levels might be diminishing slightly as the project went on, but I still felt ill when

I contemplated the prospect of facing another six strangers and having to go through the whole bloody rigmarole again. This whole thing just went against every aspect of who I was. It was now a week since the Dave fiasco (and six days since I'd posted his phone to the hospital, with no stamps on the padded envelope), and much as I'd tried my best to put it to one side, it had given me a bit of an emotional shake-up. On the plus side, at least the daydreams and nightmares had stopped. Obviously, now that I'd had real sex, my subconscious no longer felt the need to imagine it.

But on the down side, it was time for a reality check. The reality was that I was not the type of person who would, say, go on *Big Brother* and flash my baps on national telly, nor did I have any desire for fifteen minutes of fame. I liked the safety of familiarity and predictable outcomes, and much as I tried to subvert that every New Year's Eve with a declaration of intent to shake things up, the absolute truth was that I was happy being one of life's observers and didn't have the inclination or ambition to take on crazy bloody missions that put me centre stage and gave me sleepless nights.

'Stu, tell her how crazy she's being!' Trish commanded.

Above her, Stu was in manic highlight mode, wrapping little sections of Trish's hair using an incredibly quick system comprising: lift section with tail comb, slide foil underneath, dab, dab, dab with hair dye, fold foil horizontally, then fold one, two, three, four times vertically until there was just a two-inch square foil package dangling from the roots of Trish's hair. There were about fifty of them on her head now, and she looked like she should either be baked or used as a receiver for satellite television.

'I'm saying nothing.'

'Why?' both Trish and I exclaimed simultaneously.

As he stopped folding, I was puzzled by his general lack

of contribution to the conversation. Normally we'd need a gag and a restraining order to prevent Stu from giving his opinion.

'Look, no one was more opposed to this than I was when you first started, and yes, I admit that I turn into some kind of over-protective, irrational psycho when you're out with these guys, and don't rest until I know that you're home safe and not lying drugged on a container ship bound for a whore house in the depths of the Far East . . .'

'Thanks – that's a whole new worst-case scenario to add to my current list of dire eventualities.'

'But the thing is,' he conceded, 'I think Trish is right. I mean, it's six more nights and then you'll be over it and you can just enjoy the rest of your job. Leni, I've never seen you as animated as you've been in the last few months. You were so in a rut before that it wasn't healthy. Not to mention being stuck in an office day after day – do you know what that does to your health? There's the lack of vitamin D, the risk of deep vein thrombosis from sitting at a desk all day, and I don't even want to contemplate the possibility of getting Legionnaires Disease from the air-con system. At least now you're out and about, life is varied, challenging, and you're getting loads of new experiences. A recent study proved that keeping the brain active can ward off Alzheimer's by years.'

Why don't I have normal friends? Why couldn't he just have said, 'It's up to you, babe, do what you want'? Sometimes talking to Stu wasn't so much a discussion as an advisory bulletin from the Department of Health.

Even though he was reinforcing her position, Trish was getting impatient with Stu's digression, so she decided to sum it up in a clear, concise, steam-rolling manner. 'Look, put it this way, if it wasn't for the degrading, ridiculous book-research stuff, would you or would you not be really happy in your new job?'

Reluctantly, I nodded . . .

'Then you have to bite the bullet and just get on with it and stop being such a wimp.'

Thankfully for my battered sense of self, she said that last bit with something approximating a comforting grin.

'I do want you to take this though,' Stu said, as he reached into his back pocket, took out what looked like a ring box and handed it to me.

'Aaaah, Stu, I didn't know you cared. Is this a proposal? Only, if it is, can you put Cruella De Vil's hair down and do the whole bended knee thing,' I teased.

'No, honey, that's next week,' he joked. 'I want you to take this with you – it's the latest personal protection alarm, I got it from the US, it's a centimetre square and you just thread it onto your necklace. Anything goes wrong, just press it and the whole of London will hear you.'

'Stu, you are truly neurotic and paranoid, but thanks.'

'You're welcome, my darling. So anyway, what would you have said?'

'When?'

His perfect row of white teeth were glinting as he grinned. 'If I'd proposed?'

'I'd have asked when your therapy starts.'

He winked at me, making me laugh for the first time in days.

Just at that moment, the main doors to the salon swung open and in sashayed – celebrity alert – Verity Fox. *Verity Fox!*

Verity Fox was a lads' mag darling who'd been dismissed as a piece of shallow, bimbo-esque fluff when she had risen to fame after her then boyfriend, movie actor Joe Callan, had got arrested for trying to smuggle three ounces of coke into the Cayman Islands. He was doing an eighteen-month stretch where the sun didn't shine, whereas the whole incident had been enough of a publicity push to get promotions girl Verity her first topless shoot and a whole new career in the glamour industry. Her popularity really soared, however, when she was a contestant on the reality show *Celebrity IQ* and was declared to be Britain's Smartest Celebrity with an IQ of 179, beating a host of prominent and famous figures, including a much-revered captain of industry and a notoriously clever quiz-show hostess. Apparently Verity was smarter than most nuclear scientists, but she still preferred to get her baps out for the boys, her calendars garnering in millions for the mushrooming corporation that was now Verity Fox Inc.

She marched right up to Stu and gave him a casual kiss on his cheek. 'Hi, baby, I know I'm early but the shoot wrapped sooner than I expected.' She turned to us and gave a bashful, jokey shrug. 'That's what happens when you don't have to worry about wardrobe. Trish! What are you doing here?'

She fell on my other friend with air-kisses and hugs. I was starting to feel left out.

'Okay, how do you two know each other?' Stu asked, sounding just a little freaked out.

'*Great Morning TV!*' Verity shrieked. 'When Joe got arrested I was on the show every week for about two months commenting on the case, and this girl here kept me going with food and tissues.'

'You're looking great now, Verity,' Trish said warmly. 'I'm really glad everything worked out so well for you.'

'Small world,' interjected Stu. 'And V, this is Leni.'

'Ah, the one who works for Zara.'

How did she know that? How? What was I missing here?

'Stu has told me all about you. So is it worth booking a

206

session with Zara – I never know whether all this astrological stuff is for real or not. Do you think she would have predicted I'd meet you, Stu?'

Good grief, when they looked at each other with those soppy grins, the cumulative reflection of both their gleaming pearlies could cause blindness. This wasn't a romance; it was an ophthalmologist's case history.

Stu turned to Trish and me. 'I was waiting until we'd got past your latest rant' (that was to Trish) 'and your latest crisis' (me). 'So here's the news – I'm seeing Verity.'

Verity did a mock curtsey while Trish gave a congratulatory, 'Yaaaay!'

'Two weeks, one day, and we're still going strong.' Verity laughed. 'And he hasn't been arrested yet, which is always a bonus in my love life.'

Stu and Verity? Who'd have guessed it? But then . . . I watched them make eye contact again, and their bucket of mutual attraction was absolutely brimming over. There was no denying they made a stunning-looking couple. Verity was about five foot eight, but even in her four-inch Gucci orange strappy platforms with the dark wood heels (shoe of the week in *Style* magazine), she was still a couple of inches shorter than Stu. They were both wearing black jeans, Stu's loose fit, Verity's skinny, and Stu's uniform white T-shirt was a stunning contrast to Verity's black ribbed vest. Their skin-tone was a perfect match of deep caramel, and Verity's deep blonde hair with honey highlights was like the Barbie to Stu's short black Ken.

They were both interesting, glamorous, and as long as Stu didn't show the side of his personality that screamed 'Hysterical Hypochondriac' they could definitely be classed as a knockout couple.

And it made me feel . . . how?

That's when it suddenly struck me: there was nothing

wrong with looking for that. There was nothing wrong with looking for someone to have that connection with, the one who made your stomach flip and your ovaries stand to attention. There was absolutely nothing wrong with being single and on the lookout for love – apart from the fact that, clearly, I was starting to sound like a really dodgy Hallmark card.

And although the chances of meeting that person on one of Zara's dates was slim, I resolved to just get over myself and view them as being necessary evils, little blips on the road to professional and personal happiness.

Six more dates. Six more nights. Six more men. Time to bring them on . . . right after I found something to calm the nausea.

BILLBOARD

209

22

The Aquarius Date

'Will you stop checking out the room like that? You're starting to make us look suspicious.'

Millie sucked on her straw, making a noise like a lawn-mower as she drained the last of her strawberry daiquiri, all the while ignoring my advice and scanning the room like a periscope.

'I can't help it, this is exciting!'

'I think "excruciating" is the adjective you were actually going for there.'

I squirmed in my seat, making a futile attempt to pull down my skirt so that it was at least within touching distance of my knees.

'Are you sure about this outfit?' I asked the suction queen. 'It just feels a bit . . . *over-dressed.*'

'Leni, trust me, I read his application and you can get such a good feel for a guy from what he puts in a letter. He's a lawyer, he's thirty-four, he lives in Chelsea and he's taking you to the theatre. He's not going to turn up in a purple shell-suit wearing the entire contents of the Argos jewellery counter. You look perfect, so relax.'

Deep breath. Deep breath. She was right. When I'd spoken to Colin on the phone, the first thing that had struck me was his perfect diction and his long pauses between sentences. It immediately reminded me of those courtroom television shows where the prosecutor is addressing the jury and spelling out just why the machete-wielding serial killer has to get the death penalty.

Despite my resolve to be fearless about the whole trussed-up-like-a-chicken-and-meeting-strangers thing, the butterflies were back in my stomach and there was a good chance that if I tried to stand up I'd end up sprawled on the carpet, as my knees felt like they had the consistency of blancmange.

I'd brought Millie along for a pre-date drink as she'd helped me select Colin over donuts (mine) and peppermint tea (hers) a couple of days before, and was intrigued to see if she'd chosen wisely. She was dressed perfectly for the occasion . . . if the occasion involved taking to the stage to sing to our boys in the services as they departed for World War II. Her Dita Von Teese look had morphed for the evening into Ava Gardner: shocking-red lips and jet-black hair provided dramatic slashes of contrasting colour against her chalk-white skin, and she was wearing an impossibly tight dress that reached to her calves, cinched at the waist by a belt that encircled her torso, black seamed stockings and black patent leather platforms with a five-inch heel. Incredibly gorgeous she might be, but it had taken us five minutes to cross a hundred yards because her outfit limited her to steps of six inches at a time.

A sudden gasp escaped me, sending the periscope into frantic scan mode.

'Is he here, is he here, where is he?' she garbled excitedly.

'Nooooo, but I just caught a glimpse of your shoes – are they real Louboutins?'

She burst out laughing. 'On my wages, are you kidding?

They're New Look, and I just spray-painted the bottom with red enamel. Got to keep up appearances.'

Our snorts of amusement had reached a crescendo of inelegance when a tall gent appeared in front of us and stuck his hand out to Millie. 'Excuse me, and apologies for interrupting, but would you by any chance be Leni Lomond?'

'I'm Leni Lomond,' I corrected him, and then watched his almost – but not quite – imperceptible attempt to conceal his disappointment. This was definitely a man who would be good at poker.

I was consoled to see that even though I obviously didn't quite light his candle on first impression, at least my dress code was pitched perfectly to his beautifully cut, deep grey suit and – wait for it – silk tie. I hadn't been on a date with anyone wearing a tie since age ten, at my primary-school dance, and even then my 'boyfriend' Raymond Drummond's red and blue striped affair had been clip-on.

From the neck up, Colin's appearance was as striking as his attire. His slightly receding sandy hair was brushed back and rested in small curls at the nape of his neck; his nose was definitely of the Roman variety and his eyes were set wide apart and topped with eyebrows that were slightly darker than his hair. Taken singularly, his features were at best unusual and at worst unattractive, but when they were all put together the result was a weirdly commanding, handsome figure of a man who gave the impression of intelligence and authority – in a 'keep quiet, don't mention the shotgun and I'll try to get the judge down to ten years with parole after five' kind of way.

Just in time, I remembered my manners. 'And this is Millie De Prix,' I informed him. I struggled to say it without a note of amusement in my voice. Millie De Prix. She swore

212

it was her real name, despite it sounding like a cross between a porn star and a Formula One championship.

'We work together,' I added.

'And I was just leaving,' she said warmly as she shook his hand.

Gallantly, he objected. Marks out of ten for chivalry and good grace? Eleven so far.

'You're welcome to join us,' he told her. 'I can easily get another ticket. *Blood Brothers* is rarely sold out on a Thursday night.'

'Thank you, but I won't. I actually have plans for tonight,' she replied, before saying her goodbyes and walking off with short, high steps that gave anyone who was looking a prime view of her bright red soles. If nothing else good ever came out of working with Zara – although how could I dismiss the benefits of discovering how to chant affirmations like 'My body is my implement of celestial joy' – it would always be worth it just to have met the unconventional but utterly lovable Millie.

We had a quick drink – a white wine for me, while his tastes extended to a very expensive Courvoisier – before walking the hundred yards to the theatre. Even in April, a good couple of months short of London's biggest avalanche of tourists, the pavements were thronging with people making their way to the West End shows.

'Do you go to the theatre often?' he asked me as we walked down Charing Cross Road to the Phoenix Theatre.

'I do, actually, it's one of my biggest pleasures.' Why did I do that? Why? I'd been to the theatre four times in the last two years, every time with Trish and Stu, and we'd seen *Chitty Chitty Bang Bang, Mamma Mia!, Grease* and *We Will Rock You*. It was hardly the highbrow study of the arts that I had the feeling Colin was referring to.

Thankfully, we reached our destination before he could

213

ask me about the finer points of my theatrical experiences thus far.

I walked into the foyer, cool, calm and utterly in control of my faculties, safe in the knowledge that *Blood Brothers* was a musical so I was in for some toe-tapping and an all-round jolly time. Two hours later, I staggered out, crushed, devastated and with an avalanche of snot threatening to burst through my nose like a tidal wave.

I thought theatre was supposed to entertain and delight? Neither *Grease* nor *Dirty Dancing* dealt with abject poverty, family tragedy and brutal death in between the queue for the ice-cream and the lights-up at the end.

A hanky suddenly appeared in my eye-line, and not one of your common or garden disposable variety, but an actual square, cotton, 'wash, iron and re-use' proper one. I wasn't aware that anyone actually used those any more. I accepted it gratefully and then proceeded to blow my nose so loudly that a group of Taiwanese tourists (the flags on their hats gave their country of origin away) made it clear they found this hilarious.

Smashing.

I folded the hanky and was gratified when Colin made a 'you can keep it' gesture while eyeing me with concern. Unfortunately I couldn't tell if it was concern for my obviously upset state, or concern that he'd been landed with a wailing loon and the night was still young.

'I'm so sorry,' I apologised weakly, 'it was fantastic, but I just didn't expect the sad bits. I thought it was a sing-along.'

Once again, he had the manners to appear unfazed, but then I supposed that was no consolation as he spent his working day in the company of murderers, thieves, and football players who were trying to avoid another one-year ban for driving drunk on the way home from Funky Buddha.

Surprisingly, he didn't bail out there and then, and instead we walked to the restaurant that he'd booked for dinner. The beautiful, authentic little French bistro was the perfect choice: exclusive but not flash or ostentatious (although he could clearly afford that), but neither was it the local branch of Pizza Hut. Not that I'd have minded an extra-large pepperoni with a cheesy crust, because in my frame of mind I would have been delighted to pitch tent in the Camp of Comfort Food.

The maître d' welcomed him with a kiss on each cheek and a brief exchange in rapid French, before showing us to a booth upholstered in deep chocolate leather in the back corner. The walnut table was already set with crystal glasses and napkins ornately folded on silver charger plates. This was traditional French with a cosmopolitan twist, and I could see how it would impress a first date – a first date that didn't have mascara down to her chin, bloodshot eyes and sinuses that were so blocked they could bring on a migraine at any minute.

I nipped to the loo, washed my face, reapplied my make-up, and then joined him at the table looking slightly less terrifying than I had ten minutes before.

'I'm so sorry,' I repeated in an acutely nasal voice.

'Please, don't be – I thought it was rather sweet.'

Bee-baw. Bee-baw. That was my bullshit detector going into meltdown. Julia Roberts's one big fat tear at the opera in *Pretty Woman* was sweet. My hysterical interlude of grief was more of a 'keep your distance, watch for flying snot' episode.

The waiter arrived and supplied the menus and to my slightly mortified amazement, he and Colin had a full-scale discussion in French that my O-level couldn't keep up with. If anyone else had done that, I would have wanted to stamp 'pretentious plonker' on their forehead, but with Colin it was strangely, well, normal. He had a calm but commanding presence that was actually quite endearing – even if it did make me feel like I was in the presence of a real grown-up. I was impressed. And no doubt after such an in-depth consultation he'd have the low-down on the best dishes and the perfect wine choice for the meal.

'Sorry, I wasn't showing off there, but I've known the family who own this restaurant for years and they'd think it strange if I didn't take time to chat. He says his aunt isn't waitressing tonight because her varicose veins are playing up.'

So he'd known this family for years – did he mean that in a personal or a professional sense? That waiter had looked a bit shifty and the maître d's eyes were pretty close together – wasn't that a criminal trademark? What about the waitress with the über-short skirt? Prostitution? Fencing (ooooh, get me with the lingo – must stop watching reruns of *Taggart*) stolen goods? And if he was socialising with his former defendants, did that mean that he was bent? On the pay-roll? Holy indictments, did that make me a gangster's moll!!!!

One sign of a secret handshake or an unmarked brown envelope and I was out of there. We could be under surveillance at that very moment. There was no way the plump old bloke three tables away was actually on a date with the hot twenty-something sitting opposite him. They had to be undercover cops. Oh my God, we could get busted any minute. The table could be bugged. I could end up on *This Morning* telling Fern and Phil that I'd honestly had no idea my date was a key figure in organised crime. Or I could follow Verity's lead and turn an association with a criminal figure into a centre-spread in *Nuts*.

'Can I ask you something? Of course, you don't have to answer – you could take the Fifth Amendment,' I said, while running my fingers under the rim of the table to check for hidden listening devices. None. But my fingers were now stuck in a large gob of chewing gum.

'The Fifth Amendment only applies in America,' he replied with an indulgent smile, 'but yes, ask away.' Cool as an Eskimo's front door. You could just tell that he'd never crack under interrogation.

'Do you find it strange spending your days with hardened criminals? I mean, isn't it scary?'

That's it, draw him in gently – that's what Cracker always did. Robbie Coltrane never stormed in there making accusations. He always went for the softly, softly 'you can talk to me' approach. Memo to self: you're now living your life guided by old television shows – must get out more.

'Only when I'm dealing with serial killers. You always have to watch out for them.'

My eyes were bigger than the bread rolls that the reformed call girl had just slipped onto our table. That's when I noticed that in between mouthfuls of warm baguette his mouth was turning up at the edges.

'You don't deal with serial killers at all, do you?'

'Not as far as I know, although you can never be sure. Sorry, Leni, I hate to spoil the drama, but I'm a corporate lawyer – mergers, acquisitions, defamations, compensation claims . . . rather boring, I'm afraid. Are you disappointed?'

'No, not at all,' I answered disappointedly. There went the intrigue, the suspense and my *Nuts* photo shoot. Still, maybe the avoidance of criminal activity was a good thing. At least if the date didn't go well I didn't have to worry about him getting one of his ex-clients to slash my tyres or steal my identity and run up thousands of pounds' worth of debt while buying cocaine from South American drug lords. I really had to stop watching crime shows.

Why was a lawyer, albeit one who dealt in a fairly boring

area of justice, writing in to Zara Delta for a date? He was obviously solvent, undoubtedly charming, and apparently in possession of all his faculties. And he could speak French, which, given my slight crush on Thierry Henry, was undeniably sexy. I pondered the above out loud (except the crush on Thierry Henry bit).

'Spur-of-the-moment thing, really,' he shrugged. 'I heard her talk about her work on a radio show while I was in the car on the way to court and I just fired an email off on my BlackBerry there and then. I work terribly long hours, surrounded by suits, and as clubs aren't really my thing I was at a bit of a loss as to how to actually meet anyone these days.'

'So what would be your dream date then?' I asked, curious to know what a man who subjects a girl to murder and devastation on their first meeting would do if he was given a completely free rein.

His eyes flashed with anticipation. 'That's a great question. Just give me a minute, if you will, for me to think . . . a hot country, definitely a hot country. I'm wearing a cream linen suit and the lady is resplendent in white silk, toga style, falling just short of the floor. We meet at sunset, on the sand, our table the only one on the beach.'

His eyes glazed over slightly, his mind obviously going to that place in time.

I shuffled a little in my seat, unused to such elaboration and eloquence of conversation.

'We talk, we laugh, we hold hands in the moonlight as we feast on fine wine and the most exquisite seafood. And we plan for the future while never letting go of those moments, those beautiful, unforgettable moments of connection between two people who know that they are undeniably, incredibly perfect for each other.'

Silence: Colin lost somewhere in a tropical holiday resort; me lost for words.

'You know, sometimes I wonder if that lady is really out there?'

I decided to overlook the fact that he was, by default, making it clear that I wasn't 'her'. With the bloodshot eyes, ruined make-up and craving for a large Crispy Chicken Deep Pan, I figured the evidence spoke for itself.

'I mean, a woman of substance who loves to be treated accordingly. I know it's terribly unfashionable but I suppose I'm looking for that elusive lady who enjoys an old-fashioned, beautiful courtship followed by a traditional marriage.'

Who would have guessed it? Underneath that Savile Row suit was a hopeless romantic dying to break out and eat lobster on the beach with the woman of his dreams. A true romantic! It was the stuff of historical sagas and American soap operas. Why hadn't this man been snapped up? Weren't women always bemoaning the lack of windswept romance in modern men? Wasn't this the stuff of dreams (not – obviously – the strange filthy ones that I'd been having)? He was distinguished, he was intelligent, he was solvent, successful . . . why was he still single?

'Permission to be incredibly frank?' he asked.

'Granted.'

'How does one find that these days? How does one find the perfect partner? This new speed-dating thing is a mystery to me – how on earth is anyone supposed to form an attachment in such a short period of time? And I'm inherently wary about taking the Internet approach. So, to answer your earlier question with complete honesty, I thought that I'd perhaps gain some insight into current dating methods, meanwhile minimising the risks of encountering a rampant –what is the current colloquialism – ah, *bunny boiler*.'

'So this would be a bad time to tell you about my poor pet Thumper, may he rest in peace.'

It was a joke, an old stupid joke, one that I'd heard Trish use years before and had apparently lodged in my brain ready to use at an appropriate point in the future. I vividly remember that everyone at the university party back in the mid-Nineties had chuckled away quite merrily before getting up to dance to Wonderwall.

A joke. But in my dependably hopeless, slapdash hands it somehow morphed into the hand that opened the doorway to chaos.

The noise started like a tickly cough, a splutter that gained momentum until it became a moving engine, a cacophony of grunts that joined and escalated to produce an almost alien sound that was getting louder and louder and louder . . .

Colin Bilson-Smythe was single because he laughed like a jet engine that had ingested a pack of hyenas on crack. Or maybe just swallowed Celine Dion whole.

Dear God, make it stop.

People were starting to stare, shoulders were starting to shake, glasses were starting to crack, and I was starting to slide under my chair in embarrassment. And all the while, one terrifying thought was crashing through the pain surrounding my brain: thank fuck we hadn't gone to see a comedy.

When it came, the scream was so loud that it stopped Colin in mid-screech. The young woman three tables away leapt from her chair, sending it crashing to the floor, and gesticulated wildly at her sweating companion, who was now clutching his throat while making gagging sounds and writhing from side to side. I caught a flash of something red and realised that her knickers were peeking from below her white leather mini-skirt – they'd obviously been enjoying an off-menu appetiser before they had been so rudely interrupted by Colin's earth-shattering wail.

'He's choking, he's choking,' she screamed, bringing the entire restaurant to a standstill.

Except me.

People often wonder how they'll react in a life-or-death crisis, and now I know. Thank you, City Plumbing – those seven annual Red Cross first-aid training courses saved the life of an old millionaire lech who was celebrating his new mistress's twenty-fifth birthday.

Auto-pilot kicked in and, like a cartoon super-hero, I leapt across three tables, while ripping off my dress to reveal a shiny, strapless, red, white and blue basque and pants, gold wrist-cuffs and a matching belt. Okay, I'm lying. I just darted over to his table as quickly as I could, got behind him, clutched my hands together under his rib cage, and gave an almighty heave, forcing an unidentified white thing to fly from his windpipe and shoot straight into his girl-friend's platinum-blonde hair extensions.

Wheezing and puffing like a marathon runner, Sugar Daddy's head flopped onto the table, and just when I thought I was going to have to perform my second life-saving technique of the day, he pushed himself upright and roared like a beast.

'That fish was supposed to have been filleted!'

You're welcome, sir.

'Get me the bastard who cooked this pile of shit! This is a fucking outrage!'

No, not at all, it was my pleasure to save your life there, sir.

By this time the entire staff of the restaurant (minus the auntie whose varicose veins had mercifully kept her home) was gathered around and looking panic-stricken, while his bimbette was back in her chair and chewing on her bottom lip. Everyone in the restaurant was watching, and I was still standing behind the raging bull, now wondering if there was any way I could retrieve the fish bone, reinsert it in his oesophagus and let nature take its course. Colin was on his feet now, better late than never, his face a mixture of surprise, pride and, strangely, annoyance.

'Excuse me, but don't you think you owe . . . '

'Don't you fucking start! No wonder I fucking choked with that fucking noise you were making!'

Call me perceptive, but as I perused the current scene, I couldn't help but conclude that this date wasn't going well.

'Now, now, there's no need . . . ' Colin's voice had dropped about three octaves and his eyes were narrowed and focused on the obnoxious git in front of him. If ever there was a need for time travel, this was it. I'd go and track down Mr Heimlich and ask him to go invent something like painless high heels instead.

The maître d' was in the middle of it all now, frantically trying to defuse the situation.

'Sir, please allow me to . . . '

'You'll do fucking nothing!' he screamed.

Now that I realised that he wasn't going to bestow all his worldly goods on me in thanks for saving his life, I just wanted out of there, and so I started to edge my way back to my own table, passing Colin on the way.

The maître d' was near hysterical now. 'But sir . . . '

'I am going to sue your French arses off. Do you hear me?'

I thought it was probably not a good moment to point out that everyone in the neighbouring ten postcodes could hear him. 'You'd better have a fucking good lawyer because I am going to sue you fucking penniless!'

It was like listening to a male version of Trish. If I didn't know that Trish's dad was a lovely, shy, retiring baker in a village near Cornwall, I'd have sworn this guy spawned her bloodline.

There was a momentary silence as the other diners gaped in wonderment at the unfolding drama, and the staff stood speechless, while the bimbette applied another coat of lip-gloss and I surreptitiously slid down the wall to retrieve my handbag from the floor.

The only person who moved was Colin. Very steadily, his jaw clenched in an expression of utter determination, he approached the lech's table, placed both sets of knuckles down on the white damask table cover, leaned into that contorted purple face, and said in the deadliest tone I'd ever heard, 'Oh, they do have a lawyer. And I look forward to hearing from you.'

It would have taken a chainsaw to cut through the atmosphere, as every single person in the place was utterly engrossed in the drama.

I was glad.

Because it meant that no one even registered the thud of the door as it hit my arse on the way out.

PROGRESS SUMMARY: *IT'S IN THE STARS* DATING PROJECT

CONCLUDED		
LEO	Harry Henshall	Morbid fascination for simulated violence
SCORPIO	Matt Warden	Lead singer, lying arse
ARIES	Daniel Jones	Unlikely to forge career as an assertiveness coach
CAPRICORN	Craig Cunningham	Relationship therapist, incites violent urges
GEMINI	Jon Belmont	Definite potential – secret plans to see again
PISCES	Nurse Dave Canning	Avoid all future dealings with the NHS
AQUARIUS	Colin Bilson-Smythe	Lawyer, laughs like a food-mixer

EMAIL
To: Trisha; Stu
From: Leni Lomond
Re: If last night's date had a personal ad, it would read like . . .

Are you longing to return to the romantic times of old, when men were men and women were adored? Debonair bilingual lawyer, 34, regally handsome with an enigmatic presence, seeks elegant, well-dressed, well-bred lover of the classics for romantic evenings under the tropical stars. Prepare to be spoiled, prepare to be lavished with gifts and special, thoughtful surprises. If your passion is poetry, the harp makes your heart soar and theatre moves you to a place of joy, then I'm awaiting your call. I want to recreate the courtships of Shakespeare. I'm Romeo – are you my Juliet?

PS: Friends have often commented on my unique, vociferous chortle, so only those with a fondness for the noise of an industrial food-mixer should apply. Earplugs not supplied.

23

Twinkle Twinkle . . .

'Are you okay?'

Was it just my imagination or was Millie's face a picture of concern? Must be my overwrought nerves and over-active imagination – I hadn't even had a chance to fill her in on the previous night's exploits yet.

'Nothing that a fortnight in the sun with a crate of Krispy Kremes won't solve.'

She heaved a huge pile of mail up from her desk and plopped it into my outstretched arms.

'Her ladyship?' I asked.

'Already upstairs, and so is her Reiki master, her accountant and the bloke who does the feet detox. I can't believe she's got him back. That foot spa contraption that he uses leaked and blew the whole electrical system last time.'

'Smashing. I'll get the maintenance company on standby. And what about his lordship?'

'Standing right behind you.'

Was there any chance that overnight Millie had learned a party trick that consisted of deepening her voice and then throwing it so that it sounded like Conn was standing right behind me? By the way that she was struggling to contain her amusement, I was guessing not.

To his credit, he didn't look too annoyed, more subtly intrigued.

'And you know that I meant "lordship" in an endearing and reverential way,' I blustered.

'Can I have a chat to you upstairs please?'

Oh crap. He'd found out that I'd lied about the date with Dave. He knew I was therefore guilty of manipulating company records. And he'd discovered that I was still in contact with Jon, in direct breach of Zara's project rules. I looked at the huge pile of mail that I was holding. It was a moment of truth – there was no way I was carting that all the way up three flights of stairs if he was just going to fire me at the top. I had to ask . . .

'Will it be the last time I walk up those stairs?'

His brow furrowed, making it clear he had absolutely no idea what I was talking about. 'Only if you've ordered the installation of an elevator,' he replied lightly. 'Now let me carry the mail and follow me up.'

Phew. I did exactly what I was told. He climbed the stairs in front of me, his usual cloud of Eau de Hubba Hubba wafting behind him, assaulting my senses and making me so giddy that I almost took my eyes off his (thankfully fully clothed) buttocks.

After an evening with a true gentleman with old-fashioned values, I realised that such demeaning behaviour was beneath me, but walking behind him was a gift-horse/mouth situation that I simply couldn't ignore. I was so completely transfixed that I missed the top step, lunged forward and crashed into the back of his thighs.

To his credit, he laughed. 'You're not having a good morning, are you? I'll add assault to the insulting name-calling.'

I kept quiet about the fantasy sexual harassment.

He held open his office door and motioned for me to

enter. It was the absolute antithesis of Zara's workspace: monochrome, minimalist in design, with a large white leather sofa under the window and white filing cabinets stretching the length of one white wall, facing the cream leather chair and glass desk in the centre of the opposite wall. The original floorboards had been sanded and stained a deep shade of ebony, matching the gloss paint of the skirting boards and the door. If I were poetic by nature (Colin would be so proud), I'd say that the room was like Conn himself: strong, defined and striking enough to shun the requirement for any adornments or elaboration.

'Have a seat.' He gestured to the sofa and, nervously, I crossed the room and plonked myself in the middle. Then I realised that he was going to join me there, so I shimmied up, pretending to be not in the least bit embarrassed, although he probably surmised the truth given that my face was the approximate temperature that spaceships were required to withstand when re-entering the earth's orbit.

He sat at an angle, his long legs stretched across the front so that his foot was just inches from mine. Now I was sweating so much I was forced to say a prayer to the god of leather couches: bless me, Father, for I am wet – please, please do not make me adhere to this cow-hide for the rest of time.

Speak. Go on, speak. Please. Before sweat actually runs down my face and drips on the furniture. I could honestly say that Archie Botham and his ballcocks had never got me in this state. Having a boss this attractive should have been against employment legislation. Having a boss this attractive who was sitting less than two feet away from me, his deep topaz eyes fixed on my face, his easy grin relaxed, his pheromones making my uterus contract to the size of a walnut, should have been downright illegal.

'I just wondered how the project was coming along. I'm

sorry, I'm always rushing around and I never seem to get a chance to sit down and chat to you, so I just thought I'd grab you for five minutes for an update on how it's going.'

Oh.

I did that smiley shrug thing that's my automatic default when faced with any situation that's uncomfortable or involves forbidden thoughts about members of the opposite sex. Honestly, sometimes I think I got stuck in a parallel universe where my emotional maturity halted somewhere around Valentine's Day 1992, when I shoved an anonymous card through the door of the boy I fancied and then ran like the wind so he would never know it was from me.

'It's going . . . erm, okay. I've been on seven dates, so five still to go.'

'Yeah, I read the reports. Seems like you've met quite a few unusual characters.'

I loved the way he absent-mindedly ran his fingers through his hair when he spoke.

'Approximately seven. Actually, make that six – Gemini was fairly normal.'

More than normal, actually. Cute. Nice. Sincere.

'Great, that's great,' he replied. 'Well, look, I just wanted to tell you that we really appreciate you doing this and you're doing a great job. I know it can't be an easy thing to do . . . '

'It's not. To be honest, sometimes I wonder how I got myself into this.'

His eyes narrowed slightly. 'Really?'

'Just sometimes,' I blustered. Shit! What had I said that for? Do not speak. Do not speak.

'Enough to reconsider completing the project?'

'Yes.' That's what I said in my head. On the outside I stuttered a vehement, 'Nnnoooo, of course not. Definitely not. No way.'

'Great. I'm relieved about that, because this is such an important part of our plans for this year, and we want you to know that your contribution is definitely appreciated. You're a huge part of the team and we value you so much. We're under a bit of time pressure – we've got over six thousand orders now and the publisher is keen to get it out as soon as possible, so let's try to get the next five wrapped up over the next month or so. And Leni, if you have any problems or concerns you know you can always chat to me – that's what I'm here for.'

From his tone and the way that his eyes were slightly glazing over, I could tell that our little tête à tête was drawing to a close. Was that it? I'd given my heart, soul and seven long nights of my life to this project, and that was the extent of our in-depth evaluation and appraisal.

'Oh, and just one more thing . . . '

Anything. Especially if it involved nudity. Don't judge me. I'd read somewhere that women think about sex every fifteen minutes – I just seemed to save up my allocation for when Conn was around. Besides, what was the alternative? Put my romantic ponderings into the realms of reality? Definitely not. The memories of Nurse Dave and his recent gynaecological exam still made me well up with sadness and fury every time I thought about it. For now I was definitely sticking to relationships of the immature and 'all in my head' variety.

' . . . our legal team have updated all our confidentiality contracts, so can you sign this latest version?'

I quickly glanced over it, then somehow managed to keep the pen within my damp and slippy paw as I signed on the dotted line.

'Thanks, Leni. And remember, any problems at all, come and talk to me. I know my mother is pretty volatile and, well, *a departure from the norm*, but although she probably doesn't show it she thinks you're doing a fantastic job . . . '

She does?

' . . . and so do I.'

Default setting: smiley shrug. Although I'd be lying if I said my ego didn't swell just a little. Working for Zara had been a meteoric collision of craziness, and she constantly made me feel like I wasn't quite as efficient/capable/interesting as she'd like, but now Conn was telling me different and it felt great. Zara was happy with my work. She appreciated me. I couldn't give up on this project because the team were depending on me.

As if summoned by a psychic force, she took that moment to burst through the door, barefoot, wearing a pink turban and a floor-length lilac kaftan with daisies around the hem. She left a trail of damp footprints on the wooden floor as she crossed the room. She was a formidable sight – my boss, my mentor, the woman who valued me as part of her inner circle of support. I felt a moment of regret for all the times I'd ever moaned about her (when she wasn't within psychic distance, of course). How could I have been so judgemental? The woman was an ultra-successful businesswoman and a household name who was under a wealth of pressure. It was absolutely understandable that sometimes she got a little frazzled and thoughtless. And abrasive. Rude. Curt. Self-obsessed. It was time for me to suck it up and show her a little compassion and understanding. And think nice thoughts. Nice thoughts.

'Leni, glad I caught you here,' she announced. Incredible! I was going to get a motivational, congratulatory chat from her too. Today must be National Team Building Day.

'I've just had a meeting with the accountant . . . '

A pay rise! I was getting a pay rise too. Happy days!

Maybe it was time for me to fully commit to my role in Team Zara. Or Team Delta. Or Team . . .

'And he tells me that you claimed fifty-four pounds for dinner with an applicant who had already received the one-hundred-pound fee for the date.'

The left jab took me completely by surprise and I was temporarily winded. What had happened to the pep-talk? The pay rise?

'Yes, but he didn't pay and . . . '

'Leni, I don't make money so that you can throw it away. I'll let it go on this occasion, but if I come across any more blatant abuse of the expenses system it'll be docked from your wages. Am I clear?'

Conn had the decency to avoid eye contact and ponder the floor.

'Crystal,' I replied dryly, feeling a mushrooming cloud of dislike as I regarded the head honcho of Team Obnoxious Bitch.

Nice thoughts had just completely escaped me.

EMAIL
To: Leni Lomond
From: Jon Belmont
Subject: Thinking About You, Star Lady

Hey there, Leni,

D'you want the good news or the bad? Okay, first the bad news – I missed the first ten minutes of trading this morning because I was laughing so much at your email ☺. I'm beginning to think you should get danger money for that job. And the cheek of that bloke – I can't believe he didn't even thank you for saving his life!!!! Anyway, since you amused me so much I'm prepared to forgive you for costing me the thousands of pounds in commission that I lost because I missed a run on software shares.

The good news is I'm going to let you make it up to me. I think the least you can do is ply me with food and alcohol as soon as possible ☺. Kidding! I actually was thinking of just you, me and my awesome cooking skills. I'm serious! I want to make you dinner and then perhaps just get to know each other over a nice wine and the kind of upmarket, high-art entertainment that we both love: the complete box set of *CSI Las Vegas*, series seven.

And that's not all. Yes, there will also be a large box of Maltesers and a multi-pack of Worcester Sauce crisps. Have you swooned yet?

I can't wait to see you again, Leni, so when will you be free of all the very inconvenient work commitments? By my reckoning you've still got five dates to go. HURRY UP AND GET THEM OVER WITH before I lose my good-natured patience, my shirt and my job . . . LOL!!

Have a great day, my little comic one,
Jxxx

233

24

The Cancer Date

Gregory, 26, Cancer. Chosen from the pile this time with help from Zara, who'd cast her eyes over the four choices I was deliberating between and declared that she felt a 'mystic glow' the minute she'd clapped eyes on his picture. Personally, I think it was just the way she was sitting. Or maybe a spot of indigestion. Because I could quite categorically say that I'd yet to put my finger on anything either mystical or glowing about Gregory. In fact, since the moment he'd ambled up to me outside the Parliamentary Arms, he'd been a bit, well, subdued. Attentive. Yes. Polite. Yes. Monosyllabic. Yes.

Perhaps I was getting jaded and blasé (sweating palms, jelly knees, churning stomach, and two panic attacks requiring the intervention of breathing techniques and a brown paper bag – yep, I was practically casual and carefree), but I actually found it quite refreshing that he didn't waste time with convoluted introductions and instead merely grunted 'Leni?', then nodded in the direction of the bar. He opened the door and the noise of the crowd immediately ruled out an in-depth conversation about the merits of recycling plastic bags or the state of global warming. It was an awesome sight – a heaving mass of predominantly male beings, young and old, big and small, with so many shaved heads that it felt like a Right Said Fred tribute night. Gregory, on the other hand, was in possession of all his follicles. Back in the Nineties he'd have been a poster boy for Britpop, with his tall, lanky frame, shoulder-length brown scruffy hair, jeans and a black parka jacket, set off by a perfectly crafted jaw-line and green eyes the colour of a traffic light. He was Liam Gallagher's better-looking little brother, his insouciant demeanour as intriguing as it was subdued.

We fought our way through the throng of blokes that stood between us and the bar, all chanting 'Who Are Ye?' in the direction of the far right-hand corner, where, I assumed, there was either a TV screen or a newcomer cowering in fear. For a split second I wished I'd worn heels so that I could see over the heaving mass, before deciding that my Ugg boots, jeans and my old shabby-not-chic battered black suede jacket had been the perfect choice – nothing uncomfortable, nothing restricting and nothing that I'd cry over if it got damaged or stolen, unless of course I was attached to it at the time.

'Drink?' he asked when we finally got to the bar.

I ignored the fact that my head was wedged a little too uncomfortably near the armpit of a bald bloke with a stomach so distended he appeared to be hiding an Oompa Loompa underneath his blue T-shirt.

I didn't need Zara's psychic powers to deduce that a glass of perfectly chilled Sauvignon Blanc might be a bit of a stretch.

'A bottle of beer, any kind,' I hollered over the din.

While he shouted it up, I eased myself away from the gent next to me, confident that he wasn't a product tester for a manufacturer of antiperspirants, and worked my way over to the only twelve-inch-square section of unoccupied floor space, conveniently located outside the ladies toilets. After twenty minutes, Gregory managed to join me, two bottles of beer in each hand.

'Why is it so busy?' I asked. Well, not so much asked as shrieked at the top of my voice – and even then he had to bend down and position his ear six inches from my mouth to hear me.

'Chelsea,' he replied, with what I was beginning to realise was his customary elaboration, just as the natives burst into song with a beautifully synchronised classical version of, 'Ashley Cole Is a Knob, doo-da, doo-da'. Hang on – these were Chelsea supporters, and from what I'd learned from the pages of *Heat*, he was in their team. Oh my God, they were the sporting equivalent of tribes who eat their own.

'Are we going to the game?' I shouted,

Gregory replied with a loud, verbose, highly detailed nod.

Okay, I got it. It was amazing what you could surmise when spending time with a man of few words. Gregory was comfortable among the bedlam of a sporting environment – that signalled strength of character and calm under pressure. Chelsea were playing tonight, this was their home turf and that's why a pub in a normally conservative London borough was packed on a Wednesday night. Gregory obviously wasn't the type to pretend to be something he wasn't, thus bringing me into the bosom of his comfort zone. And Ashley Cole was a knob.

Yep, that pretty much summed up the night so far.

Conversation was impossible, so we stood in a strangely comfortable silence for ten minutes, punctuated only by occasional synchronised self-conscious smiles. 'Time to go,' Gregory announced, when I had barely finished my first bottle of beer. Actually, he didn't so much announce it as gesticulate to me over the thundering version of that well-known pop classic, 'Arsenal, Arsenal, bunch of dicks'.

I held up my full bottle and adopted a questioning expression. He mimed back a potential solution, and that's how I ended up leaving a London hostelry with a bottle of Budweiser down the front of my trousers. Quite exciting, really – not the bottle-down-the-trousers thing, but the whole atmosphere and anticipation. I was going to my first ever football match. Okay, so it wasn't exactly a night of luxurious pampering and ostentatious surroundings, but at least it was different. For once I wasn't worrying about what I was wearing or what to say. It made an utterly refreshing change just to be mildly fretting about inconsequential, frivolous things like getting trampled to death by a horde of boozed-up skinheads. I just hoped that the trauma of the visit to the morgue to identify my body didn't put Stu into a stress-induced coma from which he'd never recover.

However, premonitions of a suffocating death aside, the whole experience was giving me a bit of an adrenalin rush. We were carried down the street by the chanting caravan of blue, white and bald, with Gregory protectively holding my elbow the whole way. In the queue at the turnstiles, he finally found his voice. 'I hope it's okay that we're coming here, only they said the date should be my idea of a perfect night, and this is, erm, mine.' Aw, bless, he was bashful. He'd obviously borrowed 'embarrassed and awkward' from me for the night.

'No, no, it's fine, really. I'm actually quite looking forward to it.'

An elbow appeared from nowhere and I was saved from

injury by lightning reflexes and a loud 'Oi!' A middle-aged bloke in a blue tracksuit was suitably chastised. 'Sorry, love, didn't see you there.'

'Are you okay?' Gregory asked with genuine concern. He was definitely a long shot for 'Speaker of the Year', but he had a calming presence that was quite endearing in a 'monastic, vow of silence' way.

'I'm fine, really.' We were about twenty feet from the front of the queue now, so I passed the next few minutes with what I'd come to realise was the essential date preamble.

'So what made you apply for this then?'

'I didn't.'

'You didn't send an application in?'

'No.'

Cancel all of the above claims that his lack of communications skills was a bonus – this was like drawing blood out of a large parka-clad boulder.

'But I saw your application letter – it was handwritten with a photo.'

'My mother,' he shrugged.

Ah. Obviously Zara must have picked up on his mum's mystic glow.

'Your mother sent in the form?'

He nodded.

'Because she wanted to set you up on a date?'

Another nod. Shit, it would be half-time before I had a clue as to what was going on. And that was when he performed the most unexpected act of the night so far: he constructed a joined-up sentence.

'And also because she wanted to meet Zara. She thinks she might be able to contact my nan. She died a few months ago. Heart attack in Ladbrokes during the 3.15 from Aintree.'

I decided against exacerbating the pain of the memory by asking if her horse had won.

'So are you even single?'

He gave another long-winded explanation by nodding. Twice this time.

The sharing of our souls was halted by our arrival at the metal gate, where Gregory pulled out two season tickets and handed one to me with the comment 'My nan's', then flashed his at a sensor on the wall before pushing through the turnstile. I followed his lead, straight into a long corridor of concrete. I said a silent prayer of thanks that I wasn't claustrophobic or wearing five-inch heels as we worked our way up several flights of stairs, along another corridor, down a concourse hosting a menagerie of concessions selling food, drinks and merchandise, up another flight of stairs, then out into the main body of the stadium. I wasn't sure what was making the biggest roar – the thousands of hyped-up supporters or my hamstrings, which had just been subjected to the most exercise they'd had since I'd come fourth in the hundred-metres hurdles in third-year PE.

As we clambered along a long row of blue, seat after seat banged up as its occupant stood to let us pass. It was a bad time to decide that I should probably have nipped to the loo before coming this far.

Gregory stopped first, giving a nod to the people on either side of the two vacant seats. He let me clamber past him, and that's when I realised that, to my surprise, the occupant directly next to me was a very large woman in her mid-fifties, her platinum hair pulled back into a tight ponytail, her eyes rimmed with black eye-liner, lips frosted pink, in a skin-tight Chelsea shirt with 'MRS LAMPARD' printed across both front and back.

I gave her an apologetic shrug – with absolutely no idea

what I was apologising for, but I was mildly intimidated and just wanted to pre-empt any possible reason for her to take the hump with me.

'Rooney, yer a wanker, Rooney, yer a wanker . . . ' sang the crowd, alerting me to the fact that the Manchester United team had just come onto the pitch. What was protocol in these situations? Should you sing along? And was it essential to support the same team as those around me? Only I'd had a bit of a crush on Cristiano Ronaldo for years, and I didn't think I'd be able to stem the cheers if he scored and exposed any part of his anatomy during his celebratory dance.

'All right love?' asked scary woman beside me.

'F . . . fine. Thanks.'

Any attempt to swap life stories and become firm friends was nipped in the bud by the frail elderly gent on the other side of her screaming, 'Giggsy, ya big fucking poof,' in the general direction of the pitch.

Marilyn Monroe's calorifically-challenged granny gave him a swift jab to the ribs. 'Less of the fucking swearing, you old tosser, we've got a new young lady sitting next to us.'

I took that to be me, and felt truly appreciated and honoured, especially when she shot me a beaming smile. Her missing teeth didn't matter in the least.

Throughout the whole exchange, Gregory sat facing forward, watching the action on the pitch. The roars reached crescendo level when the ref blew the whistle and Ronaldo took off with the ball, dribbled past three men, and made it to within twenty feet of the opposition's goal, only to get tackled by a big bloke with black hair and go down like he'd been shot.

'Penalty!' I screeched. It was out of my mouth before I knew what I was saying. Twenty thousand heads swivelled to stare at me. Or maybe it just felt like that, but everyone in the row in front, behind and either side – including large scary lady – was definitely perusing me with contempt in their eyes.

'Sorry, shouldn't have done that,' I whispered to Gregory, who, to his credit, had casually ignored my faux pas. 'Don't worry 'bout it,' he shrugged.

'But I think I might have just shortened my life expectancy. The woman beside me doesn't look chuffed.'

'She's all right.'

'Gregory, she has LOVE and HATE tattooed on her knuckles.'

'She's harmless.'

'How do you know?' My stage whisper was developing tones of panic.

'She is.'

'Are you sure? Because I reckon if I start running now, she'll never catch me.'

'Everything okay there, love?' came the voice from the other side of me, and it was just as friendly as before.

Slowly, hesitantly, I turned to see scary lady smiling at me again. Phew. Reprieve. If I kept my mouth shut for the next ninety minutes I just might make it out alive.

'So what's your name then?' she asked me.

Oh God, she wanted to chat. It was 8 p.m. on a Wednesday night, I was in a football stadium with sixty thousand vocal, adrenalin-fuelled footie fans, sitting next to a toothless, tattooed woman who wanted to befriend me. Welcome to Planet Crazy, my name is Leni and I'll be your tour operator for the day.

'Le— Leni,' I stuttered.

'And where are you from?'

Did she mean my address? Or just in general? Maybe she lived in the same area and would want to get together for

241

yoga classes and flower arranging. Finally, and not a moment too soon, my man of few words decided to intervene. He leaned forward, craned his neck around me and shot off one of his longest sentences yet – a forthright rebuke at Marilyn Monroe's granny.

'Look, Mum, will you just be quiet and watch the game please?'

25

Women Are from Venus

'You are jesting!' Stu spluttered.

'If only I was. More steam please.'

He levered himself up from his prone position on the top layer of wooden slats and stood up, his perfectly formed torso glistening in the heat. I could definitely see why Verity was attracted to my chum – those toast-rack abs – and although his shoulders were broad, he only needed the tiniest towel to wrap around his narrow hips. He was man by Armani. I, on the other hand, was woman by Matalan, one who was surreptitiously rearranging the bikini bottoms that were currently giving me a wedgie.

Stu took the ladle out of the bucket and splashed a huge dollop of water on the hot coals. 'So then what happened?'

'We went back to the Parliamentary Arms, drank lager and sang on the karaoke until closing time. His Grandpa Jack did the best "King of the Road" I've ever heard, and his mother's version of "The Shoop Shoop Song" brought the house down. I haven't laughed so much since Trish split her leather trousers when she bent down in front of Cherie Blair at the *Great Morning TV!* Christmas party.'

'God, I wish I'd been there – at the karaoke, not at Trish's arse-flashing. Actually, I don't – the Parliamentary Arms sounds like the perfect breeding ground for botulism, the common cold and Dutch elm disease.'

'The last one only affects trees,' I retorted with an involuntary eye roll.

'My student, I've taught you well,' he laughed.

I checked out the clock. 'Okay, we've got ten minutes before Trish and Verity are finished in Tae Bo class – fancy a dip in the hot tub?'

I only asked so that I could have a chuckle at his horrified reaction. Coming to a health club with Stu, even a posh one like this, was an exercise in bacteria avoidance. Apparently the hot tub was just a whole big bucket of lethal germs, the steam room sucked the body fat out of you and deposited it in the open pores of everyone nearby, and you could get verrucas just by looking at the floor without your shoes on. I figured Stu must have really fallen for Verity to have agreed to come with us tonight, or perhaps he just felt sorry for me after I confessed I'd rather have my toenails plucked out than join Trish and Verity in a group exercise session. I'd coerced him into the sauna, but only after he'd washed the benches down with an antibacterial solution.

Stu lay back down opposite me and put his hands under the back of his head. 'I'm not rising to the bait, Lomond. You've got a sick sense of humour. So anyway, what happened next with John Boy and the rest of the Waltons?'

'Nothing. Actually, lots of things, but none that I can remember too clearly . . . although I do have a vivid recollection of singing "Islands in the Stream" with Grandpa Jack somewhere between my tenth and eleventh beer. Honestly, it was the best night out I've had for ages. I told them I'd be back next week with you and Trish.'

'Yeah, well, you'll have to wait until I check if my inoculations for Third World environments are up-to-date. So are you seeing him again?'

'Noooooo! Because here's the weirdest thing . . . '

And weird it was. The mental video of the night before played back in my head. Gregory's mother, who'd insisted I called her Glenda now that, according to her, Gregory and I were 'practically engaged', had been up on stage doing a duet to "Endless Love", featuring scarily impressive impersonations of both Diana Ross *and* Lionel Ritchie's voices. Gregory was swaying gently on his stool, I'm not sure if it was in keeping with the music or in keeping with the dozen beers he'd consumed, when he tilted over in my direction. I'd had one of those horrible moments of dread. Was I going to have to let him down gently? Was this that horrible point in the night when I would reject his advances and he'd descend into a mire of spite and petulance?

'Lied to you earlier,' he confessed with just a slight slur.

Considering he'd muttered no more than two dozen words to me all night, I was at a loss to work out which monosyllabic rant had been a lie.

'Not single,' he added.

The spattering of people still in the pub descended into laughter as Glenda turned her musical promises of everlasting devotion on two ancient little men who were sitting in the corner playing dominoes. If she didn't get off that old bloke soon we'd have to take him straight to A&E for a hip replacement.

'But that's great,' I enthused. Even through the fog of my tipsy state, I realised that this was welcome news that would delight his mother, who'd already told me at least twenty times that she was 'thrilled that you and our Gregory are hitting it off – and just think it was me who brought you both together'. Then she'd tilt her head to one side in a manner that suggested she was planning the colour scheme for the bridesmaids and working out how many sausage rolls she'd need for the buffet.

It was quite clear that it was Glenda's life's mission to marry off her shy, reserved son and live happily ever after trailing eight grandkids to every Chelsea home game. She'd dedicate her life to their education and development, welling with pride when they sat in that stadium singing 'Ferdinand, ya muppet' by their third birthday.

'So who's the lucky girl, and why haven't you told your mum, Gregory? She's obviously desperate for you to meet someone. She'll be thrilled.'

'Won't.'

'Will.'

'Won't.'

'Okay, this could go on all night. Why won't your mother be pleased – is there something wrong with . . . what's her name?'

'Alex.'

'Cool name. So, back to my question – is there something wrong with her?'

'Him.'

It took me a moment to process the information.

'What?'

Gregory didn't even reply. Instead he nodded his head in the direction of the youngest bloke left in the pub, a near carbon copy of Gregory himself, but with shaggy auburn hair and a vintage Stone Roses T-shirt.

Come to think about it, I had noticed the guy staring over earlier, but I'd just thought . . . well, one ego requiring emergency first aid yet again.

'Oh, Gregory, you're gay?'

'Sssssssshhhh,' he'd chastised me, his eyes darting to locate his mother in the desperate hope that she hadn't overheard. He needn't have worried. She was too busy asking the man behind the bar if he had a paracetamol for the old bloke she'd practically paralysed.

'But Gregory, she's a nice woman. And she obviously loves you so she'll understand.'

'Won't.'

'Will.'

'Won't.'

'Oh, for God's sake, Gregory, she will. There's absolutely nothing wrong with being gay.'

'I know that . . . '

I didn't get it.

'So what are you worried about then?'

He nodded in the direction of his special friend again. 'He's an Arsenal supporter.'

※

Stu's ornately carved torso was literally doubled up with laughter when the door opened and Verity and Trish came in. Trish had gone down the route of efficient practicality and was wearing a Speedo all-in-one swimsuit; while Verity, on the other hand, was covering her modesty with a large bath towel . . . which she then dropped to reveal a tiny leopard-print thong. It was resoundingly obvious why thousands of males (and a fair few females) across the nation were more than happy to hand over some of their hard-earned cash for the privilege of having a Verity Fox calendar. She was a goddess. Her buttocks were made of solid steel, there wasn't an ounce of fat on her perfect contours, a droplet of four diamonds dangled on her perfectly flat stomach below her belly button, and her bare, gravity-defying nipples still pointed, unsupported, in the direction of the ceiling. If those boobs could shoot nuclear warheads, Verity could eradicate an enemy air force in minutes.

Trish groaned, 'Verity, put those away before you take

247

someone's eye out,' but her objection raised only a giggle from the unembarrassed model.

I raised my eyes to heaven. Dear God, in my next life can I put in an advance order to come back looking like that?

Verity climbed up to sit next to Stu, giving Trish and me a full view of her centrefold.

'Eeeeewww, put that away too,' wailed Trish.

Stu casually draped an arm around her and kissed her swan-like neck, turning a sauna with a chum into a Calvin Klein ad.

'Gossip time,' Trish announced, bringing all eyes to her. 'But it's highly classified, so I need to confirm that none of you are in possession of a recording device.'

All eyes now simultaneously swung to Verity's tiny slither of a thong. 'If you've got an eight-millimetre reel-to-reel in there, I'm fucked,' Trish deadpanned. 'You know that Goldie Gilmartin is living with her toy-boy male stripper?'

We all nodded expectantly.

'Well, that's now expanded to a threesome situation with the inclusion of a rather gorgeous, decidedly female Amazonian lawyer.'

'Noooooooooo!' I gasped.

It would have been fine if I'd left it at that, but no, in my astonishment and sweaty, slippery, shocked state, I leaned forward, became unbalanced and slid off the bench, landing with an excruciating thud only centimetres from the hot coals. It took a few stunned seconds to realise why my pain sensors were screaming, until the water bucket that was upturned and covering my left foot gave me a clue. Oh, the pain! Three fractured toes! Okay, three stubbed and bruised toes, but in that moment it felt like amputation was the only viable option.

Further up, the news wasn't much better. There was a

sickly metallic taste in my mouth that could only come from blood, and after an investigative prod I could categorically confirm that I'd bitten my bottom lip during the slide.

The only consolation was that my friends were a picture of concern and care – right up until they realised that I wasn't seriously injured or dead, when they gave in to their trite, slapstick mentalities and laughed like drains.

It was difficult to tell what was more disturbing: their reactions, the pain, or that Verity was now rushing to my aid, running the very real risk of incurring two breast-inflicted black eyes. It was like a scene from *Attack of the Killer Bosoms*.

❊

An hour later, the stairs to my flat had never seemed so steep or so exhausting. Twenty-four. Twenty-five. Twenty-six. I stopped to catch my breath.

I was dehydrated from the sauna, had a huge bandage on my foot, and I was sure I must have lost at least eighty per cent of my blood through the hole in my bottom lip. Twenty-seven. Twenty-eight. Twenty-nine . . . I averted my eyes from the mirror on the facing wall of my landing. In my acute misery and pain, I'd boycotted the shower and come straight home for a long, soothing bath, so my lank hair was scraped back off my red, swollen, shiny face.

Thank God I hadn't met anyone I knew.

'Hello, love, what are you doing out here? Oh, good grief, what happened to you? Was it that bloody pothole outside the front door? That's it, I'm suing the council.'

'Shno, schno, ish washn't,' I replied through the pork sausage that was masquerading as my bottom lip. Mrs Naismith. I swear that at some point in the years we'd known each other she must have implanted a satellite navigation chip on my person, one that alerted her to my impending arrival and allowed her to burst out of the door for a wee chat every time I came home.

'Ish wash . . . '

The sentence hung in the air, cut off by a loud and definite noise from inside my apartment.

It took a few seconds for us to register the implications, and then Mrs Naismith's eyes widened, she disappeared into her flat and returned in a flash, clutching a video camera and an Aboriginal stick her daughter had brought back from her last diving expedition to the Great Barrier Reef. Her eyes were wide, her demeanour oozing ecstatic giddiness that the *Crimewatch* reconstruction was finally within her grasp.

Bugger. Bloody, bloody bugger. I was a physical wreck, I'd had a shit day, and all I wanted was a bloody bath, yet now I was about to confront potentially armed criminals with an Australian artefact, a video camera and an OAP who had brushed her hair and slapped on a bit of lippy for the occasion.

Using military hand signals that I'm sure she'd picked up from watching *Rambo*, she motioned for me to put my key in the lock. Slowly, gently, it went in, any friction sounds drowned out by the noise of someone moving around inside, walking down the hall now, their footsteps getting closer to the other side of the door, closer, closer, until . . . Okay, I admit it, I panicked. I shoved the key right as far as it would go, twisted it sharply with one hand, and with the other hand squeezed the tiny personal alarm that was around my neck, which emitted a deafening, piercing screech that drowned out our roars as we burst in ready to take on the burglars. Or at least capture them on film before they tied us up, ransacked the house and made off with all my worldly tat. It was definitely a plan, a really bad one that went horribly wrong when my marrow-shaped bandage caught on the door runner and I went crashing down, swiftly followed by Mrs Naismith, who landed with a thud on top of me but mercifully, by virtue of luck rather than design, somehow managed to avoid impaling me with a three-foot-long pointy stick.

I was stuck, trapped under a senior citizen, eardrums bursting with the screams from the alarm, but my wits hadn't deserted me. This was a survival situation! I opened my eyes, determined to re-evaluate the options and deploy the necessary manoeuvres to get me and my cohort out with minimal collateral damage – I think I watched the *Rambo* movie too – and that's when I saw it: the big black boot. It was coming closer, closer, its leather bending, the laces straining, the thick soles leaving indentations in the carpet. Oh no. Dear God, no. Anything but this.

Closer, closer, until it stopped only inches from my head. I didn't, couldn't look. I'd seen this before, and last time the trauma had almost derailed me for life.

The boot pulled back as the occupier bent down on one knee. Before I could stop it, his hand was on my face and his breath was hot against my cheek.

'Leni! Leni! Are you okay? Shit, talk to me, Leni, are you okay?'

I swatted the hand away, desperate to escape but knowing it was hopeless – with Mrs Naismith's arthritis it would take about a week to get her off me.

I sighed and closed my eyes again, resigned to my fate.

'I'm fine. Absolutely smashing. So . . . what are you doing here, Ben?'

26

Libra

All was back to how it should be: the personal alarm had finally been switched off, Mrs Naismith was back in her home, the Aboriginal artefact was back up on the wall, and I was lying on my couch with a cup of tea. A completely normal situation . . . if I didn't look like I'd been run over by a bus, and if I wasn't drinking my tea through a straw, and if my ex-very-married-lying-boyfriend wasn't sitting on the floor in front of me.

'Can I say sorry now?' he asked mournfully.

'Fer whatch spit?'

It took him a moment. 'All of it.'

We were having serious communication problems. He was struggling to understand me because of my facial injuries, and I was struggling to hear him over the racket of my thundering heart, my shaking legs, and the roar of the blood rushing through my head.

Ben. Two years on from his betrayal and I had been so, so sure that I was over him. I was. I'd moved on. Let go of the grief. Banished the bitterness.

'I can't tell you how sorry I am, Leni.'

'Try,' I spat back venomously. Okay, so maybe I wasn't quite ready to put him on my 'Favourite Chums' list.

My emotions were in a maelstrom of confusion. On one level I was furious and wanted him out of my house, while on another I wanted answers. There was a part of me that wondered how long I'd get for assault with a household implement, while there was another part that . . . Okay, I admit it – his sheer physical, gorgeous bloody presence was so intoxicatingly overwhelming that it seemed to have rendered me incapable of rational thought. His skin, battered by the sun, was the colour of Galaxy chocolate, his scrub of hair cropped close against his scalp, shoulders the width of my coffee table and straining against the ultra-tight khaki T-shirt, thighs clearly visible and defined under his combats. He was the incredibly handsome, perfectly formed prototype for Cheating Bastard Action Man. To my intense irritation, his voice, his smile, still had an almost hypnotic effect on me. Every movement, every gesture dragged the past into the present and caused more physical aches than a swift departure from a sauna bench.

Once he'd been everything. Trish and Stu aside, there had never been anyone that I'd connected with so completely, who accepted me for everything that I was: faults, mishaps, insecurities, clumsiness and all.

We used to talk for hours about everything, anything. Now? Silence.

'I'm sorry,' he whispered eventually.

'Good effort. I can see why it took you two years to develop your defence.'

He had the decency to look shamefaced during the next 3.5 minutes of silence, the stillness broken only by my fidgeting with the toggle on my sweat-top. If we kept up these pauses Mrs Naismith would be sending her listening device back to the factory with a claim that it was defective.

'I didn't plan to do it. When I first met you, you were just so sweet and so vulnerable and funny that I was blown away. I wanted to tell you the first time we were together, but even then I knew what you would do and I just . . . didn't . . . want to lose you.'

'I can see how that could happen,' I conceded.

'You can?' he answered, a glint of optimistic surprise in his eyes.

'Absolutely . . . if you were a low-life cheating arse.'

Two years of hurt and loss were pouring out in the form of snide vitriol.

'I *was* an arse, but you have to know that I loved you. I still love you.'

A voice in my head screamed nooooooo, don't say that! DO NOT SAY THAT! Do not come along when I'm at an all-time physical and emotional low and say beautiful things to me. Despite fierce resistance from the sections of my brain marked 'pride and dignity', I could feel my ice-maiden act begin to melt, because there was I, sitting there looking like roadkill, yet he could still look me in the eye and tell me he loved me.

To my utter horror, in amongst all the negative feelings and reactions, 'attraction and lust' began to surface in the emotional melting pot. I suddenly had a new understanding of the meaning of the phrase, 'Everything happens for a reason' because it had just become clear that the reason that God had inflicted on me a mouth like a lilo was so that I wouldn't give in to the inexplicable, utterly ridiculous primal urge to kiss Ben from the top of his crew-cut to his army supply boots.

I attempted to re-ignite 'blind bloody fury'. 'And your wife?'

He sighed as his eyes fell to the floor.

'Over. She left. Army life is tough for families and she decided she didn't want it any more.'

To my complete disgust, one of my heart valves burst into the 'Hallelujah Chorus'.

'She still lives near the base so I see my daughter when I'm home. She's seven now. Gorgeous. Funny. Amazing.'

'What's her name?' No idea why I needed to know that.

'Christy.' He smiled when he said it.

I exhaled wearily, and then winced as the cool air rushed past my lip wound.

There was another long pause. I had a vision of Mrs Naismith on the other side of the wall, panicking because she couldn't see what was going on. I decided it was time to cut to the important stuff and get it out of the way so she could get back to the *Coronation Street* omnibus.

'Why are you here, Ben?'

'Because I still love you. And I want to know if it's too late for us. Is it, Leni? I'll do whatever you want me to do to make this right, because I just can't be without you any longer. Just tell me, Leni – whatever you want.' To his credit, he didn't even seem to register the thud from the other side of the wall.

How could this be happening? On the way home I'd been looking forward to a bath, a liquidised snack that could be consumed through a straw and *Law & Order: Special Victims Unit* on the telly. Instead, the toes that weren't mummified by a crushingly tight elastic bandage were curling as my emotions were fed through a shredder.

Immediately after I discovered his heartbreaking betrayal – urgh, starting to sound like a *News of the World* front page – I'd gone through most of the stages of grief: denial, anger, devastation, etc., and somewhere along the process slipped in 'isolation and absorption in trash telly and books'. Every night I'd leave the giddy world of ballcocks, come home, take the phone off the hook, force down a cheese toastie and read masterpieces like *What Becomes of the*

Broken Hearted – how to survive the pain and *The Ex-Girlfriend's Secret Guide to Big Bastards,* until I finally fought off the breaking-heart insomnia and drifted off for a couple of hours' sleep.

My heart had been broken. In pieces. And even now, as he sat in front of me, lovingly pretending not to notice that I had a face like a space-hopper, I didn't know if those pieces could ever be mended.

I felt two fat tears squeeze from my eyes and run down my cheeks. Fabulous. Bloody fabulous. My body was now adding bloodshot eyes and puffy lids to my list of attractive features.

He leaned over and brushed them away. 'I'm so, so sorry, Leni.'

I should have left it at that. I should have taken it at face value and accepted his apology, but I needed more information. I needed to understand how and why the man I once thought I'd spend forever with had managed to lie to me so easily for so long.

He shrugged his shoulders. 'I had to. If I'd told you the truth it would have been over,' he repeated. 'Look, I know I was a selfish prick, and if you can't get past what I did then I'll understand, but I had to come back and try.'

Bravery – wasn't that what had attracted me to him in the first place? He'd disarmed the yob on the train, he loved his role in the marines and relished every mission, he flinched from nothing, and throughout our time together all my worries or fears had been quelled by the complete confidence that no matter what went wrong, he'd take care of it, he'd sort it out. Except the whole double-life thing, obviously.

My mouth opened and shut but nothing came out because I had absolutely no idea what to say. Should I tell him to get out? Talk some more? Stomp around Little

Sweden in a blind, riotous rage? Helplessness enshrouded me and, true to form, the woman who regularly spent twenty minutes trying to decide between beans on toast or spaghetti hoops was at a complete loss.

'You don't have to say anything just now. Look, why don't you go and lie in the bath and I'll phone in some dinner and then we can talk more.'

On the way there, I stopped at the freezer for a packet of frozen peas. After slipping into the lukewarm bubbles I pressed them against my lips. Twenty minutes later, the swelling had subsided a little, so I reached for my phone.

'Stu, it's me – can you talk?'

'Sure, Verity is signing autographs – we got mobbed on the way into the Ivy so I'm at the bar waiting for her. What's that noise?'

'Water – I'm in the bath.'

'Eeeew, mental picture I could live without there, Lomond,' he laughed.

'Shut up, this is serious.'

'Are you using the earphones I bought you or do you have the phone against your ear?'

'Ear.'

'Leni, get the earphones! How many times do I have to tell you that there are serious indications that mobile phones can cause brain tumours?'

The sigh was out before I could stop it. I wanted to talk about my trashed life, and Stu was busy reciting medical theories that a Notting Hill hairdresser wouldn't necessarily be expected to have on the tip of his tongue.

'Ben's here,' I blurted.

That stopped him. '*What? In the bath with you?*'

For a horrible moment I thought I was going to get a lecture on the statistical probability that two people having sex in a bath could get wedged in there, die of hunger, and their bodies could go undiscovered until a neighbour called environmental health to complain about the smell.

But no.

'Is his wife with him?' he asked, with uncharacteristic venom.

What was going on? Stu did mellow, he did funny, he did neurotic, but he very rarely did bitchy and malicious. By some weird powers of osmosis, we were both channelling Trish tonight.

'No, they've split up and he wants me back.'

'And?'

'And . . . I don't know. I have no idea. Stu, you know how long it took me to get over him, and I don't think I could ever go through that again, and . . . '

' . . . and you don't think you could ever trust him again?'

'No, I . . . '

' . . . and you're over him and you're not in love with him any more?'

'No, I . . . '

' . . . and you've moved on and there's no place in your life for him now?'

'LET ME SPEAK!'

Aaaargh, he was like Sister Stu, Agony Aunt with a cliché for every occasion. Eventually, a muted, 'Sorry, carry on,' came down the line.

'I was going to say that I'd sworn I'd never forgive him, but now, seeing him here, I'm not so sure. He was the love of my life, Stu.'

Apparently, the clichés were contagious.

'Honey, I can't help you with this one. Just know that whatever you do we'll support you. If you reject him we'll be there for you, and if you take him back we'll support that too. And Leni, I have to tell you something from the heart . . . '

His words were choked with emotion.

'You do know that after what he did to you . . . '

My stomach flipped with anticipation, his voice was so measured and thick with feeling.

' . . . I'd have kicked his ass if he wasn't a marine.'

I laughed so much I dropped the frozen peas in the bath, immediately reducing the water temperature by several degrees. What would I do without Stu? Even in the depths of confusion, pain and self-pity he could snap me back to amusement and optimism in seconds.

There was a loud commotion at his end.

'Is that Verity arriving? It sounds like chaos – I'll let you go.'

'Are you sure? I can stay on the phone as long as you want.'

'No, don't be crazy. You're with the most desirable woman in the country! Go and lavish her with affection and promises of wild sexual antics.'

'Nooooo, none of that – I could pull a muscle or get a hernia or piles,' he joked.

'G'night, Stu!'

'Call me back if you need me, babe,' he added softly.

What a sweetheart.

In the time it took to wash my hair, manoeuvre myself out of the bath, dry off and limp through to the bedroom in search of clean clothes, my plan of action swung like Verity's buttocks on a catwalk. I should tell him to go. I should tell him to stay. I should go and have a cup of tea and a Garibaldi with Mrs Naismith and ask her what she thought.

Like a robot on automatic pilot, I dried my hair and dressed in an old pair of distressed jeans (chosen to coordinate with my emotional state) and a white vest.

Back in the hall, the smell hit me before I even opened

the door to the lounge. The aroma of deep-fried wontons, crispy pork and soy noodles assaulted my senses. Although, how I was going to suck up noodles with this lip was beyond me. Perhaps I could mash them up.

He'd made such an effort. He'd set the IKEA coffee table with IKEA bamboo placemats, large IKEA wine glasses and a set of cutlery – that wasn't IKEA, my granny had bought it from QVC as a going-away present when I'd left for college (on the same night she bought a Dustbuster, a leopard-print handbag, a bust enhancer, a foot spa and a dog blanket – even though she didn't have a dog. We made her stop watching it after that). Half the set was missing, but I didn't have the heart to throw the rest out.

It was perfect. He'd remembered my favourite foods, my favourite wine, and there was a white lily, my favourite flower, sitting in a tall, thin vase in the middle of the table.

Combined with the unarguable truth that for a long time he had been my favourite man, it was a pretty compelling package.

I sat on the floor, one leg sticking straight out so that I didn't have to bend the now-unbandaged toes.

'The swelling has gone down a bit,' he said with a smile, gesturing to my lip.

'I know. Another hour or so and I'll have shrunk from "seriously swollen" to "Angelina Jolie". Some women pay good money for that look. Saves me a visit to the beautician to . . . '

One of the most important nights of my life, and there I was rambling nonsense yet again.

'I love you.' It came right out of the blue and cut right across my witterings. 'Sorry, I just had to say it again,' he explained. 'Just so that you know.'

What was he doing to me? It was like he was lining up

all my inhibitions, barriers and reservations, then obliterating them with a large AK-47.

'I'm sorry, Ben, but this is just too weird for me. Can we . . . Can we just talk about normal stuff for a while? Anything. Nonsense. Smart stuff. I don't care. Anything but us.'

If it was anyone else, they might have got uncomfortable or defensive, but not Ben. A foil container of pork was split between our plates, noodles heaped on the side, and we left the crispy wontons in a bowl so that we could pick at them throughout the meal – all exactly the way we used to do things.

My wine glass didn't spend much time on the table. The lip only stung with incredible pain for the first few slugs, before it got strangely easier. By halfway down the bottle it was only a minor twinge.

'So, how's Trish? Still terrorising the world, or did a judge do the sensible thing and lock her up for life?'

'Come on, you loved her!' In the darkest times of devastation and 'how did I not see that coming?' self-doubt, one of the things that had kept me going was that Trish, who has an entry in the *Guinness World Records* in the category of 'World's Most Cynical Woman', had been as shocked as I was when the truth had emerged. Now she hated him with a passion, but that was born of loyalty rather than anything to do with him personally.

'I did. Still do. Although I don't think I'd go within a hundred yards of her now without an armed regiment behind me.'

'Smart tactical move.'

'And what about Stu – you and him got together yet?'

It was said with a smile, but it was the same one that the bad guys in the movies use right before they attempt to cut off the hero's bollocks. My relationship with Stu had been

Ben's Achilles heel, the one and only insecurity I ever saw in him. Ironic, when in hindsight he was shagging someone else the whole time. Ouch, that hurt.

'How can you still think that? PLATONIC! Don't you get that?'

'No.' Simple answer, with accompanying shrug. 'He's gorgeous, you're gorgeous . . . ' That'll be the cataracts again. 'And I always thought you'd make a great couple. But I'm glad you didn't.'

'We didn't.'

'Did you meet anyone else?'

I shrugged my shoulders. 'No.' I speared a wonton with my chopstick, desperately avoiding eye contact.

'Never?' he replied, shocked.

'A couple of flings here and there, but no one special.'

My cheeks were burning, and not just from my Olympic wine consumption. Another glass and I'd fall into the *Daily Mail*'s category of 'binge drinker'.

'You don't want to talk about this either, do you?' His powers of observation were acutely accurate, as always.

I shook my head as I answered. 'And I don't walk to talk about us, what happened, you, your family, or anything that's happened in the past.'

His dog tags jangled as he laughed. 'Doesn't leave much then, does it?'

'Nope.' There was a pause and a break in the food consumption as we just stared at each other for a few seconds with daft grins on our faces.

'So . . . ' I eventually asked, 'banged any thugs off a train table lately?'

It was entirely un-funny, but it was enough to tip us over from surreal to ridiculous. We both creased with laughter, the raucous, uncontrollable kind that takes on a life of its own and carries on until you can't even remember what you were laughing at. My jaw began to ache, my stomach hurt, my throat became hoarse and the tears began to stream down my face. And that's when I realised that somewhere in the middle of it all my tears of hilarity had turned into great big racking sobs: heaving, wrenching exclamations of pain that I just couldn't stop.

Ben snapped back to reality, his expression morphing from joy to horror as he dived around to my side of the table and threw his arms around me. 'Leni, Leni, I . . . '

Something snapped. Two years of hurt and pain and regret exploded, and I, for the first time in years, was white-rage livid. Furious. I pushed him away, slapping his hand off my shoulder.

'How could you do that?' I yelled, just inches from his face, sobs punctuating every few words. 'How, Ben? How could you lie and lie? What were you thinking? How could you plan things with me, talk about the children we'd have and where we'd live and what we'd do when we were old, when all the time you were with someone else? How could you do that?'

'Because I couldn't let you go!'

'That's not enough of a reason!'

We were screaming at each other now, our faces contorted, mine with rage, his begging for understanding. Instinctively, without thought or reason, I snatched the lily out of the vase and lashed out with it, catching him across the chin.

Was this what it had come to? Was this really how low I'd sunk? I was hysterical, borderline manic, and attempting to batter a sergeant in Her Majesty's marines with a cut flower.

He grabbed my wrists. 'Leni, please, don't, don't do this. Leni, I'm sorry, I'm so, so sorry.'

Again, something changed, ricocheting off in another

direction. The roller-coaster of blind fury reached its peak, then plummeted down the other side, and before I could deploy rational thought he was lying flat on his back on the floor and I was lying on top of him, kissing him with a force I hadn't even realised I possessed, the pain in my lip completely wiped out by the intoxicating combination of adrenalin and Merlot.

It was Ben. Ben was back, and all I wanted to do was to cancel out every moment since he'd left and focus on right here and right now. Erm . . . apparently that was right here and right now, the X-rated version.

I pushed his T-shirt up over his head, in charge for the first time, our breathing coming in shallow, frantic gasps as we clawed at each other, an irresistible power coming into play. I'd only ever seen this in movies – angry, crazy, irrational make-up sex that I knew was a really, really, REALLY bad idea, but somehow I didn't care. My hand went to the button at the top of his trousers and with one finger I flicked it open and wrenched down the zip. Still joined at the mouth, his hands were under my vest now, my bra pushed up over my breasts as his fingers deftly, desperately massaged my nipples. He slid down, his hands around my rib cage, supporting me as his lips replaced his fingers and he sucked, his tongue flicking against the tip of my nipple, sending signals that reached my toes.

But – and oh, get me! – I wasn't ready to give him control yet.

Palms flat on the floor, I pushed myself up, pulling out of his mouth, and worked my way down his body, kissing, nibbling, licking every rock-hard inch of his chest, his stomach, his hips. On my knees and straddling him now, I slipped my hands under the waistband of his trousers and pulled them down, his bravery kicking in again as he only mildly winced at the pain of his cock scratching against his zip as it sprung to freedom and stood erect, pointing at the ceiling. My pelvic muscles contracted at the sight of it, in all its huge, glistening, that-is-never-going-to-fit glory. In the turmoil since we'd broken up I'd managed to take the memory of how well-endowed he was and pummel it to death with what had been left of my ego.

Underneath me, he kicked his trousers off the rest of the way, as I bent down, on all fours now, and ran my tongue up the inside of his thigh. Inch by inch I moved higher and higher, until I reached the base of his dick. I switched from long, languorous tongue movements to shorter, more precise strokes; slow, repetitive licks that ran from the bottom of his shaft to the tip, each one rewarded with an ecstatic groan. Eventually, when the moans had changed to desperate whispers of 'Baby, oh fuck, baby,' I rose up, clenched my lips around the tip of his cock and slid him deep inside.

Fireworks exploded in my head, but not in the way that the *A–Z of Effective Blow Jobs* would have predicted. My head jerked back with the searing, unadulterated agony of a burst lip that had started to heal but had just been traumatised by a swift and unexpected meeting with a ten-inch-long penis.

Thankfully, I managed to retreat without amputating any vital part of his manhood. Okay, so blow jobs were out, so that meant . . . Shit, my jeans were still on. To his obvious surprise I went back to my previous licking motion, this time massaging him with one hand while the other frantically attempted to push my jeans off.

Success! I just had to move forward a few feet, and then I'd be right above him and I could lower myself down, taking him inside . . .

No condom. Even in my befuddled, insane-with-hormones state, I could hear Stu's voice lecturing me on the dangers of unprotected sex and making me swear on the holy bible of the *Cosmopolitan Christmas Special* that I would never, ever, for the rest of my life, have condom-free sex with a man who hadn't arrived with a health certificate signed by an eminent doctor no more than one hour before.

No, I couldn't do it. But at the same time, I was fairly sure that there were no condoms left after my encounter with Nurse Dave.

Alternative action.

I readjusted my body position so that his cock was caught between my breasts, squeezed between them, while my tongue flicked at the tip. Up and down, up and down, faster and faster, and . . .

'Leni, stop, I'm going to come and I want to be inside you.'

Stu's voice calmly and officially recited statistics in my ear. 'Cases of chlamydia have risen in the UK by thirty-three per cent in the last . . . '

Noooooo! It was like having sex with a disapproving audience.

Ben squeezed my shoulders, trying to gently pull me up so that we would be face to face, chest to chest and nethers to nethers, but I resisted.

Only one way out of this. I clenched my breasts even tighter around his dick, and started undulating faster and faster, and – holy crap, my thigh muscles were about to snap – faster and faster until he roared my name as he came.

With other guys it would be over, but not with Ben.

'Stand up,' he whispered.

I did what he said. I saw his eyes dart to the end of the couch, where the sky-high platforms that I'd worn on my date with Colin the lawyer were lying. He grabbed them and, one by one, slipped them on my feet, their thin straps mercifully slipping right over my swollen toes. I was standing in the middle of my living room, legs apart, mortifyingly naked except for gravity-defying footwear, and the most gorgeous man I'd ever seen was kneeling in front of me.

I thought it probably wasn't the time to ask how or when he'd learned his new moves, especially while embarrassment, lust, vulnerability and sheer bloody horniness were fighting for supremacy in my head.

He took my hands, one by one, and reached up and placed them on my breasts.

'Rub them,' he whispered.

Outside: just the sound of my shallow breaths.

Inside: voices in my brain screeching a randomly confused, astonished, 'Eeeeeeeeeeeekkkkkk!!!'

An involuntary gasp escaped me as I clenched my eyes shut, trying to block out everything but the tongue that was now probing in the gynaecological area.

His hands were squeezing my buttocks, his face burrowed in front, his back glistening with sweat, the tongue strokes getting deeper and deeper and more persistent and deeper and more . . .

I came with such a shudder that I almost fell off my platforms. Not a sentence I ever thought I'd say.

I sank to my knees, into the folds of his arms, my cheek pressed against his chest, my mouth gently throbbing. After a few minutes, still intertwined, we sank to the floor and lay there, naked, in silence for what seemed like hours.

Eventually, he spoke. 'I've missed you so much, Leni.'

I put my hand to his mouth and shushed him, desperate to delay the inevitable discussions and recriminations and reality for as long as possible. Only when the goose-bumps turned to shivering did I move. He was dozing as I leaned over and kissed him gently on each eye. Once upon a time I would have given everything to this man . . . but now?

'C'mon, Ben,' I whispered, rousing him and gently tugging him upright and taking him through to bed. We climbed under the duvet, snuggled into each other, needing the heat and, in my case, the reassurance that he was really there and this wasn't all an orgasmic dream brought on by undetected concussion from the sauna episode.

My mind tried to process the situation in short, succinct bullet-points. He was back. He loved me. I'd missed him. We could be together. It felt so good. He was fan-fucking-tastic in bed, and I'd never met anyone I wanted to be with more than him.

So that must mean . . .

The hand stopped the gentle strokes on the side of my face and moved down under the cover. It was back on my overworked, tender boob now, teasing and caressing it, while my hip bone felt the pressure of a hard, demanding cock press against it.

I swatted his hand away playfully. 'Sorry, stud, no condoms so put that away.'

He was burrowed into my neck, nibbling my ear and kissing my temple, so I missed his reply.

'What did you say?' I asked him, my voice thick with pleasure and giddiness.

'I said don't worry . . . I brought some with me.'

✼

'Marry me.'

'What?'

'Marry me. Look, I brought you this.' My mouth stopped chewing, my right cheek bulging with un-masticated toast.

He leaned out of bed, reached down, and from the pocket

of the combats that were folded neatly on the floor, he pulled out a small, red leather box.

The breakfast tray that was balanced on my knees, the one he'd woken me with as soon as the sun had forced its way through the curtains, began to tremble. The orange juice was almost splashing out of the glass, the single-bud vase about to tip over, the toast and bacon clearly vibrating.

Just in time I realised that my jaw had dropped and hastily closed my mouth, fearful that the sight of my half-consumed breakfast might deter him from doing what I was sure he was about to do.

He turned to face me, his face full of fear, his halting voice a sweet, poignant reflection of his nervousness. As his anxious eyes met mine, I realised that he had never, ever looked more beautiful.

'Leni, I almost lost you once and I'm so, so sorry for hurting you, but I promise, on my life, that I will never hurt you again. Marry me, Leni. Please. And I'll make sure that for the rest of our lives you will never regret giving me another chance.'

A huge tear dropped from my face. I loved him. I could try to pretend I was over him, that I'd be happy with someone else, that another guy could make me feel the way he did, but I'd be kidding myself, because the simple truth was that he was the only man I'd ever wanted.

My head was already nodding, powered completely by invisible cords that led straight to my heart. He opened the box and there was the most dazzling solitaire diamond ring, a flawless stone ornately crafted to a simple gold band.

He eased it out from its pillow and pushed it onto my finger, both of us watching as it slid effortlessly to its resting place, a perfect fit. The tears were flowing now as I threw my arms around him and . . . CRASH!!!

For a few seconds I wasn't sure what was going on. The

breakfast tray! It must have fallen to the ground and . . . but hang on, it was still dark.

Suddenly, a light snapped on, and through my disorientated, unfocused fog, I struggled to make sense of what was going on. Ben was there, but it was still night-time, or maybe early morning. My bedside cabinet was on its side. There was no breakfast tray. There was no ring. So did that mean I'd . . .

'Sorry, babe, I didn't mean to wake you. But I knocked over the . . . '

My eyes flicked to the up-ended cabinet. 'I see that.'

I'd dreamed the whole thing. No, not again! Why was this happening? How come all the best bits of my life in the last few months had been figments of my imagination?

'I have to go. We're shipping out today and I need to be on the train back to barracks in twenty minutes.'

'Where are you shipping to?'

'Kosovo. Peacekeeping.'

I squinted in what I was sure was a decidedly unattractive manner, especially when added to the fat lip, which, contrary to my dream, actually felt like it was the size of your average baked potato.

'For how long?'

'Fifteen weeks.'

That old familiar feeling of dread and fear came rushing back. Afghanistan. Iraq. Belize. Kosovo. We'd been through them all already but the anxiety never left.

He was almost dressed now, sitting on the edge of the bed, pulling on his boots. In a minute he'd be gone, with no discussions, no resolution as to where we stood in our relationship.

Boots on, there was one last kiss before he stood up again. 'I'll call you,' he promised. 'Later today, before we leave.'

Wasn't that how so much of our relationship had been conducted? The letters, the phone calls, the packages, the wife . . . The wife.

His hand was on the doorknob now and he was twisting it. In a fraction of a second he'd be gone again, but with the promise of a return and the renewal of our relationship. Maybe it was just that I was half-sleeping, or that this whole thing was straight from Bizarre Central, but I was hearing a narration of everything that was happening in the voice of the bloke who did the voice-over for *Extreme Makeover*. I definitely needed to switch off the telly more.

The door opened, he stepped forward, he was almost gone, when Leni, 27, who'd always been self-conscious about her large nose, her low brow and her drooping breasts, blurted, 'When did your wife leave?'

He stopped in his tracks, but didn't answer.

'When did she leave, Ben? And tell me the truth, because if we're going to be together then I'll find out anyway. When did she leave?'

There was a long, tense silence, before he finally coughed up the three most painful words of all.

'A year ago.'

A. Year. Ago.

Cue sudden, blinding, nauseating clarity.

He wasn't back because he couldn't live without me. If that were the case he'd have been on my doorstep within a day of discovering that his wife was gone.

The real, unavoidable, tortuous truth was that Sergeant Ben Mathers had been here because he couldn't get his wife back, or he was bored with playing the field, or he just fancied a quickie before he went off to work. Shit, he'd even brought condoms! How bloody presumptuous was that? The selfish, self-indulgent, cocky tosser!

'But Leni . . . '

271

'Go!'

He checked his watch and obviously realised that staying to argue wasn't an option.

'I'll . . . erm . . . call you tonight.'

As the door closed behind him, I sank back on the pillow, mouth sore, foot aching, heart breaking and seething rage rising with every passing second.

A year ago.

Well, bollocks to him. I'd learned my lesson and I knew that I deserved better than him. I would not let him hurt me again. Absolutely not. No. Fucking. Way. I was stronger, much stronger than that.

'Stuuuuuuuu,' I sobbed down the phone thirty seconds later.

'I'm on my way, honey,' he replied.

27

Superstar

'Holy crap, you look like you've been in a war,' Millie blurted with her usual tact and diplomacy, although, to her credit, she did follow it up with, 'Are you okay, sweetie? Is there anything I can do?'

'Do you have a gun under that desk?'

She shook her head.

'Then no, nothing you can do.'

I'd absolutely snapped out of my post-traumatic Ben disorder – but only for about five minutes the afternoon before, when Trish threatened to hunt him down and do illegal things involving bulldog clips to his balls. Now I was right back in the mourn-zone, a raging fire of depression stoked by the dual fuels of self-pity and confusion.

I took the mail and trudged up the stairs, with Millie's reassurances trailing behind me.

'It's going to get better, you know. It might take a little while, but things will shake up and you'll be better than ever.'

God bless the powers of optimism.

'Oh, and Zara is in her office, but Conn's not in yet. Salmon bagel and cream cheese.'

'You're probably right,' I replied, not even having the

spirit to challenge her. Pathetic, yes, but I just wanted to get this day over with so that I could get back to some seriously high-grade self-doubt and oral-sex-regret.

To my relief and surprise, apart from the fish in the aquarium and the thirty-two pot plants (all of which had names – Fred the fern, Sammy the spider plant, Bob the bamboo – I'll stop in case you're feeling the urge to hurl), the office was empty when I got there. Zara must be in the loo. Bliss! I could squeeze in five more minutes of self-hatred while I opened the mail. Invitations to swanky events in a pile to the left. Fan mail to the right. Requests for postal readings in the corner pile. Requests for one-to-one consultations in the other corner. All correspondence from celebrity clients in the VIP pile. And bills in a large mound for the accountant.

Still no Zara. I pulled up her schedule – in half an hour's time she had a one-to-one with Stephen Knight, bad boy, cocaine fan, lover of high-class call girls and the A-list movie star du jour.

Haaaaaaaaaaaaaaaaaaargh.

Maybe she was preparing by meditating in a cupboard somewhere.

Haaaaaaaaaaaaaaaaaaargh.

Or pacing a corridor, fraught with nervous sexual tension.

Haaaaaaaaaaaaaaaaaaargh.

Or . . . what the hell was that noise? It sounded like some kind of native war cry. Or someone with a serious phlegm problem. And it was definitely coming from somewhere nearby.

I got up from my desk and checked the cupboards. Nope, nothing. I shuffled the pillows around on the floor – a dying animal burrowed under the soft furnishings? Nope.

Haaaaaaaaaaaaaaaaaaargh.

The window. It was coming from the open window. I squeezed past Zara's desk and wild foliage, leaned out of the huge sash and yes, there indeed was my boss, grabbing a bit of fresh air – an act that in itself wouldn't be too unusual if it weren't for the fact that she was strapped into a leather harness punctuated with huge padlocks, attached to a steel peg on the wall, and dangling – otherwise unsupported – fifty feet in the air.

Her arms were out at her sides in the crucifix position, her eyes were shut, her mouth wide open and . . . 'Haaaaaaaaaaaaaaaargh.'

'Zara!'

Her eyes snapped open and the surprised jerk of her body caused her to sway. Terrified, I instinctively reached out to grab her with the intention of steadying her, only a large windowsill and good fortune stopping me from tumbling out.

'What are you doing?' I exclaimed, in a voice three octaves higher than normal.

'New therapy – I'm absorbing the energy from the air,' she answered, completely matter of fact, conveying her utter certainty that it was absolutely normal to dangle from your office window.

'Couldn't you just have stood outside the front door?'

'The air is purer up here – I'm being absorbed by the elements.'

To be honest, I thought she'd been absorbing elements of an altogether different kind. I made a mental note to check her schedule for anyone with a name that sounded like a Colombian drug baron.

'It's time for me to come in – give me your hand.'

With all the agility of a gymnast, one that had no regard whatsoever for my personal safety, she used me as leverage to swing around and then clamber back in the window.

'Can you hand me the keys to all these padlocks; they're in a bunch on my desk.'

I reached over and lifted the large ring, in the process nudging her computer and flicking it from the screen-saver back to the program that was running. Google. And I needed only a smidgen of a second to spot the words 'Stephen Knight' in the search box. Mmm, so Zara was doing her research. Perhaps the Gods of Psychic Powers and Spiritual Connection needed a little bit of back-up every now and again.

Her long brown wavy hair brushed, deep maroon lippy applied, T-shirt and leggings whipped off, silver kaftan shrugged on, and she was ready to go just as Millie buzzed to say that Stephen Knight's driver had called ahead to say that he would be here in five minutes.

'Shall I go down and collect him?' I asked, unable to contain my enthusiasm. Stephen Knight was a physical god. Sure, he was so sexually depraved that you wouldn't touch him without double-thickness rubber gloves and a dose of penicillin, but meeting him would be one to tell the grand-children. If I ever had grandchildren. Or children. Or a husband. Or . . . A massive cloud of post-Ben depression burst over my head again and I was caught in another downpour of grief. Still, at least I'd get to meet Stephe—

'Absolutely not,' Zara snapped. 'A celebrity of his stature must be greeted personally by *moi*. You know, Leni, some-times you really lack the extra edge of professionalism that this job requires.'

On any other day I'd have kept schtum, questioned my performance and perhaps even cried, but not today. Today I was Cheating Bastard Action Man's superhero ex-girlfriend, Lethal Leni.

'*What? What the hell are you talking about???*'

Her mouth dropped wide open, clearly astonished at my uncharacteristic outburst. The secretary formerly known as Leni had been possessed by the forces of rage, rejection and sheer bloody indignation. Think nice things? Forget it! Months of humiliation, frustration and sacrifices in the line of duty bubbled over and poured forth.

'Well, I mean . . . erm, I . . . ' she stuttered, eyeing me with a face mapped in confusion.

'Unprofessional? I have conducted myself in a manner that has been completely fucking professional.'

The uncontrollable rant was out of the box and a dozen rangers armed with cattle prods wouldn't have been able to get it back in.

'The indignities that I've suffered in this role are completely over and above anything that the Department of Employment would classify as normal, yet I've put my head down and got on with the job . . . in a purely PROFES-SIONAL MANNER!'

Her shoulders shifted from a position of defence to attack and she spat back like a viper. 'Oh for God's sake, Leni, stop being so dramatic. So you had a few mishaps on a few dates – at least you're seeing some action, which is undoubt-edly more than was happening before you came to work for me.'

Why, the conniving, nasty bi—

'And let's face it, you haven't exactly been a model of efficiency. It's been months now and you're nowhere near finished with the project. Time is money, Leni, time is money, and the sooner you understand that, the sooner you might have a chance of actually achieving something in your life . . . Like finishing the task that was assigned to you!!!!'

Her flushed face was only inches from mine now, and I used my sleeve to remove the saliva that the last sentence had transferred from her gob to my face.

When I had come to work for Zara, I had known that she was volatile, irrational and prone to manic outbursts, but this was on a different level altogether. This was the premier league of bollockings – and being on the receiving end immediately burst my bubble of aggression and sent me skidding back to my default setting of defensive and nervous.

'I'm almost finished,' I blurted, before reason and fact had a chance to catch up with the whopping great big fib.

'You're only at number eight – two-thirds of the way through, Leni, and it's not good enough. I need those results and I need them soon. There is such a thing as a deadline, you know, and it's the thirty-first of May – that's less than two weeks from now. And let me tell you, lady – if all twelve reports are not on my desk on that date then I'll be reclaiming every single bonus I've ever paid you.'

My back was against the wall. I was like a wild animal cornered by a lethal predator in a tie-dyed kaftan and flip-flops. Think. Think. Think. Lie.

'Actually, I'm much further ahead than that. I had a date last night with a . . . '

What was Ben? What was Ben? Mind blank, mind blank! Then . . . of course! His birthday was 29 September, three weeks before mine, but we shared the same star sign! Shame that was the only bloody thing we had in common.

'Libra!' I blurted. 'And I've also already arranged to meet up with a –'

It was time to call on every ounce of resourcefulness, strategic brilliance and downright duplicity that I possessed – otherwise known as grasping at straws and being severely economical with the facts. Stu – what sign was Stu?

'Taurus! I'm seeing a Taurus next weekend.' Which was true – we had a long-standing arrangement to catch the new run of *Dirty Dancing* at the Aldwych Theatre.

'So that means I just need to set up a . . . a . . . ' Damn! I knew I should have memorised all this stuff.

'Virgo and Sagittarius,' she finished archly. She paused, one eyebrow cocked with cynicism. 'And have you already selected the candidates and organised the final two?'

'I have a shortlist to call this morning.'

I groaned inside as she eyed me with very obvious disbelief. What was I thinking?!! I was standing there, telling bold-faced lies to a psychic! It was like arguing with an astronaut about space. Or lecturing Stu on germs.

There was no doubt about it, she was going to fire me . . . Or, at the very least, kill me and use the powder from grinding up my bones to fertilise her Zen garden.

'Where are the applications for the two dates that I didn't know about?' she asked, her tone deadly.

'They're on my desk.'

Her lie detector screeched into life. Actually, it was just the phone – Millie saving my ass by informing us that Stephen had arrived and was waiting in reception.

'I'll look at them as soon as I get back,' she spat, obviously preferring to leave firing and bone-grinding until after her meeting with a Hollywood superstar, so as not to mess up her hair or smudge her make-up.

My resentment pushing fear aside, I lifted my chin, aped her steely glare, and spat a defiant, 'Fine.' It was a proud, bold moment of self-assurance and dignity – one that she didn't see because she was already halfway down the stairs.

I'd show her. Unprofessional? I don't think so! My professionalism and quick wit would prevail – right after I'd had a terror-filled panic and a quick cry.

How the hell had my life turned into a bad soap opera? I flicked through my phone, desperately searching for an old photo of Ben. Success. Actually, it wasn't exactly a photo of Ben – he'd always avoided the camera, behaviour that I realised now probably had less to do with modesty and more to do with minimising evidence that could find its way into his wife's hands – but I had once taken a photo of the photo on his military ID card. Found it! With a quick touch-up using Photoshop I was pretty sure I could make it look like a standard passport snap.

His application letter I could forge without a problem. I'd just skip the address and use a false telephone number. If anyone checked later I could just say the number must have changed. I wasn't too worried as these were all going to be documented as anonymous case studies anyway.

Okay, Ben was done, now Stu. The residual adrenalin from the conflict made my hands shake as I pressed his speed-dial number. He answered on the second ring. It was so sweet that he still had an iota of attention to give me considering I'd spent all day Saturday sobbing into the folds of his new Gucci shirt.

'Stu, next Saturday night – would you mind classifying it as a date?'

'Ah, babe, I thought you'd never ask. But if Verity knew what you were suggesting, she might take you out with one blow from an expertly aimed nipple tassel.'

'It's not a real date, you twat. I just want to cross off another star sign and I haven't done a Taurus yet, so I thought you could be it. I'll let you run riot in the pick 'n' mix before the show. I just need you to email me over a photo from your PDA.'

'Certainly. Would you like it to be naked or fully clothed?'

'Clothed, you perv.'

His laughter was a mellow, deep gurgle. 'You never could seize the moment, Leni, could you?'

'You're a twisted, twisted man. Now, date or no date?'

'Date. But don't blame me if you have to suffer violent repercussions from an irate glamour icon. Now, have you put the cream I gave you on that lip? Has the swelling gone down any more? Because, you know, scar tissue could be forming and that . . . '

'Sorry, Stu, have to go. Love ya.'

My fingers whizzed over the keyboard, producing two masterful, engaging application letters. I printed off Stu's photo and attached it to Taurus and put it in my pending pile. Ben's pic was stapled to Libra, and I then went on to write a full and completely fictional account of our night together. Even the lies made me wince. I created a fictional world where he wined me, dined me, and then saw me home, all the while entertaining me with subtle humour and self-effacing charm. The bastard.

I'd just added the final full stop when Zara stormed back in and stopped directly in front of my desk.

'Applications?' she demanded, demonstrating that the embers of our spat were still glowing brightly. I calmly handed over the results of the last frantic hour and she examined every word. Eventually, almost grudgingly, she threw them back on my desk with an agitated, 'Fine! Arrange the other two dates for this week, then we can finally put this whole thing to bed. About bloody time. Try to remember, Leni, that professionalism is key to everything we do here,' she concluded pointedly. With that, she turned and strutted over to her own desk.

And that's when I was faced with Zara Delta's back view in all its unexpected glory: her posture strong and proud, her long, luscious locks bouncing with the rhythm of her movements, and her flowing silk kaftan? Tucked into her knickers at the back.

In a purely professional manner, of course.

EMAIL
To: Jon Belmont
From: Leni Lomond
Subject: Making progress

Do you want the good news or the bad?

I'll start with the good. I'm two dates further along and I should be done by a week on Saturday.

And the bad? I think I've become a compulsive liar and I'll probably be unemployed by the time we finally have a proper night out.

I don't usually lie (and you can choose whether or not to believe that, but I can provide sworn affidavits from my best friends testifying to my integrity), but I faked a couple more dates. Well, when I say faked . . . I just manipulated the truth very slightly.

And here's the problem that brings up: if Zara's as good as she says she is, won't she know about this? I keep waiting for her to strut in and fire me in a dramatic fashion.

To be honest, I think the only thing that's saving me is that she's a little distracted by a certain wild, A-list movie star who's been having his chart read on a daily basis.

Anyway, I think my unemployment benefit would still stretch to two large cocktails and a packet of crisps, so hope to see you soon. Lx

EMAIL
To: Leni Lomond
From: Jon Belmont
Subject: Re: Making progress

Dear Compulsive Liar,

You're on – me, you and your giro cheque, lunch a week from Sunday. Can't wait for this to be over – soooooooo difficult knowing that you're around but not being able to see you. So I was thinking (and stop me if I'm getting carried away here) and I've had a few ideas about things we can do: drive out to the country for the day, catch a show (comedies only – don't think I could handle a traumatised woman!!!), and maybe even take the Eurostar over to Paris for the day (but be warned, my sister is demanding to accompany us on that one – something about Louis Vuitton and big price tags! She claims I owe her for hooking us up . . . actually, maybe she's got a good point!).

Sorry, am I getting a bit mushy? I'll get back to being a stern, financial type straight away!

Or maybe not . . .

Do you know how much I'm looking forward to seeing you? A huge amount. Giant. Massive.

And I never lie. J xx

28

Starman

'Fuck it, just chuck the job and get out of there – she's a fucking maniac.'

Déjà vu. My eyes automatically rolled heavenwards. 'Could you please pick an advice position and stick to it? So far you've told me to leave, then stay, then leave, then stay . . . If I was clutching on to the edge of a cliff by my fingernails and counting on your opinion on whether or not I should jump, I'd need a bungee rope.'

'Can't help it. I'm so distracted by the news that that big prick Ben showed up and you phoned Stu instead of me. Why d'you think I bought that Uzi on eBay?'

We were huddled at the back of the *Great Morning TV!* studios, watching the flurry of activity as the team descended on the sofa during the commercial break. Even in real life and in her mid-forties, Goldie radiated gorgeousness: her face incredibly tight and unlined, her body as svelte as a teenager's, her tailored scarlet suit clashing brilliantly with her copper pixie cut. Zara, on the other hand, was taking eccentricity to a whole new level, her hair a mass of pleats and ponytails so bizarre that the net effect was a demented cross between a large fern and Wyclef Jean. And that was the more conservative part of her overall look.

The kaftans were gone, and in their place was a beautiful (but frankly inexplicable) Celtic wedding dress. Yes, apparently on Planet Zara it seemed like a good idea to prepare for the unlikely eventuality that she'd run into a minister and a groom on this very day and decide to tie the knot there and then in a ceremony of ancient Scottish tradition . . . especially since, as far as I knew, her sole connection to all things Scottish was a rabid crush on Ewan McGregor.

The dress itself was breathtaking: a fine ivory jersey-silk fabric column with long sleeves and a round neck, which subtly draped over her torso before gently flaring out below her waist and falling effortlessly to the floor. Slung low across her hips was a gold chain, clasped at the front, at its lowest point, by a large gold medallion with an emerald stone in the centre. A wedding scene in *Braveheart*? Perfect. *Great Morning TV!* sofa? Barking.

I just hoped that she wasn't sending out some kind of subliminal message to her (alleged!) new man. I fully expected to hear that Stephen Knight had fled the country before the end of the day.

I dismissed Zara's agenda to the back of my mind, and pushed 'pacifying my friend' up to the top of mine.

'Okay, I'm sorry I didn't phone you first. It was Grey's weekend off – I thought you'd want time together without trivial interruptions from hysterical friends.'

'Good point. We were a bit tied up all day Saturday and all day Sunday.'

I didn't ask. Coming from a normal human being that could mean that she'd had a busy weekend, taken up with all those trivial little jobs that mount up in everyday life. Coming from Trish, there was a good chance it involved sexual deviance, chains and a gimp mask.

'*Three, two, one, cue Goldie.*'

'Welcome back. And for those of you who have just joined

285

us, Dr Craft is here with advice on coping with a prolapse, but first it gives me great pleasure to welcome the woman who knows exactly what you'll be up to this weekend, Miss Zara Delta. Good morning, Zara, so lovely to have you here, as always . . . '

Trish leaned right into my ear and whispered, 'She hates her guts, you know.'

'Who?'

'Goldie. She hates Zara with a passion. Told the producers yesterday that she wants Mystic Meg or Russell Grant in before the month is out.'

Nooooo, this was not good news! Zara would be gutted. Her morning TV slot was at the centre of her career web, and everything else spun out from there. Without her weekly publicity stunt, her market would shrink, her credibility would suffer and her ego would go into rigor mortis. I'd once overheard her saying she'd rather shack up with an oligarch than go back to feng shui-ing the homes of rich, bored Belgravia housewives. As Zara's manager, Conn would be devastated, and if they had to cut costs they might close the office, then Millie would lose her job and . . . oh, bloody hell, I really would be unemployed. Uh-uh, couldn't let that happen.

'Trish, you've got to stop that happening,' I fretted. 'If they bin Zara I'd definitely be out of a job, and . . . '

'You do know that since I passed up my role as director of television in favour of a shite job as head of hospitality, I no longer actually have a say in who is employed.'

Sarcasm dripped from every vowel. 'Anyway, don't worry, the producers vetoed the change. They say that Zara has the biggest fan base, and at the end of the day all they care about is viewing figures. Goldie was livid. Probably had to have an all-night three-way just to take her mind off it.'

My involuntary snort of laughter earned me a furious

glance and a hushing motion from the floor manager. If this job ever did end, this was the part that I would miss most: the variety and thrill of the TV stuff and the superficiality of the celebrity mingling. Being stuck in an office staring at the same four walls every day didn't even begin to compare.

Zara was halfway through the zodiac now, her hands gesturing wildly as she spoke, her voice expressive and dramatic. Goldie was nodding with a fixed smile that could either be saying 'Yes, I completely agree with you' or 'I wonder how much a hitman would cost'.

'Anyway, I've got news that trumps your leading lady's love triangle,' I said.

'You're pregnant?'

'No.'

'I'm pregnant?'

'No.' Aaargh, she was so immature and irritating – my very favourite qualities in a friend.

'Stu's preg—?'

'Will you shut up!' Another furious face from the floor manager. 'Look, do you want to know or don't you?' I asked, then winced, because the motion of pursing my lips in a disapproving manner had aggravated the cut that was almost, but not quite, healed.

'I do,' she vowed with mock solemnity.

'I think Zara is shagging Stephen Knight.'

Her eyes were the size of side plates as she grabbed my hand, dragged me out of the studio, down the corridor, into her office, closed the door and then shouted, 'YOU ARE FUCKING JESTING ME!'

'I jest not,' I replied nonchalantly, determined to milk the one and only time that I was the more interesting friend for all it was worth.

'On what evidence?'

'Last Monday he came in for a reading. Zara went into the session perfectly dressed, and came out of it with her frock tucked into her knickers.'

Trish's shrieks of laughter were so loud that if I closed my eyes I could see the floor manager's face twisting with rage.

'He's phoned her every day since – puts on a rubbish fake voice and calls himself Mr DeLongun, but I know it's him.'

'He always was a shite actor,' Trish concurred.

'And she's been sneaking out at least once a day. She even asked me to lie to Conn about where she was yesterday. I hope he doesn't find it suspicious that she just went for her second smear test in six weeks.'

Trish motioned disgust. 'That was the best you could come up with?'

I shrugged. 'I'm not cut out for subterfuge. I panicked.'

She shook her head for a few seconds, whistling as she absorbed the news. It was highly noteworthy for several reasons. First, they were both celebrities. Second, Stephen's sexual prowess and chemical exploits were legendary. Third, Zara was a good ten years older than him. The press would love this. Not that they were likely to ever find out, of course, since the protagonists were obviously intent on keeping this one well and truly under wraps.

'Well, you know what all this means?' Trish finally volunteered. 'There's no way you're chucking that job now. I don't care if she starts to beat you with a whip; you have to stay there for the insider gossip.'

I think I could quite honestly say that when Lennon and McCartney wrote 'A Little Help from My Friends', they probably didn't have a pal like Trish in mind.

✲

'Did you know that Zara was shagging Stephen Knight?' Trish demanded of Stu the minute he walked into the bar.

It was ten hours later and we'd met up again so they could bolster my pre-date spirits.

'Sssssssh, someone will hear you!' I scolded her. She swept her arm around in a semi-circular motion, illustrating the obvious truth that unless the nearby plant pot was bugged, there was no one within earshot.

We were back in the wine bar that Millie and I had sat in while we'd waited for Colin. When the next date showed up and I went off with him, the staff would definitely think I was on the game.

'Indeed I did, m'lud,' Stu answered very formally. 'Miss Lomond passed on this information earlier in the week during a highly confidential professional meeting. Your highlights look great, by the way.'

That last bit was to me. And they did – fine slivers of blonde injected into the red had lifted the colour and made it glisten like fire. Thanks to Stu's talents, at least something about me was bold and daring.

Stu wasn't exactly looking shabby this evening either. Three suited females in the corner had been staring at him since he'd entered; entranced at the sight of his black Diesel boots, battered boot-cut jeans and a black T-shirt so tight I could have flossed my teeth on his abs.

Trish, resplendent in a lime-green crepe shift dress teamed with purple platforms (not the obvious choice yet the end result was stunning), was moping now. 'I bloody hate being last to hear things. That's it, I'm divorcing Grey and coming back to singledom to join you two sad bastards. I might never have sex again but at least the gossip is better.'

A passing waitress plopped a large bowl of kettle chips in the middle of our table. Trish picked it straight back up and returned it, much to the waitress's surprise.

'Sorry, but the food fascist is here tonight,' she explained, gesturing to Stu. 'Apparently if we consume food in a public place we'll be dead within the hour and that would be really bad for business.'

The waitress backed away slowly, holding the chips out in front of her like they were unstable plutonium.

'You'll thank me one day,' Stu grinned, nudging her jovially at the same time.

'I already thank you,' Trish replied dryly. 'If it wasn't for your neurotic bloody witterings my arse would be two inches bigger.'

A crowd of city blokes in pinstriped suits, wallets bulging in their chest pockets, strutted in, and immediately the volume level in the bar rose about six decibels as they shouted for champagne and roared with arrogant, attention-seeking laughter every few seconds.

'Shit, should have brought the Uzi,' Trish muttered.

Were they the type of men that Jon worked with? No wonder he always found time to email when all he had for company were a bunch of loud, obnoxious blokes who had made it their life's mission to stoke their own egos by acting like spoiled, immature twats. Another week or so and I'd be able to ask him. I had the date tonight (Virgo), another one tomorrow night (Sagittarius), and finally *Dirty Dancing* with Stu next Saturday night. And then . . . ta da! Mission accomplished. Goodbye dates, *hasta la vista* uncomfortable silences and first-night indignities, farewell worry and stress, hello the start of my new life. And maybe more . . . I had absolutely no idea if there was anything there with Jon other than the seedlings of a great friendship, but his emails made me laugh and it was so refreshing to have someone who was genuinely interested in me and what I did. Two or three times a day now, my inbox would ping with a note from him, and even though recent events had convinced me that I fancied jumping into a new relationship about as much as I fancied herpes, at least it was a starting point to moving on from Ben. For the second time. My stomach flipped and my throat tightened. No! I wouldn't let him do this to me again. I wouldn't cry. I wouldn't.

'Oh crap, she's crying again.' Trish, still in mutter mode, pulled a tissue out of her bag and thrust it towards me. 'I told you not to think about him!'

'I know, I can't help it. He just comes into my head and my tear ducts go into meltdown.'

I blew my nose so noisily that even the pinstripes turned to stare.

'I'll be fine, honestly. It's just . . . it's just all been too crazy lately. I just need to get these bloody dates out of the way, file the reports, and then do ten years in therapy to erase the memories.'

'So who's tonight's lucky candidate then?' Trish asked, changing the subject from my desperate emotional state to the inevitably desperate night ahead.

'Kurt, with a "K", twenty-five, Virgo, comes from Brighton, now living in Camden, listed his occupation as DJ and Media Student, sounded cool but keen on the phone, no idea where we're going.'

'Personal alarm and pepper spray?' Stu asked.

'Check.'

'Mobile phone fully charged?'

'Check.'

'Promise to stay in public crowded places at all times?'

'Absolutely. And I've also notified the police, Interpol and MI5. Oh, and the coastguard, just on the off-chance that he drives me a hundred miles to the nearest beach and we get into difficulty in deep waters.'

Stu deftly stuck his fingers in my Cosmopolitan and flicked it in my face.

'Don't you dare smudge my make-up,' I laughed, 'or I'm grassing you to Millie.'

We'd had the office to ourselves all afternoon because Conn was at a meeting to discuss a potential endorsement deal and Zara was out, presumably doing that thing that ended up with her dress in her knickers. I had no idea what was actually going on with her and Stephen Knight, but I was eternally grateful to him because both her attendance in the office and her crazy quota had dropped significantly. This week I hadn't had any Third World rebirthing rituals, New Age scream therapies or a single live animal in the office.

In the quiet bliss of their absence, I'd spent the whole afternoon sitting with Millie at reception, passing the time by letting her do my hair and make-up, and the results were a lot less scary than I'd envisaged – even skin tone, pale lips and eyes on the slightly less exaggerated side of Amy Winehouse. Millie had also provided my top for the evening: a crushed silk grey shirt that was a perfect match to my skinny jeans and black boots. For once I looked like a well-groomed, successful woman of the world . . . Which meant that it was probably time for me to break a heel, fall in a puddle or contract a sudden bout of food poisoning that would result in my expunging the contents of my stomach in a public place.

Trish interrupted my musings with a sudden conversion to the power of prayer.

'God, if you're up there, please make this guy her date,' she whispered.

I spun around, more than a little terrified, to see who she was referring to. Kurt (with a K), in a white T-shirt and an old pair of Levis. Sorry, that's what he'd been wearing in his application photo. This Kurt (with a K) had been shopping in the loud and startling corner of the fashion hypermarket. Where to start? The velvet trousers in a deep shade of navy were just about passable in a dimly lit room, but his shirt? It was definitely making a statement – one that said 'I'm auditioning for the job of bingo caller in a holiday park'.

Stu let out a low, deep whistle. 'Who knew? Lamé is alive and well and living on that bloke's back.'

Noooooooooooooo, it couldn't be. This had to be Kurt with a K's evil twin, Damien with a D.

'Leni? Has to be! Gorgeous, babe, gorgeous!'

'Will you tell him or should I just deck him and leave a note pinned to his shirt to explain?' Trish asked, completely ignoring the hand that had been thrust in front of her.

'I'm Leni,' I interjected, shooting Trish a filthy look. Why did dates keep confusing me with my pals? Was it some kind of wishful thinking? There was no denying that Trish was beautiful in a 'Bond movie female baddie, I'll crack your nuts with my teeth' kind of way, but for goodness' sake, I was wearing eyebrow pencil, hairspray, and that stuff that stung like crazy when it plumped up the lips to a bombshell pout. Did all that count for nothing?

Kurt spun around to face me without skipping a beat. 'Of course you are. Gorgeous, babe, gorgeous!'

I had a horrible feeling that Ashton Kutcher and a camera crew were involved in this. It had to be a set-up. Men like this didn't happen in real life. Kurt was only in his twenties, but he had the cheesy voice, the wardrobe and the lines of a middle-aged game-show host.

As he shook my hand a wave of aftershave pinged my tear ducts. Out of his eye-line, Trish clenched her hands around her throat, crossed her eyes and pretended that she was being choked to death. I shot her another evil glare.

I climbed down from the bar stool, trying to ignore the gobsmacked stares of the three suited women in the corner, the gang of obnoxious stockbrokers, the bar staff, assorted other customers and my two best friends, one soon to be deceased if she didn't stop mocking me in public.

'So,' I asked him, unconsciously slipping into the sing-song voice of a children's television presenter, as I often did when I was nervous. 'Where are we off to then?'

'Babe, I'm going to show you a night you'll never forget,' he promised, also in an altered voice, only his was the one that you'd normally hear announcing to a housewife from Macclesfield that she'd won a brand new microwave on a prime-time phone-in show. He held out his hand towards mine. 'I promise you, Leni, I am going to float your boat!'

'Just as well she put the coastguard on stand-by,' Trish hissed to Stu.

We were about ten feet away, moving in the direction of the door, when Trish called me back. ''Scuse me a second,' I said apologetically, before returning to the table, where Trish was frantically rummaging in her bag. Triumphantly, she pulled out a pair of huge Cavalli sunglasses, then grabbed the lapel of my shirt and pulled me close to her. 'Here, take these,' she whispered.

'Why? Why would I need those when it's night-time?'

'Because after a few hours of staring at that shirt, your retinas might never recover.'

I stomped off, embarrassed and strangely defensive on behalf of Kurt. The shirt wasn't that bad. We had to (quite literally) look on the bright side – if aliens landed in West London tonight we'd be able to use Kurt's shirt to deflect the beams from their laser guns.

I held my head up high, took Kurt's arm again and strutted out. We were in the next street before the noise of the laughter behind us subsided . . .

Just in time for the demented wailing to start.

29

The Virgo Date

Who invented karaoke? Whoever it was, I hope his wife left
him (yes, it's a man – if a woman had invented it she would
have made it conditional that middle-aged men couldn't
sing 'My Way' after consuming over fifteen units of alcohol),
his kids disowned him, and he was left old, sad and broken
– close to how I was feeling, and I'd only been there for a
few minutes.

Actually, strictly speaking this wasn't karaoke in the traditional sense – i.e. the kind that was sung in pubs by hen
parties and that could, in the wrong hands (Chelsea supporters
called Glenda), put senior citizens in traction. Kurt with a K
had actually brought me to an open mike night for budding
stars in a West End club. Right now, two Goths were on stage
singing a very disturbing version of 'Tainted Love', complete
with a mock stabbing action and fake blood.

'There you go, poppet,' Kurt smarmed, as he put a drink
and a packet of Quavers in front of me. I was having serious
doubts about Kurt. If I added the clothes, the cheese and
the hugely disturbing voice to his behaviour in the twenty
minutes or so since I'd met him, he was channelling a
holiday tour rep on speed.

First of all, he'd burst into a rousing rendition of 'I've

Got You Under My Skin' just after we'd left Trish and Stu in the bar. Then he'd bombarded me with jokes until I'd glazed over, slipped off the pavement and wandered perilously close to passing cars in the hope that one of them would rescue me with a sudden and painless death.

Outside in the queue he'd entertained me with a tap dance and then he'd welcomed everyone we'd met so far in here like they were a long-lost sibling. The bizarre thing was that they were just as effusive towards him. It was like some kind of weird voyage to the Land of Exaggerated Greetings. Or musical theatre. That was it! In revenge for my recent outburst, Zara had obviously used her psychic powers to transport me to the modern equivalent of *Calamity Jane*, and as long as everyone just kept singing, slapping their thighs and heartily shaking each other's hands we'd be absolutely fine.

'Peckish?' Kurt asked after I'd polished off the crisps, more a result of nervous comfort eating than hunger. If Stu could have seen me he would have had a stroke, but I figured that the longer my hands were busy going in and out of a crisp packet, the less likely it was that Kurt would pull me up onto a table while belting out a selection of hits from Doris Day's back catalogue.

To add to the confusion, Kurt – crazed grin and Latin American Dance Champion wardrobe aside – was actually really good-looking. He wasn't exceptionally tall or ridiculously small: about the same height as me in my heels, so about five foot ten. His subtly highlighted short blond hair was swept back in the style of Brad Pitt in the *Ocean's* movies, and he had a perfectly chiselled jaw-line. Yes, he was a slightly disconcerting shade of Jordan (the glamour model, not the country), but his body was lean without being skinny, his face was smooth and his teeth perfectly straight and blinging white. He was the type of clean-cut preppy bloke who always popped up in adverts for catalogue chains and caffeinated sports drinks.

I glanced around, the casual act of checking out the ambience of the environment concealing my true agenda of pinpointing the emergency exits in case a rapid escape was called for. The room was reminiscent of an old American jazz club, but on a much larger scale. The walls were coated with ribbed, copper-coloured wallpaper, the carpet was the deepest shade of brown and, over in the corner, the bartenders all wore white shirts with waistcoats and bow ties. There were about fifty small round tables dotted throughout the main floor area, each one with a small gold lamp in the middle and two vintage wooden chairs on either side. The crowd (perhaps a slight exaggeration there) was a strange mixture of elderly couples who were obviously just there to be entertained (entry fee plus chicken in a basket for a fiver), and solo drinkers who, judging by their pained, anxious expressions, were planning on exercising their talents and seizing their heady moment of adulation in the spotlight. Directly in front of us was a stage, perhaps twenty foot by ten, on which an artist that might or might not have been a woman by birth, personally dressed for the evening by Shirley Bassey's stylist and flicking her/his waist-length curls for effect at the end of every line, was giving a thundering performance of 'The Man with the Golden Gun'.

After a few minutes of incredulous viewing, I pushed my chin back up to its original place and decided to initiate interaction with my partner for the night.

'Do . . . do you come here often?' I'd love to say that it was Kurt who'd blurted that one out, but to my eternal horror it came from me. I blame the glare from the lamé shirt. It was obviously sending signals directly from my brain to my mouth, bypassing 'interesting conversation' and 'chat-up-line taboos'.

To be fair, Kurt didn't comment on my pitiful slip into naffness, but then, this was the man who winked at me every time he caught my eye.

'Yeah, all the time,' he replied.

A voice from the stage interrupted our in-depth conversation about the meaning of life, and we turned to see a suited gent that Kurt had been chatting to at the bar.

'Ladies and gentlemen,' he announced, 'it gives me great pleasure to present a favourite here at Star Spotters, Mr Kurt Cabana!'

Cabana????? I was sure it had said Kurt Cobb on his application letter. Just like that, the night took yet another step up the unbelievable ladder. And well done me on my obviously superior judgement in weeding out the wannabes and publicity-seekers! The only way this guy would seem shy and retiring would be if he was sandwiched between Paris Hilton and Kanye West.

Kurt took the stage to riotous applause from the twenty or so people that constituted his audience. He slipped a CD into a stereo system situated at the side of the stage and then wandered over to the centre as the music started. In the space of a few bars of 'Mack the Knife', he was transformed from borderline strange to Robbie Williams in his 'swing' phase. He was actually very, very good, and if I'm not wrong, two middle-aged women at a corner table threw something onto the stage. I said a silent prayer that if it was intimate underwear it was either new or had gone through a boil wash.

When the song finished, Cabana (with a C) demonstrated his versatility by slipping effortlessly into the next track, a sultry, perfectly pitched rendition of Justin Timberlake's 'Sexy Back'. With dancing.

Another few minutes and I just might be forced to take departure from my knickers myself. He was fantastic: hitting every note, working the stage, pulling in the audience and finishing to thundering applause.

Bloody hell, he was actually really talented. If I were Louis Walsh on *The X-Factor*, I'd burst into a random ten seconds of compulsive blinking and then announce that he had 'the whole package'.

Kurt jumped off the stage, face flushed, grin like a pumpkin, and made his way back over to me. At the risk of sounding like a demented groupie, I was suddenly looking at him in a whole new light. Maybe the night wasn't quite so doomed after all.

'You were fantastic,' I enthused. 'Really great.'

'Do you think so?' His eyes glistened with excitement.

'Absolutely!'

'Thanks,' he replied, satisfied that he'd impressed my knickers off. Metaphorically speaking.

Okay, so we were on a roll now; we'd finally clicked, broken the ice and . . . Pause. Long pause. Then a bit longer. I kept my teeth clenched firmly shut. I'd already done the 'do you come here often' line, so it was his turn to soar in the conversation stakes. Eventually, he took the hint.

'Listen, I hope you don't think it's weird, but I brought you a headshot. Just in case you need it for . . . you know, *anything*.'

I didn't know.

'Anything? Like . . . ?'

I left that one hanging, hoping that he'd pick it up and run with it. Eventually he caught up.

'Like the book . . . you know, publicity shots and stuff.'

On a positive note, he'd dropped the game-show voice. On a negative note, I'd just received verbal confirmation as to what the whole bizarre performance so far had been about.

To Kurt, this wasn't a date, it was an audition. Yes, date number two with Matt, the lead singer in the band (complete with girlfriend) had been my first official encounter with a wannabe, and I'd just chalked up my second. But while Matt had been ruthlessly calculating, I suspected that Kurt's determination to impress was born more out of desperation to succeed. I could hardly bear to look him straight in the blinding blue contact lenses as I broke the news.

'Listen, Kurt, I think we might be at cross purposes here. I won't need a headshot. I hope you don't mind, but you seem like a lovely guy so I'm going to be completely straight with you: being on this date will lead to absolutely no other work in the entertainment industry. Nor will it bring fame, as the case studies in the book will be completely anonymous. I have absolutely no sway in the world of showbiz, so basically tonight will not further your career in any way whatsoever. I'm really sorry.'

To his credit, he managed not to crumble into a pile of devastation. The man could act as well! There were a few moments of excruciating silence, then he gave me a disappointed smile. 'Don't worry about it.'

The words said, 'No, it's fine, really', but his demeanour said, 'Speed-dial Samaritans.'

'Are you gutted?' I swear that if I could have, I would have awarded him a million-pound recording contract and a slot on the next Royal Variety Show there and then.

'S'okay. I'm through to the next round of *Britain's Got Talent*, I'm an extra in *The Bill* next week and I'm waiting to hear if I'm going to be a backing singer for Westlife's support act on the next tour.'

'Fantastic!'

There was another pregnant pause. 'So this really was just supposed to be a date then?'

I nodded. 'It's all to do with star signs, and, to be honest, I'm not sure how it works – I'm just the faceless researcher who has no idea what Zara is on about half the time.'

I could tell he'd lost interest now. He'd glazed over, and I couldn't swear to it, but I was pretty sure he was eyeing the exits. After he'd checked his watch for the fourth time in three silent minutes, I cracked and made the decision to rebel against Zara's project rules, number who cared? *Each meeting must last several hours, the content of which to be decided entirely by the candidate.*

'Kurt, can I make a proposal?'

'Sure.'

'I'm knackered, fed up, and I forgot to set the Sky Plus for *Die Hard* two, which starts in twenty minutes. I'm all for cutting tonight short if you are. I'll file a report saying that we danced the night away in that salsa club over the road. I'm assuming that salsa is also on your CV? Course it is. So if anyone ever calls you to check, you'll agree that's what we did. Meanwhile, you can keep the hundred quid and go and join your mates for a night on the town. Whaddya say?'

His face dropped to an expression of stunned devastation . . . for about one hundredth of a second, then it brightened and he leaned over and kissed me on the cheek.

'You don't mind?'

'Oh, I promise you, I really, really don't mind.'

'Then thanks, I'll take you up on that.' He checked his watch again. 'Rumour has it there's a scout for a new dance show checking out talent at the Embassy Club. If I jump in a cab I might just make it.'

I leaned over and reciprocated his kiss. 'Then run, my budding superstar, run like the wind.'

I slipped off my chair, made my way outside and jumped in a taxi. Twenty minutes later, my key was going in the door when I heard a slight noise from behind the door next to me: Mrs Naismith peeking out her spy-hole to check that I was okay. I leaned over and pressed my eye against my side of it, causing a cackle of hilarity from the other side. Her door swung open.

'Just making sure you are all right, love. Didn't you have a night out with one of those star-sign boys tonight?'

'I did . . . cut it short, though.'

'Right then, love, just as long as you're okay.'

'I am . . .'

She gave me a big smile as she backed into her hallway, and was just about to close the door when . . .

'Mrs Naismith, I'm going to have a glass of wine and watch a Bruce Willis film – fancy joining me?'

For a woman in her seventies she didn't half shift. Three seconds later she was back at the door with a bumper bag of Revels and a family-size bar of Fruit & Nut.

'I tell you, if I was thirty years younger I'd be outside that Bruce Willis's door in a flash. Looks much better since he lost the hair.'

'He does,' I laughed, opening my door. Nope, no marines lurking in the hallway – always a bonus.

Two hours later, world saved from destruction by the wit, charm and violence from the bald one, I covered a sleeping Mrs Naismith with a blanket, slipped a pillow under her head, took what was left of my wine and padded through to bed. My theatre date with Stu next Saturday didn't really count, because I knew exactly what to expect, so that meant that technically tomorrow night was my last night of research for Zara. One more night. Just a few hours in the grand scheme of my life. How bad could it be? I could honestly say that I didn't think there was anything that could be thrown at me that I couldn't cope with. Short of the guy turning up bollock-naked with a balloon tied to his willy, I could cope with anything and nothing could surprise me. Nothing.

Except . . .

PROGRESS SUMMARY: *IT'S IN THE STARS* DATING PROJECT

CONCLUDED		
LEO	Harry Henshall	Morbid fascination for simulated violence
SCORPIO	Matt Warden	Lead singer, lying arse
ARIES	Daniel Jones	Unlikely to forge career as an assertiveness coach
CAPRICORN	Craig Cunningham	Relationship therapist, incites violent urges
GEMINI	Jon Belmont	Definite potential – secret plans to see again
PISCES	Nurse Dave Canning	Avoid all future dealings with the NHS
AQUARIUS	Colin Bilson-Smythe	Lawyer, laughs like a food-mixer
CANCER	Gregory Smith	Shy, sweet man's man – in all respects
LIBRA	Ben Mathers	Do you want to see me cry?
VIRGO	Kurt Cobb/Cabana	Rising star in need of good stylist

Let me entertain you! Gregarious Brad Pitt look-alike, 25, Virgo, wants to show some lucky lady the stars! Multi-talented in all areas of entertainment, I'm available for wining, dining, Bar Mitzvahs and corporate functions. Seeking understanding, supportive lady (19–25) for company on tours and auditions. Must be gorgeous, fit, polished and prepared to participate in variety stage show – musical talent a must, comfort around flying knives and a transit van would be bonuses.

Administrative talents also essential, as I am current president of NSPL – National Society for the Promotion of Lamé.

Please apply in person, bringing CV and show-reel to Kurt Cabana, contestant 3432, in the queue outside *X-Factor* auditions, O2 Stadium.

30

The Sagittarius Date

Gavin West, 25, nightclub promoter. And as far as I could see he wasn't a wannabe or rising star on the hunt for publicity. Although, when Conn had spotted the application photo on my desk earlier that day, he had announced that Gavin's face was somehow familiar. However, given that Conn seemed to spend most of his nights in London clubs, that wasn't too much of a long shot.

Now that I'd managed to stop picturing him naked, I'd come to look on my interaction with Conn as being my very own personal Diet Coke ad. If he didn't have meetings, he'd strut into Zara's office first thing, smile and wink in my direction (although thankfully not a 'Kurt with a K' wink – just one of the casual, charming, non-nauseating variety). He'd take all Zara's mail, copy any phone messages, ask me to make reservations for that night at restaurants/clubs/hotels, let me know of any arrangements he'd made for her, and synchronise her schedule by copying it from my computer to his BlackBerry via Bluetooth. And, incidentally, after many years in the technologically backward world of plumbing supplies, I was borderline giddy that I even knew what that last sentence meant.

Sometimes, if Zara wasn't around he'd sit and chat for

five minutes, just surface stuff, all warm and friendly. I'd chat back, ensuring that I was always utterly endearing and beguiling. I lie. I'd sit there with a beetroot face, tongue-tied, and only when he'd left the office, got into his car and driven approximately five miles would I think of something witty and interesting that I should have said. Hopeless. Completely hopeless. He just had to look at me with those piercing eyes and I came over all self-conscious and blus-tery. And of course, I'd rather spend a month in Zara's inflatable detox-tube than discuss the problem with him.

Cleaning cupboard fantasies aside, Conn was still an enigma to me, and I had absolutely no idea what his life entailed outside the office, other than a serious social schedule that involved frequenting the flashest venues in the city and then following that up by sending multiple gifts to multiple females.

Who were his friends? What did he like to do? How did he like his tea? And what kind of women did he like? That last question was purely for anthropological purposes, of course, although I already had a sneaky hunch that Conn's type of girl would come with identical promiscuous triplets, be bedecked in designer gear, wear matching bras and knickers and never, ever step foot over the door unless her bikini line was waxed to perfection. In other words, the complete opposite of me. Just as well, really. It would be highly unusual to have a relationship with someone when the sum total of my contribution to our interaction would be, 'Sure, Conn, and would you like those reservations at seven p.m. or eight p.m.?' And even that would be said with moist palms, a red face and a light sheen of perspiration on my forehead.

Standing there waiting for Gavin, I realised that was a recurring theme. I rubbed my thumb across my palm. Yep, moist. I could feel the sweat buds popping on my forehead, and I'd bet all my worldly IKEA goods that my face was a mild shade of puce. Would I ever do anything like this again? Not even if there was a night of passion with Johnny Depp at the end of it.

Gavin the Promoter was late, so I gave Stu a quick call, anxious to prove to the Saturday-night commuters who were whizzing past me as I loitered outside the foyer of the Charlotte Street Hotel that I wasn't actually touting for business. He answered with an unintelligible croak.

'Aw, honey, you sound terrible – what's wrong?'

'Dunno. It feels serious, Leni. I checked my symptoms on the web and I think it's best-case bronchitis, worst-case lung cancer,' he answered, each word a strained rasp.

'Or it could just be a bit of laryngitis?' I suggested, with a smile that made a nearby bloke (ruddy complexion, vertically challenged, suit that strained to contain his ample curves) start to walk towards me with a leering grin on his face. He did a swift 180-degree turn when he realised I was on my phone and not flashing my Colgate smile at him.

'Definitely worse than that, Leni. Honestly, I feel like death.'

'Do you want me to come over later and mop your brow?'

'Will you? Verity is in Bermuda on a shoot for a week, so if I die in my sleep there's no one here to close my eyelids and phone the coroner.'

Sometimes it was easier just to go with Stu's neurotic flow. 'Okay, I'll be over as soon as I get done with Sagittarius. And Stu, I don't have a key so try to hold off on popping your clogs until I get there.'

'I'll try, but I can't promise. If I don't answer after five minutes, call the police, but make sure you come in first so you can check I'm not doing an Elvis. Dying on the loo would be the ultimate indignity.'

307

'What would you care, you'd be dead! It's me who'd have to . . . '

Two things hit me at once: the absurdity of this conversation, and a mental image of Stu on the toilet, trousers at ankles. 'Stu, I love you, and that's why I'm hanging up now. See you soon.'

I snapped the phone shut and slipped it into the pocket of my black leather jacket. Or, rather, the black leather jacket that I'd commandeered for the evening from my favourite new fashion line, House of Millie. Black skinny jeans, a black polo neck and my favourite black boots completed the ensemble. I was only a beret away from a World War II underground revolutionary.

The thundering of some kind of synthesised music with a thumping beat announced the arrival of a black BMW X5 in front of me. My antennae were immediately twanged by the blacked-out windows. Ooooh, a celebrity? Or a football player? My fingers tightened slightly around my phone, ready to flick it to camera mode. If this was someone I liked then I wanted a snap I could stare at on my screensaver all day. Jude Law would be fab. Matt Damon, fantastic. Josh Duhamel, be still my heart. The only preferable option to any one of that trio would be Tom Jones. Mrs Naismith idolised him and had once confessed that she was still hopeful that he'd discover her (in a one-bedroom flat on the Slough/Windsor border), whisk her off to his LA mansion and (I swear these are her words – look away now if you are easily nauseated) 'show her his love machine'. If I could somehow get Tom to speak to her on the phone she'd keep me in Garibaldis until the day I died.

The electric window on the passenger side slid down, and a voice emanated from the darkness.

'Hey! You Leni?'

Bugger. He wasn't Welsh, his voice was about four octaves

higher than Tom's, and he knew my name. Mrs Naismith would just have to put her dreams back on hold.

Crouching down, I could just about make out a face in the darkness of the car's interior. 'Er, yes.'

'Jump in.'

Jump in. I had a sudden vision of Stu, dressed in ecumenical robes, standing behind a pulpit, holding a holy book in one hand (*The A–Z of Common Medical Conditions*), thundering in a voice borrowed from a preacher in America's deep south about the dangers of getting into cars with strangers.

On the other hand, we had Gavin's name, his address and his photograph on file back at the office, and I had a photocopy of all of said details in my handbag. If I turned up mutilated in a ditch tomorrow at least CID would have a head start.

I skipped across to the car, peered in, checked that the face matched the one in the photo, and jumped into the passenger seat.

The driver held out his hand. 'Hi, I'm Gavin.'

In a well-practised motion, I surreptitiously wiped my moist palm on my jeans before shaking his hand. Yep, I had 'class' written all over me.

'Leni . . . but, er, you know that already. Or I might be someone pretending to be Leni so that I can car-jack you. But I'm not, I'm Leni.'

Stop talking. Preacher Stu, please summon all your holy powers to paralyse my gob.

To Gavin's credit, he only looked mildly disconcerted as he raised the window and slipped the automatic gear back into 'drive'.

'So, I thought we'd go to a couple of clubs first, and just, you know, check out what's happening.'

I stopped myself from telling him that I had a fairly good

idea about what was happening already. This guy had to be another 'wannabe' because there was no way he had to resort to insane television gimmicks to get a girl. Even putting the flash car to one side for the moment, from the neck down he was Vin Diesel: his T-shirt emphasising his muscle-bound bulges. From the neck up he was somewhere on the high end between average and attractive: square jaw-line, deep-set dark eyes, and short, spiky jet-black hair that was no stranger to the styling wax. His complexion was patchy, but what were a few spots between friends? Certainly not enough to make this fairly passable guy lack anything in the girl-pulling department. He was absolutely, definitely another one who was searching for a leg up the showbiz ladder.

Okay, Leni, you can deal with this. Another couple of hours with a fame-seeking star-in-the-making coming up. Just smile, be attentive, and then let him down gently before releasing him to go and chase stardom on a reality TV show. Now that *Gladiators* was back on TV he'd be a shoo-in for a leading role: the size of a Portaloo, a face that teenage girls would adore, and he didn't have to speak, thus disguising a voice that was slightly on the girly side of David Beckham.

He'd barely put his foot on the accelerator when we stopped again.

'Let's start here,' he suggested, flashing me a wide smile. The sign above the door said, 'The Devil's Den'.

Right, Leni, time for a serious conversation with self. Technically speaking (i.e. man with sore throat aside), this was my last date. I could therefore:

a)   spend the whole night in the usual state of anxious flux, feeling self-conscious and hating every minute;

b) make a conscious effort to throw off my inhibit
ions and enjoy myself, perhaps indulge in an
alcoholic beverage or two and thoroughly make
the most of what seemed to be shaping up to be
a pretty special night;

c) snog the face off Gavin the promoter in a last-
ditch defiance of Zara's project rules, number . . .
couldn't give a toss.

I decided to start with b), with the option to upgrade to
c) at a later time. Come on, enough of the self-imposed
oppression. I was young, I was free, I was single and I was
in a hot car with a hot guy sitting outside a hot club. Whey-
hey! This place was always in the glossy mags, in pictures
that featured members of girl bands sprawled across the
pavement with drunken expressions that gave no clue as
to how they'd apparently lost their knickers. Smashing.
Although given that my nethers were enshrouded in a pair
of M&S full-size briefs, I did feel a tad over-dressed.

I stepped out of the car, straight onto . . . 'Gavin, you're
on a double yellow line here.'

'That's okay – the boys will look after it for me.'

At the entrance, the two Gavin-sized bouncers – aka 'the
boys' – took it in turns to shake Gavin's hand and then
nodded deferentially to me before sweeping the door open
and waving us through. With a subtle head-nod to the teller
behind the glass window inside, we waltzed straight through
without paying. Ooh, I liked that. For a wannabe, he
certainly knew how to impress, although the raging cynic
in me did wonder if he'd popped in here on his way to
collect me, paid our entrance fee and slipped the bouncers
twenty quid each to give him the VIP treatment on his
return. If so, his plan to wow me was working. The only
thing I would change so far was the leather satchel that was

slung across his body. Sue me, but the whole metrosexual thing is just a male handbag too far for me. I prefer my woeful love-life to involve men who are rugged, masculine, and who won't blow my Christmas Top Shop vouchers on a chi-chi handbag for themselves.

Gavin strutted on in front, down a flight of stairs and into the cavernous bowels of the club. Even though it was early evening, there were already a hundred or so people in the room, many of them sitting in expansive booths upholstered in a cow-print fabric that swept around chunky ebony tables.

Over in one corner was a semicircular DJ booth, partly concealed by a smattering of barely clad young ladies who were swinging their pants (or lack thereof) on the dance floor.

'What would you like to drink?' Gavin asked when we reached the bar. Several of the waitresses that were huddled around a hatch at the end of the long stretch of marble counter glanced in our direction, smiled familiarly at Gavin and then went back to their conversation.

'A white wine, thanks.' Seconds later a glass of Dom Pérignon champagne was in my hand and he was clutching a bottle of water. No money changed hands.

'Can I ask you something?' I had to lean right into his ear so that he could hear me over the thump, thump, thump of the music. I was definitely getting old. Another couple of years and I'd be asking the DJ to turn the volume down and complaining that all modern music was just 'rubbish with no melody'.

'Sure.'

'Everyone here seems to know you and you haven't paid for anything – sorry if that's rude, but do you work here?'

He nodded. 'Sometimes.'

'So what exactly does a nightclub promoter do, then?'

He clinked his plastic water bottle against my glass. 'We just fill up the clubs and then keep them happy.'

Right then. So that was as clear as his complexion.

'I'll be back in two secs, darlin', he added, and then disappeared off in the direction of a wall, where one of the panels cunningly opened under his touch. A concealed doorway, how Cluedo was that? And yes, I was instructing my inner feminist to overlook the fact that he'd called me *darlin'* in a randomly patronising way.

Two seconds stretched to two and a half records, enough time for me to reach the half way mark on my champagne glass while subtly nodding my head in time to the music in what I hoped made me appear to be a cool, clubby, independent female, as opposed to a daft tart that was on the pull.

When he returned, he was suitably apologetic. 'Sorry, but had to have a quick chat to the manager – just setting some stuff up for next week. So . . . fancy moving on somewhere else?'

'Sure,' I nodded, relaxed now. I was beginning to doubt my initial conclusions as to Gavin's motivations. He hadn't burst into song, he hadn't recited a poem and he hadn't tap-danced all the way down the stairs. If he was a wannabe, he was hiding it well. Maybe I had it all wrong. Maybe he was just a guy who worked really hard and didn't have the opportunity to meet someone special. I thought back to the short time at college when I'd worked in a local bar to pay the rent (and to sneak illicit vodka and cokes to Trish and Stu). I'd meet cute guys all night long, but I was so busy that I never got the chance to talk to them, and by the time I clocked off they were either paired up or lying in a puddle of Pernod and blackcurrant under a table.

Perhaps Gavin shared the predicament. Back in the car (which, thanks to 'the boys', hadn't been ticketed, towed or trashed), I attempted to probe his inner depths.

'What made you write in to Zara then?'

He shrugged, then took several seconds to formulate his answer. 'Just looking for new opportunities, I suppose.'

Groan. He was a wannabe after all.

'Opportunities for what?'

This was where he'd pull the car over to the side of the road, whip off his trousers to reveal pants with a large lion on the front, and burst into three verses and a chorus of Robbie Williams' 'Angels'.

'To meet people. New people. Sometimes you get tired of seeing the same old faces every night, and I just thought this might be a way of expanding my horizons.'

Oh. Robbie Williams had left the building.

'Shocked the fucking life out of me when I got picked, though. I mean, what are the chances?'

I considered informing him that they were 3,342 to 1, the exact number of young men (or deranged specimens, depending on your viewpoint) that had responded to Zara's appeal, but my nerd attack was cut short as we'd stopped again. This time we were outside Caesar's, one of the most exclusive bars in the city, where on any given night you'd expect to find at least half the Arsenal team, two-thirds of Tottenham Hotspur, a dozen or so household-name soap stars and the current year's crop of glamour models and *Big Brother* contestants.

Again, we'd drawn to a halt on double yellow lines and we were ushered straight inside, bypassing a queue of bored revellers waiting in a line to get in. Thankfully, the envious queuing masses couldn't hear my internal mantra, repeating furious prayers that I wouldn't fall foul of a vertiginous-heeled mishap that would end with my buttocks meeting the floor.

We were barely inside the door when a tall, dark-haired gent in a beautifully cut navy suit and open-neck white shirt greeted Gavin with an enthusiastic handshake. 'Hey, my man, how's it hanging?'

'All good, Caesar, all good.'

This was Caesar! I was in the presence of London night-club royalty, the man who was a prince to Peter Stringfellow, the thong-wearing mullet king.

Caesar guided us through the throng, to a VIP bar at the back that contained, if my vision and knowledge of famous faces could be relied on, Sean Bean, Ant or Dec (I was never sure which one was which), and Ashley Cole Is a Knob. Oh, and Sven-Göran Eriksson . . . or it could be a middle-aged geography teacher from Gillingham – it was hard to tell. Even though Gavin left me there for five minutes while he had a chat to Caesar, the subtle waves of thrill and excitement convinced me that I was beginning to enjoy the whole experience of this night. Gavin wasn't exactly a conversationalist, but he was obviously one of the trendy 'scene' guys and my shallow genes were relishing the opportunity to be, for once in my life, one of the in-crowd. I wanted to process this new development in a classy, appropriate manner: by calling up everyone who'd ever known me and shouting 'Woo-hoo, I'm cooler than a penguin's arse'.

'I'm sorry I keep deserting you, but this is the kind of job where you're never off-duty,' he apologised on his return.

'That's okay, I'm enjoying myself. Usually I'd be one of those poor souls standing outside with their face pressed against the glass, so just being inside is a bonus.'

His polite laughter was tinged with scepticism, but he didn't probe any further. Maybe he was under the illusion that I was more interesting than I actually was.

Instead we switched to small talk over the beats thundering from the huge amps that were suspended from every corner of the room, and after half an hour I'd confirmed that yes, he was indeed Gavin, 25, a nightclub promoter. That was it. I hadn't learned a single new fact about him.

I'd used all of my people skills and investigative prowess, garnered from years of watching *Homicide: Life on the Street*, to come up with exactly nothing – zero, nada. This guy wasn't so much still water as a frozen puddle. But then, I supposed, in this industry, superficiality was the norm.

He'd subtly volleyed every question back to me or diverted my attention to another famous face being personally escorted by Caesar into the VIP world of three-hundred-pound bottles of Cristal and silicone breasts so huge they could suffocate a man with one squeeze.

'How about one more club and then we'll grab something to eat?'

Back in the opulent surroundings of leather seats and a state-of-the-art automotive sound system, I had another go at information extraction and managed to ascertain that yes, BMW was his favourite car, and no, he'd never driven a Nissan Micra, much less a canary-yellow one like mine. At least he seemed amused by my suggestion that he was missing out on a valuable life experience.

The Freezer was next on the list, an achingly cool club that kept its name in the gossip pages by revealing details of at least one punch-up featuring a minor royal every month. For the first time that evening, the paparazzi were in evidence, and two Amazonian creatures with straight, waist-length hair and cheekbones you could slice cheese with were standing in the middle of the pack striking a multitude of poses.

The paps didn't even flick their flashes in my direction, but a few of them nodded to Gavin. For a few seconds I got a rush of the feeling that I imagined groupies must thrive on, a vibe of fame and respect by association, although I was getting it without having to give the drummer a blow job. Happy days. Gavin, strong but silent gentle giant that he was, hadn't made a single inappropriate comment or overture all night, and (despite not knowing whether to be relieved or offended by that) I appreciated his chivalry. He'd been nothing but polite and courteous, and on the journey to The Freezer he'd actually expressed quite an interest in my job. Did he set my lust factor on gas mark eight? Mmm, nope, not even a gentle simmer. But hey, I'd been in two of London's top clubs for free, and was just about to visit another; I'd had a few obscenely expensive glasses of champagne and seen a geography teacher from Gillingham – it beat sitting at home running up my phone bill by making spontaneous, overpriced calls to vote for my favourites on *Strictly Come Dancing*.

The Freezer was an entirely different experience to the other clubs. Red lights pulsed, the music was intoxicating, and the atmosphere radiated sex from the black rubber floor to the two dozen onyx chandeliers that hung in a square formation above the main floor area. In the middle, a state-of-the-art lighting rig illuminated a dance floor that was about half full, mostly girls again, all deploying dance moves picked up during dedicated study at the Porno School of Rhythm and Movement. A bar stretched the full length of the wall opposite the entrance, but it was the action taking place against the other three walls that was responsible for my chin falling so low I could have played keepie up with my bottom teeth. Metal poles rose from black platforms, seven or eight of them along the wall and dangling from every pole was a female, completely naked, each one completely covered in a different colour of metallic body paint. Their bodies glistened against the lights as they turned, and flipped, and oh-my-God-I-couldn't-look – Miss Silver and Miss Gunmetal Grey were going to end up with friction burns on their Brazilians if they did that split descent thing again. I averted my eyes but no corner of the room was safe. Directly to my left was . . . eeeeeewwwww.

In contrast to all of the other perfectly smooth, hairless girls, if Miss Aluminium strayed too close to the light-bulbs she was in danger of starting a bush fire.

Again, judging by the smiles, the hugs and the countless handshakes from designer-clad clubbers, everyone seemed to know Gavin, and I basked in his reflected glory for about an hour as he chatted to one person after another. There was no disappearing act this time, just a steady stream of revellers who seemed anxious to say hi, most of them even having the decency to feign interest when Gavin introduced me. He might not be boyfriend material, but staying in touch and having the occasional night out with him would be a blast. Although Stu was loaded and Trish earned a really good salary, neither of them had ever been crazy clubbers, partly, I suspected, because they knew that on my marketing-assistant salary, a few cocktails and an entrance fee would swallow up a huge chunk of my weekly wage. However, so far this evening, Gavin hadn't had to put his hand in his pocket even once. There was a new private club in the West End that I regularly read about in *Hello!*, and I had a hunch that Gavin could be the passport to a free gawk at the kind of stars that demanded a huge Winnebago and charged ten million a movie.

It was after ten o'clock when we made it back to the car, my stomach pacified by four large glasses of champagne and a bellyful of celebrity spotting. Anyway, now that I was a close personal friend of Kate Moss (I was ninety per cent sure she'd been the stick-thin blonde standing next to me in the queue for the toilets at Caesar's) I no longer needed food. This was the new Leni, the one who lived on champagne and who intended to start smoking the minute she could lay her hands on a packet of Marlboro Lights.

'Are you having a good time?' Gavin asked as he clipped his seatbelt on.

318

'I am, thanks. This is the most fun I've had in ages. My mates and I have slipped down the path of Saturday-night DVDs and a takeaway so it's been a while since I was out on the town. Of course, it'll be even better when the ringing in my ears stops.'

For the first time I heard him laugh, and it was as high-pitched as his voice. I was getting a better handle now on why he'd opted for employment in the world of nightclubs: far more chance of career progression and success with the opposite sex if you spent every night in an environment that couldn't hear too much of those dulcet tones.

'Permission to blurt out something really naff?' I requested, figuring we were chummy enough now that I could drop the cool-and-collected act.

'Fire away,' he replied.

'I'm loving seeing all the famous people. I feel like I'm living in page two and three of *News of the World*.'

He was facing me now, his features slightly softened by the dim lighting and those four large glasses of champagne. Maybe I could find him attractive after . . . No! Bloody hell, I was turning into a lush. Next I'd be searching down those footballers and offering them a quickie in the toilets.

'Actually, you could return the favour.' It took me a moment to comprehend what he'd just said and work through the possible explanations until I reached a firm understanding of his meaning. Nope, no idea whatsoever. How could I return the favour? I didn't know anyone famous except Zara. Zara! Gavin didn't strike me as the obvious type, but maybe he was deeply spiritual and fancied having a personal reading. His methods were a bit strange, though – he could have saved himself the bother of trailing me around all night and just called the office for an appointment.

'Are you curious to know what's in store or is there someone on the other side that you want to contact?'

'The other side of what?'

'In the other world.'

'What, America?'

Shit, I hated these conversations. I was saying one thing, he was saying another, yet there was absolutely no connection between the two whatsoever.

'Let's start again,' I suggested. 'Why do you want to meet Zara?'

'I don't.'

How many glasses of champagne had I drunk? Had someone spiked them? Or had I somehow ingested the chemical mood enhancers that were very obviously floating around in the toilets of all three of the clubs we'd visited? That must be it – I was buzzed by osmosis.

'So how can I return the favour then? You did say that, didn't you? Or did I hallucinate the whole of the last five minutes.'

'Conn. I wouldn't mind hooking up with Conn,' he revealed.

The furrow of confusion on my brow was so deep I could have used it as a pencil holder. I was definitely stoned – or maybe this flash motor of his had a technical fault that was feeding emissions directly into the car, causing severe confusion and a departure from logical thought and comprehension.

'But why would you want to meet Conn? He's not famous.'

'Are you kidding me? He's legendary, man.'

I crossed my fingers that 'man' was a colloquialism as opposed to another confusion caused by the faulty exhaust fumes. Gavin slipped the gear-stick into drive, checked his side mirror, and we pulled out of the parking space and into the road.

'Legendary for what?'

I never got to hear the answer. A black car suddenly swerved straight in front us, perpendicular to the X5 and blocking our path. An identical one nudged our back bumper, trapping us in a black car sandwich. A third car, a silver one this time, screeched to a halt a few feet away from Gavin's door, and from each vehicle sprang at least a dozen black-clad Ninja warriors (actually, that might be a slight champagne exaggeration, but there were about a dozen blokes in total, they all seemed to be dressed in black, and in my head they were definitely of the Ninja variety), who proceeded to leap athletically around our car, two of them actually jumping over the bonnet in an action-hero-like manner.

'Out of the car, out of the car!' one of them screamed, his face contorted with rage, spittle spraying out of his mouth. I tried to comply, I really did, but my legs were temporarily refusing to receive signals from my brain.

The doors were wrenched open, and that's when I noticed the scariest development of all: every single one of the men was brandishing a handgun.

Fuck. Me. Dead.

My legs were suddenly getting their instructions directly from the cranial synapse labelled 'Shake Ferociously'.

Everything was happening like a Chinese gangster movie on fast-forward. One of the blokes wrenched Gavin out of the car, spun him around and slammed him against the back door, the other six pistols that were pointing at him encouraging him to keep his hands exactly as they were, above his head, palms clenched together.

'OUT, OUT, OUT!' screamed the large man now standing next to me.

I spun my body around, put my feet out of the door and threw the rest of me out after them, hoping my legs would at some point remember their anatomical purpose and support my body weight.

They did. Just.

Seconds later my cheek was hugging the glass of the back passenger window, and my new friend, otherwise known as 'Big Scary Man with Gun', was frisking me from head to toe.

This was definitely a hallucination. It had to be. Or a bad dream. I was actually sitting at home with Mrs Naismith watching telly and I'd nodded off and slipped into the nightmare from hell, one that a large crowd of bystanders were now forming around, all of them craning to witness the action and filming the unfolding drama on their mobile phones.

Presumably satisfied that I wasn't carrying Trish's Uzi, Big Scary Man with Gun pulled my arms down behind my back and snapped on some kind of plastic wire stuff before pulling me around to the bonnet of the car. Any minute now, I'd wake up and there would be Mrs Naismith waving a cup of tea and a ginger slice under my nose. Either that or the terror would cause a fatal heart attack and Big Scary Man with Gun would have to write up a brown paper tag and tie it around my big toe.

From my new vantage point in hell, I had full view of Gavin again, his hands also restrained, but it was his face that was the biggest shock. I expected fear, confusion and bewilderment, but all I saw were arrogance, hatred and fury, emotions that changed his whole persona from lovable large teddy bear to 'intimidation with menace'.

'Guv, got it here,' came a voice from inside the body of the car. A curly-haired guy in jeans and a black padded jacket emerged and walked towards me. Behind him, Gavin turned his head away, no interest in seeing what had been found. Curly held up Exhibit A for the men with the guns, Gavin's leather satchel, then tipped it upside down, resulting in a pile of small foil parcels forming on the bonnet. Bloody hell! Where the fuck was Mrs Naismith with that ginger slice?

A hold-all from the boot was next, opened to reveal dozens of freezer bags full of pills and about a hundred more small clear bags of what looked like high-grade oregano. I was, however, fairly sure that my guess was wrong, and we wouldn't be seeing that stuff on a deep-pan Hawaiian any time soon.

'Mrs Naismith!!!!!'

No use, I just couldn't snap out of the dream. Big Scary Man with Gun pulled me by the arm, guided me around to the car that was sitting parallel to the X5, and, pushing my head down so that I wouldn't bump it on the doorframe, shoved me into the back seat. The good news? I was out of view of the massive crowd that had now gathered on the pavement. The bad news? It gave me a perfect view of the other stuff that the men were fishing out of Gavin's car. My whole body jumped on the tremble bandwagon as they pulled item after item out of the X5. One crow bar: metal, two foot long. One machete: metal, eighteen inches long, unsheathed. One small dagger: ten inches long, extracted from glove compartment. But the biggest prize came from under Gavin's seat. One gun, large, no idea what kind.

I swear if they'd found Starsky and Hutch in the boot I wouldn't have been any more shocked.

As my car pulled away, I watched them bundle Gavin into one of the other vehicles and tried to catch his eye. No use, he didn't glance in my direction even once.

The rest of the night passed in a surreal daze, until ten long, exhausting and, quite frankly, terrifying hours later, when I once again dialled Stu's number.

He answered with a groggy voice.

'Stu, did you die in the night after all?'

'Not as far as I know,' he slurred. 'But I did exceed the recommended dose of cough medicine, so I can't be sure. Conked out on the couch and . . . shit, why aren't you here? Are you okay? Are you outside? Was I so out of it that I didn't answer the door? Oh crap, Leni, sorry, I'll come right . . . '

'No, it's okay, I'm not outside,' I said, relieved that the shock had snapped him out of his drowsiness and he seemed to have recovered full use of his faculties. 'But I do need you to come and get me, though.'

'Sure, where are you? At home?'

'Er, no . . . '

'So where are you?'

'Jail.'

PROGRESS SUMMARY: *IT'S IN THE STARS* DATING PROJECT

CONCLUDED		
LEO	Harry Henshall	Morbid fascination for simulated violence
SCORPIO	Matt Warden	Lead singer, lying arse
ARIES	Daniel Jones	Unlikely to forge career as an assertiveness coach
CAPRICORN	Craig Cunningham	Relationship therapist, incites violent urges
GEMINI	Jon Belmont	Definite potential – secret plans to see again
PISCES	Nurse Dave Canning	Avoid all future dealings with the NHS
AQUARIUS	Colin Bilson-Smythe	Lawyer, laughs like a food-mixer
CANCER	Gregory Smith	Shy, sweet man's man – in all respects
LIBRA	Ben Mathers	Do you want to see me cry?
VIRGO	Kurt Cobb/Cabana	Rising star in need of good stylist
SAGITTARIUS	Gavin West	Honest, guv, I've never seen that bag before in my life

EMAIL
To: Trisha; Stu
From: Leni Lomond
Re: If last night's date had a personal ad, it would read like . . .

Butch, square-jawed, man-bag-wearing metrosexual, big on the London club scene, would like to meet female with law degree and a minimum of ten years' courtroom experience in the defence of drug-dealers. Please apply/post bail to Gavin West, small square cell, c/o the Metropolitan Police before my hearing on Monday morning.

31

Star Maker

'Noooooooo,' Trish gasped, then popped another olive in her mouth. 'So then what happened?'

'Don't talk with that in your mouth, you could choke,' Stu nagged, miraculously recovered from his sore throat from the night before and participating in the most bizarre Sunday-morning conversation we'd ever had.

'Stu, I know that you say these things from a place of love, but I swear to God, if you warn me about my immin-ent death one more time, you may never live to imagine another life-threatening illness again. Anyway, go on, Leni – you were a bad haircut away from *Prisoner Cell Block H*, and then what happened?'

I rearranged my cushion, desperately trying to get comfortable on Stu's wildly expensive, ivory leather, angular sofa, an experience that was surprisingly reminiscent of the concrete bed I'd been lying on for the last few hours.

Stu lived in a beautiful Georgian two-bedroom mews in Notting Hill, about a five-minute walk from the salon and twenty minutes from my office. The lounge, kitchen and dining area were open-plan, light, and the epitome of under-stated class: solid oak floorboards (more hygienic, reduces dust, better for allergies and air purity), white walls (nontoxic paint), and pure wool, natural rugs (no chemicals used in the dyeing process).

'I told them everything I knew about Gavin, showed them the application form that he had sent in to be one of the dates and a pay-slip to prove I worked for Zara. They banged me back up in a cell for another few hours . . . '

'Oooh, would you listen to her? One overnight in jail and she's already picked up the lingo.'

I ignored the heckling from Trish's corner because I had a sneaking suspicion that she was just a little jealous that for once I'd managed to be the most exciting out of all of us.

' . . . until they'd gone through all their surveillance tapes and double-checked that Gavin had never been seen with me before. Turns out the police had been tracking him for weeks because he's one of the most prolific drug-dealers in the city. He only deals directly with a few of the long-standing clubs that are run by friends, but he has hundreds of pushers working for him and has a crime sheet like *War and Peace* – the detective's analogy, not mine. Assault, drugs, theft, and even an attempted murder. Apparently that one was when he was dealing steroids.'

'The voice! You said he had a really weird voice! Classic "roid user",' my medical consultant interjected.

I nodded mournfully. 'Yep, and the spots. The cop said I should have noticed it straight away. I informed him that since the only drug I've ever used is Nurofen for period pain, it was hardly surprising that I wasn't up on my "How To Spot a Drug User" info.'

'What did he say?'

'Nothing. As soon as I mentioned periods he went bright red and moved swiftly on to grilling me on everyone we'd met throughout the night.'

'I went out with a body builder who used steroids once, had a willy the size of my thumb.'

'Thank you for that highly valuable input,' Stu dead-panned, ignoring the fact that Trish was giving him a thumbs-up sign, 'but what I don't get is this – why did Gavin write in to Zara? I mean, surely a drug-dealer would want to keep a low profile? Why would he even dream about setting himself up on a blind date?'

I sighed wearily and took another sip of the cappuccino that Stu had lovingly prepared using the Dolce Gusto machine that I'd bought him for his birthday.

'That's the most depressing bit. If there could be a more depressing bit than going on a date with a potentially murderous drug-dealer, being ambushed by a SWAT team in a crowded city-centre street and being accused of being said drug-dealer's right-hand henchwoman.'

'It definitely wasn't one of your better nights,' Trish concurred.

'Both of you need to swear on my life that you won't repeat this next bit.'

They both crossed their hearts and made something approaching a pledge of allegiance. I decided to overlook that Trish's fingers were crossed the whole time.

'One of the nice policemen was talking to me while they arranged my release and he told me that their theory is that he saw it as a way of getting close to Conn. Apparently, rumour has it that Conn's group spend thousands on cocaine every night, and Gavin has been looking to get into their circle for months, but with no success.'

'That's nuts!' Stu explained. 'I mean, what are the odds of him even getting picked?'

'Three thousand, four hundred and thirty-two to one,' I said, my voice wallowing perilously close to depression, 'which means I had a three thousand, four hundred and thirty-two to one chance of getting landed with a career criminal, and yet it still happened. How crap is my luck?'

'Fairly shite,' Trish agreed. 'Fuck, so Conn's a druggie too?'

'Not necessarily,' I argued. 'The policeman just said that some of his group used drugs, and that was the only theory they could come up with to explain Gavin's behaviour. I don't think they gave much credibility to the possibility that maybe he was just trying to find a soul mate he could settle down with and live a life of crack-supplying bliss. And Gavin did mention that he wanted to meet Conn, so that does makes sense, if anything makes sense in this fucked-up saga that's become my life.'

I checked my watch. 9.30 a.m. 'Is it too early to drink?' I asked.

'Absolutely not,' Stu answered, nipping to the kitchen section and returning with three glasses of wine.

'Have you thought about how you are going to broach this with Conn?'

A ringing noise cut into our conversation and I answered the question while I searched my bag for my mobile.

'Dunno. The police were going to see him this morning so I'll cross that bridge when I come to it. Hello?'

Trish and Stu sat patiently until I clicked the phone shut again.

'Who was that?'

'Er . . . the bridge. He says he's heard what's happened and he and Zara are devastated on my behalf. I've to take tomorrow morning off . . . '

'That is *so* kind! Just think, if you'd got arrested for murder or been found bludgeoned to death in an alley, they might have given you the whole day off,' Stu raged.

' . . . and then he's going to pick me up himself at lunchtime and give me a lift to the office.'

'Well, I hope for your sake the police are wrong about Conn,' Trish murmured ominously.

'Why?'

'Because getting busted with a major drugs player once in a week is unlucky, but twice? Now that's just careless.'

✳

'Bread roll?' the waiter asked, brandishing a trendy steel square with a pyramid of hot, perfectly symmetrical, identical balls of baked dough.

'No thanks,' I replied, my face the same colour as his beetroot jacket. I pushed my hair out of my face for the fortieth time in the last five minutes. I knew I should have washed it this morning, but I thought I was going into the office for a few hours and then home for an early night. Instead . . .

'Taxi for Lomond,' Conn had announced in a chipper voice when he'd called to say he'd arrived. 'I'm sitting outside.'

'I'll be right down,' I'd replied, with just a tremor of uncertainty in my voice. At least, it might have been certainty, but I was prepared to concede that it could also have been the result of the worst hangover in the history of mankind. There were whole tribes in the southern boondocks who feasted day and night on moonshine and who, collectively, couldn't even begin to match the magnitude of my aching head and bones.

Who the hell had decided it would be a good idea to start drinking at nine thirty in the morning? By the time Grey had come to collect Trish and me, our entire blood supply had been replaced by red wine. When I'd woken up this morning the pain was so sharp that my first thought was that the ceiling had fallen on my head in the night. Then I realised that my neck hurt, my back hurt (damn Stu's couch!), even my eyebrows hurt.

One large coffee, two large painkillers and the biggest pair of specs I could find later, I was responding to Conn's breezy announcement. It was only while I was concentrating on not breathing on him, lest the fumes cause asphyxiation and loss of coordination leading to a five-car pileup, that he'd revealed he was taking me to lunch. A pizza joint I might just about have managed. The local pub would have been almost bearable. A posh restaurant on the thirty-fourth floor of a five-star hotel, complete with floor-to-ceiling windows and a panoramic view of all SW postcodes, was proving more of a challenge, especially since we'd been given a table right at the window and every time I looked down the world swam beneath me.

'Are you okay?' asked Diet Coke guy/druggie (depending on who you listened to). I nodded and tried for a smile, which probably came off as more of a crazed grimace. Conn made me tongue-tied at the best of times, but today the combination of his presence, nerves, and a jaw that wouldn't work had rendered me pretty much mute. He poured some wine into the glass in front of me and I responded in an appropriate manner: by trying not to hurl on the white damask table cover. Why? Why had he brought me here? What was going on? And did the very glamorous middle-aged woman at the next table have to keep running her eyes up and down my jeans and battered Uggs with quite such an expression of disdain? I wanted to scream 'I didn't know I was coming here, okay?!!!' at her, but I decided that I'd had enough drama in the last couple of days without asking for more.

'I can't believe what you have been through,' Conn said, his voice oozing sympathy and concern. In direct contrast to my appearance, he was looking particularly fine today in a deep grey suit that contrasted beautifully with his white shirt and pale silver tie. His jet hair was swept back, and as he spoke his brilliant white teeth danced against that perfect mouth. I congratulated myself on coming up with such a poetic description despite having killed off most of my brain cells by drowning them in red wine.

'Do you want to talk about it?' he continued.

I shook my head.

'Look, it might help. The police told me you were pretty shaken up, and Zara and I feel terrible that this happened as a result of your job. I hope you know that we would never, ever ask you to do anything that we thought might endanger you.'

I had a sudden flashback to when Conn had spotted Gavin's application letter and his eyes had definitely registered recognition. So how would he explain that, huh?

'The strange thing is,' he said nonchalantly, while buttering his multi-grain roll, 'I was sure I recognised him when I first saw that application . . . '

Holy shit! Did he have the same psychic powers as his mother?

Think nice things; think nice, fully clothed things.

' . . . and now I know why – I'd obviously seen him out and about in the clubs. Apparently, we frequent many of the same places.'

I nodded again, trying not to look down in case my eyes were drawn to the crowded pavements that were still swirling below me. However, eating gazpacho soup without watching where I was putting the spoon was a direct route to mortifying stains on my white T-shirt.

'Leni, I want to reassure you that I have never, ever met that man before.'

Aw, bless, he was so sweet when he was being earnest that I almost felt sorry for him, but then I decided that since he was the drop-dead handsome millionaire in the five-thousand-pound suit who'd travelled here today courtesy of Ferrari, I'd save my sympathy for someone who needed it far more: me.

I still couldn't get the police's theory out of my head. Whatever Conn did in his spare time was up to him, but if it was indeed his drug use that had landed me on a concrete bed in a nine-by-six cell, then he'd join hangovers and marines called Ben at the bottom of my popularity scale.

'I was devastated when the police said that they thought he might be using you as a way of establishing contact with me so that he could sell me drugs . . . '

Shit, how did he do that? Was my mind bugged?

'But I promise you, Leni, that was way off the mark. Drugs just aren't my thing. I mean, do I look like the kind of guy who sticks his money up his nostrils?'

How would I know? What did I know about anything? At the moment I was having trouble distinguishing between left and right. What was my name again? Make. This. Be. Over. Please.

'It's the same old story . . . '

It is?

'I'm the first to admit that I like to enjoy myself after hours, and yes, some of my friends are wealthy. I guess that makes us targets for anyone looking to make some cash from us. But he was wrong, Leni, and I hope you believe that.'

I nodded again, fully aware that I had morphed into one of those plastic dogs that sit on the parcel shelves of cars driven by old people.

'I do.'

I absolutely believed him. But then, right at that exhausted, pained, *desperate to be out of there* moment, I would have believed him if he'd told me he'd won the lottery, run for prime minister, or dressed as a woman while in the privacy of his own home.

334

An impeccably clad waiter removed our first courses, mine barely touched, Conn's asparagus-salad plate empty. I was handling this. I was. I could do it. I held my water glass up to my mouth as a decoy so he wouldn't notice my huge intake of breath.

'You know, I realised on my way to collect you that you've been working for us for months now and I hardly know anything about you. So tell me . . . tell me something I should know about you.'

Oh, he was good! His eyes were fixed on mine, his expression adorable, his body language open – my Diet Coke man was working his thing. And yes, in my head, that last bit was said in the voice of Tyra Banks. I really needed to lie down.

Two things happened at once. I took another deep breath at exactly the same moment as the waiter reappeared and slid a huge, complete lobster into the middle of the table. The sight, the smell, those two little eyes looking right up at me – I wasn't sure who was worse off, me or the lobster.

'Just one thing, anything at all,' he repeated.

'I think I need to go home,' I whispered. 'Right now.'

⁕

Back at my flat, he insisted on walking me up to the door. My foot had barely hit the top step when Mrs Naismith was outside. 'You okay, love?' she asked, and it's probably fair to say that Conn had never been scrutinised quite so intently. It was only when she finally switched her gaze to me that she realised I most definitely wasn't okay.

'Conn, this is Mrs Naismith,' I whispered. 'Mrs Naismith, Conn.'

'Pleased to meet you, Conned.'

To his credit, he didn't correct her.

'Come on, love, let's get you inside. You look ghastly, you really do.'

'Thanks, Mrs Naismith, but honestly, it's okay,' I stuttered slowly, words difficult now that my brain seemed to have totally disconnected. 'I can manage. I'm absolutely fi—'

And that's when everything went black.

Great Morning TV!

Goldie Gilmartin radiated her usual morning sunshine as she cut to the commercial break.

'Coming up, we have the couple who have had twenty-three children yet are still trying for more; and our beauty expert Liz Dresden will be demonstrating, live on air, what's involved in that male beauty treatment known as a back, sack and crack wax. Gents, you might want to close your eyes during that one. And, of course, it's Friday, so Zara Delta will be here with your forecast for the weekend. Back in three.'

Straight after Goldie's wink to camera, the director shouted cut, and the studio erupted into that familiar flurry of activity.

'Where the hell is Zara?' Goldie yelled.

'She's still in make-up – she didn't like the way they'd done her hair,' a young terrified girl clutching the requisite TV clipboard replied.

Goldie groaned with fury. 'That poor man over there . . .' she pointed to a male model who was standing just off set with only a towel preserving the dignity that was about to be stripped from him in front of the entire British viewing public, 'is about to have hairs pulled from his scrotum, and yet he still managed to bloody show up on time!'

'Thirty seconds,' someone wearing headphones shouted. There was a commotion at the entrance to the set and Zara strutted in and over to the sofa, the stomp of her flip-flops making it obvious that she wasn't overflowing with sweetness and joy.

'Good of you to join us,' Goldie spat, all pretence of civility gone now.

'Had to – you need all the help you can get, and it certainly won't come from Mystic Meg or Russell Grant,' Zara replied with equal venom.

One glove. Two gloves. Both off. The thirty or so people in the studio looked around frantically, as if they'd be able to spot on sight who had leaked the news of Goldie's demand that Zara be replaced. The set literally crackled with tension as the two women eyed each other with undisguised hatred.

Five seconds! Three, two, one . . . ' He pointed at Goldie and then backed away.

'Welcome back, and look who I've got here with me, the gorgeous Zara Delta!'

The camera panned to Zara, her smile beaming, presumably in the hope that if she blinded the audience with her dental brilliance they wouldn't notice what was going on at the top of her head. The premise had been great: twenty or so sections of her hair curled in individual spirals, each of them secured with a star-shaped diamanté clasp. Unfortunately, it had been a cosmic hairdo too far for the relatively new stylist back-stage, and instead of looking stellar, Zara bore more of a resemblance to a Sputnik.

'Loving the hair, Zara, loving the hair,' added Goldie, with just a hint of amusement.

The Sputnik's smile shrank to a very thin, strained line, but to her credit she recovered quickly, launching straight into her run-down of weekend predictions for each sign of the zodiac.

It was only at the end that the tension resurfaced. As soon as Zara had wound up Aries, Goldie moved in.

338

'Great, Zara, thank you, and let's hope those wild antics that you promised for us Taureans come true.'

'I'm sure that in your case they will, Goldie,' Zara replied, her voice all sweetness, her expression one of undisguised fury, 'just as long as you remember that the key to those antics is to make sure that you socialise in groups. Which I know you like to do, Goldie.'

It was immediately clear who knew about Goldie's nocturnal activities and who didn't. Those who were blissfully unaware were smiling along at this bantering interchange between the sofa queens, absolutely oblivious to the bitchy undertones and innuendo. Those who were in on the gossip had the wide-eyed, terrified expressions of doom.

'Thank you, Zara, and . . . '

Zara cut her right off. 'Yes, I know what you're going to say, Goldie, and indeed we are still looking for lucky candidates to take part in our extensive study of relationships and dating. We'll be sharing the sensational results in my new dating book It's in the Stars, and I can promise you it's going to be sensational!'

Up in the gallery the producer was doing his best to shield the audience from Goldie's very obvious irritation by shouting 'Stay with Zara, stay with Zara!'

Zara was face on to camera now, knowing full well that as long as she had the audience engaged and was in full flow, they wouldn't dare cut away from her.

'We're looking for all you fabulous Sagittarians out there, so gents, get in contact now by logging on to www.itsinthe-stars.net. Oh, and ladies, if you're single and desperate for love like our Goldie, you can place your order now and be one of the first lucky singles to find your soul mate in the stars. Log on to www.itsinthestars.net for full details.'

At the next commercial break Zara stomped straight out, leaving Goldie to vent her rage to an empty chair. For weeks, the television world would be buzzing with stories about the morning TV slot that was so dramatic, the sight of a grown man having hot wax spread on his testicles wasn't the most astonishing aspect of the show.

32

The Powers of Uranus

'Why? Why would she say that we're still open to applications when she knows that the last date is tomorrow night and that we've already picked the candidate?'

I experienced a little flip of nervousness as I finished that sentence. Occasionally, I fretted over what Zara would say if she ever found out that a couple of the dates were a little more manufactured than the others. Technically speaking, I hadn't done anything wrong: by the end of tomorrow night I would have gone on twelve dates with twelve different men, one from each of the signs of the zodiac. I'd also filed all the correct paperwork, been conscientious in my reports and only skipped bits if they involved genital interaction. And let's face it, the only reason she made public appeals for candidates was for the publicity. Suddenly I got it: she was still using the appeal to plug the book.

'She's lying from the *Great Morning TV!* sofa! That's like swearing in church!' I exclaimed. 'Trish, are you listening to me?'

'Ssshhhhh, they're just about to wax his crack – have some respect!'

Trish was sitting at her desk, feet crossed on top of a pile of paperwork, hands behind her head, every iota of her being focused on the monitor in front of her as she watched the show.

'Leni!!!!!' the voice roared from the corridor.

I poked my head out the door to see Zara thundering towards me, obviously not skipping with joy.

'Yes?' I enquired sweetly.

'Make your own way back to the office. I've got a meeting in Kensington and I probably won't make it back to the office afterwards.'

The stories about Stephen Knight's Viagra consumption must be true, I thought.

'Are you contactable if I need you?' I couldn't resist asking.

'Leni, just for once, would it be too much to ask that you deal with things on your own?' With that, she stropped off down the corridor, through the swing doors and out of sight. I just hoped that she did something with that hair before turning up for her hot afternoon of wanton lust, or she might find that her 'meeting' failed to rise to the occasion.

I absolutely understood now why her last assistant had bailed out with a boy-band member and never returned. Zara gave this illusion of inner peace and spirituality, she embraced meditation and karmic Zen, she preached love for all living things and espoused the need for the people of the world to act as one, both in this life and in the after-life (the one to which she had a direct line of communication). But the truth? She'd sell her granny for publicity, a hefty bank balance and an afternoon of jungle sex with anyone with a higher profile than hers.

'My heart is bleeding for that poor bloke,' Trish announced as the slot ended and Goldie cut to commercials again.

'Fabulous,' I muttered, 'I contracted a life-threatening virus and you barely showed an interest, yet you come over all sympathetic when a nude male is involved.'

'Have you seen him?' she replied. 'He could rob a bank, steal a pack of puppies and tell me he'd shagged my husband and I'd still feel sorry for him. He's fucking gorgeous.'

She did have a point. He looked like that Smith bloke from *Sex and the City*, before he lost all credibility by doing those Aero adverts.

'Anyway, you were getting quite enough sympathy from a certain employer who took staff perks to a whole new level.'

My grin was irrepressible because she was absolutely right. This was my first day back at work, and I'd only chosen to come back on a Friday because I knew it'd be an easy studio day. From moments after I'd fainted outside my front door, until approximately three hours ago, I'd been lying in my bed, and for a large part of that time I'd been pampered by a certain Conn Delta. Turned out my hangover was actually a horrible virus with flu-like symptoms that was sweeping the country and sending a large portion of the population under the duvet.

Trish had visited me a couple of times, bringing supplies of magazines and Lucozade. Stu had popped in daily. At least, I think it was Stu. It was difficult to tell under the bio-suit, the facemask and the latex gloves. And Mrs Naismith was my resident Florence Nightingale, right up until Wednesday night when she contracted it too and we had her bed pushed into my living room so that we could mutually take care of each other.

The man pushing the bed? Conn. It was amazing how much things could change in just a few days, how well you could get to know someone in such a short space of time. He had been truly amazing, calling in twice a day, never without something to make me smile. There was the Jo Malone body cream ('Fucking hell, do you know how much that stuff costs? He definitely wants into your knickers' – quote, unquote from Trish), the Belgian chocolates, the baskets of fruit, the beautiful orchids. He even brought Mrs Naismith a thirty-two-movie box set featuring the best action films ever made.

The awkwardness, the nervousness and the tongue-tied clumsiness that had been my standard behaviour patterns in his presence seemed to dissipate after the first day or so, when he'd seen me at my absolute worst and was still breathtakingly sweet and thoughtful.

'He's got a thing for you, you know,' Mrs Naismith would leer the minute he left after each visit. For the first couple of days I was so ill I could barely comprehend what she was saying, but by Wednesday afternoon my powers of sense were returning and I'd occasionally wonder if she had a point, before immediately dismissing the thought as ridiculous. He was the Diet Coke guy! He didn't do ordinary, he didn't do mediocre, and he definitely didn't do average-looking PAs who smelled like a landfill site because they hadn't showered in three days. It was indisputable that his actions were way above and beyond that of normal employment legislation, but I'd convinced myself that his generosity was just born of a combination of sympathy and inherent niceness. I had absolutely no idea who his dad was, but he must be a sweet guy because Conn certainly didn't get those qualities from his mother. Sometimes I despaired of my judgement skills. I couldn't believe I'd even considered for a second that he could be some debauched druggie.

'How're you feeling now anyway?' Trish brought me back to the present.

'Stop pretending you care,' I bit back with mock petulance.

'You're right, I don't,' she shrugged, leaving me to sulk

for a few seconds before she leapt out of her chair, leapfrogged her desk and fell on me in a huge hug.

'Of course I care! I care! Underneath this cold exterior is the reincarnation of Mother Teresa and, as God is my witness, I care.'

'You need help,' I told her calmly, trying desperately not to laugh.

'I know.' She removed herself from my knee and rearranged her dishevelled stunt clothes. 'It's getting up at four a.m. for the last five years – I think it's challenging my mental health. So, anyway, you never answered my question. How're you feeling now?'

'Much better. Still feel a bit giddy sometimes, but apart from that it's just the really sore head. As long as no one shouts, though, it's just about bearable.'

The last syllable was barely out of my mouth when the door swung open violently and a livid Goldie Gilmartin was framed in the doorway.

'TRISH, IS THERE ANYTHING YOU WOULDN'T DO FOR ME?' she yelled.

Trish grinned, then flicked on her solemn face, clasped her hands in front of her as if in prayer, and performed a deep bow.

'Of course not, your highness, you know my sole purpose in life is to serve you.'

'Then put some fucking arsenic in that tart Zara Delta's fucking Danish next week.'

With that, she slammed the door shut, leaving Trish and me open-mouthed but amused. Zara, Trish, Goldie . . . what was it with women in TV? They all sounded like Billy fucking Connolly after a profanity course.

'You know, I might just do that, for your sake as well as Goldie's,' Trish mused.

'How would killing Zara be for my sake?'

'Just a hunch . . . I'd hate you to have a mother-in-law that you didn't like.'

✳

She was being ridiculous. She was. Absurd. Crazy. There was no way Conn would be interested in me. Was I interested in him? Not in that way! Definitely not! But maybe I could. Could I?

Variations on the above ran through my mind all the way back to the office. I made the journey by taxi, the one we had a standard booking for every Friday. Zara would kick herself when she realised that her lowly PA had enjoyed the luxury of a fifty-quid car ride to Notting Hill instead of behaving according to her status and taking the tube. Hey ho. I was still recovering, I'd come back to work even though I still wasn't a hundred per cent, and I was still bearing a very slight grudge over the whole drug-dealing arrest debacle the week before, so the new militant me decided I deserved it.

'Hey, you're back,' Millie screeched the minute I walked in the door. 'We missed you so much!'

I gave her a huge hug, careful to breathe in the opposite direction so that I wouldn't infect her with the remnants of my plague.

'I missed you too! You're looking great!'

Today she was veering more towards her Morticia look in a purple velvet Goth jacket that was nipped in at the waist, with a high-standing collar and long sleeves that flared out from the elbow downwards. The skirt was of the same fabric, a calf-length sheath that clung to her silhouette. I hoped there was a split at the back because otherwise she'd be limited to steps of less than two inches.

'Who's in?' I asked her, reluctant to mention Conn's name in particular.

'Just Conn.'

Yes!!!! Thankfully, that triumphant exultation was just in my head.

'Leni, I have an absolutely massive favour to ask,' Millie blurted. 'I know Zara's not coming in today, so is there any possibility – just say no if you don't want to – that you would perhaps look after the desk for me this afternoon and let me knock off early? It's just I've got a . . . thing . . . I've got a thing on tonight and I'd really like to go get all my bits done. Please, please, please, and I'll owe you anything you want!'

'A "thing"?' I asked, eyebrow cocked.

'New man, long story. I'll tell you about it on Monday, but if I go now I'll be on time for the appointment at the salon that I made in the hope that you'd be pal of the year and help me out.'

'Glad you didn't resort to emotional blackmail there,' I laughed. 'On you go, it's not a problem, I promise. It's the least I can do for all the help you gave me with the dates.'

She kissed my cheek, grabbed her bag and teetered out the door. I nipped into her little cubby-hole behind reception and flicked on the kettle. The room was only about four feet by ten, and it housed a couple of filing cabinets, a small photocopier, a few paper trays, a fax machine, and all the accoutrements required in the tea-making process. While the kettle boiled, I nipped back out to reception and used Millie's computer to log on to my emails. One from Jon, just checking our arrangements for Sunday. Two o'clock at the Farmer's Arms, a quaint little village pub on the outskirts of Windsor.

My reply was brief. '*Looking forward to it. Hope you're having a great day and not getting your NASDAQs in a twist.*'

I made a mental note to ask him what a NASDAQ actually was as we lingered over our roast beef and Yorkshire puds.

I'd just pressed 'SEND' when Conn popped down the stairs with some mail.

'Hey, gorgeous, how're you? You look much better!'

You think? Must be the hour of hair straightening and full but subtle face-paint application that I'd persuaded the make-up girls at *Great Morning TV!* to provide before I'd left there this morning.

'Thanks, Conn. And I don't just mean for the compliment, although that was really nice, but for everything you've done this week. It was all very kind of you. Although Mrs Naismith is showing aggressive tendencies after watching nothing but brutal action movies for the last two days.'

Okay, okay, that was passable. A touch on the rambling side, but he was laughing so he must have been amused.

'So what's planned for the weekend then?'

'Nothing much,' I answered, and then quickly realised I was talking drivel. 'Apart from the final date tomorrow night. Oh, and lunch on Sunday, with a . . . friend.'

'A boyfriend?'

'That's right – you saw how they were all lining up outside my flat last week. Okay, one boyfriend at a time please, leave the grapes by the side of the bed and don't take any more than five minutes because there are another ten blokes at your back.'

To my eternal mortification, I did the whole of that last bit in the voice of a crazed ticket inspector. I could barely look at him.

'That's a shame, because I was going to ask you if you'd like to have lunch with me on Sunday.'

He was? Crap! How un-bloody-believable was this? For the last two years I'd been an unintentional world leader in the field of Nice Man Avoidance, and now I had two, count them, bloody TWO, wanting to take me out to lunch on Sunday.

'Maybe next week?' he added, a definite tone of hope in his voice.

'Next week would be great.' I stopped at that, determined to come out with at least one sentence that was witter-free.

He took the stairs two at a time and I tried really hard not to watch the muscles in his legs and bum flex and contract, flex and contract, flex and con— I needed a cup of tea to settle the giddiness.

Back in the cubby-hole, I treated myself to an extra sugar, then stirred and tossed the used teabag in the bin, an action that somehow unleashed chaos. I spun back round too quickly, spilt some of the tea, burnt my hand, jumped with pain, and knocked over a four-tier-high stack of paper trays, which nudged a large pile of mail and the whole lot toppled to the floor.

Bugger. How did Millie operate in this room? If Zara pissed me off even once next week I was calling Health and Safety and tipping them off about the cubby-hole.

Leaving the tea safely out of reach, I scooped up the trays and contents and shoved them back on the shelf in something approximating their original order, then I bent again to collect the mail, all still sealed except a large brown envelope, the contents of which had scattered from one side of the room to the other. It was only when I'd gathered about half of them that I realised what they were. Each sheet was headed with a different star sign: Aries, Cancer, Pisces, etc., followed by a date of birth, but it was what came below the heading that captured my attention.

Despite working for one of the country's leading astrologers (apologies to Russell Grant and Mystic Meg), I'd never managed to muster a crumb of interest in the powers of the stars. Call it cynicism, call it lethargy, or maybe it was just a lack of understanding as to how I could read the forecast for my star sign in several different newspapers and they'd all predict completely conflicting events.

But what I was reading now completely changed my mind.

The one at the top of the pile had 'Cancer' followed by Gregory's birthday as a heading, and went on to sum up his personality so perfectly it was like I'd written it myself. Sure, I'd sent in a report to Zara, but that only contained a shred of what was in here and there were so many defining characteristics that she could never have known about. The interest in sport, the love of simple pleasures and the reticence to discuss personal issues and emotions she could have got from the information I'd provided. But how had she known about the attachment to his mum; the reluctance to hurt the feelings of others; and the emotional depths that could often be confused with shyness or rudeness? I hadn't covered any of that in my feedback.

The text went on to elaborate on the subject's likes and dislikes, strengths and weaknesses, areas of improvement (wardrobe, current trends, independence) and then followed a chapter on their ideal date. The sports stuff I would have expected was in there, but so were four other suggestions (Sunday Lunch: a local, unpretentious pub; Last-minute Date: dropping in to visit family; the Romantic Date: an evening walk at the beach; and the Dreaded Date: PR launch or dinner at a fine-dining restaurant).

Even though I'd only known Gregory for a few hours, I knew that this profile was absolutely accurate. On I read, every line resonating, every recommendation ringing true, and every warning sign pitched absolutely perfectly.

I doubted if even Glenda could have summed up her boy this well. I took what was left of my tea back through to reception and studied the others. Aries – Daniel: an unbelievably accurate portrait of a self-conscious single guy who would do anything to please. Capricorn – Craig: astoundingly true, down to his strongest characteristics: smugness, smugness and more smugness. Scorpio – Matt: the lying git who would sell his soul for a shot at stardom. Virgo – Kurt: the desperate wannabe, who would, according to the predictions here, eventually make it. I stumbled a little over Jon, the Gemini, but only because I thought, using my limited-to-non-existent astrological knowledge base, that Zara had strayed from the truth and reverted in some areas to stereotypical traits for that star sign.

Like all great productions, it was the finale that assured me of its brilliance. The final sheet was headed 'Taurus' – 19 May. Stu's birthday. The same Stu who would be my date *the following night*. Zara wasn't just analysing the past, she was predicting the future.

A shiver ran from the base of my spine to the top, where it pushed up the hairs on the back of my neck. How could she know? How could she know so much about someone she'd never met, never studied, never dated? This was the *Encyclopaedia of Stu*, everything about him described in glorious Technicolor right down to every last fear and phobia. My opinion of Zara changed in a thudding heartbeat. If it was true that there was a thin line between genius and insanity, then she was on a space-hopper and bouncing back and forth across it. Suddenly, her eccentricities, her idiosyncrasies, and yes, even her dark side diminished beside these fifty or so pages of astounding talent. I'd completely misjudged her as a deluded, flaky fluke, but here was incontrovertible confirmation that she was a freaking genius.

It was also confirmation, not that I needed it, that I was off doing my HNC in Crap Boyfriends and Questionable Choices on the day that God was giving out adequate people-judgement skills.

The taste of freezing cold tea signalled the passing of

time and I realised that two hours had gone by already. It was 3.30 p.m. My internal phone buzzed. 'Hey you,' Conn's voice was smooth as a Galaxy Ripple that had been left next to a radiator. 'I'm going to head off in ten minutes, so is it okay with you to knock off early so that I can lock up?'

'Mmmm, let me see – finish work an hour and a half early on a Friday? I think I could just about manage that.'

As I hung up, my eyes fell on the pile in front of me. Crap, I hadn't processed the rest of the incoming post yet. I bolted the storm doors, grabbed all the mail and ran up the stairs, trying to mimic Conn by taking two at a time, changing my mind after four strides had almost snapped my hamstrings.

I left the mail on my very talented boss's desk, figuring at least that way she'd find it if she popped in – as she occasionally did – over the weekend. It was the lesser of two evils. Would she freak at having to use her two-hundred-pound, silk compound false nails to open it herself? Absolutely. Would she freak even more if she wanted to check what had arrived and couldn't find the post pile? Definitely. With any luck she wouldn't come in this weekend and I'd get it all opened and sorted first thing on Monday morning. With no luck, she'd launch into a tirade and Conn would come to my defence and explain that he'd made me finish early. Seemed like he was coming to the rescue a lot these days.

On the way back to the door, I stopped at my desk to grab a Kit Kat from the top drawer. Phones! I hadn't checked my phone messages all week. Bugger.

I picked up the receiver and dialled my voicemail. 'You have two new messages.'

Smashing. I was obviously an indispensable wheel in the cog of industry. I'd been off for a whole week and I had the grand sum of two new messages.

'Erm, yes, this is Detective Sergeant Phil Masters here. I

will try you on your home number, but if I don't reach you there, please call me back.'

That one was from yesterday, and when he'd called the house Mrs Naismith had croakily informed him that no, it wouldn't be a problem for me to come down to look at some mug shots at the station next week, just as long as she could come with me for moral support. I could tell the proximity to all things *Crimewatch* was giving her a thrill.

The irritatingly posh lady on the recorded message informed me that I had one more message, left this morning at 9 a.m.

'Leni, it's me.' My heart stopped. Ben. But how had he got this number?

'The message on your mobile gave this number so I hope it was okay to call here.'

It wasn't. It isn't. Why the hell had I chosen today to forget to switch my phone on after I'd left the studio? And what the hell had happened to the oxygen in this room?

'I miss you, Leni, so much. I love you, babe. And I . . . '

What? And what?

' . . . I need to go – this is a satellite phone and it costs a fortune. I'll call again.'

Aaaaaaaaargh. I slammed the phone down, furious with him for spoiling my happy karma. Satellite my buttocks! He was probably in the desert camp right now, shagging a buxom blonde behind the supplies tent and telling her he was young, free and single, which, strictly speaking, was true, but that wasn't the point.

I grabbed my chocolate fix and was just about to leave when I realised that a button was still illuminated on the phone. This bloody system was older than me. It was unreliable, regularly unusable, and if Zara wasn't so bloody tight, professionalism would have forced her to renew it years ago.

I snatched up the receiver and cut straight into another

call. I realised immediately that Conn's voice had a distinct edge to it, so I hung up straight away in respect of his privacy.

Or should I say, if I'd had an ounce of decency I would have hung up immediately, but curiosity had batted decency right out of the ballpark, so I covered the receiver with my hand to silence the noise of my breathing and carried on listening.

'Where are you? You've been out of touch all day.'

'Smear test,' she blurted, forcing me to stifle a laugh. Apparently someone else panicked under pressure too sometimes.

'Anyway,' she continued, cutting off any questions he might have had. 'How's our problem?'

'Don't worry, I told you I'd take care of it and I am.'

'I hope so, Conn, because any publicity about that little debacle last weekend could blow our plans apart. Not to mention what would happen if she sued us for putting her in danger. The lawyer said we should have vetted those blokes before we sent her out there.'

His voice was exasperated now. 'I've already told you. I've taken care of it. She won't go to the press, she'd never have the bottle for that, and anyway, her confidentiality contract forbids it. And she definitely won't sue. Look, she's a mouse, and she's a mouse who, right now, would do anything I asked her. Don't worry, I'll keep her sweet . . . but I'm telling you, if I have to screw her then you owe me something big. How about that Marbella weekend you've been promising?' he said, his laugh conveying that he found this highly hilarious.

'If you keep her quiet, you can put it on expenses,' she replied dryly.

'Deal. I'll see you later.'

With that, one of my bosses hung up on the other one.

With a shaking hand I replaced the receiver . . . then I ran . . .

33

Mercury Rising

'We're going.'

'No, we're not.'

'Yes, we are.'

'Not.'

'Are.'

'Not.'

'Leni, I have a thirty-foot-long pink limo outside, waiting to whisk us away to the theatre. We're going.'

I lifted my head from under the IKEA pillow and squinted at Stu's suited form as he stood over me.

'Pink, you said?'

'Pink. With leopard-skin seat covers and Bacardi Breezers in the minibar,' he replied smugly, so sure of his triumph that he was practically doing a lap of honour around Little Sweden.

It was like the bit in romantic comedies where the hero says exactly the right thing and the heroine capitulates then runs down a fire exit to snog him. Every year, roughly a month before my birthday, I would point out to Trish and Stu that I'd never been in a limo in the hope that they'd pimp my ride for my birthday treat. So far it had all been to no avail – although, thanks to Trish's connections in the fire service, we had once hitched a lift home in a fire engine after a night at a Mongolian barbecue ended with flames, flashing blue lights, and several men in plastic yellow trousers. It had been one of my better birthdays.

But now, Stu, bless him, had finally taken the hint and arranged a very classy, elegant, screaming-pink limo with faux animal-print upholstery for our faux date. How thoughtful was that?

'Does it look really, really naff?'

He nodded. 'Couldn't be more tacky if it had fake tits stuck to the bumper.'

'Okay, I'm coming.'

As I dragged myself out of bed he had the courtesy not to comment on my comfort pyjamas, the ones that were flannel, tartan, and only came out in times of acute upset.

Getting taken for a manipulative, duplicitous ride by Team Delta had caused upset that definitely qualified as acute.

How could they? For the last twenty-four hours I'd mentally replayed that conversation hundreds of times, trying desperately to find another conclusion other than the obvious one: evil wanker genes are hereditary.

I'd been conned. Duped. Taken for the kind of ride that didn't involve pink bodywork and an extra-long wheel base.

The most ironic thing was that it was all so unnecessary – I hadn't even considered the possibility of Zara being personally responsible for my near brush with a criminal record last week, and I certainly hadn't considered going to the press. Why would I? Why would I possibly want my gran to read about my new life as a London drug mule? She'd never be able to show her face down the bingo again.

The most depressing thing about the whole situation, though, was just the resounding familiarity of it all. Is the Pope a Catholic? Do bears shit in the woods? Do I completely misjudge people time after time after bloody ridiculous time?

Ben – didn't spot he was married.

Matt – didn't spot that he was only in it for the fame.

Nurse Dave – didn't spot that he was the type of bloke who would shag me while he had a girlfriend.

Gregory – didn't spot that he was gay.

Gavin – didn't spot his connections to half the drug-dealers in London.

It had never even crossed my mind that Conn might have an agenda. Oh no. He was just being lovely and decent and kind. It was only a small consolation that, where he was concerned, I wasn't the only one who had got it wrong. Mrs Naismith had popped in that morning with my mail and I'd told her the whole story. After she'd threatened to mobilise the lethal forces of her regiment of Help the Aged to march down to his office and provide cover while she gave him a 'piece of her mind', I reminded her that she'd once told me that she could sense that Conn 'had a thing for me'.

She shook her head woefully. 'And there you have it, love.'

'Have what?'

'The reason that the only man in my life is Bruce bloody Willis.'

Well, no more. I had taken off my rose-tinted glasses and smashed them to sand-like particles. From now on I was going to make a point of honing my perception skills so that I'd never waste another day languishing in despair under an IKEA duvet, berating myself for my chronic lack of insight. I, Leni Lomond, from this day forward, would be smart, savvy, and never misjudge anyone's motivations again.

'Hon, do you think there's any chance of you shifting your tartan arse so that we can get there before Baby gets shoved in the corner? Or before I berate you mercilessly for giving me whatever virus you had last week.' Head tilted to one side, he squinted as his fingers gently massaged his neck. 'I feel brutal today. Did your head hurt when you had that virus? And your chest? And did you feel all breathless and exhausted?'

I nodded to all.

'Great. Next time you want to share, can you forget the viral infections and make it something out of Oddbins instead? Now hurry up, before I break into panic mode and rob Mrs Naismith of her stash of antibiotics.'

To my credit, I only groaned once as I dragged myself from the bed and headed to the bathroom for a quick shower. I'd just snapped the shower cap on my head when the phone rang, so I popped my head back into the bedroom to tell Stu to ignore it and let it go to voicemail.

'No problem,' he said, retracting the hand that was only inches from my Motorola. 'Incidentally, that look really works for you. I don't think I've ever wanted you more.'

He dialled into the answering machine and put it on loudspeaker.

'Hi Leni, it's Conn. Didn't get a chance to say goodbye yesterday, got caught up on a call, so just wanted to say have a good weekend. Hope all's good with you and see you Monday.'

Click.

'Stu, what's the current sentence for murder?'

'Prisons are overcrowded, so you'd probably be out in ten years.'

'I could plead PMT.'

'A hundred hours' community service at the most.'

I dipped back into the bathroom, musing that a hundred hours of cleaning chewing gum off the streets might just be worth it.

Five minutes later I showered, dried, and plodded back into the room to find my dress laid out on the bed, shoes sitting on the floor below it.

'How did you know that's what I was wearing?' This man was so special. He just inherently understood me, knew me, sometimes even better than I knew myself.

'It's the only dress you've got.' Okay, so my new perception skills hadn't quite kicked in yet.

Stu fixed my hair, make-up and mood in the time it usually takes me to unclog my mascara brush, and then swept me downstairs into what could only be described as a vulva on wheels. It was truly, truly splendid. I'm sure the driver must have been used to the shrieks of delight and irrational reactions, because he didn't even raise an eyebrow when I stuck my head out of the sun roof and screamed 'Weeeeeeeeeeeeeeeeeeeeeeeeeeeeeeeeee' all the way down my street.

To hell with Conn and Zara. I didn't give a flying, bright pink, leopard-skin-upholstered fuck about them any more. In the last few months I'd experienced more drama, more upset and more terror than the collective disaster quota for the whole of my preceding twenty-seven years, and do you know what? I'd survived. I'd done it! I was still in one piece. I'd felt the fear and bloody done it anyway and I'd lived to tell the tale (probably at my imminent therapy sessions).

Life was fine. I had my health, my friends, my house, and my very own Neighbourhood Watch officer. I had a lunch date tomorrow with a lovely young man, and sometime after that I'd decide whether to maintain a dignified silence and carry on with my job for the sake of my career, or deck Conn first thing on Monday morning with the hand that wasn't clutching my resignation letter.

In the meantime, I was going to have fun. For the next few hours the city and this bright pink limo were mine, and I intended to enjoy them.

I retracted my upper body from the sun roof, plonked myself back down on the seat next to Stu and grabbed a

Bacardi Breezer from the minibar. I took Stu's hand and rested my head back on the leopard-skin seat, closing my eyes and letting all the strains of the last few months evaporate. This was bliss and nothing could spoil it.

'Thanks, Stu, for doing this,' I murmured softly.

He squeezed my hand, conveying an unspoken understanding of just how much this meant to me.

We sat like that for a few seconds, in perfect peace, just savouring the moment, then Stu's hand squeezed mine again. And again. Then a little tighter.

'Leni,' he said, his voice strained, anxious. My eyes snapped open as my head spun towards him.

'I think . . . I think . . . ' he began haltingly, obviously struggling to get the words out. 'I think I'm having a heart attack.'

For weeks, perhaps months, the swarms of people leaving Slough General Hospital would talk about the night they were wandering back to their cars after visiting time, only to see a huge pink limo screech up the long driveway and almost raise onto two wheels as it skidded around the last bend to the doors of Accident & Emergency. However, the rumour it was carrying a comatose Amy Winehouse would never be substantiated.

A few seconds of barely coherent hysteria at the desk (me) was enough to motivate two nurses, a doctor and a porter to come rushing out pushing a trolley to the car, where the patient (Stu) was slouched down in the back seat, sweating profusely, struggling to breathe, his skin a stomach-turning shade of grey. Communicating almost silently while acting swiftly and efficiently, they deftly manoeuvred him onto the stretcher, slipped an oxygen mask over his head and then manually pumped on an inflatable bag thingy that I'd seen many times in the revered hands of Dr Luka in *ER*.

360

I grabbed Stu's fingers as the trolley crossed the pavement, and ran with it, through the doors once again, past rows of people waiting and straight into the bowels of the hospital, all the while struggling to take in the reality of the situation: my best friend was having a heart attack.

A red light flashed above the doors as we barged through, and that's when a large, stern-faced nurse stopped me, forcing Stu's hand to slip from mine. 'I'm sorry, we'll need to work on him so you can't come through.'

'But I can't leave him!' My eyes swivelled frantically to Stu's face, the look of sheer terror on it amplified by the terrifying rasps as he struggled to breathe. 'Please, please, let me go with him, I beg you, please don't make me leave . . . '

'I'm sorry,' she replied, her hand out in front of me, making it clear that if I wanted to get past I'd have to wrestle her to the ground in a fight to the death. Mine, I suspected.

Shit! I staggered back to the seating area, ignoring the rows of eyes that seemed to be focused directly on me, and sat down in between an old lady with a bandaged foot and a budgie in a cage next to her, and a teenage skinhead in a Kappa tracksuit, holding a white, blood-soaked pad to his forehead.

The tears fell like rain. This couldn't be happening. It couldn't. Not to Stu. Stu was only twenty-eight, he was the fittest guy I knew, and, raging hypochondria aside, I didn't think he'd had a day's serious illness in his life. He ate well, he exercised, he avoided pollution. For fuck's sake, he was the only person I knew who had a special machine that purified the air in his house on a two-hour cycle. Stu couldn't be sick. Sure, he got stressed, but . . . The irony hit me. What if the stress of worrying about getting sick had actually made him ill? Oh, the controllers of the fates were some twisted fuckers if that's what had happened here.

Shaking, I pulled out my phone to call Trish. 'No calls in here, dear,' said the bird woman, gesturing to the sign on the wall featuring a phone with a big red cross through it. If there was such a thing as cosmic equality, a large poster with a crossed-out picture of a budgie would transpire any second.

I raced over to the automatic doors, stepped outside and tried again. Answering machine. Fuck, fuck, fuck. I left a message in which I'm sure I said 'Fuck' several more times.

Back inside, I found it easier to pace than sit. Come on. Come on. Why weren't they telling me anything? What was wrong with him? Was he okay? Was he scared? Was he . . . He was *not* dead. He couldn't be dead. Stu had better not fucking die on me or I'd kill him.

We shouldn't be here. It was a mistake. Last time I'd been here was after the high-heels crash-down on the first of those ludicrous bloody dates, and Stu had rushed to collect me, oozing panic, concern and antibacterial spray. And now . . . He had to be okay!

Three hours later, bird lady was gone, the skinhead was gone, and almost everyone else who had been waiting when I'd arrived had been replaced by another broken or bloodied specimen. I was standing against the side of a vending machine, terror and panic now morphed into a zombie-like state.

'Leni Lomond?'

It didn't surprise me in the least that I recognised the voice. It had crossed my mind already that there was a fifty per cent chance that Nurse Dave would be on duty. That was those fuckers in the fate department again.

'You can come through now.'

Why? Why could I come through? Was he okay? Was he stabilised? Was he . . .

I didn't even meet Nurse Dave's eyes, just stared straight ahead through the door he was holding open for me.

'He's in here.'

He showed me to a curtained cubicle, and as I entered a gasping sob escaped from my lungs and my hand flew to my mouth. On a bed in the centre of the room lay Stu, his face white, eyes closed, absolutely still . . . absolutely dea—

'You can wake him if you want, but I'd leave it for now and let him recharge his batteries. A fright like that can really take it out of you.'

Nurse Dave had been replaced now by a female doctor with an Eastern European accent who looked like she should still be playing for her school netball team.

'Doctor Gratz,' she introduced herself.

'Leni,' I replied.

'You're his . . . ?'

'Friend. Is he going to be okay?'

'He's stable, but we want to keep him in overnight for observation and do more exploratory tests tomorrow. I can tell you that, going by his results so far, we don't think it was a heart attack, but we need to investigate further. You can have five minutes with him and then you can come back tomorrow after three p.m. We should know more by then.'

Off she went, presumably to finish her homework, update her Bebo page and buy her first bra.

He looked so vulnerable lying there that I wanted to climb in beside him and just be with him until they told us that he was definitely going to be okay. He had to be okay – because he was Stu and he was important and nothing could take him away from us. My throat tightened again, and my hand trembled as I ran a finger very gently across one of his perfect eyebrows and then the other, then softly, barely touching, ran the same finger down the side of his cheek. This was my Stu and he was going to be fine.

He had to be.

34

The Big Bang

In the taxi, I switched my mobile back on and the force of the vibrations almost made it jump out of my hand.

I checked the answering machine: six new messages, and I was pretty sure they'd all be from Trish.

I called her back straight away and her phone didn't even ring before she yelled, 'For fuck's sake, WHAT'S GOING ON? Is Stu okay? And why the fuck didn't you tell me where you were? I've phoned every fucking hospital in London and he's not there.'

'Didn't I say where we were?' Shit, no wonder she was frantic. 'Sorry, I was seriously freaking out when I phoned you. We're back in Slough General. We were barely out of my street when he got sick, and then he . . . ' A massive sob stuck in my throat again and it was a few seconds before I could speak, leaving Trish to scream, 'What? What? WHAT? *WHAT HAPPENED?*'

Speaking in two-word sentences, in between sobs, I started to fill her in on everything that had happened over the last four hours. I was up to our arrival at casualty when she pleaded, 'Leni, honey, stop crying, I can't understand a thing.'

I pulled a large ream of hospital toilet roll out of my bag

and blew my nose so violently that the taxi driver's toupee fluttered in the resulting draught.

Composed now, I continued, eliciting an impatient 'and then what?' at the end of every sentence. My house was in sight by the time I got to the bit where the prepubescent doctor told me to come back tomorrow afternoon.

'Fuck.' Trish sighed, emotionally drained. 'Do you want me to come over and stay at your place tonight?'

'Thanks, Trish, but you sound as exhausted as me. Come over tomorrow and we'll go to the hospital together. I wish I knew Stu's mum's number. I feel we should let her know.'

'We'll ask him tomorrow, and in the meantime I'll get a hold of Verity. I'll nip into the office tomorrow; we'll have her number on our database.'

'Thanks, Trish.' We were drawing up outside my flat now, and the thought of going into an empty house, the one that Stu and I had left only a few hours before, filled me with dread. Maybe I should tell Trish to come over after all. No, that was just being too selfish – it would take her at least an hour to get here, it would be crazy to drag her across the city at this time of night, and if she got car-jacked on the way here I'd never forgive myself. God, Stu had only been in hospital for a few hours and already I was taking over his mantle of irrational and morbid worry.

I trudged up the stairs, my feet as heavy as my heart, but when I got to the landing outside my door I paused and stared straight into my neighbour's peephole.

'Mrs Naismith, are you there?' I whispered.

I barely had the last word out when the door swung open. 'Leni, love, you look terrible. Are you okay?'

I slowly shook my head from side to side. 'Can I sleep on your couch tonight?'

She didn't even probe any further. 'Course you can, love, on you come in. I'll just put the kettle on.'

✳

The sleep part never came.

It took an hour or so to bring Mrs N up to speed, and then – spotting that sleeping might be hard for me – she sweetly offered to slip on an Indiana Jones movie and stay up with me to watch it. I graciously refused and sent her off to bed.

Illuminated only by the soft light radiating from her pink lava lamp, I stared at the ceiling until daybreak, four hours of utter silence and (apart from the rising and falling of large pink balls of wax) complete stillness.

Only a few months ago, Trish, Stu and I had brought in the New Year with an optimism and enthusiasm for change. Now, Stu lay in the hospital, my career lay in tatters, and we'd yet to achieve the happiness that we'd been so determined to find. Except in each other, that was.

As the sun came up, so did my spirits, fuelled by realisations that somehow had become clear in the dark. I knew what I had to do and it was time I stopped being the unfocused, inactive bystander in life and took the actions I needed to take to sort myself out. If I'd learned nothing else since I started working for Zara, it was that nothing should be left to destiny because that's when it all goes ceremoniously tits up.

Six a.m. I got up and, as noiselessly as possible, slipped back into my own flat, showered quickly, and threw on a pair of jeans, my cream chenille jumper (the one that was two sizes too big for me and came second only to the tartan pyjamas on the comfort scale) and my old Uggs and jumped in my car. I never took the car in to central London, but I figured on a Sunday morning at this time the chances of my slightly nervous driving causing a six-car pile-up on the M4 were minimal. In just over half an hour I was opening the office door with the keys Zara had given me to use only in the case of an emergency. Clearly, they didn't trust me to open up and lock up on a daily basis, but if the building was on fire it would be fine for me to use them to charge in, ignoring the warnings of the emergency services, and rush up to Zara's office with the sole purpose of saving her collection of African mongoose skulls.

Ignoring the deep sensation that I was doing something illegal that would bring the police storming in at any moment, I sprinted upstairs to my office and flicked on my computer. I printed off a couple of files that I wanted to preserve, typed up a quick report, then set about writing the easiest letter of my life.

Dear Zara,

I regret to inform you that I have decided to end my employment with your company as I feel that recent events have made my position here untenable. I will not work the required notice period, however I feel that my commitment to the role warrants that my salary for this period be paid in full. If it is not, then I shall not hesitate to take this matter further.

Yours sincerely,

Leni Lomond.

PS: My report regarding my Taurean date is attached. Job done. Bonus expected.

A sarcastic 'Ta-da!' slipped out as I pulled the letter off the printer and strutted over to Zara's desk, placing it front and centre where she couldn't miss it.

I was about to turn and leave for the last time when I

noticed that the mail that I'd left in a neat pile on Friday night was now scattered all over the floor to the left of her desk. Bugger, it must have fallen off. The devil on one shoulder was on a major defiance strop. Leave it. Just leave it. What did I care? Let her ladyship hitch up her Celtic wedding frock and get down on her knees and pick it up herself.

Unfortunately, the angel with conformist issues on the other shoulder had beaten her to it and was already on all fours, pulling the envelopes into an organised bundle.

Only one more envelope, a large, thick manila one, and then I could walk out of there, head held high, and move on to the next stage of my life, one that would be smarter, happier and designed and controlled by me alone. God help me.

But at least I wouldn't have to spend another day on the highly volatile, highly corrupted, suffocating world of Planet Zara.

Lessington Publishing.

With everything bundled together, I heaved the pile up onto the desk and then clambered to my feet.

Lessington Publishing.

I tapped the resignation letter again for luck, and then . . .

Lessington Publishing.

Nope, no good, I couldn't ignore it. Lessington was the publishing house that was releasing Zara's new book. I knew that contracts and financial stuff pertaining to the book got sent directly to Zara's accountant, so if they were sending a large manila envelope then I was guessing it must be something to do with the book. The cover? The artwork? The very tidy and orderly angel didn't want to know, but the wee devil decided that, sod it, I was leaving anyway, so it would be rude not to rip open the envelope.

I pulled out the sheaf of papers inside. Too thick to be just the cover images, so it must be the artwork. I flipped it over so that it was face up, and there was the . . .

Hang on. My eyebrows met in the middle as I tried to attain some level of understanding.

The top page was an index listing of the star signs, with various sub-headings and titles such as 'First Dates', 'Under the Covers', 'Rock His World' and 'Turn It Off', but as I flicked through the pages I discovered four things:

1. It only featured six of the star signs.
2. This was an actual draft of the first half of the book.
3. It featured case studies that were almost word-for-word identical to the reports I'd filed of the dates.
4. The analytical content bore absolutely no resemblance to the stuff I'd read on Friday.

In fact, as I read on I realised that this was on a whole different level, one that was miles away from the acutely perceptive, beautifully worded prose that I'd stumbled across just two days before and left right . . . My eyes darted around the desk. Nope, no sign of it. I fell to my knees and searched underneath and around the trees, careful not to catch my favourite jumper on a wayward branch. Still no sign of it. Perplexed, I came up empty-handed. I was sure I'd left it there. Definitely. The only explanation was that Zara or Conn must have come in and taken it. Perhaps Zara wanted to work on it some more over the weekend. And as for the variation between that version and this . . .

It suddenly came to me. Maybe the stuff I was reading now was just a mocked-up version of the book, a combination of date reports and chapters dummied up by someone at the publishing house as a working example of how the book would look. That made sense, sort of. This was a rough draft, just to give everyone involved a feel for the layout and aesthetics of the final version, and the actual content would only be finalised after Zara had analysed my last report and used it to develop her Taurean chapter.

There was a certain logic to that, but then what did I know? The closest I had ever come to the publishing world was devouring a Marian Keyes or a Carmen Reid novel on a rainy weekend.

Anyway, why was I even, to coin a Zara term, 'giving this headspace'. My head was quite full enough, thank you; full of worry about Stu, full of resolutions, and full of new plans for the future.

I replaced everything in the envelope, added it to the pile, then marched downstairs and out of the door for the last time. Little did I realise that just a couple of hours later my headspace would be filled with sheer, unadulterated panic.

35

Star Central

My watch said 11 a.m. but my body clock said it was hours later. This had already been the longest day of my life, and I still had four hours to kill until I could go back to the hospital. The inside of my cheek was raw and bleeding, thanks to my subconscious nervous chewing as my optimism pendulum swung wildly between 'he's going to be absolutely fine' and . . . I couldn't even bear to go there. Fine. He was going to be fine.

At 11.05 a.m. I took the slip road off the M4, heading back home. At 11.10 a.m. I stopped for petrol. At 11.11 a.m., while aimlessly waiting for my tank to fill, I suddenly remembered – bollocks, bollocks, bollocks – that I had a lunch date with Jon at noon. As soon as the pump clicked off, I dragged my handbag from the front seat and rummaged for my phone. It was 11.14 a.m.: I still had time to cancel and I was sure that under the circumstances he wouldn't mind. I'd just give him a quick call. As soon as I . . . Bugger, where was my phone? At 11.15 a.m. I mentally retraced my telecom steps: I'd spoken to Trish in the taxi last night, then gone upstairs, phone still in hand, into Mrs Naismith's, put phone and bag on floor, and sometime during the night I'd switched the phone off because I was afraid the 'low battery' beeps would wake Mrs N. Then this morning I'd grabbed my bag and tiptoed out.

At 11.16 a.m. I realised that the phone was still lying on the floor beside Mrs Naismith's couch. I also realised that I was only five minutes away from the pub where I was supposed to meet Jon in approximately forty-four minutes. No point in going home, retrieving phone and calling him, because he'd probably be on his way by now, so there was really no option other than to go as planned.

On the negative side, the last thing I felt like doing while my best friend was in hospital was having a lunch date. On the positive, it would at least pass some of the time until I could get back in to see Stu at three.

At 11.18 a.m. I made my way into the petrol station to pay, glanced at the rows of newspapers on the stand; and then, at 11.18 a.m. and a few nanoseconds: shock. Just complete and utter shock.

DELTA PORN, WHO'S THAT ACTOR YOU'VE GOT ON? screamed the headline.

I just screamed. I snatched the top copy of the *Daily Globe* and gasped at the picture that covered half the page: a black and white shot, taken through a car window, grainy but still clear enough to make out Zara, naked, obviously kneeling, the front of her body pressed against the reclined white leather front seat that she was spread-eagled across; and Stephen Knight, A-list movie actor, pressed against her back in what was obviously a sexual position taken from the *Canine Book of Puppy-Making*. And, judging by the ecstatic look on her face, Fido Knight was getting it just right.

Oh. My. God. How?

How had this happened? There must be earth tremors on Planet Zara today, and I'd no doubt whatsoever that she'd be reaching a ten on the Richter scale right about now. I should go to her. She'd need help, she'd need calming down, she'd . . . er, she'd need a new assistant because I didn't work for her any more. The phone conversation between her and Conn replayed in my mind again, firming my resolve.

Delta Porn was just going to have to deal with this one herself.

My defiant attitude lasted until I was sitting in the pub shortly afterwards and about halfway through the story. It wasn't good. It wasn't just the facts: the debauchery (kinky sex in public places), the deviance (suggestions of swinging and group sex) and the sordidness (snaps taken of them entering a premises known to operate as a high-class brothel), but the innuendo, hints and blatant reminders about Stephen Knight's drug use jumped off the page. Zara was a family celebrity – middle Britain had a precedent for overlooking sex scandals (thank you Camilla Parker-Bowles), but you had to be Kate Moss or Pete Doherty for your career to flourish after a proven connection with drugs.

I was almost at the end of the story, however, when a sentence made my blood run cold.

While her extra-curricular activities keep her very busy, Zara still has time to publicise her forthcoming book It's in the Stars, *a relationship guide based on the zodiac system. Concerns regarding the authenticity of the book and the rumours of fabrication of case studies have yet to be confirmed, as have the whispers that Zara continued to encourage the public to apply for a date via her website and premium-rate phone number even after the study was concluded. Perhaps when Zara isn't quite as busy she'll find time to give us a call and predict just what the outcome of this story might be?*

'Hey there, Star Lady, how are you?' The voice caught me just as the wave of panic came crashing down.

His eyes went from my shaking hands to my stunned face.

'I'm really sorry, Jon, but I don't think I've ever been worse.'

✳

'Yes, but how? How could they know this stuff? Zara and Knight? Fabrication of case studies?' I repeated for approximately the fortieth time, and again, for approximately the fortieth time, Jon shook his head helplessly. He'd been such a sweetheart. He'd shrugged off his deep caramel leather jacket (if I hadn't been blinded by fear and confusion I would have noticed how well it looked with his cream T-shirt and faded jeans), sat back and, over pre-lunch coffee, he'd listened as I recounted the story of Stu's hospital admission and current condition. In the calm, confident manner that had attracted me to him in the first place, Jon had taken my hand and reassured me that Stu would be fine. Yes, he used all the well-worn clichés (Stu was in the right place, the doctors knew what they were doing, etc. etc.), but his intentions were good and I appreciated the effort.

When the starters arrived, the conversation switched to the front-page splash, sending my anxiety back up to a level that could involve NASA, but again, Jon had listened to several blurts of, 'But how? How could they know this stuff?', then soothed me from 'sheer terror' down to 'deeply horrified' just by listening and caring and saying soothing words. He even had the decency not to laugh too loudly when I filled him in on all the actual details of her exploits with Knight, going right back to the knickers in the frock incident.

Cue several more variations on, 'But how? How could they know this stuff?'

Over our main course, a barely eaten penne arrabiata for

me and a steak for him, I'd focused on the line about fabrication of case studies and encouraging applications after the event. The latter was all on Zara – when she'd done that live on morning TV I'd been astonished. But there was no denying my involvement in the first accusation. Yes, I'd been economical with the truth, and yes, the little arrabiata I'd forced down was flipping over in my stomach every time I considered the consequences. It was a bit late to fire me, but could . . . could I get charged with fraud? Holy shit, I was going to end up in jail, and it would all be because of this fucking newspaper.

How? How could they know this stuff? My mind was banging itself against a brick wall in frustration as the same phrase ricocheted time and time again in my head. There were only two people who knew about the slightly underhand manipulation of the dates involving Nurse Dave, Ben and Stu – Trish and Stu – and those two people would never, ever, not even on pain of death, sell me out.

Unless . . . Oh crap, had Stu been gossiping at the salon? Had his love of passing on a great story blinded him to the sensitivity of my situation and he'd unwittingly blurted all to the wrong person? Or maybe he'd casually told Verity over a long weekend in bed (I mean, there was only so much sex a couple could have), and she'd revealed all to a team of stylists while stuck in the boring waiting periods during a photo shoot.

Or Trish, had she been indiscreet and blabbed to her colleagues at *Great Morning TV!*? Had Goldie overheard and used the information to trash her nemesis?

How? How could they know?

We were on our coffees now, mine a creamy latte that I nearly spat across the table when Jon surprised me by taking my hand and whispering, 'I like you.'

His flaw had suddenly become clear: his sanity was questionable.

375

'Are you kidding me? Jon, when we met I was serially dating other guys, and now I've just sat and sobbed through a two-hour lunch while regaling you with the kind of drama that would make any sane, rational guy head to the nearest embassy to apply for emigration. I could double the population of some small countries just by being me.'

'Well, I like you. And, if it's okay with you, I'll come home with you and hang around, just in case you need me in the couple of hours before you go to hospital. No telling what the fallout from these stories is going to be.'

'You would?' Oh, bugger, *nice alert*. I was just about holding it together, but now that he was being so sweet and concerned my tear ducts were threatening to go wild.

'Sure.' His hand stretched over as he pushed my hair back off my face and swept away the one solitary tear that had so far made a bid for freedom.

If Jon wanted to go out on a date with me after this then he must be crazy. Insane. Certifiable.

'I'll just go and pay at the bar and I'll be right back.'

'Wait! Let me share the bill with you,' I objected, diving under the table for my bag, but it was too late, he'd already wandered off. Getting back up should have been a simple reverse manoeuvre, but for a female who had clumsiness at the top of her list of defining characteristics, it was a little more convoluted than that, culminating in a head-banging-under-the-table incident, a loud 'Ouch', a jerking sideways movement and a toppled chair. The diners at the surrounding tables did, however, have the decency not to laugh directly at me. Mortified, I reached over and attempted to lift the chair back up, but with the weight of Jon's leather jacket it was impossible to do that with only one hand. Face beaming, I slid off my seat, performed a successful two-handed lift, and was just about to return to my seat when I realised that one of my Ugg boots was standing on something. A ribbon! I jerked it towards me and the small white card that was attached to it followed suit.

A security pass? We weren't far from several large company HQs, so perhaps this had been left after post-work drinkies the night before.

One side was just a mass of standard text, so I flipped it over.

The two words in bold red capitals caught my attention first: PRESS PASS. Next came the photograph below it, a familiar face that seemed to mock me as it returned my stare. Finally, I registered the two lines on the sub-heading.

The Daily Globe.
Ed Belmont – Reporter

36

Cosmic Explosion

I took the stairs to the flat two at a time, desperate to get inside so that I could finally howl without the risk of crashing my car or forcing concerned passers-by to call the police.

Ed. He'd even lied about his name.

'Did you put your steak on expenses?' I'd spat as I'd passed him on my way out, the shock lowering my tone to somewhere around 'homicidal'.

It hadn't taken long to get the whole story out of him, just a dash to the car park, a face-off next to my Nissan Micra and a threat that I was going to call the police and report him for breach of the peace.

'I haven't breached the peace!' he'd shouted, trying to manoeuvre in front of me so that I couldn't get into the car.

'No, but you will when I boot you in the bollocks!' I'd screamed.

'Let me explain, Leni, please!'

'No!'

'Yes!'

'No!'

'Yes!'

Victory was his unless I could suddenly summon the strength to drag a fully grown man off the driver's door of a small yellow car.

And so I got the gospel according to Ed Belmont, lying bastard and reporter for the *Daily Globe*.

'We've been after Zara Delta for months, sure that she's a con artist and a scammer. Some of our people had readings with her, we tracked her for a while, we even infiltrated her organisation by getting ears on the inside, but then that person left and we were back to square one.'

'The PA before me?'

'I'm sorry, I can't say.'

'*NOW YOU'RE DISCOVERING INTEGRITY?!!!*' I'd blasted.

Elderly couples out for a quiet pub lunch were now pulling into the car park, spotting the scene, and reversing straight back out again, no doubt muttering about the ineffectiveness of the ASBO system.

'Okay, it was! Then you took her place and we were going to talk to you, but then this dating thing was announced and it just seemed like too good an opportunity . . . Dozens of guys on the staff sent in multiple applications, but I got picked.'

My rage was turning from red to white. 'Get away from my car.'

'Come on, Leni . . . '

'Don't you dare use my name! I don't even know you! I knew a guy called Jon Belmont . . . '

'My brother,' he interjected.

'Who was a stockbroker . . . ' I spat.

'Also my brother.'

'Who used to write me lovely notes . . . '

'They also came from my brother – but only because I routed them through him so that they'd look more official.'

'Notes that I now realise were nothing but fishing expeditions for gossip. You. Evil. Prick. And I suppose that the sister you claimed sent the application in doesn't exist either?'

He shook his head, as I realised that a couple more things weren't adding up.

'Why did you want to wait until I'd finished the dates before going out again? I would have thought you'd have wanted to wheedle your lying arse in there as much as possible.'

'Too much of a danger that I'd get caught out – it was safer to get the info over email.'

'But I never told you about Zara and Knight. How did you find out?'

His desperation was tinged with weariness now. 'You mentioned in one of your emails that she was sneaking out with an A-lister. We just put a new tail on her and had the photos within days. I'm sorry, Leni.'

'Sorry you did it, or sorry you got caught?'

At least he had the decency to ignore the question rather than to lie.

'Get away from the car,' I'd told him again.

'Come on, Leni, we could turn this around and get something out of it for both of us. This story has been brilliant for me . . . '

That had stopped me dead in my tracks. Maybe he had a point. Perhaps I could forget that he'd completely used me, lied to me, implicated me – albeit not by name yet – in a fraud. Perhaps I could retract my resignation, go back to work for Zara and slip every little juicy nugget of scandal or suspicion to Jon/Ed. For a small fee, of course.

Perhaps I could do all that, and perhaps I should.

However, the next second of my life ruled that option out. He never even saw the fist coming, as I, for the first time in my life, punched a grown man in the face and then watched him go down like a whirligig in a hurricane.

I stepped over him, wrenched open my car door, battering him on the back of his head as I did so, climbed into the car and turned on the ignition. Before I closed the door, I looked down on him in all his pathetic glory. 'You know, it's a shame I didn't meet your brother – I think I might have liked him.'

And as I had driven off, one resounding wish had come into my head: I just hoped someone had nicked his leather jacket.

Now the adrenalin, rage and despair was fuelling every step I took up those stairs, ending with a thump as I kicked my front door in protest because my shaking hands couldn't get my key in the lock.

Mrs Naismith's door flew open. 'Leni, love, here's your phone, you left it under my couch last night, nearly ended up in the Dyson, so it did.'

'Thanks, Mrs N – I'll pop in and see you later.'

I needed to get inside. I couldn't speak, couldn't think, couldn't function. I just needed to be on my own so that I could find a way to make sense of all this.

'Okay, love, but you've got a visitor here.'

She swung her door back against the wall and stood to one side, allowing my visitor to step forward.

'Leni,' said a very tear-stained, crumpled face. 'I've been fired!'

An instant response to something like that just didn't come immediately to mind – unless, of course, you were Mrs Naismith. 'Millie, love,' she told the tall, weeping woman standing next to her, 'you go on into Leni's and tell her all about it. I'll go and put the kettle on and be over in ten minutes.'

The key cooperated this time and Millie followed me in,

launching the explanation of her predicament with a question.

'Did you find some papers at reception on Friday and put them on Zara's desk?'

I nodded. What was the problem with that? She'd been fired for envelope opening? For not sending the envelope up to Zara sooner? If that was the case, she'd definitely win at tribunal.

'The chapters for her book,' I clarified, and was rewarded with a bout of head shaking.

'They weren't Zara's, they were mine! I wrote those!'

Yep, and any minute now Matt Damon was going to walk in the door, followed by Johnny Depp, and they'd have a punch-up on my walnut IKEA table to decide who deserved to whisk me off to Necker for a fortnight of serious shagging. And that would be the least surreal of the scenarios that were currently playing out in my life.

She spilled the whole story. Millie De Prix, it transpired, came from a long line of psychic De Prixes, but she was the first one to follow this up with a degree in astrology in the hope of using her gift in conjunction with traditional astrology. She'd erased the degree from her CV so that she wouldn't seem over-qualified to be a receptionist at Zara's office, a job she'd hoped would give her valuable experience and insight into the industry. After a year, she'd been about to resign and develop her own career when I'd joined and embarked on the dating experiments, a project that she thought would be a great test of her skills. It was. If what I'd read on Friday was anything to go by, she'd proven that she was truly gifted.

Zara, on the other hand . . .

'She's a fake, Leni. She researches everyone she gives a reading to prior to meeting them, does her homework, uses subjective language . . . She's all smoke and mirrors. Even the date book, I'm sure that was all a big scam: advertise for dates because that generates public interest, gets masses of free publicity, and also gives you an opportunity to rake in the advance orders. Then she would have turned out a book that looked great but had no substance whatsoever, and people would buy it anyway because it had Zara Delta on the front or because they were desperate to find love. She was just playing on people's vulnerability and taking advantage of their emotions. I honestly don't feel that she has any kind of talent at all – except for making money, of course.'

It was all clearer than the glass on Mrs Naismith's lava lamp. Millie was absolutely right about everything: to Zara this was nothing but a cash exercise, and I'd just been a tool in her methods to generate publicity. Even my reports had been used almost verbatim to fill a few more pages in the book. If it wasn't so depressing it would be quite brilliant.

'So what happened when she fired you?'

Millie shrugged. 'She just turned up at my door last night, ranting, raving, going crazy, waving my stuff in front of me, accusing me of sabotaging her career and trying to undermine her by stealing her ideas and then writing my own stuff.'

'I'm so sorry, Millie, this was entirely my fault. I saw the envelope in your back office on Friday and I read it and thought it was part of the mail delivery, and that's why I put it on her desk. But then this morning . . .'

I filled her in on my discovery of the other manuscript. This was all starting to make very horrible sense now. The disparity between the standard of the stuff I'd stumbled across on Friday and the manuscript I'd opened in the mail this morning wasn't because one had been mocked up by a publisher; it was because one had been cocked up by Zara.

There was a loud knock at the door. That'd be Mrs Naismith using the tea tray as a battering ram. Distracted by the ongoing discussion with Millie, I pulled it wide open, but instead of a pensioner with a tray of PG Tips and packet of chocolate digestives, Zara and Conn stomped in. Or, rather, Conn stomped and Zara glided, her gold kaftan so long that it completely covered her feet, giving the impression that she was travelling on a skateboard.

'Leni, thank God you're okay,' Conn blurted, putting on what I had to admit was a pretty convincing act. 'We just got your letter and we came straight over. Why would you resign?'

'You resigned?' Millie gasped.

'I resigned,' I confirmed to no one in particular.

'But why?' Millie asked, a question I suspected pre-empted Conn and Zara's next words.

'Because these two are completely without scruples or morals.'

'Leni!' Conn feigned incredulity well.

'Oh, don't give me that crap. I heard you talking to Jackie bloody Onassis over there . . . ' At which point Zara snapped off her huge black sunglasses, revealing two red, swollen eyes. Good.

' . . . about "keeping me sweet", and let me tell you, sunshine, I'm worth far bloody more than a weekend in Marbella!'

He didn't even have the decency to look shame-faced.

'He was taking you to Marbella?' Millie asked, perplexed.

Aaaaaaaaaargh! 'No. They realised they were on shaky ground after the drug-dealing thing, and Zara sent rent-a-cock round to make sure I didn't sue them.'

'You devious bitch,' Millie spat at Zara.

'Don't you dare speak to me like that,' Zara fought back. 'You try to muscle in on my operation, and then when I fire you, you get straight on to the press and sell stories on me! How did you do it? How did you get the photos? Did you plan all along to damage my reputation so that you could make a name for yourself?'

'Actually, that was me.'

The world stopped and all three sets of eyes spun to me.

'And I didn't sell the stories – one of the dates was a press plant. They'd been trying to get you for years.' I decided to omit the small matter of my unwitting compliance. 'But then, if you'd checked the guys out before you sent a vulnerable young woman out onto the streets with them, you'd have known that, so actually, you set yourselves up. Hope that feels great. Now get out of my house. I'm not coming back to work because you two are lying, cheating scum. Millie isn't coming back to work because someone with her talent doesn't care to be in the same building as two commerchants, and we'll both be expecting full salary and references or the press will be hearing about his drugs, your mistreatment of staff, and whatever other things Millie and I can think up or make up.'

Yes! Anxious, nervous, people-pleasing Leni had now well and truly cracked, and oh, it felt so, so good (and only a little terrifying) to finally speak my mind.

'Don't you dare think that you've got one over on me, missy,' Zara hissed, speaking up for the first time. 'I don't think they'd be interested in a story from someone who was caught misappropriating company funds.'

The tension in the air could have powered the National Grid as Millie gasped, her eyes darting from Zara to me and back again.

'What funds?'

Zara pulled a few sheets of paper from her Gucci Positano bag and threw them at me. 'No address, fake phone numbers – we know that this was the fabricated date that the press story talked about, and we suspect there were more, yet the one-hundred-pound fee for each date was still withdrawn. So what did you do, Leni? Get your pals to say they'd go out with you and then keep the money for another pair of cheap shoes?'

I was outraged! The accusations of theft I could just about deal with, but my shoes were not cheap! These were genuine Uggs, and I had the eBay receipt to prove it.

Stomping over to the door to retrieve the bag I'd dropped there on the way in, I tried not to look at Ben's photo at the top of the document Zara had just thrown at me. Bloody typical – he was making a habit of cropping up when I didn't want him to. The banging on the door started just as I reached it, so I pulled it open, allowing Mrs Naismith and her assortment of confectionery delights to step forward. She stopped dead when she spotted Zara and Conn.

'What's that cow doing here?' she growled.

'Don't worry, Mrs N, I'm on it.'

As I pulled the file I'd brought from the office out of my bag, I felt empowered, I felt strong, and for once I felt absolutely confident. It was all I could do not to put one hand on my hip, jut my chin out and cockily shake my head from side to side in the manner of Mary J. Blige.

It was my turn for document-brandishing: three emails, all from different charities, all confirming the receipt of one hundred pounds in the name of Zara Delta. I might be clumsy, I might not have the strongest judgement skills, I might make terrible choices – but I, Leni Lomond, was an admin whiz. I'd realised when I first fabricated the report on Nurse Dave that if the money didn't come out of the account then Zara, with her finance obsession, would notice, so after the fake dates with Dave and Ben, and before my date with Stu, I'd sent the money off to a good cause instead.

Strangely, the National Association for Shit Psychics wasn't one of them. These receipts were ones I'd printed off in the office that morning as a little insurance policy against exactly this kind of scenario. Was it wrong that holding my own in all this duplicity was giving me a minor thrill?

'Accuse me of anything and I'll just say that those dates were planned with your knowledge, and you, out of the goodness of your fucked-up heart, sent the money off to charity. You cannot prove I did a single thing wrong here.'

I honestly thought she was going to explode. The gold kaftan appeared to be inflating as rage made her even more animated and volcanic than usual.

'You devious little fucker,' she shrieked.

'DON'T YOU DARE SPEAK TO HER LIKE THAT!' came a voice from Betty Naismith, 74, resident of the Slough/Windsor border, former yellow belt in Tae Kwon Do, who strutted straight over to the nation's most famous paranormal expert, intent on committing assault with a lethal packet of digestive biscuits.

Conn stepped between them, hands out, trying to calm everyone down with a 'Hey, hey, hey, let's all just take a deep breath here. Mother, just keep it zipped for a minute and let's see if we can all sort this out amicably.

'Leni, we're prepared to overlook the *discrepancies,* and we'll agree to your notice pay and references for both of you, just as long as you agree to walk away, no fault on either side.'

A bizarre sound, like that of a cat being strangled, came from Zara's direction, and was rewarded with a warning glare from Conn.

It should have felt like a victory. It was a victory. But the new me, the one that had been recently possessed by Mary J. Blige, suddenly wanted more.

'Are you still going to publish the book?'

387

He spluttered incredulously. 'Of course.'

'Then no. I'm going to the press.'

'You can't! You signed a confidentiality agreement!'

Millie joined Mary J. in the fray. 'My boyfriend is a lawyer and he says that's not worth the paper it's written on: not witnessed, not official, and we could allege that our signatures are forged. Oh, and good luck going up against him – he's one of the top lawyers in London.'

My, my, my, she was a dark horse – this was the first I'd heard of a boyfriend.

Bitch Delta and her Satan spawn were temporarily stunned, giving me the opportunity to exercise my newfound skills in negotiation and underhand tactics.

'So here's where we're at – our requests have changed. We want six months' salary, excellent references, and the book never sees the light of day. Now get out of my house and don't ever, *ever* contact anyone here again.'

'Don't you . . . !' Zara still had a fight left in her, but fortunately a new opponent was standing in the open doorway. Bloody hell, the population of Little Sweden was rising by the minute.

'I think that she asked you to leave,' Trish said, her voice like ice. 'And if I were you I'd do that immediately . . . or I swear on Lorraine Kelly's life that I'll have Goldie give an interview reliving the horrific moment that she caught Stephen Knight sniffing coke out of your muff behind the *Great Morning TV!* sofa.'

They didn't even bang the door on the way out.

37

It's in the Stars

It was 3.30 p.m. Trish had gone to Heathrow to collect Verity, who'd abandoned the shoot as soon as she'd heard about Stu and caught the next flight home. I'd been waiting in the hospital reception for thirty minutes now and no one was telling me anything. I was shaking like Zara on her cosmic vibrating ball, and despite an adequate personal hygiene regime, very unattractive sweat patches were forming under my arms while I rocked back and forward repeating an internal prayer of, 'Please God, make him be okay, please God, make him be okay, please God, make . . . '

'Leni, isn't it?' It was teen-doctor, who'd probably given up cheerleading practice to keep our meeting. She took me through the double doors and then stopped outside a door at the end of the corridor. Why was she stopping here? Was this where they delivered bad news? Had they moved him to a ward? To another hospital? Or to the . . . Nope, couldn't even think that. He wasn't dead. He was fine. He was fine. He was . . .

'Stuart is going to be fine. We've run comprehensive checks and we are fairly sure it was just a very severe panic attack, one that was exacerbated by an influenza virus. The likely scenario is that the virus caused the tightening of the chest wall, this triggered the panic attack, and the combination of the two symptoms mimicked that of a heart attack.'

Mimicked? She made it sound like an act at a comedy club. *Hi, I'm your aortic valve and I'll be your compere for the evening.*

Elation soared from the pit of my stomach, destroying the knot in the back of my throat on the way up. Stu wasn't dead; he was just having a little bout of 'mimicking'.

'Thank you, doctor, thank you so much, and I'm sorry if we've wasted your time, but I just panicked.'

'No, not at all. Given his history, you were absolutely right to come straight here. We're just preparing the discharge paperwork and then you can take him home. He's already dressed and waiting.'

She opened the door to a little private room, motioned me to go through and then went off in the other direction.

Stu lay on a bed in the middle of the room, his hair wild and unkempt, his face pale and gaunt, his eyes red-rimmed and puffy, yet I didn't think he'd ever looked more gorgeous.

'Hi,' he croaked. 'Sorry we missed the show.'

'S'okay, I know how it ends. But I can't promise I won't jump off the sideboard and make you catch me later.'

His laugh degenerated into a full-scale coughing fit.

'You're absolutely fine,' I told him, great big dollops of tears falling again and landing on his five-hundred-pound shirt.

'I know. Sorry if I scared you.'

'You did,' I whispered. 'But I'm just so relieved you're okay, Stu. I love you.'

'I love you too,' he replied, smiling for the first time.

'You do?'

He nodded.

'Good. Then you can tell me what that twelve-year-old doctor was talking about when she referred to "your history"!'

'Sudden Adult Death Syndrome.' Never before had I seen the devastated expression on Stu's face, or heard the raw, searing pain in his voice.

It was early evening now and we were back in his flat. Trish and Verity had arrived minutes after we had, and now all of us sat utterly still as we listened, only slightly distracted by the fact that Verity was wearing the standard uniform for most people on a lazy Sunday afternoon: a pink sequinned boob tube, white leather skinny trousers and platforms the size of my car.

'My dad died of it when I was ten.'

Trish's eyes widened, mirroring mine. We knew that Stu had been raised by his mum but I couldn't remember him ever mentioning his dad, other than saying that he had 'never been in the picture'.

'Him and Mum had separated, but I was still gutted when he died, and I suppose it freaked me out that no one could ever tell me why. Doesn't take a genius to work out that's where the hypochondria started, although I wasn't really aware of it at first. Michael Jackson wore a facemask and slept in an oxygen bubble, so I didn't think compulsive germ avoidance was such a bizarre concept.'

My heart was breaking for him. All this time we'd laughed and joked about his bizarre idiosyncrasies and it transpired that they were rooted in tragedy.

'Remember I took some time out when we were in college?'

Trish and I nodded as he sighed. 'History repeated itself.

391

My dad's brother died too, and again there were no symptoms, no explanations – just Sudden Adult Death Syndrome recorded on the certificate. I was away for a few weeks because my doctor had me admitted so they could run tests to check for anything hereditary.'

'I thought you'd won a few quid, discovered dope and sex and gone on a month-long shagathon with your childhood sweetheart?' Trish exclaimed.

'I think I might have told you that at the time,' Stu said with an apologetic grin that turned to mischief. 'Did it make me seem more interesting and wild?'

'Not enough to make me want to have sex with you,' Trish retorted.

'Then out of tragedy came a blessing.'

Thankfully, the health scare hadn't diminished his ducking reflex, which came in handy in avoiding the cushion that Trish launched across the room.

'That's where I got the money I used to buy the salon. My dad's brother was a scrap merchant, one with no kids and a stockmarket hobby. He left me five hundred grand.'

'Fuck, now I want to sleep with you,' Trish moaned.

I stopped myself from gasping out loud. So that's where the money had come from! And so much!

'He also left me with an inherent fear that I'd be next. The doctors say there's absolutely nothing wrong with me, they've done every test possible and I'm healthy, but I suppose that it just all sits in the subconscious.'

'That's completely understandable, Stu,' I piped up, desperately sad that I hadn't known, and hadn't been able to help him through what must have been a terrifying time.

'Would you have slept with him if you'd known about the dosh?' Trish asked glibly, causing us all to crease into laughter.

'Erm, excuse me, can I just point out that you are in fact

392

talking about my boyfriend and I'd thank you to keep your manipulative sexual longings towards him to yourself.'

Verity was laughing, but, well, she had a point. Stu was her boyfriend. And girlfriend/boyfriend gazumped best friends every time. Much as all I wanted to do was cuddle up on the sofa with him and hold him tight for the rest of the night (an act completely unmotivated by the extent of his recently revealed windfall), Trish and I should leave and let them have some time together.

As we left, I kissed him lightly on the forehead.

'*Dirty Dancing* next week instead?' he asked.

'You're on.'

'Good – it's a date.'

'Stu, I promise you something – I am never, *ever* going on a date again.'

❊

The dancers were still shaking their pants to the last verse of 'I've Had the Time of My Life' when the credits started to roll. I sniffed inelegantly and reached for the huge bucket that had been full of popcorn a few hours earlier. Now there were only a few edible pieces among the corn kernels that had resisted the microwave and sat like tiny little militant nuts in the bottom of the bowl.

Comfort movie. Comfort food. And . . . glug . . . comfort wine.

Two empty bottles lay on the coffee table in front of me, but in my defence, one of them had been consumed by Mrs Naismith, who'd joined me when I'd come home from Stu's and shared a cottage pie while we watched *Rocky IV*. She'd headed off to bed around nine, when I'd insisted on putting on 'that girly rubbish'. Obviously we'd never know the outcome now, but my money would have been on Mrs

Naismith if Zara had taken her up on her offer of a bout of armed combat.

Notting Hill and the *Sex and the City* movie DVDs sat in their boxes in front of me, but I felt decidedly ambivalent now about watching them. I played aimlessly with the remote control, throwing it up and catching it in the popcorn bucket. I felt aimless, bored, bizarrely agitated. What to do? Moving through to the bedroom held no appeal, and since I didn't need to get up for work the next morning I could do pretty much anything that I wanted. That was the problem: what, exactly, did I want?

A new job was probably at the top of the list, although there wasn't a massive rush since Millie and I would be financed by the Bank of Zara for the next few months.

Maybe I should travel, get out and see the world. After all my experiences over the last few months, a solo global expedition held no fear now, and in a weird way I had Zara to thank for that. She might have pimped me out without a single thought for anything but her bank balance, but every aspect of it – from the nerve-racking dates to the final showdown – had given me another nugget of confidence. However, if I did go travelling I would have to pay close attention so I didn't mistake serial criminals for upstanding members of the tourist community. I had indeed made definite progress in the fields of confidence and self-awareness, but my people-judgement skills were still up there with my fashion sense and my interior design prowess.

But would a few months of escapism really solve anything? What was wrong with me? I should be elated, but instead I felt like someone had put *me* in a corner and then had buggered off and forgotten all about me.

The remote control missed the bucket and ricocheted under the couch, but when I blindly fished in after it, my hand made contact with paper: Ben's profile, the one that Zara had thrown at me only a few hours before.

Don't cry. Don't cry. Glug.

I stopped the tears, but I couldn't bring myself to scrunch up the offending article and launch it at the nearest bin. I ran my index finger across his photo, touching his hair, his face, his smile, the movement slowed by melancholy and wine.

After more minutes than were psychologically healthy, the knock at the door snapped me out of my mental fug. Mrs Naismith with a nightcap, no doubt, hell-bent on staging an intervention that would get me off the 'girly rubbish' and back on to decent, uplifting cinematic treats like *Platoon* and *Armageddon*.

'Hi,' said the languid, gorgeous voice at the door – definitely not Mrs Naismith.

'Hey,' I replied, surprised. 'Coming in?'

He shook his head. 'I need to tell you something first.'

Was it just the wine, or was my best mate standing in my doorway, acting very strangely.

'What?'

'I think . . . I think you made a mistake.'

The giggle was out before I could stop it.

'Which one? I always make mistakes – I'm a serial fuck-up,' I replied, my hilarity taking the edge off the element of truth in there.

'You're not. You're beautiful, and kind, and funny, and the most amazing female I've ever known.'

'I am?' Hello? Just when I thought I'd departed from Weird Central, it seemed like I was taking a one-way ticket back there.

Stu nodded thoughtfully. 'Last night, in the hospital, one of the nurses sat with me for hours and we talked and talked, and I think I know now who you should be with.'

'You do?'

'I do.'

'Who?'

Why did I feel like I was the lead actor in a romantic comedy but no one had given me the script?

'Me.'

Wow.

Wow.

Wow.

Sorry, I was stuck on 'wow' there for quite a while, but not because of anything that Stu had said . . . it was more to do with the man who was standing next to him.

'Nurse Dave?' I blurted. Process, Leni, process. I was trying, but I kept going back to 'wow'.

'You were wrong, Leni – he doesn't have a girlfriend. He told me all about it last night: she was his ex and she had issues, and when you answered the phone she just decided to mix it up a little. I promise. I called her and checked it out.'

'You're kidding me!'

They both shook their heads, their grins splitting their faces in half.

'So why didn't you tell me this before?'

'I tried,' Nurse Dave argued. 'But I didn't have your phone number and every time I came here you were out.'

Smashing. Mrs Naismith had somehow managed to avoid interfering in my life on the few occasions that might just have made the most incredible difference.

'So you really don't have a girlfriend?'

He shook his head.

'And you don't have a fetish for weapons, aspirations to be in a band, dreams of stardom, a wife, a passive personality, or a secondary career as a drug-dealer?'

'Definitely not.'

My smile mirrored his now, as I stood to the side and opened the door wider.

'Then you'd better come in.'

CONCLUDED		
LEO	Harry Henshall	Morbid fascination for simulated violence
SCORPIO	Matt Warden	Lead singer, lying arse
ARIES	Daniel Jones	Unlikely to forge career as an assertiveness coach
CAPRICORN	Craig Cunningham	Relationship therapist, incites violent urges
GEMINI	Jon Belmont	Duplicitous prick with a press pass
PISCES	Nurse Dave Canning	Now providing services over and above those routinely offered by the NHS
AQUARIUS	Colin Bilson-Smythe	Lawyer, laughs like a food-mixer
CANCER	Gregory Smith	Shy, sweet man's man – in all respects
LIBRA	Ben Mathers	Who?
VIRGO	Kurt Cobb/Cabana	Rising star in need of a good stylist
SAGITTARIUS	Gavin West	Drug-dealer – currently serving eight years
TAURUS	Stuart Degas	Hairdresser, hypochondriac and the best friend ever . . . just don't tell Trish

EMAIL
To: Trisha; Stu
From: Leni Lomond
Re: If last night's date had a personal ad, it would read like . . .

Sorry, that's between me and my boyfriend.

Great Morning TV! – New Year's Day

'*Welcome back to our* Great Morning TV! *New Year special, and if you've just tuned in, the beautiful Verity Fox is here, talking about her engagement to our very own* Great Morning Television! *hair expert, Stuart Degas.*'

The studio erupted into a round of applause and, at the back wall, Trish and I ducked as one of the cameras swung round to catch Stu's grinning, bashful reaction.

'*Tell me, Verity, when did you know? When did you absolutely know for sure that he was the one?*'

Verity flicked her gorgeous long blonde tresses off one shoulder and flashed twenty thousand pounds' worth of teeth at Britain's breakfast tables. '*The first night I met him.*'

'*Nooooo!*'

'*Goldie, I swear it's true! It was a freezing cold night and I had on the most fabulous, but smallest dress you've ever seen . . .*'

Goldie nodded knowingly.

'*. . . and when he collected me, he suggested that I might want to put on something thicker so that I wouldn't get a chill. It was the first time in my life that a new boyfriend had actually asked me to put clothes on.*'

Cue more spontaneous whooping and cheering.

Goldie grabbed Verity's hand for the second time that morning. '*And then last night, at the stroke of midnight, he asked you to marry him. One more look at the ring before* 'you go.' She held up Verity's perfectly manicured paw and flashed the four-carat, princess-cut, square diamond mounted on a gleaming platinum band into the camera.

'Aren't you worried her ex-boyfriend is going to get out of jail and kick your arse?' Trish whispered to Stu.

'Nah – I've got enough money to flee the country at short notice.'

Back on camera, the slush-fest continued.

'So this is forever?' Goldie asked softly.

Verity nodded and whispered, 'Forever.'

Trish made vomiting motions beside us, earning her a swat from Stu.

'Verity, thank you so much for sharing your story,' back to camera now, 'and remember, Stuart will be with us later when he gives Betty Naismith from Windsor a whole new look for the New Year. Soon, and I can hardly contain my excitement about this, we'll be meeting the incredibly talented, sensational new Great Morning TV! astrologer. But first, straight from his latest stint supporting Westlife on tour, is Britain's Got Talent *winner KURT CABANA, with his new number-one hit, "Loving You Is Easy"'.*

Up in the gallery, the director switched to the right stage cameras and Kurt launched into his act.

'Just think, you could have been Mrs Cabana,' Trish whispered.

'That's enough of that! She did perfectly fine with what she got, didn't you, Leni, love?' came a voice from behind us.

One of the junior producers had brought Mrs Naismith out from the green room, and now she bustled past, dressed in a white terry robe, her hair soaking wet, to left stage, where Stu was now setting up his stuff, ready to transform her on air. It was all part of her master plan to reinvent herself and get a new action hero of her very own – even if his action only extended to the occasional game of bowls down at the social club.

Great Morning TV!'s *new astrologer, who also had the misfortune to be my new boss, joined us to wait for her call.* 'Nervous?' I asked her.

'Terrified,' Millie replied.

'Come on, you know you'll be great,' Trish encouraged her.

'Actually, you're right – I think it'll all go really well,' she concurred with a knowing smile. None of us doubted her. We'd all realised over the last few months just how brilliant Millie really was. I couldn't believe that I hadn't noticed before: the lunch predictions, choosing the right clothes for my dates, instinctively knowing when things were good, bad or ugly. And hadn't she perfectly documented every one of the twelve guys – even noting that Jon had a dark side to him long before I sussed him out. Her inherent psychic gifts combined with her genius in the field of astrology had already raised her to the top of her field, and she was now the proud president of Millie De Prix Inc.

On the other hand, Zara had always been so vague about her techniques, so guarded about her methodology, and now we knew why: she was a kaftan-wearing, movie-star-shagging, obnoxious big fake, one who'd been caught up in a scandal this year that had started with Stephen Knight and ended with a full confession about her sordid addiction to sex, drugs and New Age therapies. Zara had been forced to reveal all in return for the Daily Globe's agreement not to publicly brand her a sham. Anyway, now that Stephen Knight had buggered off back to Hollywood and most of Zara's clients had dried up, she was happy to live by the mantra that any publicity was another few thousand in the bank. And according to rumours of her and Conn's burgeoning coke habits, they needed every penny they could get.

Zara's publishers had, however, still got a revolutionary dating guide after an anonymous source (me!) sent them Millie's manuscript. Incredibly detailed, the Zodiac Guide to

Love shunned the generalised star-sign groupings that Zara had offered, and instead contained an individual analysis for every day of the year. Millie's six-figure book deal and lucrative TV contract had been brokered by . . .

'Holy fuck, what is that noise? The floor manager will fucking kill him!'

. . . Colin Bilson-Smythe, Millie's boyfriend and the lawyer who'd called Delta Inc. in an effort to track me down and apologise for our disastrous date, realised he was talking to my beautiful companion from the night before, and asked her out instead. He and Millie had been married before the month was out . . . apparently it was in the stars. Strangely, she didn't seem to mind that his laugh sounded like a food-mixer.

Today, as a personal favour for her PA (also me), Millie was giving a reading, live on air, to Glenda Smith, who was at that very moment suffocating Goldie in a bear hug and hoping that she'd get a message from her dearly departed mother – the one who had keeled over two years ago in the middle of the 3.15 from Aintree. Her son Gregory and his 'special friend' Alex were watching back in the green room. Glenda had taken a while to get used to the idea, but she was coming round to it now that Alex had converted from Arsenal to Chelsea.

'So what are your New Year's resolutions for this year then?' Trish whispered. 'Grey said to remind you that "avoiding fire raising" should be one of them.'

I laughed quietly, in no way mimicking the sound of a kitchen implement.

Grey had given me several lectures since the day, just a few months before, that I'd inadvertently set fire to a garden shed, three wheelie bins, two skateboards and a goal post, all of which resided in the communal gardens of our apartment block. Who could have predicted that the unfortunate combination of a self-help-book bonfire and a strong westerly wind would have caused so much damage?

But, arson aside, this year there would be no resolutions. It would be greedy, really, since I'd achieved so much more than I could ever have hoped for when I'd made those semi-drunken declarations just twelve months ago. I'd finally exorcised Ben from my life; I'd finally landed a great new job that I loved; I'd finally grown out of so many of my fears and insecurities; and I'd finally realised that my people-judgement skills weren't completely hopeless – hadn't I fallen for Nurse Dave right from the start?

Oh, and I was also a massive YouTube star, thanks to some video taken of me being wrongly arrested in a London drugs swoop. Thankfully, no one had yet shown it to my granny. This year I wanted calm and a drama-free existence – not because I'd reverted to my old personality traits of plodding and predictability, but because I was now genuinely, truly happy. We all were.

'Happy New Year, Leni!' The hands came round from behind me, encircling my waist and squeezing me tight.

'You smell of hospital,' I murmured blissfully to Nurse Dave, who had – as promised – come straight here after his all-night shift.

Trish made the vomiting gesture again.

I ignored her.

Millie nudged me and then spoke softly, determined not to upset the tortured floor manager. 'After the show I could do a reading for you, Leni. Do you want to know what will be happening for you this year?'

I thought about it long and hard . . . for about a second and a half.

'No, thanks, Millie – I think I'll just wait and let the stars surprise me.'

THE END

New Year, New You.

It's one minute past midnight, you've had a couple glasses of wine and you find yourself swearing to eat healthier or spend less on shoes. But come the morning after and suddenly the craving for a full English breakfast followed by a stroll down the high street just can't be ignored.

Find out how likely *you* are to stick to your resolutions by answering the questions below.

1. When do you start thinking about your New Year's resolutions?

a) At the chime of midnight, normally between martinis.

b) The day before, when Tarmararia deGlutenfreebia from your office starts whining about how it's *so hard* to stay a size 6 when she's taken out for dinner *every* night.

c) At least two months beforehand. After all, you're running out things to improve about yourself, and will need to design a spreadsheet to monitor your progress. It needs planning, and a *lot* of lists.

2. An example of a typical resolution would be:

a) 'I really should reply to mum's answerphone message from last week . . . '

b) 'I *must* lose 5 stone, stop drinking completely, never bite my nails again, and become overall perfect goddess worthy of office and friend envy.'

c) 'I will run the London marathon, again, but this time at least *ten* minutes faster than last time. I will also be promoted. *Again*.'

3. **When you mention your resolutions to your friends, the general response is:**

a) Silence. Maybe a snigger/cough.

b) Sympathetic hugs and smiles as they all remember how badly last year's '*find fabulous boyfriend and get engaged*' pledge went . . .

c) A round of serious nods. They too have decided to shave their heads for Ugandan orphans whilst cycling up Ben Nevis.

4. **In your opinion, celebrating the New Year means:**

a) Wearing sparkly tights, getting drunk and pulling a hottie. In that order.

b) The opportunity to change completely and become the person you always wanted to be: lean and mean, with manicured nails.

c) Challenging and really pushing yourself to the limits. There is no bigger satisfaction than achieving a goal. If someone else has done it, you *will* do it better.

5. **The downside of your resolutions is:**

a) Everybody asking what they were the morning after: of *course* you don't remember, and why does it even matter? What *does* matter is where you left your Louboutin wedges . . .

b) The feeling of complete failure when, the next day, you consume an entire chocolate gateaux by accident.

c) Having to think up bigger and better ones year after year in order to amaze your friends and colleagues.

If you answered:

MOSTLY As- You have a fairly blasé attitude towards New Year's resolutions, to put it lightly; seeing them as mainly for the driven or miserable. Your long-term plans consist of where to go on Friday night, and whether or not a boob-tube with miniskirt really *does* break the 'either legs or breasts out' rule. Whilst it *is* fun living in the moment, and you don't feel the need to change anything, you should really have a go at thinking about the future and where you want to be in a year's time.

Recommendation: Make a list of goals. Start small. For example 'I will get to work on time tomorrow.' Or 'I will cash my birthday cheque from 6 months ago'.

MOSTLY Bs- Enough! It's time to stop trying to be someone you most definitely are *not*. Come on, when was the last time you saw yourself in your pants and thought the reflection looked pretty good? You are the kind of girl who refuses to buy any more bin bags because you've spent your wages on a Mulberry purse . . .

Recommendation: Sit down and write a list. *Not* one of those that you always make, lose, and don't follow anyway, but a sensible one, like so: Remind myself that I *am* a goddess worthy of envy.

MOSTLY Cs- You are either a robot, or suffering from a very well disguised lack of self-confidence. Whilst the targets you reach *are* impressive, and a large percent of developing countries have you to thank for new water-pumps, there are some questions you should ask yourself about the never-ending competition between you and everyone else. Why is everything always a contest? Are you challenging yourself for the right reasons? And, most importantly, are you *really* happy when you achieve your goals?

Recommendation: be disorganised for a day, just to try it out. This involves waking up no more than 20 minutes before work, leaving your phone behind, and on *no account* may you write a list.

n.b. This is not a challenge.

FREE new<id MAKEOVER FOR ALL READERS

new<id is the UK's leading provider of exceptional makeovers and photo shoots, having served over 37,000 clients in the last 12 months alone, their vast experience in the world of beauty and photography makes them successful in their aim – to make every client feel and look gorgeous!

We are offering AVON readers a free half-day new<id makeover and photo shoot session where dedicated experts from the world of fashion and beauty will create your perfect look: beautiful hands, stunning make-up and a gorgeous hair style. Step onto the photographic set to enjoy a fashion photo shoot. You'll get one free print to keep as a memento of the day and the opportunity to purchase more during your viewing session.

This free offer includes:

A consultation	Hand and beauty treatments
Make-up application	Hair styling
A professional photoshoot	One 5x7 print

Locations: London, Birmingham, Manchester, Cardiff and Newcastle.

To claim this fabulous prize, readers need to call 0844 800 8884 and quote "MABNM75". On arrival to your photo shoot, readers will need to present a copy of "A Brand New Me", which will act as the voucher.

new<id MAKEOVER TERMS & CONDITIONS

1. This offer is open to all UK residents aged 18 years or over. This offer is not available to employees of HarperCollins or its subsidiaries, TLC Marketing plc or agencies appointed by TLC and their immediate families.
2. The offer entitles the bearer to a half day makeover and photoshoot session. This includes consultation, hand beauty treatments, skin refresh, make up applied, hair styled, professional photoshoot, and a 5 x 7 print.
3. Proof of purchase is required, therefore a copy of the book "A Brand New Me", which also acts as a voucher, must be presented on arrival at the venue. If this is not produced, you must pay the full price for the makeover and photoshoot.
4. Only one voucher may be used per person. The voucher claimant may not claim another offer at a participating venue.
5. All additional customers will pay the full price and all future bookings will be charged at the full price.
6. This offer expires June 30th 2009. This offer is subject to availability, so redeem soon to avoid disappointment.
7. Offer excludes Public Holidays and Bank Holidays.
8. The offer is based on advance bookings only and is subject to promotional availability at participating venues.
9. Customers must call the venue in advance of their visit, stating that they are in

possession of a "TLC New ID Makeover session voucher", to check availability, discuss the usage of the offer (restrictions may apply) and book their session.

10. A fully refundable booking deposit of £25 is required to secure each appointment on Monday to Friday, and £50 on Weekends and bank holidays. Appointments are available 7 days a week. All dates and times are subject to availability. 72 hours notice is required for booking alterations. Each alteration is subject to a £5 administration fee.

11. The terms and conditions listed at the back of the book and on the Avon website at www.avon-books.co.uk form part of these terms and conditions.

12. If you fail to cancel your booking within 48 hours of the appointment, or do not show at the venue, a cancellation charge may be incurred.

13. The list of participating venues remains subject to change. Please contact your chosen venue to confirm continual availability of the offer.

14. Participating venues are all contracted to participate in the New ID makeover session offer.

15. Participating venues reserve the right to vary prices, times and offer availability (e.g. public holidays).

16. Prices (if any) and information presented are valid at the time of going to press and could be subject to change.

17. Neither the Promoter, nor its agents or distributors can accept liability for lost, stolen or damaged vouchers and reserves the right to withdraw or amend any details and/or offers.

18. The book may only be shown once. Photocopied, scanned, damaged or illegible books will not be accepted.

19. The New ID makeover voucher has no monetary value, is non-transferable, cannot be resold and cannot be used in conjunction with any other promotional offer or redeemed in whole or part for cash.

20. In the event of large promotional uplift, venues reserve the right to book voucher holders up to 4 months from date of calling to make a promotional booking.

21. Neither TLC, its agents or distributors and the Promoter will in any circumstances be responsible or liable to compensate the purchaser or other bearer, or accept any liability for (a) any non-acceptance by a venue of this book or (b) any inability by the bearer to use this book properly or at all or (c) the contents, accuracy or use of either this voucher or the venue listing, nor will any of them be liable for any personal loss or injury occurring at the venue, and (d) TLC, its agents and distributors and the promoter do not guarantee the quality and/or availability of the services offered by the venues and cannot be held liable for any resulting personal loss or damage. Your statutory rights are unaffected.

22. TLC and HarperCollins Publishers reserves the right to offer a substitute reward of equal or greater value.

23. The terms of this promotion are as stated here and no other representations (written or oral) shall apply.

24. Any persons taking advantage of this promotion does so on complete acceptance of these terms and conditions.

25. TLC and HarperCollins Publishers reserves the right to vary these terms without notice.

26. Promoter: HarperCollins Ltd, 77-85 Fulham Palace Road, Hammersmith, London, W6 8JB.

27. This is administered by TLC Marketing plc, PO Box 468, Swansea, SA1 3WY

28. This promotion is governed by English law and is subject to the exclusive jurisdiction of the English Courts.

29. HarperCollins Publishers excludes all liability as far as is permitted by law, which may arise in connection with this offer and reserves the right to cancel the offer at any stage.